PRAISE FOR GEMMA TOWNLEY

Praise for *The Hopeless Romantic's Handbook*

"A witty, sweet tale of finding true love."
—*Romantic Times*

"A hilarious spin on finding Mr. Right . . . From the
delightful characters to the tantalizing inside peek of the drama
found in the world of television and celebrity gossipmongers,
Gemma Townley's fourth novel is an absolute treat."
—*FreshFiction.com*

"A wonderful and entertaining tale of true love and the
obstacles to finding it. [Townley's] characters are interesting,
fun and richly drawn. The plot is unique and fast-paced . . .
This is a romantic comedy with sizzle."
—*Armchair Interviews*

Praise for *Learning Curves*

"Townley shines at creating characters who
are engaging and realistic."
—*Booklist*

"Charming."
—*Publishers Weekly*

"[The] family dynamic is fascinating . . . Jen is an appealing
character who is sure to please readers."
—*Romantic Times*

The Importance of Being Married

The Importance of
Being Married

A Novel

Gemma Townley

Ballantine Books New York

A Ballantine Books Trade Paperback Original

Copyright © 2008 by Gemma Townley

Published in the United States by Ballantine Books, an imprint of The Random House Publishing Group, a division of Random House, Inc., New York.

BALLANTINE and colophon are registered trademarks of Random House, Inc.

Library of Congress Cataloging-in-Publication Data
Townley, Gemma.
The importance of being married: a novel/Gemma Townley.
p.   cm.
"A Ballantine Books Trade Paperback Original."
ISBN 978-0-345-49980-6 (pbk.)
1. Marriage—Fiction 2. Inheritance and succession—
Fiction. 3. Chick lit. I. Title.
PR6120.O96I47 2008
823'.92—dc22   2007043771

Printed in the United States of America

www.ballantinebooks.com

10 9 8 7 6 5 4 3 2 1

Book design by Julie Schroeder

TO ATTICUS: THE BEST BABY IN THE WORLD

ACKNOWLEDGMENTS

Many thanks as always to my agent, Dorie Simmonds, and my editor, Laura Ford, for their unstinting enthusiasm and patience when pregnancy and baby got in the way of deadlines. Thanks also to Val Hoskins for all her input, to Mark for making numerous cups of tea, to Oscar Wilde for inspiration, and to Atticus for sleeping three times a day when I really needed him to. . . .

The Importance of Being Married

And the most lucrative. Remember, we're talking about £4m here.
That's not to be sniffed at.
I'm not sniffing. I'm just planning what I'm going to do when it all goes wrong.
It won't go wrong.
Easy for you to say. You're not the one who has to do any of this.

Key features of product (positive): Um . . .
Small waist. Nice legs. Bit too serious, sometimes. And seriously crap when it comes to men.
Thanks.
You're welcome.

Barriers to rebrand/issues to tackle:
1. Target audience has so far shown no interest in product.
2. Product not remotely interested in target audience, either.

The gorgeous Anthony Milton? Come on, you must be slightly interested.
Not even a little bit. He's not my type.
You have a type? You never go on dates. How can you have a type?
I don't have a type; I just know who *isn't* my type.
That'll be men in general, then . . .
This is a bad idea. Maybe we should rethink . . .
Oh no you don't. You agreed to do this. You can't back out now.
Yes I can.
No, you can't. Anyway, you don't have a choice in the matter. We've already gone over the alternatives and they don't exist.
Thanks for the reminder.

Strategies:
↬ Could I delegate this? Hire a supermodel to marry Anthony instead?
↬ *Kind of defeats the point, doesn't it? Look, it's not that hard. You just*

Chapter 1

The product: Jessica Wild

I'm a product now?

Look, either we do this my way, or we don't do it at all.

Fine. I'm a product. Whatever . . .

Project mission: To rebrand product in order to make it irresistible to target audience, prompting target audience to declare its undying love for product and to propose marriage.

Timescale: 50 days

Target audience: Anthony Milton (product's boss and gorgeous-looking advertising world A-lister)

Objectives for new brand:

1. To be attractive to Anthony Milton.
2. So attractive that he asks product out.
3. And then asks product to marry him.
4. Oh, and this all has to happen in 50 days. Including the wedding.
5. This is the most stupid project I've ever worked on.

need a haircut. Some new clothes. To learn to smile properly. And a bit of training in the art of seduction.

↝ *I like my clothes. And my smile. And I'm not interested in the art of seduction.*

↝ *You will be when I've finished with you.*

↝ *You're finishing with me? Is that a promise?*

My flatmate Helen screwed up her nose. "Why do I get the feeling you're not taking this entirely seriously?"

"I have no idea," I said innocently. "Because I'm taking it very seriously indeed. In fact, I'm thinking about going to the library and researching marriage over the past two thousand years. You know, to glean top tips."

Helen rolled her eyes. "Come on, Jess. This isn't a joke. Are we doing this or not?"

I sighed. "Look, maybe we didn't think this through properly. I could just call the lawyer. Come clean. Apologize and then forget all about this ridiculous idea."

"Is that what you want to do? Really?" Helen demanded.

I went red and shook my head. There was no way I was calling up the lawyer and admitting the truth. It would be too awful, too humiliating. It just wasn't an option.

Helen shrugged. "So then tell me exactly what you've got to lose, Jess. I mean it."

"My dignity," I said immediately. "My independence. My . . ."

"Debts?" Helen suggested. "Your nonexistent social life? Come on, Jess, when was the last time you went out?"

"I don't want to go out. Going out is highly overrated. As are marriage and relationships."

"How would you know? You never have relationships. And anyway, this isn't a relationship; it's a business proposition."

I bit my lip. "Anthony won't know it's a business proposition. You're saying you're going to make him fall in love with me, but it's never going to happen. This really is a huge waste of time."

Helen narrowed her eyes and stared at me. "You're not scared, are you?"

"No!" I said defensively. "Of course I'm not scared. I just think it's a crazy idea."

"I don't believe you," Helen said, shaking her head. "You're scared. Jessica Wild, Miss 'I Hate Marriage,' is scared of rejection. Admit it."

I rolled my eyes, irritated. "I'm not scared of rejection," I said, pointedly. "I just know Anthony is never going to fall for this . . . this project. Or me, in fact. And I don't particularly want him to, either. I've got better things to do with my time than go chasing after some womanizing man."

"Better things to do than inheriting four million pounds? Don't be silly. Anyway, I think it would do you good to have a boy-friend."

"I bet you do," I said. "But I'm afraid that's neither here nor there. Contrary to your belief system, I don't think that men are the answer to everything. I don't want a boyfriend. Don't need one to validate me. I'm perfectly happy on my own." The words came out like a mantra, I'd said them so often. And I believed them, too. Marriage was fine for pretty young things who were happy to depend on a man, but it wasn't for me. I knew better.

"On your own and broke, you mean. So, fine, you're happy on your own. But if this works out, you don't just gain a gorgeous husband; you make four million pounds. I mean, come on. That's got to be worth a shot, right?"

I shrugged uncomfortably. She had me there. Four million was huge. It was a life-changing amount of money. "I'd still be married," I said.

"You could always get divorced."

I frowned. Sure, I didn't believe in marriage, but I didn't much like the idea of divorce, either. It smacked of failure, of having made a bad choice. Maybe Anthony and I could separate, I found myself thinking, then kicked myself. I was beginning to believe Helen's hype. I wouldn't be separated or divorced, because I wasn't getting married. I might be humoring Helen, but Project Marriage was never going to actually work. "I guess."

Helen smiled at me. "So you'll do it? You'll give it a go?"

"I'll give it a go," I said hesitantly. "But I'm not doing anything I'm not comfortable doing. And I still think it'll never work."

"Well, if it's not going to work, you've got nothing to worry about," Helen said. "Have you?"

I sighed. "You think this is funny, don't you?" I said accusingly. "You think this is just a game."

"It is a game." Helen grinned. "It's a game show. And the prize is huge. Come on, Jess. Lighten up."

I caught her eye and frowned. I didn't want to lighten up. I wanted this all to go away. But I knew it wasn't going to. So instead I shrugged. I knew when I was defeated.

"Yay!" Helen clapped her hands together. "So, then, let's go and get your hair cut," she said, handing me my coat. "Before you change your mind again."

Chapter 2

I SHOULD PROBABLY EXPLAIN about Project Marriage. And the four million pounds. The lawyer, too. I mean, you're bound to have a few questions. Just promise not to judge before you've seen the whole picture. And even then, I'd appreciate it if you'd cut me just a little slack.

The story started a long time ago, in the tradition of all good fairy tales. Not so long ago that goblins were roaming the earth, but long enough for it to have gotten a little bit out of hand—two years, two months, and six days ago, to be precise.

In fact, it started the day Grandma died. Well, not when she died so much as when she installed herself in a retirement home because, she kept saying, no one—meaning me—was going to be able to look after her properly if she didn't. Grandma and I didn't always get on so well. She got left with me when I was two, when my mother died in a car accident, and as she regularly told me she could have done without another child to bring up, at her age. And once I was brought up, I did my best to be suitably grateful, to look after her, to visit her regularly and check everything was okay, but every time I saw her she found a new thing to criticize me for—my hair, my job, my friends, my car . . . I mean, sure, I was used to it—I'd grown up with her raising me, but when she mentioned the retirement home idea, I have to confess I jumped at it.

It seemed to suit her, too. She had new people to criticize, new reasons to complain. The staff hated her, the other residents were scared of her, and her venom for them meant that when I visited her we actually had something to talk about, which meant that we had the odd conversation that didn't focus on my failings, which was very novel and incredibly welcome.

But that wasn't when the story starts. The story starts when Grace Hampton, Grandma's next-door neighbor in the retirement home, happened to pass her room one day when I was visiting, and poked her head around the door. I was just telling Grandma about a new job I'd gotten at Milton Advertising, working for Anthony Milton, the golden boy of the advertising world, and in walked Grace and offered us both a cup of tea. Which was pretty surprising since Grandma had only had bad things to say about her skittish neighbor who read "stupid" romance novels and watched far too much television (Grandma preferred long, turgid books that gave her headaches). Grace didn't seem to notice Grandma's wide eyes, or her slightly brittle tone when she arrived back a few minutes later with three cups of tea, sitting down on the sofa with me and asking me all about my new job. Actually, for a sweet old lady she had very thick skin, and before I knew it she was always there when I visited Grandma, smiling expectantly at me, asking me about my life, like she was actually interested.

Then, a few months later, Grandma died and everything changed. Suddenly I was free. Suddenly I was completely on my own. Suddenly I had a funeral to organize. And pay for. Actually, it wasn't the only thing I had to pay for. Grandma hadn't thought to mention her failing heart to me; she also hadn't thought to mention that she'd run out of money and owed Sunnymead several thousand pounds for her care. Grace was there when they told me, when they delicately put Grandma's final bill in front of my nose. I did my best not to go white as I gripped it rather too tightly; as my eyes swam at the figures in black and white.

Twenty-five thousand pounds in total. And right then Grace put her hand on mine, and she said, "You know, Jess, I wonder if you would do me a favor." To be honest, I wasn't really in the mood to do anyone a favor—I was seeing my life flash before my eyes, a life of debt, of being broke. But I didn't say that; I just smiled and said, "Sure." And then she said, "I wonder if you'd let me pay for your grandmother's funeral. It would make me so very happy."

I said no, of course, but she had a way of not taking no for an answer, and I knew that really it was her doing me the favor, but she was adamant all the way that it was the other way around. The funeral was beautiful, too—far more beautiful than it would have been if it had been left to me. Grandma might have been a strict Presbyterian, but Grace managed to turn the stark church into a beautiful place; turned a serious service into a huge celebration of Grandma's life. She turned up in a pale pink suit, smiling at me and telling me that no one should ever wear black to a funeral, and she held my hand through the whole thing, giving me a handkerchief when to my own surprise I started to cry. "She loved you," she whispered as Grandma's body was lowered into the ground. "When you weren't there, she couldn't stop talking about you. She was so proud." And I wasn't sure if she was telling the truth or not, but it was nice to hear.

Obviously, I offered to pay Grace back. But she always said no. She said that money didn't matter, that what mattered was people, and company, and laughter and love. And that's when she said that if I wasn't too busy, she'd love it if I'd visit her from time to time. So I told her that of course I wasn't too busy; I'd love to come and see her. Which was why, just days after Grandma was buried, I found myself back at Sunnymead. And the week after that, too. You see, Grace wasn't much like Grandma, and visiting her didn't seem like a chore at all; more like popping in to see a friend. All of a sudden I found myself looking forward to walking down Sunnymead's corridors, to sitting beside Grace as we watched television and read magazines together, and discussed her favorite books. She'd tell me about her childhood—about Sudbury Grange, the house she grew up in, the house that had been in her family for generations. It was a large, rambling house in the country, she told me, full of little passages and surrounded by a huge garden where she and her brothers used to play all summer long.

I'd listen wistfully, wondering what it must have been like, to live somewhere like that with brothers and dogs and friends and trees to climb and places to hide. Even without Grandpa, who left a week after I arrived—he'd been having an affair, Grandma told me later at his funeral (he'd only survived a year without her, she pointed out victoriously, as though he'd brought his cancer on himself), but it was my arrival that sent him over the edge—Grandma's house had been small and cramped. The few toys I'd owned weren't allowed to leave my bedroom, weren't allowed to clutter what little space she had. It wasn't a house for children, she'd tell me in a way that let me know I had intruded. It wasn't a house that could cope with laughter or shouting or games or loud music, either. It appeared to be a house for reflection, for sitting quietly. Solitude, Grandma would tell me, was something to be valued. Friends couldn't be trusted, men would always let you down, but you could depend on yourself. If you were happy on your own, then your life would always be satisfactory. And satisfactory was a good state of affairs, she'd add. Satisfactory was as high as one should aim for.

Grace, on the other hand, didn't believe in solitude one bit. She loved people and noise and gossip. And I came to love her. Every time I went to see her, I left feeling slightly happier, slightly more comfortable in my skin. She always seemed to be interested in what I had to say, remembered things I said from one week to the next, and she never made me feel like I was inadequate or a failure; in fact, she made me feel like anything was possible. She was one of those people who assumed that everything would be a success—as opposed to Grandma, who assumed that things would fail. And if she was rather too fixated on my love life (or lack thereof), it wasn't a big deal. At least I thought it wasn't.

Grace's fixation would generally manifest itself halfway through my visit, when she would ask me if there was anyone special in my life. I'd give her a slightly incredulous smile and then, not wanting to upset her by admitting that the last thing I needed in my life was a man making demands on my time, I'd change the subject. It wasn't like I didn't like men. I mean they were fine, in their place. I just didn't want one as a boyfriend. Didn't have time for one. Romance, in my opinion, was a dangerous drug that turned sensible, independent women into gooey love-struck teenagers, and that was never going to happen to me. Not if I could help it. I had no interest in obsessing over some man who would only walk out on me. The fact that men very rarely asked me out—or in fact showed any interest in me at all—was really quite convenient.

But Grace didn't let it go. To her, the only thing that really mattered was "finding that special someone." Every time I came to visit, she'd press her hand onto mine and ask me if that nice boss of mine had asked me out yet (her favored romance novels were the sort where secretaries would be asked to take off their glasses and let down their hair, before their bosses would sweep them into their arms and declare their undying love), and I'd roll my eyes because that was never going to happen. I was fine on my own. More than fine. It was the way I liked things.

And so a little stalemate situation developed. When Grace asked me about my love life, I'd tell her about a project at work. When she asked me if my boss was still single, I brought up the coffee machine Helen and I had splurged on in an attempt to save money on lattes (for the record, don't try it—they're expensive and we still ended up buying coffee every morning). One visit I managed to spend nearly the entire two hours telling Grace about a campaign I was working on, and after all that, she fixed me with those twinkling eyes of hers and said, "So, Jess, how's the husband hunting going? Has that golden boy of the advertising world noticed you yet?"

I kept thinking that eventually she'd get bored, that she'd give up, that she'd accept that she was fighting a losing battle, but not a bit. Instead she just upped the ante, asking me about every single man I worked with, analyzing them as potential husband material.

And then, finally, after months of avoidance, months of subject changes, incredulous eyebrow raises, and determined shrugs, I did something I'm not proud of. I invented a boyfriend.

Okay, I know how bad that sounds. Inventing boyfriends is what you do when you're thirteen. But you have to believe me when I say I didn't have a choice. Or, if I did have a choice, it wasn't really apparent to me at the time.

Fine, so most people probably would have thought of something else. But someone else probably would have had a boyfriend, too, so that isn't exactly relevant.

But back to the story. It was a really warm, sunny day, and I arrived at Sunnymead Retirement Home a bit earlier than usual. There were doctors in the room, so I waited outside because, well, doctors freak me out a bit, frankly, with their tubes and their serious faces. So there I was, standing outside in the corridor, and I heard one of the doctors say, "I'm afraid, Grace, that it's not looking good. The situation is worsening."

And I didn't know which situation was worsening, or what exactly didn't look good, but when doctors use words like that the details don't tend to be too important, do they? I shrank back and found myself getting all breathless and panicky because I didn't want anything to happen to Grace, couldn't bear it, and then the doctors left, and I forced myself to calm down and put a big smile on my face, because I figured she was going to need cheering up after news like that, and she looked so pleased to see me, and I wanted that cheery look to stay on her face and not to be replaced by fear, or despondency, or anything else bad.

The first thing Grace said was: "So, Jess, how are you? Any exciting news? Any nice men asked you out recently?"

And I was about to say, *No, of course not,* when I saw the little glimmer of hope in her eyes and knew suddenly that I couldn't disappoint her again. Not now.

So instead what I said was: "Yes, actually! Guess what? I've got a date!"

You should have seen her face. It lit up like a beacon—her eyes were shining, her mouth was smiling, and even through my guilt I couldn't help but feel pleased with myself for making her so happy.

"Who with?" she asked. Immediately I started to rack my brain for a name, any name, but I've never been that great under pressure and my mind just went blank, so I just smiled, awkwardly, and Grace gave me a mischievous grin and said, "It isn't with your handsome boss, is it? Anthony? Oh, tell me it's Anthony Milton, please!"

In retrospect it would have been really easy to say no. When, later, I replayed this scene to myself, I realized there were a million and one things I could have said that would have been infinitely better than my actual answer. But I panicked. I'd just made up a date—I didn't have the imagination to come up with any new information. "Anthony Milton?" I found myself saying. "Um . . . Yes, that's right. That's who my date's with."

I should probably mention at this point that me going on a date with Anthony Milton was about as likely as me going on a date with Prince William. Or Justin Timberlake. Or James Bond. Anthony Milton was the proprietor and chief executive of Milton Advertising. He was tall, blond, handsome, successful, and everyone loved him. A week didn't go by when he wasn't photographed in *Advertising Weekly,* a year didn't go by when he wasn't nominated for some award or other—mainly because his presence at an awards ceremony would guarantee that everyone in the advertising world would want to be there, too. Also, a day didn't go by when he wasn't fawned over by every woman in a four-mile radius.

He'd interviewed me for my job at Milton Advertising—he and Max, his deputy, who fired questions at me while Anthony smiled winningly as he told me how great the company was, making me lose my train of thought several times. Then, when I got up to go, I caught Max's eye and he grinned at me, and the next thing I knew I'd walked into a glass wall. When I say *walked into,* I mean it literally: bang slap, sore head, the whole works. Luckily Anthony had seen the funny side and still offered me a job; Helen helpfully pointed out that he'd probably been worried that I was going to sue him for dangerously placed glass walls and my physical and emotional distress after walking into one.

Of course, news spread about my interview, and by the time I actually started at Milton Advertising I was known as the girl-who-walked-into-walls. But that didn't bother me—after several years working in data processing (Grandma had told me regularly I was lucky to have a job, and that it was very selfish of me to complain when some people hadn't had half the chances I'd had in life), I finally had a job with prospects, one that might earn me a decent wage. Anthony had given me a chance, and I was going to grab it with both hands, even if I started out a bit of a laughingstock.

But I digress. The point was, Anthony wasn't just out of my league, he was in a different stratosphere. Even if I was interested. Which I patently wasn't.

"Anthony Milton?" she twinkled. "I knew it! I knew it the moment you told me you walked into his glass wall."

So that's how it all started. Just a date, just a little story to cheer

Grace up. I never meant it to snowball. I never meant for it to go any further than that at all. But somehow, it did. Somehow it all got just a little bit out of hand, bit by bit, layer by layer, until there just wasn't any going back.

Not that there was ever the possibility of going back. I mean, I couldn't come in the following week and say the date had been canceled. It would have broken her heart, or she'd probably have had a relapse, and I would have been responsible. So instead I told her about our date. Actually, I told her about my flatmate Helen's date with a director of a record company, substituting my and Anthony's names in their place, except it didn't end up with us having sex in his office but with us sharing a chaste kiss at my door. Anthony, it turned out, was honorable, interesting, and, most importantly, crazy about me. And I know it sounds stupid, I know it's humiliating to admit it, particularly since I looked down on people who spent their time obsessing about getting boyfriends, but I quite enjoyed telling Grace all about it. Free from the constraints of reality, it was the best date I'd never been on. So good, in fact, that I wouldn't have been able to bear it if he hadn't called afterward. So he did call. Two days later, in fact— just like the music executive. Only while Helen let her date leave message after anguished message, I agreed to a second date. Figuratively speaking.

If I had any doubts back then, I managed to bury them, convincing myself that it was all just a bit of harmless fun. Just some silly stories to feed Grace's desire for romance. And if I'm being honest, I quite enjoyed it, too. I mean, sure, I knew it was ridiculous; the logical, sensible side of me knew that it was no more realistic than "Snow White and the Seven Dwarfs" or "Cinderella." But that's the thing with fairy tales—they're warm and fuzzy and full of happy endings, and even if you know life isn't like that, it's still nice to suspend your disbelief, just for a little while.

Grace, meanwhile, could not have been more excited. She had

a good feeling about it, she kept saying. So good that she could barely wait for my visits for each installment of the story. It was keeping her going, she told me.

Keeping her going. I mean, how could I tell her that it wasn't true?

Every time I visited I would steel myself, would be determined to tell her the truth, to admit it was all made up. But every time her eyes lit up as I walked into her room and she'd say, "So? Tell me! Tell me everything," and I'd bottle it, would tell myself that the truth could wait, that now wasn't a good time, that the truth didn't matter if my stories were making Grace happy.

And when I told Grace that we were going on holiday together (I was actually going on a week's course on "Boosting Your Profile at Work and Getting the Promotion You Deserve"), she looked at me, her eyes shining, and she said, "You know what he's planning, don't you?" And I frowned, and said no, and then she smiled and said, "He's going to ask you to marry him."

Sure, I froze slightly. Sure, I did think to myself then and there that maybe things were getting a bit out of hand. The idea of getting married, even in imaginary fairy tale land, brought me out in a cold sweat. But I'd never seen Grace look so excited. She was almost trembling with anticipation.

So I rolled my eyes and said, "Oh, I doubt it."

"I don't," she said wistfully. She sighed, brushed a tear from her eye, and took my hand in hers. "Jess, I want you to promise me something."

"Really?" I asked tentatively. "What is it?"

"I want you to promise me if and when someone offers you everything they have, you'll take it," she said.

"What?" I raised my eyebrows. "What do you mean? I don't want everything Anthony has."

Grace smiled sadly. "Jess, I know you're very strong and very independent. But don't turn someone down who wants to help just because you don't think you need it. We all need help, we all need love, we all need . . . Just promise me, won't you?"

I frowned. "Okay, sure," I said.

"No," she said, shaking her head. "This is serious, Jess. I want you to promise."

I looked at her uncertainly. "Promise?"

"Promise." Grace nodded. "Promise that you won't run away. That you won't reject it out of hand."

"Reject what?" I asked, perplexed. "I don't know what you're asking me to promise here."

"You will," Grace said, a little smile on her face. "You will."

"Fine," I relented, figuring that it didn't matter, since what I was promising related to something that didn't actually exist. "Then I promise."

"Wonderful," Grace said. "And let's see what happens on your holiday, shall we?"

He proposed. Of course he did. Grace was so excited, she borrowed a nurse's mobile phone to text me while I was away and to find out "how things were going." If I'd come back without a proposal I think her heart would have broken. And an imaginary fiancé wasn't such a great leap from an imaginary boyfriend. He proposed on the beach. Which is, I know, a total cliché, but I couldn't think of anything else. He had the ring already—a perfect square-cut diamond, beautiful and delicate (that's when I bought a paste ring. Sure, it felt pretty depressing, buying my own fake engagement ring, but I did it online so I didn't have to think about it too much or face a real-life salesperson. And Grace thought it was the most beautiful thing she'd ever seen). The moon was full and bright and he had suggested a walk after a lovely dinner. He'd started saying how he couldn't believe how lucky he was to have met me. I'd obviously told him that no, I was the lucky one, and then he'd gotten down on one knee and asked me to be his wife, and I'd just nodded because I couldn't speak, I was choking up. In truth, I got the whole story from a cheap magazine I'd picked up at the dentist, and I did wonder at one point whether I was going too far, whether Grace could possibly believe such a load of old tosh, but she did. She even started crying. She said that it wasn't just me who was the happiest person in the world. She said that she'd been hoping and praying for this moment ever since she met me, that it was everything I deserved and more, and that she wished me—us—as much happiness as she'd had over the years. And yes, I felt uncomfortable. Yes, my stomach twisted in knots slightly. But I kept telling myself I was doing the right thing, even if it didn't always feel like it.

In the event, we eloped. It just seemed like the easiest solution. Grace was upset, of course—she'd wanted to come to the wedding—but not when I told her that it had been Anthony's idea to forgo a big wedding so we could give the money to charity instead, and that our little register office affair had been exactly what we'd both wanted—intimate, low-key, private.

The next week I went back online and bought myself a wedding ring (silver, twenty-five pounds), and every week when I went to see Grace I'd put it and my engagement ring on, and would make up stories about my married life to my own Prince Charming.

And now she was gone. Now it was all gone.

Chapter 3

IT WAS GRACE'S LAWYER who told me she had died. He turned up unannounced to give me the news. It was the one Sunday I hadn't been able to visit because of a work deadline. He told me that she'd died in the morning, and so I wouldn't have gotten there in time anyway, but it didn't help much.

I'd arrived home that day at 6 PM to find Helen in the sitting room, watching *Deal or No Deal*. As I poked my head around the sitting room door, she held up her hand to stop me talking. "No deal!" she shouted at the television. *"No deal!"*

Helen and I had met at university where we'd found ourselves next-door neighbors in our first-year hall of residence. I'd never had a best friend before—I told myself I didn't have time for one, but the truth was that Grandma had scuppered my chances at female bonding very early on by refusing to let me watch television, buying me only extremely unfashionable clothes, and imposing a strict curfew of 8 PM, all of which meant that I could only ever be an embarrassment to anyone who gamely attempted to befriend me for any length of time. She'd made a mistake with my mother, Grandma used to tell me constantly, giving her too much freedom, allowing her to become fixated by clothes, by makeup, by boys and television programs, and she wasn't going to make the same mistake with me. By the time I got to university, I saw it as a good thing: it meant I had more time for work, more time to focus on getting straight A's.

But Helen, I soon discovered, wasn't like other people. Wasn't like me, either. In fact, she was the opposite of me in almost every way—she was beautiful, rich, impulsive, and sociable—but for some strange reason she didn't dismiss me, or befriend me only to dump me a few weeks later. Instead she took to storming into my room on a regular basis to tell me about her latest conquest or agonize about an essay that was invariably several weeks overdue. She thought it was funny when I rolled my eyes and told her that I'd never heard of any of the bands she listened to; she made me spend the whole weekend watching *Friends* DVDs when I told her I'd never seen an episode, and didn't even seem to mind when I sneaked away from parties early to catch up on my studies. We were an odd couple, but despite my best attempts to show her just how inappropriate I was as a friend, we were still close years later. Not just close—roommates.

Helen worked in television as a researcher, which meant that she worked very intensively on a program for several weeks, then had a few weeks off "resting" before she got her new contract. Recently her "resting" period seemed to be extending rather longer than usual, which meant that the only income she had coming in was my rent (the flat had been a "gift" from her father. I'd have been jealous, only she invited me to move in with her and charged me far less than I'd pay elsewhere, so instead I was just hugely grateful), which nowhere near covered her living expenses. But whereas I fretted on her behalf, it didn't seem to worry her too much. Instead, while she rested, she considered it her duty to watch as much television as possible so that when she finally got around to applying for a job she'd be clued up on whichever program she was potentially going to be working on.

The contestant said, "Deal," and Helen threw her arms up in

despair. "Idiot!" she yelled, then turned the television off. "Can't bear it," she said, shaking her head. "I just can't watch these people. So, what's up with you?"

I didn't get a chance to answer—at that moment the doorbell rang and I got up to answer it.

"Jessica Milton?" a man's voice asked over the intercom, and I jumped slightly.

"Um, who is this?" I asked tentatively. I didn't tend to get many visitors. Not male ones. Not on Sunday evenings. And certainly not ones who called me "Milton."

"It's Mr. Taylor. I'm Grace Hampton's solicitor. I have some bad news, I'm afraid. I wonder if I might have a word?"

"Grace Hampton?" I said, curious, then reddened. She'd found out about Anthony, I thought with a thud. She'd found out it wasn't true. Then I kicked myself. She'd hardly send her lawyer around, even if she did find out. "Um, come up."

As he came through the door, the credits were rolling for *Deal or No Deal,* and Helen evacuated the sitting room, telling me that she was going to make a chili for supper. I smiled gratefully and ushered Mr. Taylor in.

"Sorry," I said quickly. "Please, sit down."

The sofa and chair were strewn with Helen's magazines and my work projects, so I hurriedly cleared some space for him, then sat down myself.

"So, is there something wrong with Grace?" I asked tentatively.

Mr. Taylor looked at me sadly. "I'm sorry to tell you that Mrs. Hampton has . . . passed away."

It took me nearly a minute to digest this information. "Passed away?" I gulped eventually, and my eyes widened.

"Last night. In her sleep. I'm very sorry."

I stared at him openmouthed, then I felt myself stiffen. "I think you've made a mistake," I said quickly. "Grace is fine. I saw her just last week."

He gave me a sympathetic look. "I'm sorry," he said again.

"Sorry?" My throat caught as I spoke. "Well, you should be. Because this isn't happening." I turned away from him like a petulant teenager. People were always dying on me—my mother, my grandmother, my grandfather (even if I never met him I still went to the funeral, so I figured he counted), and I wasn't going to have Grace die, too. I just wasn't.

He nodded sadly. "I'm afraid it is. I believe the situation took a turn for the worse quite suddenly."

"A turn for the worse?" I shook my head, incredulously. "She's dead and you're calling it *a turn for the worse*?" I regretted saying the word *dead* as soon as it came out of my mouth, as though saying it made it real. I could feel tears pricking at my eyes, tears of indignation, of anger, of sadness. And of guilt. Because I hadn't felt like this when Grandma died. When Grandma died, I listened to the news with an attitude of resignation, kept my voice low and somber because that's what you did in these situations. I hadn't felt like my world was breaking into two; hadn't wanted to rewind time to make it untrue.

"Perhaps I can get you a drink of water?" Mr. Taylor offered. I shook my head.

"I don't want water. I want Grace." I rushed to the phone and dialed Sunnymead's number. "Yes. Grace Hampton, please. I'd like to speak to Grace Hampton."

"Grace Hampton?" The voice was uncertain, preparing itself to give me bad news.

"Yes, Grace Hampton," I said impatiently. "I want to talk to her please."

There was a pause. "I'm . . . I'm afraid to tell you that Grace . . ."

I put the phone down before the woman on reception could finish, before she could repeat what Mr. Taylor had already told me. Grace was dead. I wasn't going to see her again. Ever. Slowly,

I walked back to the chair I'd been sitting on, eased myself onto it, pulled my legs up and hugged them into my chest.

"I understand that the two of you were very close. I'm truly sorry to be the bearer of such bad news," Mr. Taylor was saying.

"Yes, we were close," I said. I was angry suddenly. Angry with this man who dared to come into my flat on a Sunday night and tell me that there would be no more little chats with Grace over tea and biscuits, no more Sunnymead. And no more fantasy love affair. From now on it was just me.

"Very close." I felt tears in my eyes and wiped them distractedly. "I should have been there," I heard myself say, anger suddenly being replaced by sadness, emptiness. "I should have known."

"I'm very sorry." The lawyer didn't seem to know what else to say. I looked up at him and realized how badly I was behaving. It wasn't his fault. None of this was his fault.

"No, I'm sorry," I managed to say. "It's just . . . well, it's a bit of a shock."

"Indeed," Mr. Taylor said sagely.

An image came into my head of Grace on her bed, just like Grandma had been when she died, her skin almost translucent, her spirit ebbing away. I saw her being taken out of her room, her things being packed up, someone else taking her place, as though she'd never existed in the first place. Forcefully, I pushed it out.

"Do . . . do you know when the funeral's going to be yet?" I found myself asking. "Do you need a hand with anything? I mean, I know what her favorite flowers were, if that helps? And she loved 'I Vow to Thee My Country.' You know, if you're wondering about hymns . . ." I trailed off, trying to keep my voice level.

"Thank you, Mrs. Milton. I mean, Jessica. That's very kind. In actual fact, Mrs. Hampton had very . . . specific ideas about her funeral. All written down. They don't allow me much leeway at all."

I managed a rueful smile at that, imagining Grace detailing her requirements like a shopping list. She had a wonderful way of coaxing people into getting her exactly what she wanted without ever seeming to impose herself—the nurses brought her not just tea bags but Twinings English Breakfast, and I brought her not just apples but English Coxes, and only in season.

"Okay," I said, nodding awkwardly, not sure what I should be saying or doing. I wanted to be on my own. Wanted to feel angry and sad in privacy. "Well, thank you for coming to tell me. And you'll let me know where and when, won't you. And if you need anything else . . ."

I waited for him to stand, but instead he gave me a funny sort of smile.

"Actually, there is something else," he said, clearing his throat. "There's the matter of Mrs. Hampton's will."

"Will? Oh, right." I sat down again with an inward sigh. I knew all about wills. Grandma's will had been read to me two days after she died. I hadn't expected anything—I knew she'd sold the house to pay for her care at Sunnymead. What I hadn't banked on was that wills worked both ways—that instead of inheriting money, I was inheriting all her debts.

"Mrs. Milton," Mr. Taylor said seriously, pulling out a folder and handing it to me. "You are the primary beneficiary of Grace's will, and you're going to be inheriting her estate. I can run through the details now, if you'd like, or if you'd like to come to my office one day next week, we can sort out the paperwork then and there."

I put the folder to one side. "Okay. I mean, I'll look at this later, if that's okay. When I'm . . . better able to . . . you know."

"You're not interested in the contents of the estate?"

I looked up. "Contents. Yes, of course. You mean her personal effects?" I sniffed, forcing myself to concentrate. She hadn't had much in her room—a couple of pictures, a few books. Still, it would be nice to have something to remember her by.

"Ah. Yes, well, I suppose that I do," Mr. Taylor said uncertainly. "But it's the house that forms the largest part of the legacy."

"The house?" I looked at him blankly.

Mr. Taylor smiled at me as if I were a small child. "The house has been in her family for several generations. I know that she was very keen for it to come to you." He handed me a photograph of a crumbling stone house. I say house, but really it was a huge mansion, surrounded by land. And suddenly I knew what it was; could see Grace as a young girl tearing along the corridors with her brothers, spilling out into the garden.

"Sudbury Grange?" I gasped. "She left me Sudbury Grange?"

"So you know the house? Well, that's good," the lawyer said, nodding. "In addition to the house there are some not insignificant investments, along with various paintings, jewelry, and so on. Obviously you'll be wondering about death duties and I'm happy to tell you that Grace also provided for those, with a trust of one million pounds that should be ample to cover all your taxes."

My eyes widened, then I grinned. "Oh, you're joking. For a moment there you had me. A million pounds for taxes. That's good. That's very good."

Mr. Taylor didn't smile. Instead he cleared his throat awkwardly.

"The liability is reduced because of various trust arrangements," he said. "Without them, I'm afraid that the bill would be even higher."

"Higher?" I repeated stupidly. My skin felt prickly and I was getting rather warm.

"Grace thought a great deal of you," the lawyer said. He was smiling benevolently at me, like he was talking to a small child. "With no . . . no family of her own, I think she rather thought of you as . . . kin."

"Me, too," I said. "But there has to be some mistake. She wouldn't leave me her house. No way."

"Oh, but she did." Mr. Taylor smiled. "You do know who Grace Hampton was, don't you?"

I looked at him impatiently. "Of course I knew who she was. I've been visiting her for nearly two years."

He looked relieved. "The estate, then," he said, seriously, taking some papers out of his briefcase and passing me a photograph. "There is a husband-and-wife team who currently work full-time and live in one of the cottages. I understand that they're happy to continue if you'd like them to. Then there's a team of gardeners, a cook, and two cleaners who work on an ad hoc basis."

I was staring at the photograph. It was even more incredible in real life than Grace had described, with ivy growing up the walls and acres of land around it with secret gardens and outhouses and places to hide where no one would ever find you. When I'd lived with Grandma in her small terraced house in Ipswich, I used to imagine that my mother hadn't really died; that she was still alive somewhere, living in a crumbling house like the one in the photograph (only about a quarter of the size), and that one day she'd come and find me and take me home. Not that she ever did. And I knew it was just a dream, not real. But this house in the photograph was completely real. And it was mine?

"It's . . . very big," I said tentatively.

"Yes, I suppose it is," Mr. Taylor said, nodding. "Now, I've got all the information here, along with details on the furniture. It's all staying with the house, so you can go through it at your leisure, along with Lady Hampton's personal effects."

"Lady . . . Lady Hampton?" My voice had become a squeak.

"So you didn't know?"

I shook my head. Maybe I hadn't known her as well as I'd thought.

"Then you had no idea that her will in total amounts to in the region of four million pounds?"

"Four million?" I couldn't see properly. I felt like the world was closing in on me.

Mr. Taylor started to open his briefcase, but I held up my hand. "I'm sorry," I said, my voice now several octaves above its usual register. "Can we just rewind slightly. I thought you were talking about Grace having left me a few books or something. I didn't know . . . I mean, an estate? I . . . And she was a lady? She never said. And I don't want her money. That's not . . . I mean . . ."

"Grace considered it very important that someone she trusted take over the estate," the lawyer said, gently. "Someone who would nurture it, perhaps have a family there. Someone whom she could trust with her possessions, too," he said. "Grace was a very . . . private lady. I know that when she met you, a great weight was lifted from her shoulders, because she knew that you would be a good and trustworthy heir. That by leaving her estate to you, she would protect it. I know that this knowledge made her very happy. Very happy indeed."

"But . . . but . . ." I said redundantly. "Isn't there someone else? Family? Someone other than me?"

The lawyer nodded. "Lady Hampton did have a son. Does have a son. But they are estranged. She . . . disinherited him many years ago. He left home when he was eighteen."

My eyes widened. "She had a son? She never mentioned a son."

"She didn't consider herself to still have a son," Mr. Taylor said, the flicker of a frown crossing his face. "They . . . father and son argued, as I understand it. He left home when he was eighteen. I believe they haven't been in touch since."

"But won't he want the money? The house?"

Mr. Taylor shook his head. "I understand that he's gone abroad. I assure you, he has no claim on the will." He was looking just to the right of me, as though he couldn't quite look me in the eyes.

"Right," I nodded, my mind spinning. Grace had never mentioned a son. Then again, she'd never mentioned the four million pounds, either. Or the house.

"Mrs. Milton, you are going to be a very rich woman," the lawyer said. "And with wealth comes responsibility. It's a lot to take in, so I suggest you take this folder, perhaps discuss it with your husband, and try to give some thought to what you'd like to do."

"To do?" I asked hoarsely. I was having trouble assimilating the information being given to me. I was going to be rich. Seriously rich. Which meant no more debts. No more anxiously checking my bank balance at the end of each month as I teetered precariously toward my overdraft limit. I'd never expected to be rich. Never hoped for it. And I couldn't believe Grace really wanted to leave it all to me.

"Whether you wish to move in to the estate, or . . . or dispose of it."

"Sell it?" I asked incredulously.

The lawyer shrugged.

"Sell the estate that Grace left to me specifically so that I could look after it?" I demanded.

Mr. Taylor smiled. "I'm glad you see it her way," he said. "Grace always prided herself on being a good judge of character. Still, I will leave these papers with you, if I may, and perhaps you would like to visit me in my office to discuss the transfer of assets—say, next week?"

I nodded, my mind still racing.

"Why was she at Sunnymead?" I asked. "I mean, if she was rich—couldn't she have had a team of doctors and nurses at her estate or something?"

The lawyer looked thoughtful for a moment. "She was lonely," he said, eventually. "Grace always liked to be around people. And after her husband died, she wanted to leave the estate. She said that the house felt too empty, felt too full of memories."

"And she really left it all to me?"

"She said that you were like the daughter she never had. Or the granddaughter. I know that it was very important to her that you inherit the house, in particular. She said that otherwise it would go to the government and get demolished by developers. Or turned into an ugly conference center."

He was smiling again, wryly this time, and I smiled back. That was exactly the sort of thing Grace would say.

"As I was saying," Mr. Taylor continued, "you'll want to come to my office, I should think, to sort out the paperwork. I can go through the details of the estate and financial arrangements then."

"Paperwork," I said, nodding vaguely.

"Nothing too onerous. Just need your proof of identity, signatures, that sort of thing," he said, smiling. "There is one rather strange but significant clause to the will, which is that the inheritance must be claimed within fifty days or it will be forfeit."

I frowned. "Forfeit?"

Mr. Taylor nodded. "It's a Hampton peculiarity—all the family wills have the same clause. It was introduced to avoid family wrangles—if anyone disputes a will beyond the fifty-day limit, the entire inheritance is lost. It's rather an effective mechanism, actually."

"Fifty days." I nodded again; words were suddenly a bit of a struggle. "That sounds . . . okay."

"It's rather a lot to take in, isn't it?" Mr. Taylor said kindly, and I kind of nodded and gulped both together, and shot him a smile so he wouldn't think I was rude.

"I can't quite believe it," I heard myself saying. It was like an out-of-body experience.

"Well, you should. Mrs. Milton, you are going to be a very wealthy woman."

Mr. Taylor stood up then and held out his hand. "I look forward to hearing from you. Thank you for your time. I'll be in touch shortly about the funeral—it will be in London. Kensington. Sometime next week. Perhaps you'd like to bring your husband."

"My husband?" I looked at him strangely, then remembered. "Oh, yes, my husband, of course. Well, yes. I mean, if he's free. He's very busy, you see."

Mr. Taylor nodded, and I shook his hand, using all my strength to keep calm, to not yelp, to act like inheriting four million pounds was no big deal at all. Inside, I was screaming, though, screaming and dancing and shaking my head in utter bewilderment. I was going to be rich. Rich beyond my wildest dreams. I couldn't believe Grace had never said anything, never even given me a clue.

And then, suddenly I thought of something. Something that made my stomach turn upside down rather violently.

"Um, so, the will," I said, trying to keep my voice casual. "Grace left everything to Jessica Milton, did she? I mean, you know, to me. In my married name?"

"The papers cite a Mrs. Jessica Milton, that's right."

I nodded, managing somehow to keep a fixed smile on my face, and suddenly needing desperately to sit down again. "It's just that . . ." I paused, my mind racing. "Well, I didn't actually change my name. So, I'm still Jessica Wild. Officially, at least. Is that . . . is that okay?"

"That's perfectly all right," Mr. Taylor said, and I felt relief rush through me. "I'll need proof of identification in your maiden name—a passport or birth certificate, and then you just need to provide me with a copy of your marriage certificate so I can adjust the paperwork."

"Marriage certificate?"

"That's right. Anytime next week, Mrs. Milton. Just call this number and my secretary can arrange a time. Again, I'm so sorry to disturb you and your . . ." He looked vaguely back toward the kitchen. "Your cook?" he suggested, and I found myself nodding.

"Well, I'm sorry to disturb you on a Sunday evening. I just thought you should know. Please, do send my regards to your husband, who is more than welcome to join us in my office. Thank you again. I'll see myself out. Oh, and do you have some contact details? A telephone number?"

I looked at him blankly. "Yes. It's . . . oh-two-oh seven-six-oh . . ." I frowned. Oh-two-oh seven-six-oh-three. No, four. Seven-six-oh-four . . ." I smiled, weakly. I couldn't even remember my own phone number. I could barely remember my own name. Sweating slightly, I reached for my bag and pulled out a business card. "Here," I said. "My number's on the card."

"Thank you." He took the card, stood up, and left; two seconds later Helen appeared at the sitting room door.

"So?" she demanded. "What did that man want? And why did he say he wished he had someone at home like me?"

I smiled nervously, unsure I trusted myself to speak right now. Then I shook myself.

"Nothing," I said eventually. "He just . . . He just came to tell me Grace had died."

"Grace? Oh, poor you. Oh, Jess, I'm so sorry," Helen said, rushing over to give me a hug. "Oh that's really sad news."

"Sad?" I said, hardly trusting myself to speak. "Sad doesn't even begin to cover it."

Chapter 4

I woke up in the middle of the night to find myself sitting bolt upright. I was totally freaked out. I'd dreamed about Grace—although it was more of a memory, really. I was in her room and we were watching some cheesy film, I can't remember which one, and Grace turned to me and said that I should get my hair cut like the girl in the film—I think it was Drew Barrymore. And I rolled my eyes because I thought I had far more important things to think about than haircuts, and then Grace passed me a hairbrush and asked if I'd brush her hair. So I did, and she was smiling and telling me that her husband used to brush her hair, that some of her favorite moments were leaning back in his arms as he brought the brush down gently over her head. And she said that she hoped one day I'd find someone who'd brush my hair, and I don't know why but I found a little tear pricking at my eye, which was ridiculous, I knew, but when I wiped it away, another one came up straightaway to take its place. Of course, I stopped the tears in their tracks; told myself off for being so utterly pathetic. In reality, I mean. When it actually happened. In the dream I didn't have time to wipe my eyes or give myself a stern talking-to, because the door suddenly opened and Mr. Taylor walked in and pointed his finger at me and looked at Grace and said, "She's the one. She's the one who's been lying to you." And I jumped up off the bed and Grace was looking at me, wide-eyed, and then she was crying, shaking her head and whispering that I'd let her down, that I was a big disappointment, and then suddenly she wasn't Grace anymore, she was Grandma, and now she wasn't whispering, she was screaming, shouting, telling me that I was a waste of space, that she wished she'd never set eyes on me, that the sooner I learned to fend for myself the better because she'd had enough, she was sick of looking after me.

That's when I'd woken up to find my sheets drenched with sweat, and I was staring at the wall in front of me. I took a few deep breaths, got a drink of water, went back to bed, and had a little think. I didn't want to go back to sleep, didn't want to reenter the nightmares that waited for me. And that's when it hit me— the nightmare wasn't in my head; it was here, in the real world, and of my own making. Four million pounds was more than I'd ever dreamed of having. It was incredible, tantalizing. But I couldn't claim it. Whatever I did would be wrong.

I mean, I wanted to come clean. That was the right thing to do—to admit my mistake, to tell Mr. Taylor that I wasn't who Grace thought I was. But what if it meant I couldn't claim the money? Grace's beautiful house would go to the government, or developers, or something, and I'd probably get arrested for impersonation.

But the alternative was . . . well, there wasn't an alternative. Not unless I could come up with a certificate proving that I was married to Anthony Milton. If only I hadn't told Grace I'd married Anthony. If only . . . Then I frowned. If I hadn't told her I was married, perhaps she wouldn't even have left the house to me. Didn't she want a family in her house, not Helen and me rattling around and watching DVDs?

My mind raced until early the next morning, which was why, as dawn broke over London that Monday, I got out of bed tentatively, heavy bags under my eyes, a despondent stoop to my shoulders; why I barely managed a good-bye to Helen as I slowly left our flat to go to work and mooched my way to the tube station; why I flinched every few seconds as thoughts and memories flooded my brain, of opportunities I'd had to correct my mistake, to tell Grace the truth, to avoid this living nightmare. Opportunities that I'd failed to take. Perhaps work would provide some solace, I found myself hoping as I approached the office. And then I rolled my eyes at my stupidity. Work meant Anthony Milton, a constant reminder of my stupid, stupid little fairy tale. Solace wasn't going to be an option.

Milton Advertising was situated in Clerkenwell, a part of London that had somehow morphed from a fairly dull area that was close to, but cheaper than, the city's financial district into a not-so-dull area that was close to, but cheaper than, Hoxton, the center of New Cool in London. Under both guises the area was filled largely with city types and media people (pronounced *meedja* by those who worked in the field), but whereas before they walked around in pseudo Savile Row suits, they now walked around in pseudo punky-art-student garb, sporting hairstyles that were, in my humble opinion, best left to the twenty-something artist, and really rather ill advised for slightly overweight men in their thirties and forties.

The company itself was situated in a squat two-story building nestled between two higher-rise blocks, making it look both defenseless and defiant at once. Inside, both floors were open-plan with a large sweeping staircase in the middle leading from the first floor to the second. On the ground floor were the private offices

(Anthony Milton's large one and Max's smaller one), along with the "account" people (that was the account directors, who were responsible for managing and "nurturing" accounts—otherwise known as "persuading clients to give the firm more business") and the account executives, of which I was one, who were responsible for doing all the work, meeting all the deadlines, running up and down the stairs to talk to the "creatives," and getting blamed whenever anything went wrong. It wasn't the best job in the world, but it had prospects—I could, Max told me at my interview, make account director within three years, if I worked hard enough, if I made an impression. I had no idea if I was making an impression or not—no one really seemed to have time to notice whether I was making one or not—but I certainly worked hard. Evenings, weekends, you name it. Account directors made serious money and had an expense account. The hard work was really a no-brainer.

The "creatives" did the design work; they had the upper floor to themselves, and Mac computers on which they would design logos and argue among themselves over whether a particular shade of red said *vivacious* more or less than one that looked exactly the same to me.

My desk was situated about fifteen feet to the left of Anthony's office and ten feet to the left of Max's; more significantly, it was right opposite Marcia's desk. Marcia, who had joined the company several months after me and who had already been given more accounts to lead, even though she was an account executive like me.

Slowly, I made my way through the lobby to my desk, where I sat down heavily, put the bottle of water I'd bought at the tube station down in front of me, and turned on my computer. If I could lose myself in work, I told myself, the answer to the whole will issue would just come to me out of nowhere. The trick was not to focus on it.

Fortunately, Marcia didn't seem to be interested in giving me any thinking time, either. Marcia didn't much like working, or, in fact, anything that interfered with her busy schedule of manicures, blow-dries, and facials. As far as I could tell she had gone into advertising in the hope of getting free stuff—she spent most of her time flicking through fashion magazines and only seemed to come to life for clients who were marketing shoes, handbags, clothes, or makeup.

"So do you have the style sheet I gave you on Friday?" she demanded as soon as I sat down. "You know I needed it this morning, so you'd better have . . ."

I forced a smile. Marcia had a way of talking to me like she was my boss or something. It was Max who had given me the style sheet to finalize, not her. But I told myself that now wasn't the time to quibble. "It's here," I said quickly, pulling it out of my bag. "I'll send you an electronic copy, too."

Her eyes narrowed suspiciously. "You did this over the weekend?"

"Yes. I came in yesterday." Yesterday. I almost felt like taking out a guitar and singing the Beatles song about all my troubles being far away.

Marcia raised an eyebrow. "Really. So, good weekend? Other than working, I mean?"

I shrugged. "It was . . . fine. How about you?"

"Me?" Marcia smiled. "Oh, it was good, thanks. Dinner out, lunch with some friends, hit the shops. You know, usual sort of thing."

I raised my eyebrows quizzically. It always amazed me how much effort Marcia put into shopping, how excited she'd be about each new purchase, even though as far I could see each one looked pretty much the same as the ones that had come before. Belts, bags, shoes, sweaters, skirts . . . for what? Money down the drain, Grandma used to say. Money that could be spent on something useful.

"Aha, I see Anthony's out and about," Marcia said suddenly as Anthony Milton's door flew open and he and Max emerged. Immediately I went slightly red and turned back to my computer screen, while Marcia waved, flashing Anthony a huge, beaming smile, just like she always did. They started walking toward us and I glanced up to see Max staring at me. Anthony was, too. I blanched slightly; Anthony never stared at me. He usually barely seemed to notice me. Had I done something wrong? Had I made a mistake on some major account?

They were just a few feet away. Max's face was serious; Anthony's, quizzical. And then, suddenly, I felt my heart sink. Not just sink, but fall like a lead weight to the bottom of my stomach. I'd given Mr. Taylor my business card. He'd probably called the office, asked for Mrs. Milton, been put through to Anthony . . . I couldn't believe I'd been so stupid. Couldn't believe my house of cards was about to come crashing down so quickly.

Getting hotter by the second, I wiped my palms on my trousers and focused on my breathing. I had to think of an excuse. That, or I had to get out of the building before they could say anything.

They stopped at Marcia's desk, their eyes still on me.

"Hi, Anthony," Marcia breathed, and he smiled at her. I looked up at Max, caught his eye, then looked down again, quickly. He had blue eyes. Really deep blue. But it was hard to notice them because he covered them up with glasses most of the time. He was slightly shorter than Anthony—which wasn't hard, bearing in mind that Anthony was well over six feet—and managed to make even expensive suits look somehow crumpled. Most people avoided Max if they could help it; they thought he was an obsessive workaholic who had no sense of humor, but it wasn't true. When he smiled—which wasn't that often, admittedly—his whole face lit up, his eyes crinkled up so you could hardly see them, and you couldn't help grinning back stupidly at him. Not that I liked him or anything. I mean sure, I liked him. But just as a colleague. And anyway, he certainly wasn't interested in me. Max wasn't interested in anyone.

I wiped my forehead, which was now perspiring.

"You okay, Jess?" Max asked, coming over. "You look terrible."

"I do?" My face fell slightly. "I mean, really?" I said quickly. "Because I'm fine, honestly."

"So how was your weekend?"

I took a deep breath—I could feel my chest constricting. Did he know? Was he playing with me?

"Not so good, actually," I said, my heart pounding. "Grace . . . my friend Grace . . . well, she died, actually."

Max's eyes widened in alarm. "Oh, Jess. I'm sorry. Oh, God, that's awful."

I looked at him uncertainly, then felt my entire body relax. He didn't know. If he'd known about the will, he'd have already known Grace was dead. I was safe.

"It's okay," I said breathlessly. "Thanks, Max."

"So, Max," Anthony said, raising an eyebrow. "Are you going to explain to Jess why we're over here?" His face was suddenly serious again and I felt my heart thudding in my chest again.

"The . . . reason?" I gulped.

Max shrugged uncomfortably. "Maybe now's not a great time," he muttered.

"Not a great time? Max, business is business."

I stared at him. "Is there something wrong?"

"Very wrong, I'm afraid," Anthony said seriously.

My eyes widened. "Really? What? Look, it wasn't my fault. I didn't mean to. I . . . I . . ." I could feel my chest constricting again.

Anthony arched an eyebrow. "That might be the case. But would you mind telling me what that bottle of Evian is doing on your desk?" he asked me.

"Seriously, Anthony, not the time . . ." Max said, but Anthony silenced him.

I looked at the bottle anxiously. "The water? It's . . . I mean, it's just for me. I . . . I . . ." The room was beginning to spin. I couldn't see properly. Couldn't speak properly.

"Better hide it when the Eau Best people come around later, eh?" Anthony's face broke into a huge smile. "Our new client! Max won the pitch last week. How about that?"

Marcia threw her head back and laughed. "No way! God, that's great. Really exciting."

I stared at Max, who rolled his eyes.

"Um . . . that's great," I said, feeling my heart begin to slow slightly. I put the bottle in the trash bin. Then I realized how thirsty I was. "I might just go and . . . get some . . . water. From the cooler . . ." I said, standing up on unsteady legs.

"Jess?" I could hear Max behind me calling, but I didn't stop. I felt out of control. I needed to splash water on my face, to cool down. Needed to get away from people. And then I heard my phone ring. My mobile phone. Which was on my desk.

Immediately I stopped, panic rising up through me again. Then I forced myself on again. It wasn't going to be Mr. Taylor. Sure, my mobile phone number was on the card I gave him, but that didn't mean that every time it rang it was going to be him. And even if it was him, no one would pick it up. It would go through to voice mail.

And then the ringing stopped. Too soon for voice mail to have picked up. Cautiously, I turned around; then I went white. Max had my telephone receiver in his hand, pressed to his ear. And he looked confused.

He caught my eye and looked over at me curiously. And suddenly I felt sick. Quickly I ran toward my desk, but already it was too late and as I ran I felt my legs begin to buckle under me. It was all over. Mr. Taylor was probably explaining right now why he'd asked to speak to Jessica Milton. Mrs. Jessica Milton. My life was over. Max knew. Anthony would know. Everyone would know. I'd be a laughingstock throughout London.

I reached for my desk anxiously, to steady myself. I couldn't seem to breathe in and out; I was gasping, like a fish, my chest compressing my lungs and heart as I clutched them and fell to the floor.

"The phone. It's for me?" I managed to say just before my head collapsed onto the ground beneath me.

"Jess? Bloody hell, what's wrong?"

Max was looking at me strangely, but I ignored him.

"Who . . . was it? I can explain. I . . ." I gasped, but the words barely came out.

"Jess, slow down. Just breathe in and out. In and out. Get her a paper bag," Max said firmly, snapping my phone shut. Marcia handed him the bag from her croissant and Max held it over my mouth; a few seconds later I was choking from a croissant crumb that got lodged in my trachea.

"I'm fine," I said quickly. "I must have . . . um . . ." Gasping for breath, I felt Max pull me up. Then Anthony looked at me worriedly. "Jessica?" he said, his face filled with alarm.

"She needs to go home," Max said seriously.

"No, I . . ." Max's arms were wrapped around me and they felt soothing. "I'm fine."

"See? She's fine," Marcia said.

"No," Max said, looking at me uncertainly. "No, she's not. Come on, Jess, let's get you into a cab." His arms tightened around me and he walked me toward the door; I just had time to grab my phone and bag on the way out.

"The . . . the call," I managed to say, as he maneuvered me onto the pavement and hailed a cab. "Who was it?"

Max looked at me strangely. "Oh, right. Yes. It was someone called Helen wanting to ask you something about *Murder, She Wrote*. Seemed rather . . . vexed."

"Helen?" I got into the cab, my face flushed with relief. "She's my flatmate," I said.

"And she's at home?" Max asked.

I nodded.

"Good. Then maybe you should call her and let her know that you're on your way. Who knows, you might get there in time to find out who dunnit."

"I'm fine, really," I said, attempting a smile. "I don't need to go home."

"I think you do," Max said, closing the door, his face impenetrable. "Can't have the staff collapsing on us like that. Bad for morale."

I opened my mouth to say something, to try to explain, but there was nothing I could say and before I could even say *thank you* or *see you tomorrow*, the taxi moved away, Max walked back into the building, and I slumped back on the seat wondering what on earth I was going to do.

Helen was waiting for me when I got home, all wide-eyed and serious. I'd called her from the cab, but I hadn't said much—just that I was on my way, just that I wasn't feeling so good. She put the kettle on. Made some tea. Then we both sat down.

"You're not . . . ill, are you?" she asked nervously.

I shook my head. "No, not ill."

"Oh, thank God. Okay, then," she breathed. "So, what is it?"

I opened my mouth to speak, but nothing came out.

"You *look* ill," Helen said seriously. "Actually, you look awful. Are you sure you don't have some horrible disease or something? There was a program on yesterday on Living TV about people who died from illnesses they didn't even know they had . . ."

"I'm not ill," I said firmly. "Not physically, anyway."

"You're ill mentally? Oh, God. Okay, so what is it? Depression? Psychosis? Look, so long as you're not dangerous, I'll totally help. I worked on a documentary about psychologists once, so actually I know quite a bit about—"

"I'm not mentally ill, either," I interjected. I could feel my breath quickening. "I . . ."

"Yes?" Helen's eyes were huge now, and curiosity poured from her every pore.

"I did a bad thing."

"A bad thing?"

"And now I'm in trouble and I don't know what to do."

"Oh, God. Okay. I think I know what this is." Helen stood up and nodded, seriously.

"You do?" I asked curiously.

"It's to do with the rings, isn't it?"

"The rings?"

Helen nodded. "I saw the rings in your jewelry box the other week. Diamond rings. You stole Grace's jewelry, didn't you? Oh, Jess, I was worried this might happen. So what, was her lawyer here last night looking for them? Look, it's fine—we'll get you a really good lawyer. I mean, you really shouldn't have taken them, but I'm sure you won't have to go to prison."

"Prison?" I looked at Helen incredulously. "I'm not going to prison. And I didn't steal Grace's jewelry."

"But the rings. I saw them," Helen said, wide-eyed. "And then that man turned up . . . Oh, God, is it worse than that? Have you been smuggling diamonds or something? Was Grace running a crime ring?"

I raised my eyebrows. "I think someone's been watching a little bit too much television," I said.

"Fine, so tell me what it is," Helen said impatiently. "If you didn't steal the rings or smuggle them, then why have you got an engagement ring and a wedding ring in your jewelry box? And why are you home from work early? You never come home from work early."

I sighed. "I bought the rings."

"You bought them? But you're broke. I thought you were broke?"

"They're paste."

Helen frowned. "Paste? Jess, I don't understand."

I took a deep breath. Then I let it out and took another one, and another one. And when I was sure that I could open my mouth without my chest clenching up, I told her. Slowly, but surely, cringing as I spoke and avoiding Helen's eyes entirely, I told her about the lie that had gotten out of hand, about the fake wedding, and the lawyer; about the estate and all the money. And then Helen didn't say anything.

Perhaps I should have mentioned that Helen wasn't known for her silence. She talked during films. She talked to the television when I wasn't there (I knew this because I'd walked in on her several times having quite fierce debates with the newsreader). She called me up at work when she was bored and had been known to keep me on the line for over an hour. The girl had things to say, all the time, about everything.

Except now.

Instead Helen leaned down and picked up her tea, taking a big swig.

"So, let me get this straight," she said eventually. "Grace was Lady Hampton. She left you her entire estate worth in the region of, what, four million pounds?"

I nodded. "Four million or thereabouts."

"Or thereabouts," Helen said, nodding, pulling back her long brown hair, her deep brown eyes slightly dazed. "Only, she thought you were married to your boss, so the money was left to

Jessica Milton. Mrs. Jessica Milton. Who you aren't. Who doesn't actually exist. Stop me if I'm getting any of this wrong . . ."

I shook my head. "So far, pretty much spot-on."

"And you have a moral obligation to claim the money, because otherwise Grace's lovely house will get sold off by the government and turned into flats. Or a casino. Right?"

I nodded. "It's the most beautiful house in the whole world. It's been in her family for generations. She wanted someone to live there, the lawyer said. To raise a family."

"Of course," Helen continued, slowly. "A family. With your imaginary husband, I suppose?"

I smiled nervously.

"And you can't actually claim the inheritance because you're not Jessica Milton? I mean, the house, all that money . . . and you can't get your hands on it?"

"That's pretty much it," I said, attempting a smile. I was putting on a front, trying to make light of the situation, but I was still covered in a light sweat and finding it problematic to just breathe in and out.

Helen nodded slowly. "You can't just claim it as Jessica Wild?"

"He said I needed to show him my marriage certificate."

"What if you told him the truth?"

I shook my head. "I can't," I whispered. "I just can't. It might get out. It would be so humiliating. And I probably wouldn't be able to claim the money anyway. There's a fifty-day rule—if it isn't claimed within that time frame, it's all forfeited."

"So the money will just . . . disappear?"

"To the government. Yes." Deep breath in, I told myself. Now breathe out.

"All four million pounds?"

I nodded, focusing on my breathing, and Helen let out a long, deep sigh.

"Bloody hell," she said, taking another swig of tea. "I mean, seriously. Bloody hell. I can't think of anything else to say."

"There is nothing to say," I said morosely. "I'm an idiot."

"*Idiot* doesn't come close," Helen said, shaking her head incredulously. Then her eyes lit up. "You say you've got fifty days?"

I nodded.

"Okay," Helen said excitedly. "In that time I bet you can change your name by deed poll."

I stared at her. "Deed poll. Of course! Oh my God, Helen, you're a savior. Deed poll! Why didn't I think of that?"

"Jessica Milton. Actually, it's a nice name," Helen said. "So can I come and live in your big house? Can we have a butler? Oh, please, Jess, let's have a butler. A good-looking one. And we can have parties all the time . . ."

She caught me shaking my head and frowned. "What? What's the matter? Fine, no butler. But we can still have parties, right?"

I sighed. I was looking at the folder Mr. Taylor had left me.

"Mrs.," I said, glumly. "It specifically says Mrs. Jessica Milton."

"So change your name to that, then," Helen suggested. "First name Mrs."

"First name Mrs.? Now who's being an idiot? And he said he needed a passport or driver's license. I'll never get it in time. Anyway, I told him I hadn't changed my name. If I suddenly turn up with ID for Jessica Milton, don't you think he'll smell a rat?"

Helen slumped back against the back of the sofa. "Okay, but there has to be another way. Come on, Jess, this is huge. We have to work out a way to claim the money." She caught my eye and blanched slightly. "To claim *your* money, I mean. But seriously, if we think hard it'll come to us. It has to."

She frowned, suddenly picking up the phone, dialing a number, and, when I looked at her worriedly, waving me away. "Rich? Hel . . . Yeah, hi . . . ! I know, sorry, been really busy. Listen, I've got a quick question for you. You know about wills, right? . . . Yes, I know you're a banking lawyer, but you must have done family law at some point, no? Fine. So, look, let's imagine that a will's been written, leaving the money to a . . . oh, I don't know. A Mrs. Jones. And let's say that Mrs. Jones isn't actually Mrs. Jones at all; she's Sarah Smith. Only the person who left her the money thinks she's called Mrs. Jones. Could Sarah Smith still claim the money? . . . Uh-huh . . . Right . . . Okay . . . Well, great. Thanks, Rich. . . . Yeah, a drink would be lovely. Give me a call? Okay then. Bye."

She turned to me. "That was Rich."

"I gathered that. And Rich is?"

"Richard Bennett. The lawyer I slept with a couple of weeks ago."

My eyes widened. "He's a lawyer? What did he say?"

Helen grimaced. "He said Sarah Smith could get the money if she could prove that she was in fact the person that the will maker considered to be Mrs. Jones, but it would probably have to go to court."

"Court?"

Helen bit her lip. I, meanwhile, pulled up my knees and wrapped my arms around them. "I can't go to court. And anyway, there's no time to go to court. God, I can't believe I'm such a total loser."

"You're not a loser. I mean, not a total one. Just a little one," Helen said, trying to look reassuring and failing completely. "I can't believe it, though. You, the total cynic, the woman who hates men, and all the time you had this little fantasy marriage going . . ."

"I don't hate men," I said, sighing. "I just think relationships are a waste of time. And I didn't have a fantasy marriage going. I just did it for Grace. It was her fantasy, not mine."

"You're sure you didn't want a boyfriend, too? Just a little bit?"

"No," I said stiffly. "Of course I didn't want a boyfriend."

"Just a husband?" Helen smirked.

"No! Hel, I do not want a boyfriend or a husband. You know I don't."

"How can you know you don't want something if you've never had it?"

"I have had a boyfriend," I said, hotly. "I've had two, actually."

"One at university and one three years ago. Yes, you're quite the man-eater." Helen was shaking her head at me, and I rolled my eyes irritably.

"Just because your life revolves around men, it doesn't mean that everyone's does," I said quickly. "I am just not interested in making small talk on dates, waiting for the phone to ring, feeding the ego of some man so that he'll like me and then watching him swan off with someone else a few months or a few years later. Romance is a myth, Hel. Love is just a hormonal reaction. Two out of three marriages end in divorce and the rest of them are probably miserable. Everyone ends up alone; why spend half your life chasing a chimera?"

"A chimera? You mean something that doesn't exist?"

I nodded.

"You mean like an imaginary husband?" Helen's eyes were twinkling, and I reddened.

"So you're not interested in Anthony Milton one little bit," she continued, smiling at me mischievously. "Isn't he the one who's, like, incredibly good looking? He was in that article you showed me."

"Yes, he is," I admitted. "But I'm still not interested."

"Really?" Helen looked dubious. I shook my head.

"No," I said firmly. "Trust me, if I was looking for a husband, which I'm not, it certainly wouldn't be Anthony. He's too . . ." I wrinkled my nose, trying to think of the right word.

"Successful? Gorgeous?" Helen suggested.

"Flighty," I said, then shook my head. "No, not flighty. Too . . ." I sighed. "Oh, I don't know. He's just not my type. Not serious enough. Goes out with models. Girls who look like models, anyway."

"You mean he's not your type because you don't think he'll fancy you?"

"I mean," I said sternly, "that he isn't my type because I don't fancy *him*." I paused and reddened slightly when I saw Helen looking at me, one eyebrow at least half an inch higher than the other. "Or anyone else, for that matter. And he certainly doesn't fancy me."

"At the moment," Helen said.

"At the moment?"

"I'm just looking at this laterally," she said thoughtfully. "Grace thought you were married to Anthony Milton, right?"

I nodded.

"And Anthony Milton is good looking and successful? I mean, objectively speaking, he's quite the catch."

"I guess."

Helen grinned. "So, then, the way out of this mess is staring us right in the face. You need to marry him for real."

I laughed. "Of course!" I said drily. "God, why didn't I think of that. Great idea. I'll just ask him tomorrow."

"I'm serious," Helen said. "I mean it's worth a shot, isn't it? Pull it off and you've not only married Mr. Perfect but become a millionaire four times over, and you've saved Grace's house."

"He is not Mr. Perfect. And you've forgotten something. I don't want to get married."

"Ah, but that's not important. You don't want to get married because you don't see the point in it, and you think that romance is a waste of time. But this is different."

"It is?" I asked, dubious.

"Of course it is. You're not getting married to live happily ever after. You're getting married to earn four million pounds. It's like an anti-marriage. Actually, it's really just a business deal. You have to pitch to your client and get him to give you the deal."

"Anthony's my client now?"

"Yes!"

I frowned. "But . . ."

"But what? Do you have any other ideas?"

I looked down at the floor.

"And do you want the money? Do you want to look after Grace's house like she wanted you to?" Helen continued.

I nodded. "Yes, but . . ."

"Stop with the buts," Helen said, standing up. "Does Anthony Milton have a girlfriend?"

"Not that I know of."

"So it's settled then. Project Marriage is under way."

My shoulders slumped forward. "Helen, please try to understand. What you're suggesting is . . . is madness. It's like you saying you're going to marry Tom Cruise. And let's not forget the fifty-day timetable."

"Tom Cruise is already married. Anthony Milton isn't. And a lot can happen in fifty days."

"I can't do it," I said helplessly. "I just can't."

"No such thing as *can't,* only *won't.* Don't tell me you're scared?"

"Scared?" I said, a little too defensively. "Of course I'm not scared. I'm just not a model, I'm no good with men, and I think the whole idea is completely insane."

"You aren't much good with men, that's true," Helen agreed. "But we can work on that. And your clothes."

"My clothes? What's wrong with my clothes?" Now it was my eyebrow shooting up.

"Everything," Helen said with a shrug. "And your hair."

"I like my hair."

"This isn't about you. It's about Anthony Milton, and I bet he doesn't like your hair."

"I doubt he's ever noticed my hair," I said crossly.

"Exactly."

"I'm not changing my hair for a man." I could feel myself stiffen. "Or my clothes. I'm not . . ."

Helen sighed. "Give it up, Jess. Look, I know your grand-mother was a bitch and that you're obsessed with being all self-sufficient, or whatever it is you bang on about all the time. But that doesn't mean you can't have a bit of fun sometimes. Putting on lipstick doesn't reduce your IQ. Going on a date doesn't turn you into a pathetic creature who can't live without a man."

"This has nothing to do with my grandmother," I said hotly.

"Whatever. All I'm saying is that you need new clothes and new hair. This Anthony Milton may not notice you now, but it's because you do everything in your power *not* to be noticed. And you don't fancy him because you won't let yourself," Helen said, firmly. "Because you're convinced he'll never fancy you, so it's easier to rule him out yourself. You know, if you were as ambitious with men as you were with your bloody job, you'd have men queuing down the street by now."

I laughed despite myself. "Hardly."

"Look, Jess. The way I see it is you either give this a go, or you don't. And if you don't, then you're saying good-bye to an awful lot."

"But . . ."

"No buts. Jess, just think of what you'd miss out on if you don't at least give it a try."

"It is a nice house," I said tentatively.

"It's a fabulous house," Helen agreed.

"And I'd be able to pay off all my debts."

"You'd be rich, Jess. Rich beyond your wildest dreams. Which means self-sufficient."

"And married."

"Fine. But not in a romantic high-hopes way. You'd be rich, independent of your husband, and you'd also be protecting Grace's legacy."

I felt a twinge at the mention of Grace's name. "I know. But I still don't see how I'd do it."

"Get Anthony to fall madly in love with you, you mean?" Helen asked. "Well, you need to do a . . . what do you call it when you change a product? Like when they launched the KitKat Chunky?"

"Rebranding," I said.

Helen's eyes lit up. "Yes! We're going to rebrand you."

"As a KitKat Chunky?"

"As perfect marriage material."

I snorted. "And then we'll turn back the tide, shall we?"

Helen shot me a look. "I'm going to ignore that," she said archly. "Look, Jess, you've got to promise to take this seriously. This is Deal or No Deal. Everything or nothing. So which is it going to be? Deal or No Deal, Jess? Which one?"

"This isn't a gamble, Helen, it's pure madness. It's impossible. It's . . . it's ridiculous."

"Deal or No Deal?" Helen repeated, fixing me with her eyes.

I looked at her for a moment. "You know this is the stupidest idea I've ever heard?"

"Deal or No Deal? Yes or no?"

I let out a long, painful sigh.

"I can't . . . I . . ."

"You can if you want. Come on, Jess. Take a risk. Give it a go. Do it for Grace."

I looked down at the floor, remembering how excited Grace had been when I'd first told her Anthony had asked me out. Remembered the excitement in her eyes when she told me he was going to propose on holiday. And then I frowned.

"What?" Helen said. "What is it now?"

I bit my lip. "Nothing. It's just . . . something Grace said. Ages ago."

"What?"

My forehead creased in concentration. "I thought she meant . . . I mean . . . But maybe she didn't. Maybe she actually meant that . . ."

"What?" Helen said impatiently. "What did she say?"

"She made me promise . . . she made me promise that if someone offered me everything they had, I'd take it," I said quietly. "I thought she meant Anthony. I thought it was one of her silly romantic dreams."

"And now you think she meant her inheritance?"

"I don't know. Maybe."

"And you promised that you would?"

I nodded.

"So does that mean . . . Are you going to do it? Are you?"

I looked at Helen for a few moments, then nodded. "Deal," I said, so softly I barely heard it myself.

"What was that?"

"Deal." My eyes were wide with trepidation. I couldn't believe what I was agreeing to.

Immediately Helen fell upon me and embraced me, tightly. "You won't regret this, Jess. God, it's going to be brilliant."

"It's a campaign, right?" I said nervously. "I'm just running an advertising campaign?"

"Project Marriage," Helen agreed. "Project Four Million Big Ones."

"And if it doesn't work, we'll just forget all about it and I'll change my name to Mrs."

I met Helen's eyes and a second later we both exploded into laughter, although mine was rather more hysterical than hers.

Then, a few minutes later, Helen picked up the phone and dialed a number, winking at me as she did it. "Hi, it's Helen Fairbrother. I need to book an appointment with Pedro. Only I need it for this afternoon. You can? Fantastic. And can I book a few beauty treatments for afterward? Yes, pedicure, leg wax, tan, and a facial. With eyebrow shape. Two PM? Fantastic, we'll see you then. It's for my friend Jessica. Jessica Wild."

Then she turned to me. "Right, I think we need a project plan, don't you? Go and get a pen and paper. We're launching Project Marriage."

Chapter 5

PEDRO, IT TURNED OUT, was a small Spanish hairdresser who worked in a tiny salon above a shop close to Islington High Street, barely visible from the road—which was, according to Helen, the whole point: this was very much a word-of-mouth place, she told me confidently, and they did the best threading in London.

I had no idea what threading was, and I didn't want to have my hair cut, but—I was swiftly learning—resistance was futile.

"Helen! Hiiiiiiiya! Ohmygod I love your boots!" The man who turned out to be Pedro came racing toward Helen as soon as we arrived at the top of the narrow staircase leading up to the salon. "I didn't know you coming today! What we doing?"

"Actually, we're doing my friend Jessica," Helen said, moving to the side so that Pedro could look at me properly. "We're doing a makeover."

Pedro's mouth fell open and I felt myself getting hot as everyone's attention turned to me—*everyone* being three immaculate women who, until my arrival, had been staring at themselves in the mirrors.

"A makeover? I love a makeover! What kind?"

"The total-transformation kind."

"Just a haircut," I interjected worriedly. "Nothing too dramatic," but I could see Helen shaking her head behind me.

Pedro grinned, then put his hand up to my hair, rubbing it between his fingers. "Short? Color?"

"Blond," Helen said firmly, just as I said, "No color, thanks."

Pedro nodded as my face drained. "Blond?" I gasped. "I can't go blond."

"Of course you can," Helen said dismissively. "So, Pedro, what do you think?"

He frowned. "Yes. I think so. But peroxide funky blond or highlighted chichi blond?"

Helen glanced at me. "Highlights," she said. "Expensive looking."

"Not just expensive *looking,* honey." Pedro laughed. "Okay. So we go natural-looking highlights. And the cut?"

They frowned and stared at my head, neither of them appearing to be remotely interested in my thoughts on the matter. I felt my hands clench into fists. I'd promised to go along with whatever Helen suggested, but *blond*? Seriously?

"Just a trim, please," I heard myself saying. "I had it cut only a couple of weeks ago."

"I think layers might be nice," Helen said, ignoring me.

"Layers. Yes, I think so," Pedro agreed, maneuvering me into a chair. "Layers and a long fringe. Like this . . ."

He lifted up the front of my hair so that I had a sweeping fringe cascading down my face.

"Perfect!" Helen squealed, clapping her hands. "God, Jessica, it's going to be great. Now, Pedro, she's also having her eyebrows and legs done, and we've also got to go shopping, so don't keep her too long."

Pedro grinned. "Okey dokey. You sit right here"—he pointed out a chair next to a sink— "and we get started, huh?"

I sat down rigidly, gripping the sides of the chair. Blond layers. I was going to look like Lassie. I was going to look ridiculous. I was going to look like one of those loose women Grandma used to shake her head at in the street. Women in miniskirts, women in pastel pink, women wearing too much makeup. "They'll end up like your mother," she'd mutter, darkly. "And so will you, if you don't watch out. Men look at women like that and they see a conquest, they see a victim. They'll walk all over you, mark my words. Leave you before you've even noticed they're gone." I'd nod seriously, determined that I would never be caught out like that, determined that I would never allow myself to be a victim, or a conquest. Not that I'd allow myself to think of my mother in that way, either. Grandma had her wrong, I'd tell myself. She didn't mean to leave me behind. Didn't mean to get killed in a car crash.

But even without my mother to act as a warning, Grandma was proof enough. After forty years of marriage, forty years, she'd tell me again and again, Grandpa left her for a woman half her age. Just walked out, without a care in the world. That's when Grandma stopped wearing makeup. That's when Grandma stopped smiling, too—at least, I was fairly sure it was. All the photos of her with Grandpa showed a different woman—a happy, cheerful-looking one with eyes that twinkled. But after he left, she had a permanent scowl. He left one month after my mother left me with Grandma for the weekend. One month after my mother got into a car, drove down a street, and ended up in a crash. She could so easily have not gotten into the car, I used to tell Grandma. She could so easily still be alive, if only she hadn't gotten in, if she'd stayed at home instead. Grandma disagreed about that. My mother had been wearing a miniskirt, she told me, as if that explained everything. A woman her age wearing a miniskirt was asking for trouble.

But before I could explain about highlights and short skirts to Pedro, the seat moved, throwing my legs up in the air as he pulled it backward toward the sink. He grabbed my hair and started rubbing something into it—not shampoo, but something else, something oily.

It was oil, I discovered a few minutes later.

"For condition," Pedro helpfully pointed out. "Before we putting on peroxide, yes?"

"Peroxide?" was all I managed to gasp before I was whisked out of the chair, moved to another chair, given a copy of *Vogue* to read, and told to look straight ahead while Pedro focused on my hair, picking out a few strands, covering them in white gunk, wrapping them in tinfoil, and then doing the same all over again. I concentrated on an article about the ongoing drive for exclusivity in the fashion world and tried not to think about my burning scalp.

As soon as my entire head was covered in foil, I was whisked downstairs to Maria, a stout woman who turned out to be Pedro's mother, who looked me up and down sternly, ordered me to undress, got me lying down on a narrow bed, and then went to work on my legs, laying on hot wax before ripping it off with what felt like most of my skin. It was agony, but I didn't want to say anything, so I just clamped my teeth shut and closed my eyes against the pain.

Next, she turned her attention to my eyebrows, wrapping two pieces of cotton together then letting them unravel, quickly, ripping out my eyebrows as they did so in a way that seemed so haphazard I was fairly sure I was going to look like something out of a horror movie by the time she'd finished. She handed me a mirror to inspect her handiwork but I was too scared to look in it, so I just handed it back and nodded, forcing a smile onto my face so she wouldn't suss me.

Immediately she pulled me off the bed, yelling "Pedro! I finish!" Then she sent me back upstairs to have my hair washed before I was plonked down in front of a mirror.

"Ah!" Pedro said, his eyes lighting up. "Ah, yes. Is better, yes?"

I looked down at my knees and nodded. It was just too humiliating. I felt like a turkey being basted for Christmas.

"So, now we cut," Pedro said, picking up his scissors and flourishing them like a matador's flag.

"So now we cut," I repeated, nervously. As soon as the scissors started to snip I closed my eyes and tried not to think about the pieces of hair that kept plopping into my lap, onto my hands, up my nose. I could always buy a scarf, I told myself. I could start wearing hats. I could shave my hair off and tell everyone I had that stress disease where your hair falls out.

And then I felt the heat of a hair dryer on my scalp, felt my hair being tousled and primped.

"Okay you have to look now."

I opened my eyes, slowly, and directed them toward Pedro's face in the mirror. "Great!" I said. "Really great."

"But you haven't looked," Pedro said, a hurt look on his face.

"Oh. Right." I blushed and forced my eyes toward my own reflection, steeling myself for the surprise, preparing a smile that probably wouldn't quite reach my eyes but would at least get me out of here with minimum fuss.

Except it wasn't surprise I felt when I saw myself properly. It was shock.

"Oh my God."

Pedro looked at me in alarm. "You don't like?"

My eyes widened. "I don't look like me," I said. I looked again. I resembled the sort of girl who walked down the Kings Road talking loudly into her mobile. The person staring back at me was the sort of person I poured scorn on—the sort of girl who sat outside cafés on a Saturday, eating lunch with a gaggle of friends, talking about boys, about shoes, about inconsequential things that didn't matter at all. My hair was sun-kissed honey blond with long, chunky layers softening my jaw. My eyebrows hadn't disappeared, either; they were just thinner, higher, arched, and they made my cheekbones suddenly stand out, turning my face into a kind of permanent question mark.

"She no like," Pedro said, his face falling. "She no like the makeover."

"No," I said quickly. "I mean . . . I don't . . . it's just . . . I . . ." I cleared my throat. "I just never thought I could look like that," I managed to say, eventually. "It's just different, that's all."

"Good different?" He had so much hope in his face, I couldn't tell him how shocked I felt, how doubtful. I looked down at my hands, which were covered in cut hair. My hair. I felt like Samson. I felt like Cinderella. I felt thoroughly confused.

"Good different," I agreed, uncertainly. Pedro, having decided that everything was okay after all, beamed.

"Yes!" he agreed. "Different is good. Is all good."

"Good? She look good?" Maria appeared behind him and stared at me in the mirror. "Ah, yes," she said approvingly. "Now pretty girl, huh? Now much better."

I nodded weakly, still trying to equate the reflection in the mirror with myself.

"Wow," Helen said, raising her eyebrows at the commotion as she pulled herself away from her magazine. "You are an amazing man, Pedro," she murmured, surveying my reflection.

"And Maria, you're an amazing woman," she added quickly, when she noticed Maria glaring at her.

Pedro put his hands on my shoulders. "People, they have surgery," he said sadly, "but all they need is hair cut."

"And eyebrows," Maria pointed out. "Eyebrows more than hair, in fact."

Everyone digested this thought for a few moments, unwilling to argue with her, and then Helen pulled me up. "Okay, time to go. We've got shopping to do."

"Shopping? But I hate shopping. And I haven't got any money."

Helen rolled her eyes. "Think of it as an investment," she said impatiently.

I stood up slowly, and in a reflex action pulled my hair behind my ears. But it wouldn't stay. It was shiny and soft, and immediately bounced back to its cascading fringe.

"A Jessica-proof haircut." Helen smiled as she pulled me out the door. "It really is a minor miracle."

Chapter 6

"I CAN'T DO IT."

It was the following morning, and suddenly what had been one of Helen's crazy ideas was now beginning to be very real and very scary.

"You can *so* do it."

I swallowed nervously. Helen and I were standing in front of her full-length mirror as she put some finishing touches on my makeup. Makeup! I'd never worn makeup to work before.

It wasn't just the makeup, either. I'd been up an hour and a half already, being tutored by Helen on the arts of flirting (you have to stay in the same room as the person you're trying to flirt with), smiling (push lips out before allowing corners of mouth to go up, and don't show too many teeth), accepting a compliment (look up seductively, and say "thank you," then smile; don't raise your eyebrows as if to suggest that the person complimenting you is an idiot), and what not to do with hands (drum fingers on the table, gesticulate vigorously), and it had just hit me that this wasn't a game; this was real.

"I really can't," I said, taking a deep breath. "Honestly, Helen. And I don't need the money. I mean, money doesn't make people happy. Friends and love make people happy, right?"

Helen smiled and wrapped her arms around me. "Jess, I'm your only friend. Trust me, you need the money."

I grimaced, then, shaking myself, focused back on my reflection. I was perched on two-and-a-half-inch heels, my legs clad in the thinnest of nude tights, my thighs encased in a skin-skimming skirt that didn't even attempt to reach down to my knees. A soft, cashmere sweater covered my top half, and around my face my new, swingy mane of hair was glistening like I was in a hair spray ad.

Helen clocked my expression. "You don't like it?"

I frowned. "No, I look like . . . like . . ."

"Like someone who people might actually be attracted to?" Helen asked, her eyes twinkling. "Someone who allows herself to have some fun from time to time?"

I met her eyes and reddened slightly. I'd been going to say *like a brain-dead floozie*. "Look, I have to go," I said instead, looking down at the floor quickly, wondering why it seemed such a long way away.

"Okay," Helen said. "Just remember, mouth shut when you smile, and no hiding behind your computer."

I raised an eyebrow, and she hit me on the shoulder. "Come on, Jess. You've got to put yourself out there. You've got to be open and friendly."

"Got it," I said quickly, figuring resistance was futile.

"Then prove it. Stop fidgeting and looking in the mirror like you're staring at a freak show," Helen said firmly.

"I'm not fidgeting," I said defensively.

"Put your arms by your side and stand up straight. You are Jessica Wild, hot babe. Who are you?"

I shrugged awkwardly. "I'm Jessica Wild," I mumbled.

Helen rolled her eyes. "You are Jessica Wild, a hot babe, who Anthony Milton is going to fancy madly," she said crossly. "Say it."

"No. You've had your way with the hair, and I'm wearing the makeup. But I'm not saying that I'm a hot babe."

"Yes you are. If you don't say it, you won't believe it. So until you do, you're not leaving," Helen commanded.

"But I don't believe it."

"Look, Jess, we can do this the easy way or the hard way. You can say it and go, or . . . or we can stay here all morning until you do."

"You can't make me," I said flatly.

"I've double-locked the front door and hidden your key."

My eyes widened. "You haven't . . ."

"Say it."

I stared at her pleadingly for a few seconds, but her face remained impassive. Eventually, I slumped. "I am Jessica Wild," I mumbled. "Hot babe."

"*Who*—? Come on, finish the sentence."

"Who Anthony Milton is going to fall madly in love with," I muttered. "Except he won't. Helen, this is stupid."

"No it isn't. Come on, again. I'm Jessica Wild, hot babe, and I'm charming, impetuous, and gorgeous."

"I am Jessica Wild," I sighed. "Hot babe. I'm charming, impetuous, and . . ."

"And gorgeous."

"And gorgeous," I repeated uncomfortably. I could imagine Grandma shaking her head at me.

"Now say it like you mean it."

I looked at Helen irritably. I was going to be late to work at this rate. "But I don't mean it."

"You better mean it. What time are you meant to be at work?"

I looked at my watch. "I have to go now," I said. "Right now."

"So say it again."

I narrowed my eyes, doing a quick calculation of being late to work versus the humiliation of doing what Helen was telling me to do. Then I shrugged. "Fine. I am Jessica Wild." I tossed my hair. "I am a hot babe, and Anthony Milton is going to fall madly in love with me."

"Who are you?"

"Jessica Wild." Big toothy grin.

"And now with the smile we practiced?"

"Jessica Wild." I pouted, for effect.

"And what are you?"

"A hot babe, who's charming, impetuous, and charming." I gave Helen a little wiggle of my hips just for good measure, just to make sure she let me out.

"And who's going to fall madly in love with you?"

"Anthony Milton."

"Good," Helen said, taking out her key. "And now you can go. No you can't. You can't take that handbag. Here, have one of mine."

I looked at her incredulously as Helen decanted the contents of my bag into one of her latest acquisitions.

"Like the bag matters," I said, rolling my eyes.

"The bag? Of course it matters. Bags are your calling card," Helen said, firmly. "Bags say everything that needs to be said. Well, bags and shoes."

"Great, I'll remember that," I said dismissively, grabbing the bag and waiting for Helen to unlock the door. Then, cautiously (there's no other way to walk in two-and-a-half-inch heels), I made my way down the road toward the tube station.

By the time I got off the tube at Farringdon, my feet felt like they were bleeding. For all I knew, they probably *were*. Whoever had designed the shoes that Helen had forced on me either hated women, hated feet, or never actually wore shoes themselves.

Irritably, feeling about as far from "Jessica Wild hot babe" as it was possible to feel, I hobbled into the coffee shop on the corner for my usual (small cappuccino, no chocolate, since you ask), and waited in line.

"Coffee?"

I smiled. "Just the usual, thanks."

Gary, the man behind the counter, frowned. Then he grinned. "Is you? You different."

I blushed awkwardly. He thought I looked ridiculous. And he was right.

"You do your hair? Is nice!" he continued. "Very glamorous lady."

"Hardly." I bit my lip. "It's far too shiny. Not practical at all."

"No, is good." Gary was still grinning at me. "Is very good. I like." He wasn't actually called Gary, he'd told me once; he was Polish and called Gerik but whenever people asked him his name, he'd had to repeat himself about a million times and then the person he was talking to still seemed to think he'd said "Gary," so eventually he'd given up correcting them.

He turned around and started to make my cappuccino. Then, when it was finished, he handed it to me. "No money," he insisted when I tried to hand him two pound coins. "And you take this pastry, too. From me. Present."

"Present?" I looked at him in alarm. He felt sorry for me. That was the only explanation. "No, no, you have to take money, Gary Here . . ."

But he held up his hand. And then he winked. Frowning, I turned around to see whom he was winking at. But there was no one there, and when I turned back he winked again. "On the house," he said, firmly.

"Really?" My eyes widened in surprise.

"Really. For brighten up the day." Brightening up his day? I'd never, to my knowledge, brightened up anyone's day before. Gary shot me a big grin and I managed to smile back, sort of, before turning uncertainly and making my way out.

"I'll brighten up your day if you give me a free croissant," I heard a woman offer as I pulled open the door.

"Bright enough, thanks," I heard Gary say gruffly. "And you keep smiling like that, I make you pay double."

Unsteadily, I made my way down the road toward Milton Advertising. As I approached the door, my phone rang and I transferred my coffee and pastry to my left hand, then pulled out my mobile. HOME was flashing on the screen.

"Hello?"

"I forgot to say, keep your head up. You always look at the floor. So don't."

I sighed. "Aren't you meant to be applying for jobs today?" I asked.

"I am," Helen said quickly. "But you're my priority."

"Well, thanks," I said. "And I'll keep my head up if you get your résumé together."

"If you make this work, I won't need a job. You'll be a millionaire and I can be your paid companion," she said.

" 'Bye Helen." I put my phone back in my pocket. As I did, I saw Anthony through the glass doors. He was on his way out; immediately I felt myself tense up.

Awkwardly, I pushed the door in front of me, but Anthony pulled it at the same time and instead of walking through, head held high, I fell forward, knocking into him. Quickly I pulled myself backward, but my legs, unused to balancing on high heels the width of a pin, swiveled under me; as I reached out to grab something—anything—to stop me from falling, I let go of my cup of coffee, which tumbled, as if in slow motion, toward the floor, toward Anthony, splashing his shoes, missing his trousers by about an inch. I would have followed it, too, if Anthony hadn't reached out to catch me.

"Fuck! I mean, oh God. I'm sorry." My face drained of blood.

Anthony looked at me for a moment, his clear blue eyes slightly bigger than normal, a startled expression on his face. Then he grinned and held out his hand, steering me into an upright position.

"Jessica. Feeling better this morning?"

I gulped. "Yes. Thank you," I stammered. "And sorry. About the coffee."

"Don't be," he said, still smiling. "It was my fault. Nice shoes, by the way. Are they new?"

I nodded, uncertainly, as he held the door open for me.

"See you, then." He winked at me, then turned and strode purposefully toward his office, leaving me staring after him. Shoes? Why on earth did he like my shoes?

"Jess?"

I arrived at my desk to find Marcia staring at me.

"Hi, Marcia." I sat down heavily on my chair and turned on my computer.

"You've . . . you've done something." She was looking at me suspiciously.

"I just had a haircut."

"What, yesterday? I thought you were ill?"

My face flushed. "My . . . flatmate did it. To cheer me up," I lied.

Marcia's eyes narrowed. "Your flatmate?"

I nodded, hoping she wouldn't ask any more questions. Luckily she picked up a file instead.

"So I take it you're better now? No more fainting fits to get attention?" she said, archly.

I nodded, checking that my phone was safely in my pocket. "I'm fine."

"Good." She sighed and leaned back in her chair. "So, listen, you know the Jarvis account?"

I slipped off my shoes. "Sure. The bank." It was a new account that Marcia had taken on, in spite of her protestations that she knew nothing about finance.

Marcia nodded. "It's just that I need a PowerPoint presentation done," she said. "And you're so good at them . . . You wouldn't help me out, would you?"

I looked at her archly. "Marcia, I've explained how to use PowerPoint. It's really very simple . . ."

She smiled. "I know, I know. But you're so much better than me. I just thought, since you were out all day yesterday, you might give me a hand . . ."

"Fine," I said, sighing and taking the file. "So when do you need the presentation by?"

She flinched slightly. "Ten AM."

"Tomorrow?"

"Today."

I stared at her. "Today? That's in . . . like . . . one hour."

"I know, I know." Marcia's eyes widened like a puppy's. "I should have gotten it done before, but I've been so busy. I mean, *I* haven't managed to have *my* hair cut in weeks . . ." She looked at me hopefully and I reddened. I knew the haircut was a bad idea.

"Sure," I said levelly. "I'll see what I can do."

"Thanks, Jess. You're a star." Marcia winked at me, waited for me to smile back, then picked up her phone. "Hi, Net-A-Porter? Yes, I wonder if you could tell me a bit more about a Marc Jacobs dress I've got my eye on . . ."

I opened the file. Inside was a twenty-page spec from Jarvis Private Banking, which was planning to launch a new investment fund specifically aimed at women—young professional women who had never considered investment funds before—and it wanted an advertising firm to come up with a name, a brand, and a concept that would make it sound fun, cool, aspirational, and desirable.

Attached to the spec were two sheets of A4, on which Marcia had scribbled some barely legible notes. They read:

- Chester Rydall, chief exec. From New York. Smart suit.
- Blue chip, needs weight.
- Women—young. Colors? Logo? Bright, not cheap, not tacky. Expensive.
- Aspirational? How to . . . ?
- Organic farmers market—find out what kale is??
- Angel book. Do I have Guardian Angel? Can I harness?
- Sample sale, Kensington Church Street, Sat. 12 PM. MUST REMEMBER!!!

On the other page, she had helpfully written a shopping list of all the things she was hoping to buy at the sample sale, including a pair of black trousers and a cocktail dress that worked with her new handbag.

I stared at the list. These weren't notes for a pitch. They weren't even close. Was this some kind of a joke that I didn't understand?

"Working hard?" I lifted my head to see Anthony leaning over me and quickly closed the file again. "Only I thought you might like one of these. You know, since your other one got . . . knocked over. I'm terribly sorry about that, by the way."

He put a coffee down in front of me and I stared at it, uncomprehendingly. "You . . . you got this for me?" I asked.

"I didn't know how you took it," Anthony continued easily. "So I brought you some sugar."

"Sugar," I repeated blankly. Anthony Milton had just bought me a coffee. It was just so . . . unexpected.

"That's right. I hope you don't mind?"

"Mind? No, no, I don't mind," I managed to say. He smiled at me; immediately Marcia appeared next to him.

"Anthony," she chided flirtatiously, "Jessica has work to do. And we need to talk about Chester Rydall."

He turned, and I hurriedly looked back at Marcia's notes.

"Of course," he said. "My office?"

"Perfect." Marcia smiled and stood up, brushing her skirt down in a seamless movement.

"You're going?" I said quickly, looking in her direction. "Only . . . before you go, I think you gave me the wrong notes."

"The wrong notes?"

"For the presentation. I don't have the information I need."

Marcia rolled her eyes. "It's all in there," she said irritably, before shooting another smile at Anthony. "Look, just be a bit creative, can't you? I mean, this is a creative agency."

"Be creative?" I raised an eyebrow. "Okay, but . . . are you absolutely sure I've got the right file? Or do you want me to base the presentation on the spec instead?"

Marcia glanced at the file on my desk. "Yes, it's the right file. And why would anyone want a presentation based on a spec that the client gave us in the first place? Look, Anthony and I have got some important things to discuss. So I'd really appreciate it if you'd just put a presentation together for me like I asked. Okay, Jess?"

"Fine," I said, with a sigh. "Fine, I'll just type them up then."

"Thanks, Jess." Marcia smiled sweetly before marching off. "That would be really great. And I do love the hair. Really suits you."

By 9:50 AM Marcia was back at her desk and I'd managed to come up with a whole six slides, one of which, to my immortal shame, said BRIGHT, NOT CHEAP, NOT TACKY. I cringed slightly, imagining Marcia's face when the slides came up in front of a team of serious bankers, but it wasn't my problem. Checking the spelling one last time and trying not to look at the presentation too closely, I saved it and e-mailed it to Marcia, then turned back to get on with some of my own work.

But two minutes later Marcia was at my side of the desk, her face white.

"Is this it?" she asked, staring in horror at the single sheet of A4 that contained all six slides.

I nodded.

"But there's nothing to it!" she said, her voice barely audible. "I've got to present in ten minutes. In front of Jarvis's chief executive. This isn't a presentation. It's . . . it's a joke! Jessica, I thought I could trust you to put this together. I was counting on you."

Carefully, I pulled out the notes she'd given me. "Marcia, these are the notes you had me work from. I followed them precisely."

Marcia picked up the notes and stared at them. Then she moved her hand out to my desk to steady herself.

"Oh fuck. Oh bollocks, wrong notes. These were . . ." Her eyes were focusing on the bottom of the second page, the bit where she'd started to write out her shopping list. "These were just . . . I mean, they were the preliminary . . ."

"So, ready for the meeting? Anthony says you're really confident about this pitch, Marcia. Anything you want to share with me?"

Marcia and I both looked up at once to see Max right behind us. Marcia's face was now slightly greenish. Mine immediately went red. It always did when Max wandered over, I noticed. I was thinking about getting treatment for it.

"No, no, everything's fine," she said, looking anything but. Then she looked at me, a funny look in her eye. "Actually, Max, I was thinking that maybe Jessica should be in on this one. You know, come to the meeting."

I looked at her in surprise. She never invited me to any of her pitch meetings.

"Good idea. Where is she, by the way? Is she in today?"

I raised an eyebrow at Max and forced a grin. "Very funny."

Max frowned and stared at me. "Jess?" He came closer and peered at me. "Bloody hell. It *is* you! What happened? What did you do to your hair?"

"She had her hair cut," Marcia said. "And she's got some great new clothes, too. Amazing that she had the time, considering how ill she was."

"I thought you were a new intern or something," Max said, frowning, ignoring Marcia's jibe.

I forced a smile. "No, just me."

He looked at me suspiciously for a few seconds, as if to reassure himself that it really was me.

"Anyway, what do you think, Max?" Marcia persisted.

"About Jess's hair? I like it. I suppose. I mean, it'll take a bit of getting used to . . ."

"About her coming to the meeting." Marcia sighed impatiently.

Max flinched slightly. "Right. Of course. Well, I think it's a great idea. Jess, you up for it?"

I nodded. "Of course. I mean, it would be really useful . . ."

"Good," Marcia interjected, "because Jess has been working with me a lot on this pitch and it could be a really great development opportunity for her to give the initial presentation."

It took me a few seconds to register what she'd said.

"No . . . I mean . . . I couldn't . . ." I stammered.

"Of course you can. I mean, you virtually wrote it," Marcia said, avoiding my eye.

"I didn't! I didn't at all . . ." I stared at her in horror.

"Great idea!" Max said, easily, ignoring my protests. "I'll okay it with Anthony, but as far as I'm concerned Jessica's more than welcome on the team. I'll see you both in a few minutes, then."

Before I could say anything else, he had disappeared. I immediately rounded on Marcia.

"I can't give that presentation!" I protested. "There *is* no presentation. Plus you know I can't talk in public. Marcia, you can't do this to me."

Marcia grabbed my shoulders. "Come on, Jess. Please. You're always asking for more involvement—and now you're getting it."

"But I can't present this. It isn't even a presentation. It's a load of drivel!"

"I know," Marcia said, pulling herself upright. "But that's not my fault. You did put it together, Jess. You have to take some responsibility."

"Me? I was doing you a favor. I had nothing to do with—"

"Look, this is your first presentation," Marcia interrupted flatly. "If it's crap, everyone will just chalk it up to inexperience. I'll defend you. It'll be fine. But if I screw it up . . ." She sighed, dramatically. "Max is already gunning for me. He'll use any excuse to get me fired."

"You won't get fired," I said desperately. "But I will be if I present this. Marcia, I can't. I really can't. You *have* to do it."

"No," Marcia said, shaking her head. "No, I don't. So if I were you, I'd start practicing. Okay?" She smiled awkwardly, then turned back to her desk. As for me, for the second time in as many days, I wished I was dead.

Chapter 7

I WALKED INTO the meeting room on unsteady legs—and it wasn't the shoes' fault. Immediately Max came over.

"So, your first pitch, huh?" He smiled, which would usually make me feel better, but this wasn't usually. "About time, too."

"Right," I said, trying to stay calm. "So which one's Chester Rydall?"

Max pointed to a man with silvery hair and tanned skin talking to Anthony—he looked like he'd just stepped off a yacht. Around him, everyone was fluttering—offering him coffee, offering him orange juice, asking him if he was hungry. Only Anthony and Max seemed unfazed by this giant of the financial world.

"Max! Come and meet Chester Rydall." Anthony appeared beside him and grabbed him by the shoulders.

"Of course. And Jess should meet him, too," Max said immediately. "She's presenting today, after all."

"Absolutely!" Anthony smiled at me benevolently, and I looked back uncertainly. It was the second time he'd smiled at me today, and it was slightly unsettling. "Love the hair, by the way," he whispered. "Suits you." I stared at him in surprise, but before I could say anything he'd put his arm around Chester. "Chester, meet Max, my deputy. And Jessica. Jessica Wild."

"Anthony, can I have a quick word?" Marcia appeared at his side, suddenly, her face one big simpering smile.

"Sure. No problem." Anthony nodded and disappeared, leaving me and Max alone with Chester.

"Jessica Wild," Chester said, shaking my hand. "Great name. So, you been with the firm long?"

I cleared my throat. "Um, well, awhile," I managed to say. "You know, a couple of years."

"Jess is one of our best account executives," Max said, seriously. I looked at him in surprise. He'd never said that to me before.

"She is? Well, great," Chester said, smiling. "In that case I look forward to hearing your presentation, Jess."

"The presentation. Right." As I spoke, my heart sank. It was bad enough that my presentation was going to be appalling; now I had to contend with high expectations, too. It was the worst of all worlds. I could already picture Max's stern stare as I messed up the pitch, could already feel the weight of his disappointment.

But before I could say anything, think of an excuse to run from the room, or even have another fainting fit, Anthony appeared again. "Right guys, it's ten fifteen. What do you say we get this show on the road? Ready to present, Jess?"

I felt my heart thudding in my chest; I nodded weakly.

He guided Chester to the table, then sat down next to him. Marcia sat next to Anthony, and Max sat opposite with two men Chester had brought with him. I took a chair next to Marcia and tried to calm my heart rate even though I knew the only thing that would really slow it would be my leaving the room and never coming back.

"I've loaded your presentation onto the projector," Marcia said to me, smiling. I gulped.

"It's not really my presentation," I said, feeling everyone's eyes on me. "I mean, I wasn't really involved in it that much."

"Don't be silly Jess, you wrote it," Marcia said sweetly, and I felt a wave of nausea wash through me. I was having one of those out-of-body experiences, looking down at the situation from the ceiling and shrugging at the Jessica sitting at the table. All the work I'd put in since getting this job was about to be forgotten. Any dignity I'd managed to carve out for myself was about to be decimated.

Anthony looked thoughtful for a moment, then flashed Chester a smile. A few seconds later he stood up and walked toward the window. "Milton Advertising," he said, after a pause, "is not an ordinary firm. Sure, we do some ordinary things, but we like to think that we do them in an extraordinary way. When we work for a client, they become part of our family, part of our raison d'être, if you will. Their problems are our problems, their successes our triumphs. We don't just assign client directors; we embed them. We work *with* our clients, not *for* them. We go the extra mile; we're available whenever we're needed, not simply when our office happens to be open. And when you task us to develop a new brand, we don't just think about logos and typefaces. We think about core values. We think about what a company stands for, what its brand needs to communicate—with customers, with rivals, with shareholders, with the media, the public . . . We help you to discover who you are, what you're about, and then we make sure that everything you do reflects your values, from the way your receptionist answers the phone to the way your online sales are handled. We're big-picture people who are passionate about the detail. We are tireless, committed, insightful. Sometimes we may tell you things that you don't want to hear, but we'd rather tell you the truth than have you discover it elsewhere. In a nutshell, we care. Deeply. And you'll see that care in everything we do—from today's presentation right through to our brand development, should you hire us. Which"—at this point, Anthony turned to Chester—"I sincerely hope you will."

The room felt electric, all eyes on Anthony. I knew he hadn't really said anything—nothing of substance, anyway—but it had worked nonetheless. Even I felt myself thinking I'd hire him if I were in Chester's shoes.

He sat down silently. No one said a word. A few seconds later, Chester cleared his throat expectantly, but still no one said anything. Was this a tactic? I wondered. Was this what you did in a pitch to unsettle your clients, to keep them guessing? And then I felt a kick to my ankle. Quickly I swung around to see Marcia glaring at me. "The presentation," she hissed. "You're up."

My eyes widened. Now? I had to give the worst presentation ever made right now? After that introduction? Smiling awkwardly, I stood up, and Marcia thrust the PowerPoint remote control into my hand.

"Good day," I said, clearing my throat, then coughing desperately. Good day? What was I, an eighteenth-century salesman?

"Good morning, I mean," I said quickly. "I'm Jessica Wild, and today I'm going to be talking to you in general terms about our interpretation of Jarvis Private Banking's new venture."

I smiled brightly, trying to disguise the abject fear making my legs tremble beneath me.

"You're far too modest, Jessica," Anthony said, encouragingly. "I'm sure that you've got more than generalities to share with Chester and his colleagues."

I blanched. "Right. Yes, of course," I said. Already I was writing my resignation letter in my head, wondering what other career options might be open to me.

Hesitantly, I pressed a button on the remote control, and my presentation flashed into life. I wanted to spend as long as possible on the first slide—the one with the title on it—because it was undoubtedly the best; once it left the screen, things would go downhill all the way.

"Jarvis Private Banking," I said as authoritatively as I could manage. I looked over at Max; he was looking at the Jarvis Private

Banking client file, his eyes serious, those little lines he got between his eyes furrowed and focused. I looked away again quickly. My whole body was shaking, and I was sweating lightly all over. Desperately, I thought about what Anthony had said, trying to think of something I could say to make this presentation slightly less bad than embarrassingly awful. Anything to pad it out just slightly.

"What . . . um, what values do we associate with Jarvis Private Banking?" I asked, eventually, then left the question hanging for a minute. Everyone was looking at me expectantly, and I realized I had no idea what their values were. So I decided to throw in another question.

"Which values are the pivotal ones? And which values need to be carried over to the new investment fund?"

I was seriously hot now, and lifted my hand to my forehead to wipe away the beads of sweat glistening there. I cleared my throat. "Quality," I managed to say. "Quality, and . . . privacy."

I snuck a quick look at Chester, who was looking slightly baffled.

"Quality, privacy, and . . . luxury," I concluded. "Luxury products, luxury service. For those who are looking for . . . luxury."

I smiled, but it wasn't a happy one. It was a smile of desperation. And then I noticed Marcia's mouth. She was smirking, I was sure of it. As she caught my eye, her face turned suddenly serious again, but I'd seen her mouth creasing upward. She actually thought this was funny. She thought it was a joke, me standing here making a fool of myself.

I pressed a button on the remote control and brought up the second slide.

Key stakeholder: Chester Rydall, chief exec.
What we know: New Yorker, smart, taste for luxury

Chester was looking like he was expecting me to tell him the punch line, like he knew this was meant to be funny but he wasn't sure why.

"The reason that this slide is important," I said, forcing myself to look at Chester seriously, "is that as the leader of the brand, your values are inevitably going to both influence and demonstrate the core values of the brand. If we understand you, we will understand the brand and vice versa. And when I say *we,* I don't just mean Milton Advertising, I mean the world at large." I could feel myself getting hotter and hotter by the minute. All eyes were on me, and not in a good way.

Chester smiled weakly and I cleared my throat again. There was no going back, I told myself—I was like an out-of-control lorry on the motorway. All I could do was watch the road and try not to hit anyone.

Quickly I brought up the next slide.

Investment fund for women

"And here," I said brightly, "is the concept that we're here to discuss today. An investment fund aimed at women. Let's just think about that, shall we?"

Everyone stared at me blankly. It was like that nightmare where you're in an exam and the questions keep changing as soon as you've answered them. Or the one where you turn up at the school prom only to discover that you forgot to get dressed.

"You see," I said, desperate now, mentally dragging up some facts and figures from the Jarvis spec, "there are a million and one investment funds. More, probably. Investment funds are ten a penny. Investment funds are really not terribly exciting, are they? But an investment fund for women? That's different. That's specialized. That's . . . brave. Innovative. Pushing back boundaries."

I heard a snort from Marcia's side of the room and bristled. Steeling myself, I flicked to slide four.

Usual market for investment funds: high-income, sophisticated investors

It wasn't much, but at least this slide had more than four words on it. Slowly, I read it out loud. All I could hear was Helen's voice ringing in my ear like a pantomime dame, telling me I was a hot babe. A hot babe? God, I wished I hadn't come to work this morning. There I was, a few hours ago, standing in front of the mirror while Helen ummmed and ahhhed over which of her many handbags I should use today, when all the time destiny was planning my total destruction. In fact, handbags were a bit of a running theme in this horror story; Marcia's shopping list cited at least three that she was hoping to buy.

"So," I said, tentatively, remembering the first thing Max had taught me about advertising: clients will always expect you to have the answer, but usually *they* do—so keep asking questions, because eventually someone will reveal it. "How many people in this room have money invested in investment funds?"

Slowly, Chester and his two colleagues raised their hands, along with Anthony and Max.

I figured I had about twenty seconds before they'd call security.

"Well, that's interesting," I said, taking a deep breath. "All men. All high earners . . ." I reddened slightly at this point, not sure that it was the done thing to refer to your potential client's salary level at a pitch . . . "And all . . . sophisticated."

I caught Anthony's eye and he raised an eyebrow quizzically, making my blush deepen.

Quickly I flicked to the next slide.

Colors? Logo? Bright, not cheap, not tacky.

I stared at it, feeling the blood drain from my face. It was over. It was all over. Slowly, I turned off the projector. I was going to have to apologize and give up. I had nothing to say, no pitch to present.

I picked up my bag—Helen's bag—aware that everyone was staring at me, aware that in a few seconds my career at Milton Advertising would be over. As for Project Marriage, I figured that Project-Getting-Anthony-to-Speak-to-Me-Again would be hard enough.

"Jess? Is everything okay?" It was Max, his face creased with concern.

"Of course she's okay," Anthony said quickly. "Come on, Jess, don't keep us waiting. I bet you've got something in that bag of yours, haven't you?"

I hesitated for a second. Then I bit my lip. Maybe it wasn't over quite yet. Anthony didn't think there was anything wrong. He thought I could pull it out of the bag, quite literally. And maybe I could. Helen was right—sometimes you had to go for it. Deal or No Deal. And this job was too important for me to give up. It was going to be Deal all the way. Purposefully, I put my bag back down.

"Sorry about that," I said, as the silence around the table deepened uncomfortably. "But no slides are going to get to the nub of the issue here."

"The nub?" Chester asked tentatively.

"The nub," I confirmed. It was all or nothing, I decided. Sink or swim. And I was going to do what I could to stay afloat, even if it meant doggy paddle. "And the nub of the issue is that women, particularly the ones who've got enough money to invest in an investment fund, would probably rather spend the money on . . ."

I looked at Marcia, and my eyes were drawn to something on the floor next to her. Something made of the softest, buttery leather. Something that, I had no doubt, had cost upward of three hundred pounds. And then I had an idea.

". . . on a handbag," I concluded firmly.

"A handbag?" Chester was staring at me now.

"A handbag," I confirmed. "Or a great pair of shoes."

"Instead of an investment fund?"

I nodded. If I was going down, I was going to fight all the way. "Marcia," I said, seriously, "how many pairs of shoes do you have?"

"Jessica, I'm not telling you that." She glanced around the table with a slightly baffled look on her face.

"No, tell us," Chester said intently.

She looked at Anthony, who nodded, and she sighed. "Oh, I don't know. Thirty, maybe."

"Including the ones you don't wear much?" I asked her.

Marcia smiled uncomfortably. "Okay, maybe more like forty. No, fifty. Something like that, anyway."

"And bags?" I persisted. "How many bags?"

Marcia was looking very uncomfortable now. I'd seen her with at least ten designer bags in as many months.

"Fifteen," she said with a shrug. "Twenty. What does it matter? We're talking about an investment fund, Jessica, remember?"

"Fifty pairs of shoes and twenty handbags. Average cost of each, three hundred pounds. That makes . . ." I frowned as I did the calculation, unsure how many zeros to add . . . "Twenty-one thousand pounds! Twenty-one thousand pounds that could have been secured in an investment fund, but only if that investment fund made Marcia feel as good as if she'd bought a new pair of shoes, or a new bag."

"Twenty-one thousand pounds on . . . on accessories?" Chester said, busily scribbling on a piece of paper. "And this is normal?"

"Completely," I said confidently, thinking of Helen's wardrobe back home. "Some women will have a lower budget, of course, but the proportion of salary will be similar."

"Really? So how do we do it? How do we make a fund as desirable as a handbag?" Chester asked, leaning forward and picking up his pen. Anthony grinned at me and I felt my shoulders relax just slightly.

"Well," I said, playing for time. I suddenly remembered the *Vogue* article I'd read when Pedro had been trussing my hair up like a chicken being prepared for Sunday lunch. It had been discussing the key items of the season, pieces of clothing that had waiting lists as long as your arm, and which items fashion-conscious women would fight over. At the time I'd been amazed that anyone would pay over a thousand pounds for a green sweater, but now it was giving me ideas. "Explaining the benefits and the growth potential isn't going to work, is it? Because plenty of funds do that, and Marcia still prefers to spend her money on handbags."

Anthony laughed and Marcia grimaced slightly; it was all I needed to spur me on. "No," I continued, getting into my stride, "to make an investment fund as sexy and aspirational as a handbag, it has to be difficult to get hold of—which means waiting lists. It needs visible benefits—maybe a limited-edition purse given out free when you open the fund, so that those in the know recognize it and it becomes a little club. Make it expensive—minimum investment of, I don't know, two thousand pounds a month or something, so that not everyone can afford it. Don't call customers 'customers' or even 'clients'—call them members, so they feel a sense of ownership. And don't aim your public relations at the finance pages; aim it at *Vogue* and *Harper's Bazaar*. Get a couple of celebrities to join and get them to mention it in a *Hello! Magazine* interview."

I took a deep breath and looked at Chester. For what felt like forever, he didn't say a word; just looked down at the notes he'd scribbled, scratching his head. Then he lifted his head.

"I love it."

I looked at him uncertainly. "You . . . you do?"

"I really love it," he said again. "You've managed to get to the . . . what did you call it? The nub? Yes, you got to the nub of the issue so succinctly. You're right—a formal presentation of slides was all wrong for this. I have to hand it to you, Anthony, this was one hell of a presentation. Off the wall, had me guessing there for a while, but I guess that's what you meant by *extraordinary*. It certainly wasn't ordinary, that's for sure."

I was getting goose bumps on the back of my neck. He loved my idea?

"Of course it wasn't ordinary," Anthony said warmly, winking at me and causing Marcia's eyes to narrow. "Jess, you've done us proud. Thank you." I looked over at Max to see if he was smiling, too, to see if he was looking at me proudly, but his eyes were fixed downward and I felt my shoulders fall slightly.

"Thank you," I forced myself to say, the words sounding alien in my mouth. "I'm so glad you liked it."

I grinned, then felt Marcia's gaze on me. She had a very fixed smile on her face. "That all sounds so great," she said. "But what about the branding? I thought we were going to cover that, too, Jess."

"And I'm sure she's got it covered," Anthony said reassuringly, his eyes twinkling. Suddenly he didn't look quite so plasticky. He was actually quite attractive, really, in a blond, blue-eyed kind of way. "What were your thoughts on the branding, Jess?"

I shook myself. "Well, obviously," I said, "the branding would need to reflect these . . . these values and . . . and . . . aspirations."

"And they would be?" Marcia asked, wide-eyed.

"I thought you'd know that, Marcia," I said smoothly. "The values are luxury, membership, and exclusivity."

"Exactly," Chester said, grinning.

"What about visuals, Jess?" Max asked suddenly.

"I . . ." I looked up to see him smiling appreciatively at me and

I felt a surge of happiness zip through my body. Then my eyes flickered back to Anthony, who was grinning ear-to-ear. "I thought that the logo might be a handbag," I found myself saying, like I'd spent a week prepping for the question. "Or maybe a pair of shoes. Something that tells men that this isn't a club for them."

Chester was still looking at me expectantly, so I decided to continue. "It could have a tagline that plays on the logo," I said, my eye flicking up to meet Anthony's again and feeling immediately reassured by his confident smile. "Something like *All you need to carry with you* or *Keeping you walking tall all the way.*

"All you need to carry with you. This just gets better and better," Chester said, standing up. "So listen, I'm hooked. I can't stay now—I've got another meeting. But I'm going to keep in touch. I have a good feeling about this." He looked at me. "Jessica Wild, huh?" he asked. I nodded. "Good to meet you," he continued. "Good to have you on the team."

And with that, he and his flunkies left Anthony's office.

"Marcia, see him to the door, will you?" Anthony asked. Marcia opened her mouth as if to complain, then shrugged and half jogged out of the room.

Immediately Anthony rounded on me, enveloping me in a huge bear hug. "Jarvis Private Finance. We've got fucking Jarvis Private Banking! Jessica Wild, you're an asset to this company."

"I am?" I asked breathlessly.

"Yes, you are," Anthony said. He clapped Max on the back. "Jarvis Private Banking," he said, shaking his head. "That's not just blue chip. It's royal blue chip. Think of the money! No more problems, Max. It's going to be plain sailing from now on."

"Let's hope so," Max said, picking up his papers. "A good job all around, I think."

Anthony rolled his eyes. "A brilliant job," he said, turning back to me. "So, Jess. Handbags, eh? Inspired. Ingenious. And that

whole charade at the beginning—amazing. Risky strategy, but totally worked. Kept us all guessing, didn't she, Max?"

His eyes were twinkling at me, like we were sharing a private
joke.

Max nodded. "She certainly did," he said, but he wasn't grinning anymore. I looked at him uncertainly, expecting a big smile,
a nod of congratulations, but instead he didn't meet my eyes. He
simply walked toward the door.

Anthony, on the other hand, couldn't stop slapping me on the
back.

"Our new best executive," he said as Marcia reappeared
through the door. She looked at him, happily, then her expression
blackened slightly as it dawned on her that he wasn't talking about
her. "And well done, Marcia, for suggesting that Jess do the presentation," he continued. "That shows real insight."

Marcia smiled weakly. "Well, yes, it does," she said, after a
slight pause. "I thought it would be a good idea. And I'm sure
she'll be of great help to me on this account."

"You're . . . I mean . . . you're still leading the account?" I said,
before I could stop myself.

"Well of course I am," Marcia said. "After all, it was my pitch."

"I thought you said Jess wrote it," Max said, hovering in the
doorway, a little smile playing on his lips.

Marcia frowned. "Well, she did, I mean she put it together,
technically, but it's still my account. Isn't it, Anthony?"

Anthony looked at her for a moment, then turned to me.
"Well," he said thoughtfully, "if Jess wrote the pitch, it makes
sense for her to take on the account, doesn't it?"

"Really?" I stared at him in delight. God, I loved Anthony. You
know, in a not-wanting-to-marry-him kind of way. Oh, what the
hell, even marrying him was beginning to seem like a good idea.
"Me, leading the Jarvis Private Banking account? Are you serious?"

"Of course I am," he said immediately. "The Project Handbag account. What do you reckon, Marcia? Means you don't have to lead a . . . what did you call it? A boring finance techie account?"

That was it. I was in love. Marcia stood stock-still. "Project Handbag?" She swallowed awkwardly, then forced a smile onto her face. "That's not really finance, is it? I mean, not anymore."

"Not once our star turn Jessica Wild got her hands on it, no!" Anthony said, grinning at Marcia. "So that's settled then. And I know you'll help Jess out if she needs it, right, Marcia?"

"Right! I mean, if you think it's the right thing to do, then yes. Of course!" Marcia smiled weakly, as Anthony winked at us both.

"Nothing like great teamwork, is there?" he asked benevolently.

Marcia and I both smiled back brightly. "Teamwork," she said. "Nothing like it."

Chapter 8

"SO?" HELEN WAS WAITING for me at the door when I got home that evening.

"So?" I replied nonchalantly.

"So what happened? Did you talk to him? Did he notice your hair?"

My face broke out into a huge grin. "Helen, this was the best day ever. I'm leading a *major account,*" I squealed. "I presented to Chester Rydall, who's the chief executive of this huge private bank, and it was nearly the worst hour of my whole life, but I thought about your handbag and had all these ideas and now I'm leading the account. And Max told me I was the best account executive."

Helen looked slightly nonplussed. "He did?"

I gave her a quick hug, and as I took off my coat I told her everything. "It was the best day ever," I concluded happily. "And if it wasn't for you, I never would have thought of any of it."

"An account director," Helen said flatly. "So, what, that'll be more money?"

I nodded. "Lots more. At least ten thousand pounds a year more."

"Wow. So that'll really make a difference, then."

"Loads," I agreed, then frowned when Helen flicked me in the forehead.

"The same difference as four million?"

"Helen, this is real, not some crazy plan," I said seriously. "If I make account director, I'll be set for life."

"Project Marriage is not some crazy plan, Jess. And if you inherit four million pounds, believe me, you'll be more set."

I rolled my eyes. "Fine. Don't be pleased for me. See if I care."

"I am pleased," Helen relented. "But tell me more about the coffee. Tell me more about Anthony."

"Anthony?" I said, a little smile playing on my lips. "Well, he was the one who gave me the account. And he was great, too—I mean, he really knows how to get people excited about the company—"

"Not the pitch," Helen said, wearily. "Tell me about you and Anthony. You know, Project Marriage?"

"Oh, right." I blanched slightly. The whole "I love Anthony" thing seemed a bit childish now, but I figured I owed Helen something. "Well, um . . ."

"Yes?" Helen said impatiently.

"He bought me coffee!" I said suddenly, a note of triumph in my voice as I remembered. "And he said he liked my shoes. And my hair."

"He did?" Helen asked excitedly. "Really?"

I nodded. "And he smiled at me a lot, too." I looked encouragingly at Helen, who appeared mollified.

"Did anyone else notice your hair?" she demanded.

"Everyone," I assured her. "Max didn't recognize me. And Marcia wanted to know who my hairdresser was."

"You didn't tell her, did you?" she asked accusingly. "Pedro's my secret."

"I told her you did it."

"Me?" She was smiling now. "And she believed you?"

"I think she might be giving you a call sometime."

"Good. She's competition. I'll give her a crop."

"See?" I moved closer to Helen and leaned back on the counter next to her. "It's been a good day. A really good day."

"Fine," she said with a sigh. "But you have to focus, Jess. This is not about work, this is about Anthony Milton falling madly in love with you."

"Sure, I know." I pulled out two mugs and put tea bags in them. "But the better I do at work, the better Anthony will like me. You know, he was so excited about my presentation, whereas Max didn't say anything about it," I said casually, as I boiled the kettle. "He didn't even smile once."

"No?" Helen asked. "So what? Why do you care what Max thinks?"

"I don't," I said quickly. "I don't care."

"Good. Because you have to stay focused on Anthony here."

"Sure, I know that," I said just as the phone rang. Helen immediately swooped on it.

"Hello? Oh, yes. Just one moment."

She handed it to me, pulling a face as she did so, and I pressed the receiver to my ear.

"Hello?"

"Mrs. Milton? It's Robert Taylor here. Of Taylor and Rudd."

"Mr. Taylor." Immediately I reddened. "Hi. How are you?"

"It's about the funeral, Mrs. Milton . . . I mean, Ms. Wild. It's on Wednesday afternoon—er, tomorrow—at three PM. I do hope that's convenient."

"Oh, the funeral," I said, reddening even more. "Tomorrow? Yes, of course."

"I'm so pleased. It's at All Saints Church, in South Kensington. Do you know it?"

"Yes. Yes, I think so."

"And perhaps if there's time afterward, we might discuss the paperwork? Around Grace's will?"

I swallowed nervously. "Right. Um, yes. I mean, I'm not sure how long I'll be able to stay—work commitments, you know. But let's see, shall we?"

"Indeed," said Mr. Taylor. "Let's."

I put down the phone and returned to the counter.

"Shit. That was him, wasn't it? The lawyer," Helen asked worriedly. "I knew it was as soon as I heard his voice. I should have said you were out."

"It's okay. He just wanted to tell me that Grace's funeral is tomorrow," I said quietly.

Helen nodded sadly. "Oh, right."

I bit my lip. "He was also hoping we might go through some paperwork."

"You can't!" she said quickly. "You can't go. You'll have to think of an excuse."

"I have to go," I said crossly, folding my arms. I felt tawdry, all of a sudden, planning Project Marriage with Helen when poor Grace wasn't even buried yet. "Some things are more important than money."

"But you'll have to leave early," Helen continued. "I mean, you have to get out of signing anything."

I raised an eyebrow. "I don't want to talk about it now," I said, turning on the television. "Don't worry about Mr. Taylor. I'll think of something."

Chapter 9

The day of the funeral was a washout—it started out dark, gloomy, and rainy, and it got progressively worse as the hours ticked on. After a brief attempt to flirt with Anthony had been foiled when Max came over and started talking to him about outstanding loans, I'd given up all thoughts of Project Marriage and instead focused on getting to the church and avoiding Mr. Taylor instead. It was only when I got off the tube to find the streets of South Kensington full of people hunched over under umbrellas while the rain tipped down like several thousand buckets of water being turned over at once that it hit me—today I was going to be saying my final farewell to Grace. I wasn't sure I was ready to say good-bye, wasn't sure how I'd react to seeing her buried.

"Ah, Jessica. I'm so glad you're here."

As I walked through the door, I immediately saw Mr. Taylor walking toward me, and bit my lip.

"Hi, Mr. Taylor. How are you?"

"I'm very well," he said graciously. "I'm so glad you could come."

I managed a smile. "Well, of course. I mean, I wouldn't have missed it. No way."

"Of course. Now, we must make an appointment to sort out the paperwork around the will. Are you free afterward? Perhaps we could go to my office?"

"You know," I said carefully, "today isn't that great."

I saw Mr. Taylor's eyes narrow slightly in curiosity and I swallowed uncomfortably.

"Not great?" he asked.

I nodded. Then I sighed. "To be honest," I said, "I'm just not sure I want to discuss Grace's inheritance on the same day that . . . well, you know . . ." I looked up toward the altar, and Mr. Taylor smiled.

"Oh, I quite understand. But believe me, Grace wouldn't mind. She'd positively encourage it."

"She would?" I asked hesitantly.

"Absolutely. So, later?"

"Later?" I gulped. "Well, maybe. I mean, I do have to get back to work, so maybe not, but . . . well let's see, shall we?"

Mr. Taylor smiled. "Of course. And Mr. Milton?" he asked.

"Yes?" I asked, my heart stopping briefly.

"Is he here with you?"

I could feel myself getting hot. Of course. I should have my husband with me. Mr. Taylor was going to get suspicious. "Mr. Milton? Oh. No. No, he couldn't come, I'm afraid. Business, you see. He's . . . away a lot," I said awkwardly.

"Yes, I see," Mr. Taylor said understandingly. His eyes flickered down to my left hand and I blanched. My fingers were bare.

"God, look at that. Always forgetting to put my rings back on,"

I said uneasily, quickly pulling the paste engagement ring and cheap wedding ring out of my coat pocket. I'd put them there that morning, thinking that I'd remember to put them on before the funeral. Which, of course, I hadn't.

"Back on?" Mr. Taylor asked curiously. "I thought people usually wore their wedding rings all the time."

"They do," I said, flustered. "Of course they do. As do I. Except I was . . . washing up earlier. You know."

"Indeed." Mr. Taylor smiled, and I wiped a trickle of sweat from my nose. "And your husband is away, you say?"

"Yes, that's right. Away working. It's a nightmare, actually." I forced a smile, wishing fervently that Mr. Taylor would leave me alone, wishing I'd never started this conversation. "He's away a lot, Anthony. Always busy, busy, busy."

Mr. Taylor nodded sympathetically, then he smiled. "Shall we?"

He motioned toward a pew just ahead, and, relieved that I didn't have to talk anymore, I followed him, taking a seat next to him.

Music started to play, organ music—I think it was Bach. And then the vicar walked in and everyone stood up, and he said something about peace or God or something, and then everyone sat down again. Then, just as he was saying the immortal line (*Dearly beloved, we are gathered here today*) that seems to start all the major services—weddings, funerals, christenings—I felt someone squeeze in next to me. I turned around in slight annoyance—there were plenty of spaces around and no need to sit quite so close.

My mouth fell open in surprise. "Max? Max, what are you doing here?"

He shrugged. "I just thought . . ." He picked up a hymnbook. "Thought you might like some company. Funerals are shitty things, aren't they?"

"Yes, they are," I said uncertainly. "But you came all the way here? You left the office to come?"

He shot me an enigmatic smile. "I do leave the office on occasion, you know."

The organ started playing and before I could say anything, before I could interrogate him further, everyone stood up to sing another hymn—"Lord of All Hopefulness." Duly, Max stood up; I followed. We were standing close together, and I felt his coat sleeve brushing against mine as we peered at our hymnals. My heart started to beat rapidly in my chest. I did my best to ignore it.

Instead I decided to focus on the talk at hand, namely trying to sing in tune. After all, I told myself, I didn't like Max. The object of my attentions was Anthony. Or no one. It certainly wasn't Max. And even if I did like Max a little bit, it didn't matter. It wasn't like anything was ever going to happen. I knew better than to get carried away. Getting carried away was dangerous. It led to heartbreak, to loneliness, to all sorts of problems. I was far too professional, far too . . .

"Actually," he whispered, "I did have an ulterior motive, coming here today."

My stomach did a flip-flop. "You . . . you did?" I looked up at him, held his gaze for a second.

He smiled, and I found the corners of my mouth turning upward. "The style sheet you did for Marcia," he said. "She appears to have lost it, and we're seeing the client today so we need a copy urgently."

I stared at him for a second as his words sank in. Then I cleared my throat, aware that there was suddenly a big lump in it. It served me right, of course. God, I was an idiot.

"You couldn't have called me?" My voice sounded tight, strained.

Max frowned. "I tried," he said. "Your phone must have been turned off."

"Right. Of course." I swallowed uncomfortably. "So, the style sheet," I heard myself say. "I . . . well, I sent it to her by e-mail. So she should still have it . . ."

Max raised his eyebrows. "If Marcia had it, I wouldn't have had to come all this way," he whispered loudly to be heard over the singing.

"Right," I said stupidly. I wanted to sink into the ground. Instead I shook myself and forced a smile. "Sorry, I forgot we were talking about Marcia. It'll be in my sent folder. I'll give you my password if you want?"

"Thanks, Jess. You're a star."

I wrote down my password on a scrap of paper and handed it to Max, who put it in his pocket. Then he picked up a hymnbook and started to sing loudly.

"He managed to get away, then?" Mr. Taylor asked, leaning in closely so he could whisper in my ear.

I looked at him vaguely. "Um, yes, I guess so," I said, only realizing too late what he'd meant. "Not that he's . . . I mean, this isn't . . ." I whispered, frantically, but Mr. Taylor was already singing again and didn't hear me.

Then the hymn came to an end, and the vicar said a prayer, then started to talk about Grace. And gradually, I forgot about Max sitting closely next to me, forgot about Mr. Taylor and the will and the rings. Grace had been named perfectly, the vicar said—she had been full of grace, but also, as anyone who had met her knew only too well, full of determination and strength. He told stories about her—stories I'd never heard before—and talked about the many years she'd done the flowers in this very church, every week, without fail. And then, as the funeral march started to play, and Grace's coffin suddenly appeared at the back of the church, it hit me like a boulder. She was really gone, and she wasn't coming back. My sweet friend, sweet Grace, would never tell me about the joys of coral lipstick again; would never tell me that happiness was around the corner if you could only make yourself turn it; would never laugh at my silly stories or write down little recipes for me to try. She was dead—not away on holiday, not out of town, but dead. And I was on my own. Like I always knew I would be.

Gripping the pew in front of me, I felt large, fat tears begin to cascade out of my eyes.

"You okay?"

I turned around to see Max looking at me concernedly.

"Fine," I said quickly. "Look, you should go back to the office. You've got a meeting to go to." I didn't want his pity, didn't want him pretending to care.

"I can stay," he said, frowning. "The meeting's not until this afternoon. Come on, you don't want to be at a funeral on your own."

"Maybe I do," I said, sniffing. "Maybe I like being on my own."

"Really?"

"Really." I nodded just as the hymn came to an end. Immediately Mr. Taylor turned around and held his hand out toward Max, who shook it uncertainly.

"So, you finished your business early, did you?" he whispered, smiling.

"Business?" Max asked.

"Jessica said that you were very busy and couldn't make it. I just wanted to say how good of you it was to come."

My face drained of blood; Max looked at him curiously. "She did?"

"Yes, but you're here now, which is all that matters." He smiled again and sat back, as the vicar told everyone to kneel. Gulping, I pulled out a prayer cushion from in front of me and Max followed suit.

"What was all that about?" he whispered, as everyone started saying the Lord's Prayer.

"That?" I asked, weakly. "Oh, that was just Grace's solicitor. I wouldn't worry about him. He's just a bit . . . batty, I'm afraid. He must have thought you were someone else."

"Someone else? Who?"

"Who?" I repeated vaguely. "Um, well, I'm not exactly sure. I mean . . ."

"He said you thought I was too busy to come. He can't have just made that up."

I smiled weakly. "He . . . he probably thought . . ." I said, racking my brains, "he probably thought you were my . . . boyfriend."

"Boyfriend?"

"That's right," I whispered uncertainly. "He was going to come, you see. But then he couldn't. And I told Mr. Taylor, so I guess he just thought . . ."

"You've got a boyfriend?"

"Yes. Yes, that's right." I nodded, then looked away, willing my face to lose its beet-root hue.

"Oh. Right. Sorry, didn't know."

"No, well, there you are."

The prayers ended and we sat back down as the vicar introduced one of the readings.

"Well, look, I'd better go really," Max said, leaning forward to pick up his umbrella.

"Right," I said, trying not to feel disappointed, telling myself it was a good thing.

"Yes. I mean, work to do, preparation for this meeting, you know . . ."

"Of course." I nodded. "You go. I'll be fine here."

"Good. Well, I'll . . . see you later. Or tomorrow. Whenever."

He got up and shuffled out; I forced myself not to watch him go. After all, I told myself, the empty feeling in my stomach had nothing to do with Max; it had to do with Grace. I was at a funeral, for heaven's sake—I was *supposed* to be feeling empty.

"That's a shame." said Mr. Taylor, shaking his head. "Your husband had to go, did he? I was rather hoping to meet him properly."

"Yes," I said weakly, "it is a shame." Then I turned around quickly. "But that's my husband," I said, forcing a big smile onto my face. "Busy, busy, busy."

I didn't stay for the drinks and nibbles that Mr. Taylor had organized—partly because I couldn't risk him bringing over the paperwork for Grace's will and partly because I needed some time alone. So instead I walked around the churchyard, then around the surrounding streets, looking around at everything and seeing very little.

I kept thinking about the promise I'd made Grace, thinking about all the stories I'd made up for her about me and Anthony. Wondering what advice she'd give me now, if she were still alive. Would she tell me to come clean? Or would she want me to make good my lies? Maybe this was my penance for engaging in deceit. That's what Grandma would have said. She'd have shaken her head and told me that I'd gotten exactly what I deserved.

Grace, though . . . she hadn't believed in penance. She'd believed in people, in romance, in love. She'd believed in me. Whenever I'd doubted I could do something, whenever I'd been tempted to throw in the towel, she'd looked at me with those glistening eyes of hers and told me that I could do anything I set my heart on, so long as I stayed focused and didn't doubt myself. And she was always right. At Grandma's funeral I didn't think I'd be able to make a speech—not one that would do her justice, not one that wasn't tinged with anger, with recrimination, with the desperate need to shout out, *"It wasn't my fault, it wasn't my fault"*—but I did. When I got landed with her debts, I was convinced I'd never be able to pay them off, that my life was for all intents and purposes over, but again Grace disagreed. She took my hand and squeezed it, and she said, "You know, your grandma was a proud woman. She wouldn't have wanted you to know about the debts. But she was proud of you, too." And I raised my eyebrows because if anything I was a disappointment to Grandma—though until I turned up on her doorstep she didn't even know I existed. But Grace just smiled and said, "She didn't know how to tell you. But she told me. She told me all about you. You got Grade Five piano when you were just thirteen. She kept the certificate, you know. She kept everything." And just like that I stopped worrying about the debts. Because I was proud, too. Proud to finally be able to help Grandma, like she'd helped me all those years.

And now . . . now I wanted to help Grace. Wanted to pay her back for being a friend, for making the world a bit brighter. Slowly, I dug out my mobile phone and dialed home. "Helen? It's me. So, tell me what to do next."

Chapter 10

"OKAY, SO WE NEED to up the ante."

It was Friday night, and Helen and I were sitting in a smoky bar. I wrinkled my nose. Despite my following Helen's advice to the letter for the next two days, wearing lipstick, flicking my hair, and generally behaving like the sort of person I loathed, I had gotten no further in securing a date, let alone a marriage proposal, from Anthony.

"Okay," I said carefully. "But remember, Rome wasn't built in a day."

"I'm not expecting you to marry Anthony in a day, either. But you had fifty, and I'm sorry to say it but you seem to be frittering them."

"I'm not frittering them," I said defensively. "But Anthony's barely been there . . ."

"Barely? So he has been there a bit?"

"I guess, but he's been in meetings."

"Meetings? Who with?"

I sighed. "I don't know. Clients. Marcia. People."

"So then set up a meeting of your own."

"Me?" I frowned.

"Yes! Set up a meeting to talk about that handbag thing. Or to complain about the fax machine. Anything."

"The fax machine," I said uncertainly.

"It doesn't matter what the meeting is about," Helen said patiently. "The point is, you want some one-on-one time with him."

"Ah," I said. "I see."

Helen shook her head. "God, for someone who's meant to be clever, you are a total moron when it comes to men."

"I'm not a . . . ," I started to say, then shrugged. "It just seems like wasted effort when there are so many other things to do."

"You mean Max?"

I looked up with a start. "Max?" I asked, reddening. "What are you talking about?"

"I'm talking about the fact that you had the hots for Max, didn't you? You used to talk about him all the time. And he never asked you out."

"That was ages ago," I said defensively. "And I didn't have the hots for him. I just . . . I just respect him, that's all. I think he's really good at what he does, and . . ."

"And you fancy him?"

"No!" I protested, shaking my head vigorously.

"Just a little bit?"

My blush deepened; I said nothing. I didn't fancy Max. And even if I did, it wasn't important.

"Fine, deny it. But just imagine if he liked you back. Wouldn't that be nice?"

"Nice?" I rolled my eyes, trying to push the image of Max kissing me from my head. "Look, Hel, trust me, I don't like Max. Really I don't. Not at all."

"So you keep saying," Helen said with a sigh. "I'm just trying to make you see that having a boyfriend isn't such a terrible thing. It's not a sign of weakness."

I looked down at my drink. I remembered the funeral, remembered the little smile on my face when Max had turned up unexpectedly, the crashing disappointment I'd hidden when I realized he was only there to get a style sheet. Of course love was a sign of weakness. Wasn't it weak to feel the prick of tears just because someone didn't like you back? It was pathetic. And I wasn't having any of it.

"Helen, if I'm going to do this ridiculous Project Marriage thing, I want you to understand that it has nothing to do with love, romance, or the desire for a boyfriend. Or husband. Got it?"

"Got it." Helen shrugged. "So, let's get on with it, shall we? Because we're losing time every day. There's no time for coyness or a gradual buildup. You have to swoop in. You have to figure out the competition, make your move. Now is the time to really get in there and seal the deal, so to speak."

"Seal the deal?" I raised one eyebrow. "Helen, do you watch anything other than *Deal or No Deal* these days? What happened to *Murder, She Wrote*?"

"You have to get him to ask you out," Helen continued, unabashed. "Come on, that's the baseline requirement here if you're going to get him to marry you. Am I right?"

"I suppose," I said, squirming slightly. "But it's not that easy. I mean, you can't just get someone to ask you out, can you? He has to want to."

Now it was Helen's turn to raise an eyebrow.

"You could ask him," she suggested.

"No. No way." I shook my head for added emphasis.

"I guess you're right," Helen said thoughtfully. "You want him to chase you. Okay, so you have to get him to ask you, then."

"Brilliant!" I said archly. "Well, that's all sorted then."

Helen sighed. "God, you're annoying sometimes. Okay, watch this."

She stood up and walked over to the bar, shaking back her long dark hair that was absolutely gorgeous, in a slightly messy, boho way. Helen was only five foot two, but you'd never know it, because she always wore shoes with heels so high the city could use them to build bridges.

She stood at the bar for a few moments, turned around and winked at me, then let her gaze revert to the bar, slowly. Before it got there, though, she seemed distracted by something to her right. She looked at it kind of curiously, smiled, looked down, then looked back at it. Next, she kind of lifted her head so she was looking down at it, and, finally, she turned back to the bar. Two minutes later there was a guy next to her, offering to buy her a drink. Evidently the *it* had been a *him*. I saw her shake her head and point me out, then I saw him call over the barman, giving him a ten-pound note, before handing Helen a business card, giving her a meaningful look, and then walking away, stopping at least twice to turn back and stare at her some more. I had to admit, it was impressive.

Five minutes after that she was back at our table, carrying two drinks.

"See?" she said triumphantly.

"You got a number, not a date."

"I could have gotten a date." Helen shot me a withering look. "So, now it's your turn."

I laughed. "You have to be kidding. There is no way I'm walking up to the bar and asking some guy to buy me a drink."

"You don't ask someone. You just wait for him to offer."

"Helen, I am not going up to the bar to get some stranger's number. It's indecent. It's . . ."

"It's what you have to do if Anthony's going to give you a second glance," Helen said. "Come on, if you can't flirt with a total stranger who you're never going to see again, what hope do you have with Anthony?"

"But . . ." I said, searching for a good reason why I couldn't do it—a good reason that Helen would buy.

I looked at her imploringly, but she wasn't in a sympathetic mood.

"Jess, you do realize what's at stake here, don't you?" she said before I could come up with anything. "This is about changing your life. But if you can't be bothered, then I guess we may as well go home . . ."

She picked her bag up and started to stand up, looking all fiery and mad.

"Helen, don't," I said quickly, tugging at her arm. "Helen, it's not that I can't . . . I mean . . . look, I will if you want me to . . ."

"Good, because I do."

"Fine," I said resignedly. "Fine, I'll do it. But if you ever tell a single soul, then I am moving out of our flat and will never talk go you again. Okay?"

"Okay." Helen shot me a thumbs-up, and I started walking to the bar. Then I turned back.

"On second thought, you can move out of the flat."

"Whatever."

I started walking again. Then I hesitated and nipped back to Helen.

"You don't think I should start with something easier? I mean, like baby steps, leading up to the bar? Maybe I could just smile at people to start with, get used to that and then—"

"Go," Helen ordered.

I made my way over to the bar, then stood there for a few seconds, gripping the wood with my hands. This was crazy. I just wasn't the sort of person who flirted with strangers. Or with anyone. It was such a waste of time. So humiliating. And dangerous. Potentially, at least. For all I knew these people could be ax-wielding homicidal maniacs. Still, I had to at least pretend to try, for Helen's benefit, to get her off my case. It was all right for her—she loved this stuff. Getting her to *stop* flirting was the tricky part. Taking a deep breath, I edged around until I was facing the room. There was a group of men to my left, several groups of men and women dotted around, a couple of small groups of men to my right, and in the far corner a man on his own, drinking a pint, looking very uncomfortable and out of place. He was in his forties, I guessed, wore glasses, and looked like he'd have been happier in his local pub than a trendy wine bar. Immediately I smiled at him. He looked at me suspiciously, then looked around to check whether I was looking at someone else close to him, before looking back at me. Nervously, I raised my chin, trying to remember whether I was meant to keep eye contact or not while I did it, but by the time I decided that eye contact probably was a good thing, he was gone.

Well, I told myself, at least I'd tried.

I caught Helen's eye and shot her an *I-told-you-so* look, when I felt something on my shoulder. I turned around to see the man from the corner, still clutching his pint.

"Hello!" he said.

I gulped. "Hello."

"Are you . . . I mean . . . I didn't think you'd be . . . Well, your description didn't do you justice. Didn't do you justice at all."

"My . . . my description?"

"On the website. You know, I was worried that you'd stood me up. I've been over there an hour, you see. Not that I mind your being late. Not at all. Woman's prerogative, my wife used to say. Oh, probably shouldn't mention her, should I?"

"Shouldn't you?" Now I was thoroughly confused. "And what website?"

"SecondTimeAround dot com. That is . . . I mean, you are . . . Oh God. Oh, you're not, are you? Oh I should have known. Beautiful young woman like you, and I think that you're here to meet me? Look, I'm sorry. Really sorry. I . . ."

He looked even more upset and humiliated than I'd felt just a few moments ago, and somehow it seemed to diffuse my embarrassment.

"I'm not from the website, no," I said gently. "But there's no need to apologize. You . . . think you've been stood up?"

He shrugged. "Of course I have. I mean, look at me. I don't fit in here. Don't know what I was thinking, really. It was my mate Jon who put me up to it. Said it would be good for me—meeting new people. The divorce . . . it was a year ago now, you see. She's shacked up with someone called Keith in South London, and I'm just here like a sad git, trying to be something I'm not . . ."

He trailed off, helplessly, and I felt a stab of recognition.

"You know, I don't think you're a sad git at all. I think you're very brave," I said firmly, holding out my hand. "I'm Jess, by the way. Jessica Wild."

"Jessica Wild? That's really your name?"

He looked surprised. Everyone always looked surprised by my name, like I was somehow traversing the trade description act. And I guess I was. I wasn't wild at all—didn't want to be. I was sensible. Disciplined. At least I always used to be . . .

"Really," I confirmed.

"Suits you," he said.

"No it doesn't," I said on reflex. "I mean, look at me. I'm not wild. Not one bit."

"I think it suits you really well. Jessica Wild. Very glamorous. Tiny bit dangerous. You're lucky."

I looked at him incredulously. My name had always struck me as entirely inappropriate. My grandma blamed the surname for my mother's waywardness; I'd spent my life doing my best to make sure I didn't go that way as well. "I am?"

"My name's Frank," he said. "Frank Werr."

"Frank Verr?"

"That's right. Only with a hard W, not a V like it sounds. I got called Wanker a lot growing up," he said. "People said it was just rhyming slang."

"Right," I said, feeling suddenly very sorry for him. "Yeah, that's not great, is it. So, look, can I . . . can I get you a drink?"

Frank shook his head. "I think I'll probably just go home, actually. I mean, my date's not coming, is she? And you're a million miles out of my league, plus there's a match on the telly that I might get home for if I leave now."

"A million miles out of your league? I am not," I said indignantly. "Not even one."

Frank looked at me uncertainly. "You're *so* out of my league. You're gorgeous. You're, like, a nine. I'm probably a five. Maybe five point five. I mean, everyone likes to think they're just above average, don't they? I'm not in bad shape. No beer belly or anything. I think that gives me point five, wouldn't you say?"

"You're a seven," I said firmly.

Frank shook his head. "No. Not a seven. Six tops."

"Six, then," I relented. Then I looked at him curiously. "So you really think I'm a nine?"

"Nine point five. I was trying to be cool before."

I grinned. "You're mad. But look, don't go. Come and join me and my friend for a drink."

"Really?" he asked, smiling nervously. "You mean it?"

"Of course I do." I nodded, leading him toward our table. Helen looked at him as we approached, a quizzical look on her face.

"This is Frank," I said. "Frank, this is Helen."

"Helen." Immediately, Frank went red and held out his hand uncertainly before deciding it wasn't such a good idea and retracting it. "Very nice to . . . Can I get you a drink?"

"Love one." Helen smiled graciously. "A white wine, please."

"White wine." Frank nodded. "Yes, of course. Right away. You, too, Jess?"

I nodded, smiling, watching as he pushed his way to the bar, his back suddenly a little straighter.

"Well, you took your time," Helen said, grinning. "But you got us both a drink so I think you passed the test."

* * *

Two hours later, and a little bit tipsy, I was amazed to find that it was already 11:30 PM. Not once had I looked at my watch, not once had I been tempted to make my usual excuses and leave early. I'd actually enjoyed myself. Frank was funny and interesting and although I wasn't interested in him in the slightest (or him in me), the three of us were still laughing as we made our way out of the bar and out into the cold, crisp air outside.

"Well, it was lovely to meet you," Frank said as we paused briefly on the sidewalk.

"Likewise," Helen said.

"Definitely," I agreed. This meeting-people lark wasn't as hard as I'd thought. It was almost kind of fun. Maybe Helen was right. Maybe I should enjoy myself more.

We waved Frank good night, then made our way down the street. The bar was in Soho, which meant walking up to Oxford Street to attempt to find a cab. The road was full of drunk office workers shrieking, clusters of girls wearing next to nothing, and groups of lads taking up the whole pavement and leering at anything female that crossed their path, but tonight they didn't worry me too much; tonight I almost felt like someone else, like I almost lived up to my name.

"I just started talking to him," I said to Helen, linking her arm in mine. "And he wasn't a weirdo or anything. He was nice."

"Yes, he was," Helen agreed. "Very nice."

"And he said I was a nine point five," I continued. "I mean, I'm sure he didn't mean it, but it was nice all the same."

Helen stopped and looked at me quizzically. "You are a nine point five, Jess," she said seriously. "Honestly you are."

I grinned sheepishly. "I'm not," I said firmly. "But thank you. And thanks for getting me out. It was . . ."

"Fun?" Helen prompted.

"Kind of." I nodded.

"And now you're going to start flirting with Anthony Milton?"

"Yes," I said, nodding again. "Yes, I am. I'm going to do it, Hel. I'm just going to walk up to him, and I'm going to smile, and I'm going to—"

I was interrupted by the rush of a car as it sped past me, making me lose my balance and fall onto the pavement.

"Jess! Are you okay?" Helen jumped down, her face indignant. "What a maniac."

I nodded—my leg hurt a bit, but it was shock that I felt more than anything.

"You stupid bastard," Helen shouted, chasing after the car, which had screeched to a halt at the traffic lights just behind us. "You should look where you're going."

"And you should walk on the sidewalk, not the road," a woman's voice shouted back. Evidently the driver's friends were as rude and inconsiderate as he was. As Helen continued to argue with him, I pulled myself to my feet and hobbled over, taking Helen's arm.

"Leave it," I told her. "It's not important."

"Yes, it is," Helen said crossly. "He nearly drove into you. He should be more careful."

I shrugged and tried to pull Helen away. But not before taking a curious peek into the car. There was a girl in the passenger's seat with dark, sleek hair—her face was obscured by large sunglasses, which considering the time of night struck me as faintly ridiculous.

I looked past her to the driver. And then I felt my mouth fall open.

"Come on, Hel, let's go," I said quickly, my eyes widening as the driver clocked me.

"Go?" she said defiantly. "Not until they say sorry. Not until—"

"Now," I insisted, dragging her away. "I want to go home."

I saw an empty cab and stuck my hand out; seconds later it drew to a halt and I pulled Helen in.

"What was all that about?" she rounded on me crossly as we drove away. "You could have brought charges against that driver. He was obviously drunk."

"Yes," I said uncertainly. "But I'm not sure if that would really fit with our game plan."

"Game plan?" Helen's face twisted into an expression of incomprehension. "What are you talking about?"

"Project Marriage," I said quietly. "The driver, you see, was Anthony Milton."

Chapter 11

THE NEXT MORNING, when I woke up and wandered into the kitchen, Helen was at the cooker, frying eggs.

"What's this for?" I asked curiously.

"Fuel." Helen grinned. "How's your leg, by the way?"

I shrugged. "It's fine. I've got a bruise above my knee, that's all. Fuel? What for?"

"For today's activities," she said firmly. "So eat up, because you're going to need your energy."

"Not more shopping?" I asked worriedly. "I'm broke, Hel. I can't afford anything else."

"Not shopping. Anthony Milton owes you. He owes you big. And when he apologizes profusely for what he did to you yesterday, you need to be prepared. You need to be so great at flirting that you fell him in seconds."

I felt the hairs on the back of my neck stand up in trepidation. I had a bad feeling about whatever Helen was planning. "Hel, he's not a tree, you know," I said, attempting a smile.

"Nevertheless, he is going to be felled. And I've got someone to teach you how." Helen grinned. "So there's no getting out of it now."

"Teach me?"

Helen nodded excitedly. "The idea came to me last night, on the way home. She's amazing. She was working in one of the bars

we filmed in for that *London Uncovered* program I did last year.
Remember? Anyway, her name's Ivana, and what she doesn't
know about seducing men isn't worth a thing. And she'll teach
you for free, too. Well, free for now. I said you'd bung her a thousand pounds when you inherited the money. I told her it was like
an investment."

I looked at Helen closely. "Ivana? Are you talking about the
Ivana you interviewed for the piece on lap dancing?"

"Yes, but she wasn't the lap-dancer. She was the escort. It's different. These girls don't dance, they just flirt and seduce and convince men to buy drinks for fifty pounds a pop just to spend more
time with them."

"She's a prostitute!" I exclaimed. "You've asked a prostitute to
teach me? You're mad. Forget it. There is no way on earth—"

"She's not a prostitute," Helen interrupted crossly. "She's an
escort."

"Who has sex with her clients."

"Who sometimes might have sex, yes, but that's not the job.
The job is to seduce. God, Jessica, I'd thought you'd appreciate
this. It wasn't exactly easy to convince her, you know . . ."

She looked really hurt. "I'm sorry," I said quickly. "I didn't
mean to be so negative. But . . . I'm just not sure she's . . . right. If
you know what I mean?"

Helen shook her head. "She's right, Jess, believe me. If anyone
can get Anthony to propose to you, Ivana can. Now eat up, because we've got to be at hers by eleven."

Ivana, it turned out, lived in a flat on Old Compton Street in
Soho. *Flat* was probably an exaggeration—it was a room, on the
second floor, with a large mattress, a cupboard that, when opened,
revealed a teeny-tiny kitchen, and another cupboard that mas-
queraded as a bathroom.

She was beautiful in a kind of sleazy-exotic way—full lips, soulful brown eyes, silky brown hair, and a figure that was petite and curvaceous in one. Her eyes were green, her hair was cropped into an angular bob, and she was dressed in a tight black dress and wedges at least four inches high. On Helen's insistence I had dressed up in my best seduction outfit—high black heels, tight pencil skirt, all bought after my makeover at Pedro's—and I still felt like a frump.

She and Helen exchanged kisses and held a quick, animated conversation about the program they'd worked on, and I found myself mesmerized by Ivana's Eastern European tones ("I heff so much business after theees program. The police, they come to see me. I know! They don't do nothing, though. They just come to *see* me, you know what I mean?").

And then she turned to me, looked me up and down, and folded her arms.

"You not know how to be sexy?" she asked, and I blushed awkwardly. "You need seduce men and get him ask you to merry him?"

I nodded, awkwardly, my face probably now an attractive puce color. Somehow, laid out like that, my predicament sounded utterly pathetic.

"Then we need coffee," she said, looking at Helen. "I will have a macchiato, which you will order in Café Boheme downstairs, and wait for me. I there in five minutes. Good?"

Helen looked at me. "Good," I confirmed. "Very good. We'll . . . um . . . see you there."

We traipsed down the narrow stairway and out onto the street, stepping over two men sleeping in the doorway, and nipped across the road to Café Boheme, where we ordered coffee and waited. And waited. And then waited some more.

An hour later Ivana finally emerged and took a seat next to us.

"So," she said, turning to me accusingly as though the intervening hour hadn't happened. "How you seduce a man? What you do?"

She looked with distaste at her cold macchiato, and Helen quickly ordered her a new one.

"I don't know," I said awkwardly. "I mean, I guess I don't. Not really."

"Your last boyfriend was when?"

My face filled with humiliation. "Look, I've been kind of concentrating on my career lately."

"When?" Ivana demanded.

"Two years ago, maybe," I said quietly. Suddenly my usual defense—that I was focusing on my career, that I didn't need a man in my life—seemed a little pathetic. Ivana was right—I didn't know how to be sexy. I didn't even know where to start.

"Two year?"

"Maybe three." I cleared my throat.

Ivana looked at Helen and rolled her eyes. "So, I have my work cut out, yes?"

She was looking at me now, so I kind of half nodded and tried to smile, but then decided against it when I saw her eyes were smoldering and not in a *come-hither* way.

Ivana's coffee arrived and she downed it quickly, then turned back to me.

"Okay," she said, sighing loudly. "Tell me how you talk to men."

I frowned. "How I talk to them?"

Ivana nodded.

"Well, I guess, like I talk to anyone else. I mean, it depends on the context, but you know, I'd just . . ." I looked at her helplessly. "I don't know. I really don't know."

Ivana nodded again. "I think as much. Okay, so a few basics you must know. First, you no talk to men how you talk to woman. Men, they like to speak. End they like you to listen.

Everything he do is fascinating, everything he do, you find sexy. Okay?"

"But what about what I've got to say?" I asked. Ivana glowered at me and immediately I reddened. "Fascinating," I said. "Fascinating and sexy."

Ivana looked at me uncertainly. "You disagree, he move away."

"But then he'll think I'm facile," I said, feeling myself get agitated. "And anyway, I'm not going to agree with someone just to make him fancy me. Have you not heard of feminism? Of female emancipation? I'm not prepared to look stupid."

"Men prefer stupid," Ivana said flatly. "Anyway, agree with man, he think you're clever."

"But . . . but . . ."

"But nothing," Ivana said firmly. "Trust me. So, next, you have to touch a little bit. Too much and is over; too little and he is looking away. Okay? Just on arm, on face when you lean in to say something. Little brush here, little touch there. You want him focus on you. Not anyone else. Okay? So, you hanging on every word, and then you lean. Like this." She demonstrated by draping herself over Helen. "This I think biggest challenge for you, no?"

I rolled my eyes. "What, and I'm going to do this where? Over the watercooler? Very professional."

The tone of my voice was distinctly sarcastic, and Ivana frowned. "You will find opportunity," she said abruptly. "But is problem with your voice. You need to change."

"My voice? What's wrong with my voice?"

"It no sexy."

"Well, I can't change it," I said stoutly. "It's my voice. I'm kind of stuck with it."

Ivana shook her head. "You can always change your voice. Listen." She took another sip of coffee and began to talk in what I could only assume was her native language. Her voice was coarse, angry, spiky, and guttural. Then she pulled a different face and started whispering in English, her voice as silky as a siren.

"You see? In Russia, I no heff to seduce. Here, I heff. Here, I heff better voice. Yes?"

I nodded in admiration, then checked myself.

"Now you try," she demanded.

"I can't." I squirmed.

"Go on," Helen urged me. "Give it a go."

I sighed. "Fine, but don't laugh," I said, then cleared my throat. "Hi," I said, attempting to imitate Ivana's sultry tones. "Hi, my name is Jessica Wild."

"Wild? Your name is Wild? For real?" Ivana was smiling now, revealing at least four gold teeth. "I kill for name like thet," she said, shaking her head, and I found myself hoping that she only meant it as a figure of speech. "Your name Wild, you use that, no? Say W-i-l-d."

She purred my name so suggestively, I looked around to see if anyone else had heard.

"Wild," I repeated, achieving none of the sexiness.

"Wiiild," Ivana said again, looking me right in the eye.

"Wiiild," I said back, this time sounding slightly less like an English schoolgirl but still nowhere near sexy.

Ivana frowned. "We need breathing exercise," she said. "We go to park."

"Park?"

"Park."

Twenty minutes later we were in Regent's Park.

"Now," Ivana said firmly, "you run and scream at same time. We watch."

I stared at her. "I'm not running and screaming," I protested. "There are people here."

"You want husband? You want money? Less my cut, of course."

I studied her face to see if she was joking, but apparently she wasn't.

"No," I said. "I mean, this isn't about money. It's about . . . well, this friend of mine, Grace, who died. She thought I was married, but . . ."

I trailed off as I caught a glimpse of Ivana's stony stare. "You want merry, you run, and you scream 'Wild,' okay?" she said abruptly.

"Helen?" I looked imploringly at my friend, but she stared at her feet. "You could at least try," she suggested without meeting my eye. "I mean, what harm can it do?"

"Harm? What, other than humiliating myself in a public place, upsetting the tourists, and potentially getting myself arrested?"

Ivana looked at her watch. "Quickly," she ordered. "Is getting late."

Her eyes were stony, and I realized with a jolt that I wasn't going to get out of this, that one way or another I was going to be running around Regent's Park screaming my name. Slowly, I took a deep breath and jogged away from Helen and Ivana—or, more to the point, away from the couple on a park bench and the man walking his dog nearby—then ran, and shouted "Wild." Maybe *shout* was a slight exaggeration, but I definitely said it quite loudly.

"Thet vos crap," Ivana shouted after me. "I no hear you. You heff to scream."

Gritting my teeth, I started to run again. "Wild," I snarled. "Wild," I shouted.

"Run faster. You no run fast enough." Ivana jogged over to me and started running alongside, her spiky heels sinking into the grass until she stopped, whipped them off, and carried on barefoot. Wondering why I hadn't thought of that, I immediately followed suit. Then, realizing that Ivana was about to overtake me, I upped my pace. It was almost fun, trying to stay ahead of her, feeling the wind fill my lungs.

"Wild," she shouted. "Come on, Jessicaaa. Is wiild." As she ran, she opened up her arms and screamed with a guttural force that made birds fly away.

"Wild," I shouted, louder this time. "Wild."

"You're wild, I'm wild," Ivana shrieked.

"We're all wild," I yelled, closing my eyes and breathing in deeply. I was, I realized with surprise, actually beginning to enjoy myself. Somehow I didn't care if people were staring, or if my feet were killing me—it was liberating to be running around, screaming, in a sedate London park; exciting to be behaving so outrageously, like a child who hasn't yet learned to be self-conscious.

"Wild," Ivana shouted at the top of her voice.

"Wild," I screamed back, flinging my arms open and tossing back my head. "Wiiiiiild."

I carried on for another five minutes, and only realized as I ran back toward Helen that I'd been doing it on my own for most of that time; Ivana was now back in her shoes and standing next to Helen, smoking a cigarette.

Immediately I felt stupid again and looked down at the ground.

"That vos better," Ivana said, throwing her cigarette to the floor and stamping it underneath her stiletto heel. "But you heff long way to go before you gonna seduce men into merry you."

"I thought you were really good," Helen said, noticing my crestfallen expression. "You were totally wild. I mean, really."

"Okay," Ivana said, walking off toward the park entrance. "I heff to go now. Your homework: to tell yourself in mirror that you are Jessica Wild, that you are sexy woman. You tell your friend, too."

"That's it?" Helen asked. "No other tips? It's just that time is . . . well, short."

Ivana stopped walking. "You prectice this today. I see you again soon. You tell me about touching."

I looked at her uncertainly. "But . . . but I can't. I mean, I don't know how to. I'll look ridiculous," I protested.

"You do right, you look sexy," Ivana said, walking away as though that settled the matter.

"But how do I do it right? You haven't even shown me," I called after her, then immediately regretted it when she stopped walking. With a sigh, Ivana looked at her watch and slowly turned around.

"I heff appointment," she said irritably. "But okay, two things. Licking lips like this."

Her tongue flicked out of her mouth and languidly made its way around her lips.

"See? Now you do."

I reddened and tried to imitate her. Ivana looked distinctly unimpressed and raised her eyebrows at Helen.

"Do in mirror," she suggested. "Better to see yourself when doing. Now for touching," she continued. "Is better to show you close. Come here."

I did as she told me and approached her.

"Now talk," she barked.

Uncertainly, I started to babble about the weather. As I spoke, Ivana stretched out a hand and lightly brushed mine. "You know," she whispered, "it vos very nice to meet you today." Then she leaned down to take my hand in hers. She touched it so tenderly, and I suddenly realized that underneath her fierce façade, Ivana was actually really sweet. And gentle. I squeezed her hand back, affectionately.

"Thanks, Ivana. It was really nice to meet you, too."

"Where are your eyes?" she demanded.

"Um . . . ," I said, not wanting to admit that my eyes had, just that minute, been drawn to admire her amazing cleavage, which had shot into view as she bent over. Then she pulled away, and I found myself frowning. I didn't want her to go.

"You should be looking at my breasts," she said, looking up to check that I was. Neither Helen nor I could look at anything else. "And the touching. It was nice, yes?"

I nodded, speechless. "You put that on? That was all part of the seduction?"

"Of course." Ivana shot me a withering look. "Getting a men attention—is game, you understand? You come close, they get interest, you step away. Make them want, then make unavailable, then they want more, yes? So, you prectice this. And you prectice bending over—you fix shoe, you pick something up, it no matter; what matter is where he looking, yes?"

"Yes." I nodded. I couldn't believe games like that actually worked. There I'd been thinking that love and lust were a matter of natural chemicals and the power of attraction, when in reality it was all about the right touch and flashing a bit of cleavage. I wished I'd brought a notebook now, there was so much to remember.

"Thanks, Ivana," Helen said quickly.

Ivana looked at her, then at me, her face impenetrable. "This not going to be easy," she said, with a sigh. She gazed at my feet as though she'd never noticed them before. My feet that were now uncomfortably wedged back inside my black heels.

"You need better shoes," she said matter-of-factly.

"Shoes? But these are new."

"You no think Anthony deserves girlfriend with good shoes? You think he should put up with unsexy shoes? Is that what you tell me?"

I reddened slightly. Frankly after last night I wasn't sure Anthony deserved a girlfriend, let alone one with good shoes. "These aren't good?" I asked, looking down at my shoes.

"They no sexy," Ivana said, shrugging. "Thinner heel. Color. Your face need color, too. No bleck, I think."

"No black?" I gulped. My whole wardrobe was black. The only way Helen had persuaded me to buy this ridiculously tight pencil skirt was because it was black and I'd convinced myself that no one would really notice how it clung to my thighs.

But Ivana wasn't listening—already she had nodded her good-byes and I watched, silently, as she strode off, her high heels clacking on the path.

"I'm screwed, aren't I?" I said to Helen as we watched her go.

She took my hand. "Come on. Let's go shopping."

Chapter 12

To do
1. Listen to Anthony with fascinated look on face.
2. Flirt your socks off.
3. Be Jessica Wiiiiiiiild.

Marcia was in Anthony's office when I got in on Monday morning—I saw her sauntering out five minutes after I sat down at my desk.

She stopped at my desk and looked me up and down. I was wearing a lime-green cardigan that Helen had insisted on. It made me feel like a nighttime cyclist.

"That's bright," she said.

"Yes," I agreed, trying to suppress the urge to take it off immediately and, instead, checking my calendar for the day. Nothing all morning. Meeting with Max at 2 PM. "So, good weekend?"

She raised an eyebrow. "Great, thanks. You?"

"Oh, really good." I forced a smile, trying to feel like Jessica Wiiild and failing miserably.

"Really?" Marcia looked surprised. "Oh, and before I forget, someone called for you," she said. "A Mr. Taylor."

"Mr. Taylor?" The blood drained from my face. "When?"

"This morning. About half an hour ago."

"And did he say . . . what he wanted?"

Marcia looked at me, wide-eyed. "Of course not—I didn't ask." She smiled curiously at me. "He left a number, though." She handed me a scribbled note.

"And he didn't say anything else?" I asked anxiously.

"Should he have?" Marcia asked, her eyebrows raised slightly. "He sounded quite old for you," she continued. "I didn't realize you were into older men."

"I'm not," I said, about to explain that Mr. Taylor was not in any way a romantic prospect, then decided not to bother. I had other things to worry about. Much more important things. "Right, well, thanks," I said.

Trying to breathe normally, I turned on my computer. Marcia had spoken to Mr. Taylor. There was no need to panic. Obviously he hadn't said anything because if he had, Marcia would have told everyone in the office and would now be laughing in my face. It was fine. Everything was fine.

Moments later Marcia stalked off toward the kitchen and I quickly dialed Mr. Taylor's number.

"Good morning, Mr. Taylor speaking."

"Mr. Taylor! Hi, it's Jessica Wild."

"Oh, Jessica. Yes, thank you for calling me back. I was just hoping to get a meeting in the diary."

"Yes," I said, biting my lip. "About that. It might be tricky. I've got a . . . a lot on, over the next few weeks, I mean."

"The next few weeks?"

I looked down at the floor guiltily. "Actually, I'm going away. Out of the country."

"A holiday?"

"Yes. Kind of. Work and holiday. That's why I'm going to be gone for a while."

"That is a shame. And you're not free later today?"

"No. No, I . . . I leave this afternoon," I said, feeling my cheeks getting hot. "Last-minute thing. But I'll call you when I get back. Right away."

"That's very good of you. And bon voyage."

"Thank you. Thanks, and . . . and speak to you in a few weeks."

I put the phone down and let out a deep sigh, then let my head hang backward.

"Jess?"

I jumped as Anthony appeared from behind me.

"Sorry, didn't mean to startle you," he said, seriously. "It's just that I think I owe you a very big apology."

"An apology?" Easily, elegantly, he leaned against my desk.

He looked right at me, his expression one of dismay. "It was you on Friday night, wasn't it? I didn't realize what had happened until too late, and then you and your friend just ran off . . . I'm really so sorry. Did the car hurt you?"

"No," I said quickly. "No, not at all. Really, it's no problem."

"It is a problem," Anthony said, shaking his head as his blue eyes twinkled into mine. I could see Marcia returning to her desk, straining to hear what we were talking about, and I felt the surprising satisfaction of being the person Anthony wanted to talk to ripple through me. "And I want to make it up to you."

"You do?" My hands moved to straighten some strands of hair that had fallen across my forehead.

"I was thinking maybe lunch. Do you think you could bear to let me buy you lunch?"

"Lunch?" I looked at him uncertainly. "You want to have lunch with me?"

"If you're not too angry. You're not too angry, are you?"

I shook my head. "No, no, I don't think so."

"Good. Shall we say one-ish?"

He was smiling mischievously now, and I grinned up at him. I had totally misread him. Anthony wasn't rude. He was really sweet. He felt really bad. And he wanted to have lunch with me.

"Um, okay. One-ish." I nodded.

"Great. Well, I'll see you then."

He gave me a little wave, then wandered off back toward his office, leaving me reeling slightly. I was having lunch with Anthony Milton. Just the two of us.

"Oh, so Anthony found you, did he?" Marcia said, sitting back at her desk. "He said he wanted to talk to you. Was it about Jarvis? Something to do with the account? Tell me if you need any help, won't you? I mean, what I don't know about handbags isn't worth knowing."

"Um, something like that," I said uncertainly, quickly digging out my phone to send Helen an incredulous text. "And thanks. I'll let you know."

Lunch was at a little wine bar just a few hundred yards down the road, where we were ushered to a small corner table. If I'd been self-conscious leaving the office, then I was even more so when we sat down. The table was so small, our knees were almost touching. Me and Anthony Milton.

As soon as we sat down, Anthony pulled out a cigarette.

"You mind?" he asked, suddenly catching my eyes on him. "Because I don't have to."

"No," I said quickly. "No, it's no problem at all."

"What a relief." Anthony lit up two cigarettes, passed one to me, then leaned back in his chair. "People are so funny about smoking, aren't they? I mean, give it a few months and I'll be banned from doing this. No one's allowed to have any fun anymore. I mean, would *Pulp Fiction* be any good without smoking? Would Camus have written such great books if he hadn't been able to sit in Left Bank cafés breathing in nicotine?"

I was as surprised by the Camus reference as I was by the cigarette, which I surreptitiously stubbed out.

"You like Camus?"

His mouth creased upward slightly. "That depends. Do you?"

I nodded. "Actually, I do. I think *The Outsider* is one of the best existentialist texts around."

"I see. Well in that case I'll have to confess that I've never read any Camus. I was hoping you hadn't, either, in which case I'd have gotten away with pretending that I had."

He grinned and I looked at him uncertainly. "And *Pulp Fiction*?"

"Seen it. Loved it."

"Me, too." I smiled nervously.

"Well, that's something we've got in common then. So, Jessica, what do you fancy eating? You're not a vegetarian or anything, are you?"

"Vegetarian? No, not me," I said, picking up the menu and relaxing slightly.

"Glad to hear it. The steak here is wonderful, if you fancy it?"

"Sounds great!"

Anthony called the waiter over and ordered, adding a bottle of red wine as an afterthought. Then he turned to me and grinned.

"You're going to have to help me drink that, you know," he said. "We don't want a repeat performance of Friday night, do we?"

I smiled. "No. No, we don't want that."

Anthony nodded and a slightly awkward silence descended.

"So I'm meeting Max later to talk about the Jarvis account," I said brightly after a minute or two. "I can't tell you how excited I am to be leading it. It's such a great opportunity."

"Yes, it is," Anthony said. "But that's work and this is lunch, so we'll hear no more about it until we're back in the office. Okay?"

"Okay," I agreed. "No work."

There was another pregnant pause.

"It was really cold today, wasn't it?" I heard myself say.

"Was it?" Anthony frowned. "Can't say I really noticed."

I swallowed awkwardly. God, I really was boring. But if I wasn't allowed to talk about work, what else was there?

I picked up the menu again, my eyes scanning the words but not taking any of them in. And then, suddenly, I could hear something in my head. *You heff to ask questions. You heff to find everything he says fascinating.*

Nervously I looked up. It would never work. Not in a million years. I didn't *want* it to work—it made me feel like a 1960s airhostess. But it wasn't like I had many other options. I cleared my throat, again. "Um, you . . . You must be so proud of what you've achieved at Milton Advertising," I said. "I'd love to hear about how you set up such a successful firm."

Anthony raised an eyebrow at me. "You would?"

"Oh yes." I sounded phony. Completely ridiculous. I knew I did. Anthony was going to think I was weird, and he'd probably eat quickly, and . . .

"Well, in that case, I'd be delighted."

"Really?" I asked, slightly taken aback. "I mean . . . you would?"

Anthony looked at me quizzically. "You're really interested?"

"Sure. I mean, definitely."

"Well, okay then," he said, sitting back in his chair. "You asked for it. We started about ten years ago. But you know that, I'm sure. What you may not know is that for the first three months of its existence, Milton Advertising sat above a fish-and-chip shop . . ."

"Fish and chips?"

"We smelled awful. Had to hang our suits out the window before every pitch so we didn't turn up smelling of overcooked oil."

I laughed, the wine arrived, and Anthony carried on talking.

"Max and I were working for rival firms, and we both wanted a new challenge. So we both sweet-talked as many clients as we could into jumping ship with us, moved above the chip shop, and tried to make enough money to survive. We made a point of selling ourselves as the real deal, you know? An advertising agency that took what it did seriously. Promoting our clients but in a truthful way, getting to the core of their offering, getting the details right."

"You mean like grammar," I said.

"Grammar?" Anthony asked uncertainly.

"Getting grammar right," I said, seriously. "You know there was an article in *Advertising Today* a month or so ago on how advertisements are full of poor grammar these days. Like putting apostrophes in the wrong place, or saying *less than* when it should be *fewer than*—that sort of thing."

"Exactly!" Anthony said, banging his glass down on the table. "Exactly, Jess. Grammar. Details. Getting things one hundred percent right. A hundred and ten percent right. Going the extra mile."

"And your strategy worked?"

"It certainly did. I think our track record speaks for itself. We grew, bit by bit, and before too long we got a proper office space, right next to a brothel in Soho."

"A brothel?" My eyes widened in shock, then I remembered Ivana's advice. "I mean, how amazing!"

"It was, rather," Anthony said, grinning. "The girls were great fun. And actually, it worked in our favor. One of my former colleagues threatened to sue us for poaching clients, and we . . . . discovered, shall I say, that he frequented the brothel. Once I let him know that I knew that . . . well, the problem went away."

"No way!"

"Way. I tell you, those were the days. Adrenaline city, every day. Each pitch was make or break."

"You did really well," I heard myself say, feeling the warmth of the wine hit my stomach. "You're one of the top London firms now."

Anthony smiled. "I suppose we are."

The food arrived, and as we ate and drank Anthony told me how he'd grown the firm, how they'd pitched for their biggest clients, how they'd become successful. And by the end, hanging on his every word was becoming the most natural thing in the world; with every ooh and aah that came out of my mouth he seemed to relax, to enjoy himself more. By the end, I wasn't even pretending. I was warm, I was comfortable, and Anthony's blue eyes were twinkling away, looking right into mine.

"It's so impressive," I said when we'd finished eating. "I mean, so many people talk about launching their own businesses, but so few people actually do it."

"You're very kind." Anthony shrugged, then looked at me quizzically. "You know, it's been really good fun talking to you, Jess. You're a very interesting person. You have quite hidden depths."

"I do?" I smiled bashfully, thinking of pointing out that I'd said nothing indicative of any depths all lunch, then deciding against it.

"Yes, you do." He held my gaze for a fraction longer than was entirely comfortable, and I reddened slightly. Then he asked for the bill and flashed a smile at me. "So look, thank you again for being so understanding about Friday night. It was apalling behavior and I am truly sorry."

"Oh no!" I said immediately. "It wasn't your fault. I was walking in completely the wrong place."

"You're very kind." Anthony smiled. "So, out in Soho. Does that mean you live centrally, or is Soho just your Friday-night stomping ground?"

"My stomping ground?" I looked at him in surprise, then forced a smile onto my face. "It's my flatmate's stomping ground really. We live in Islington."

"Islington!" Anthony nodded thoughtfully. "Lots of nice bars in Islington. I keep meaning to get up that neck of the woods."

"It's nice," I said. "You know, if you like that sort of thing."

"And what would that sort of thing be?"

My blush deepened; he was looking at me flirtatiously and I suddenly felt like a schoolgirl. If he'd told a crap joke, I would have laughed like anything. "Oh, you know. I mean, it's busy. Lots of people."

"I love lots of people," Anthony said, smiling mischievously. "Don't you?"

"Sure." I nodded. "I mean, you know, in moderation . . ."

The bill arrived and Anthony looked at it for a moment. "You know what?" he asked eventually, his eyes twinkling conspiratorially.

"What?"

"I'm rather enjoying myself. What do you say we get ourselves another bottle of wine? We can sit here and I can smoke and you can tell me all about the people in Islington."

"More wine?" My eyes widened. "Oh no. No, I couldn't. I mean, I've already drunk far too much. And I've got a meeting with Max at two o'clock to go through my project plan. Actually, I should probably get back now really."

"Max?" Anthony raised an eyebrow. "Max can wait. After all, there's more to life than work. More to success than work. It's a little-known secret, Jessica Wild, that the people who work hardest end up working for people who know how to enjoy themselves."

"They do?"

"You're looking at the living proof," Anthony said. "So, more wine? Trust me, it'll be a better career move than sitting in Max's office going over the fine print of your project plan."

I looked at him, biting my lip. I knew I should leave, knew that Max would be waiting for me. But then again, would it be such a bad thing to let him wait? All I ever did was work. Right now I was here with Anthony Milton. I was having fun. And I didn't want it to end.

"More wine," I said, feeling the thrill of being badly behaved zip around me.

"Good decision," Anthony said, winking, and called over the wine waiter.

Chapter 13

MAX CAME OUT of his office just as Anthony and I sloped back in to Milton Advertising. I'd never, to my knowledge, sloped any-where before, but there was no doubt about it—our eyes were cast down, our expressions nonchalant, we kept giggling for no reason whatsoever, and it felt great. I realized I'd become way too serious. I really had to lighten up a bit. Meeting people was fun. Flirting was fun. Drinking at lunchtime was fun, too.

"So how was lunch?" Max asked. I looked up semi-guiltily; Anthony gave us both a little wave and disappeared into his office.

"Lunch? Good. It was good." My voice was slurring slightly and I beamed at Max. His hair was messy—it always was by this time of the day because he put his hand through it when he con-centrated, pulling it from side to side until it sat almost upright. He was wearing a stripy shirt and navy-blue V-neck that high-lighted his broad shoulders. I thought of pointing this fact out, but decided against it. Max was too serious, too, I decided.

"Right," he said uncertainly. "I thought we were meeting at two, though?"

I nodded vaguely. I wanted to reach out and pat his hair down, to work out whether it sat better on the right or the left. "We were," I said, instead. "But work isn't everything, Max. Not hard work, at least. Successful people . . ." I frowned, trying to remember what Anthony had said. "Successful people don't work hard," I concluded.

"They don't?" Max asked wearily. "Are you sure about that?"

"Absolutely." I staggered toward my desk. I hadn't felt this drunk when we were in the wine bar. Even walking down the street, I'd felt kind of okay. Sure, I'd bumped into Anthony a few times, but I'd thought that was his fault, and he seemed to think it was funny so I hadn't really worried about it. "You have to learn to enjoy yourself, Max. That's the trick."

"Have you been smoking?" Max, who had followed me to my desk, creased up his face in distaste. "You smell hideous."

"Smoking . . . Smoking is . . . ," I said, then forgot what I was going to say. I hadn't really been smoking; Anthony had offered me another cigarette and I'd tried it out, that's all. I only had a few drags. To be honest, I couldn't see what all the fuss was about.

"Right. Well, while taking your advice that I need to enjoy myself more, we do have some work to do I'm afraid. Can we say my office in five minutes?"

I looked up at him, but my eyes were finding it hard to focus; instead I turned to my computer and turned it on.

"Marcia's not here," I said, suddenly noticing her absence. "She's not at her desk."

"No," Max said, looking at me strangely. "She's at a client meeting. So, five minutes?"

"Five minutes would be no problem at all," I said, concentrating on each word.

"Glad to hear it."

As soon as he'd gone, I rushed to the kitchen and drank a pint of water. Then I rushed to the loo. After that, I made myself a coffee, drank a bit more water, just to be on the safe side, picked up my notebook, made my way unsteadily to Max's office, and sat down at his meeting table.

"Right," Max said, sitting down next to me, "the situation is this: in just under two weeks, Chester Rydall will be here expecting us to have firmed up our proposals. Which means we need visuals, we need a full concept, and we need the target audience analyzed."

I nodded seriously.

"So?" Max asked expectantly.

"Sounds great," I said, wondering what Anthony was doing, just the other side of Max's wall. He had a little crease above his eyes, I'd noticed over lunch, that got deeper when he smiled. "You know, you don't smile enough, Max, do you?"

"I don't smile?" Max stared at me in surprise.

"Not *enough*," I corrected him. "People like people who smile. Although you shouldn't show too many teeth."

"Right," Max said, his brow furrowing slightly. "I'll bear that in mind. So, look, I've been talking to the creatives about your logo idea."

"The handbag," I interjected, pleased to be able to remember it.

"That's right," Max said, frowning. "The handbag. And they've got some nice ideas. Look."

He pulled out some mock-ups on whiteboard, and I did my best to focus on them.

"That one's nice," I said, pointing to a pink one.

"Jess, are you okay? You're acting kind of strange."

"Strange?" I shook my head vigorously. "I'm not acting strange. Anyway, you should have said strange*ly*. Grammar is very important." I sat back on my chair triumphantly. That would show him how fine I was. How absolutely and completely . . . I realized Max was looking at me and shot him a quick smile.

"Grammar," he said. "Right. My apologies. So, anyway, these are just first draft—once we have our concept firmed up a bit more we can get some more work done. Which is where you come in."

"Me?" I should ask him questions, I realized suddenly. I should act all interested in him and then he'd be flattered and he'd forget all about concepts or whatever it was he was talking about.

"The concept. And the research. Jess, what the hell's the matter with you? This is your account. You do realize how important this is? For us and for you?"

"Absolutely," I said. He was looking vexed. Annoyed, even. Perhaps I needed to ask him a few questions. Perhaps I needed to turn on the Jessica Wiiild charm a bit. "I'm just pleased, because that's exactly what I wanted to talk to you about." I smiled, pouting as best I could. "The visuals, and the concept. By the way, Anthony was telling me about how the two of you started this company. It sounds amazing. You're so talented. I'd love to hear your side of the story."

"What?" Max looked at me curiously.

"You. Starting this firm together. You know, against all the odds, smelling of fish-and-chips, winning over clients . . ."

"Yes, well, you make it sound very romantic, but really it was just a lot of hard work."

"Hard work and getting prostitutes to do you favors," I said, smiling with what I hoped was a mischievous glint in my eyes.

"Getting prostitutes to do us what?" Max's eyes widened. "There were no prostitutes doing any favors as far as I knew."

"No, not you. The guy who was going to sue you." I rolled my eyes. "Anthony told me all about it."

"He did," Max said. "Well, then, he might also have told you, it turned out the girl got it wrong. That we discovered she was talking about someone else. And that the meeting we had with the right man subsequently was one of the low points of Milton Advertising's existence."

I frowned. "He didn't say that, no."

"Well, he wouldn't have, because it rather ruins a good story," Max said, rolling his eyes. "But let's not digress. I think you were about to talk to me about the research and concept for Project Handbag."

"I was?"

"Yes, you were. So?"

"So," I said, realizing crossly that none of Ivana's tactics was going to work on Max. "So, I suppose I've been looking at the concept in the round, really. You know, thinking through the implications to the research . . ."

"In the round." Max looked skeptical.

"Yes," I said defensively, "I mean that I've been considering the wider angles. You know, thinking through the key issues."

"And they are?"

I shifted awkwardly on my chair and took off my cardigan. I suddenly really needed to pee again.

"They are the key elements in this campaign," I said tentatively.

"I was hoping for a little more detail." Max's eyes were narrowing; I could see the frustration in his expression.

"Detail?" I crossed my legs. "What sort of detail?"

Max stood up. "Okay, I don't know what's going on here, but I do know that we're getting nowhere. How about I tell you what I think the issues are, and you tell me if you agree?"

"Good idea," I said, biting my lip and trying to stay focused on what he was saying.

"Okay," Max said, his face suddenly serious. "So, we need to get some thorough research done. Desk-based, but also maybe a focus group or two. We need to be clear what the proportion of spend should be on print advertising as opposed to web advertising; whether we're aiming at direct results or brand awareness; the parameters of the logo; and anticipated take-up . . ." As Max talked, I found myself counting to ten over and over again, hoping it would make the time pass more quickly.

". . . The key is to get people to sign up, right?" he concluded eventually. I nodded uncertainly; my forehead was now covered in small droplets of sweat.

"Right," I said, uncrossing my legs then crossing them again. I realized I hadn't opened my notebook, so I picked it up and started to write in it but for some strange reason I appeared to have two right hands writing two different things. Realizing that I was also apparently unable to write in a straight line, I carefully put my pen down again. "Yes. Getting them to sign up."

"So we need to consider when to advertise in the glossies and how best to reach potential clients post-launch to generate interest," Max continued, frowning slightly. "Direct mail, sponsorship, that kind of thing. Then we need to work out a strategy for engaging the trade press over the same timescale—we need financial advisers to recommend the fund to their clients, don't you think?"

I nodded weakly. My pelvic floor muscles were working overtime.

"Good," Max continued. He evidently wasn't finished yet, I realized with a thud of disappointment. "So . . ."

Several minutes later, he stopped and looked at me expectantly. I nodded brightly, having no idea what he'd been talking about—it had taken every bit of my brain power to concentrate on holding out until I got to the bathroom. "Okay, then," I said. "Well, if that just about wraps things up, I'd better get on with it."

"What, now?"

"No time like the present. When did you say Chester's coming in to hear about this stuff?"

"Not next Monday but the one after," Max said. "You've got it in your diary, right? Because this is going to be a very important meeting."

"Well, then, I'd better crack on," I said, smiling and clenching my fists.

Max looked at me levelly. "Are you sure everything is okay? You're acting very oddly," he said.

"No I'm not," I said slightly defensively. "I'm just being a bit less serious, that's all. A little less boring. Life is for living, Max."

"Life is for living. That's your new mantra?"

I nodded. "It's the new me."

"I think I prefer the old you," he said flatly.

"Well, that's your prerogative. But actually it's nothing to do with you. And as for Project Handbag, it's perfectly under control," I assured him, little beads of sweat trickling down the back of my neck. If I didn't get to the bathroom soon, I was going to lose control completely. "Work is all very well, but it's also important to have fun, Max. Very important indeed."

"Fun is overrated in my opinion," Max said, his eyes narrowing. "So you'll let me know if you need any help?"

I nodded.

"And remember, we don't have much time."

"Will do," I promised as I half walked, half ran out of his room. "I'll get it done super-quick."

He followed me to the door.

"Oh, and Jess?" he called after me. I was so close to the bathroom I could almost touch it, but I forced myself to turn around and smile.

"Yes, Max?"

"I think you meant you'll get it done super-quickly, didn't you?" he said, a wry little smile playing on his lips. "Grammar, you see. It's very important."

Chapter 14

When I woke up the next day with a terrible headache it felt like aliens had moved into my head overnight, taking out my brain and replacing it with a heavy iron machine with nails sticking out of it that pressed into my skull. I'd been too drunk to eat when I got home, and my stomach felt like it was concaving inward; a quick look in the mirror revealed a pallid complexion that suggested I'd been underground for several months. I could barely remember the day before. I remembered having lunch with Anthony—remembered asking questions and watching his eyes light up, remembered feeling little twinges of excitement zip around my body as his eyes twinkled at me, mischievously. But after that my mind drew a bit of a blank. I vaguely remembered having a meeting with Max—although not what the meeting was about or what we discussed. I remembered (vaguely) getting home, remembered Helen whooping when I told her about lunch, remembered clambering into bed . . . and that was about it.

"You can't go in," Helen said firmly. "You look awful."

"I have to go in," I croaked. I wanted to go in. I wanted to see Anthony, wanted him to grin at me again.

"But you're sick."

"Hungover isn't sick."

"Even your hair looks tired."

"It is tired." I sighed. "But you can do your magic, can't you?"

"You mean perform a miracle? Look, don't go in. Pull a sickie."

"I have to go in. I want to."

We continued this circular conversation for forty minutes or so, during which I managed to have a shower, drink two cups of coffee, eat a bowl of milk-drenched Weetabix that seemed to avert the worst of my stomach cramps, swallow slightly more than the recommended dose of paracetamol, and put some makeup on. Actually, Helen did the makeup; my hands were shaking too much.

"Did I tell you about my lunch with Anthony?" I asked her as she brushed concealer under my eyes.

"Several times, yes."

"Did I tell you that he said I had hidden depths?"

"I think you might have mentioned it, yes." Helen smiled. "Although you weren't terribly coherent. I've never seen you so pissed. Actually, I've never seen you pissed."

"And I had a cigarette," I said proudly.

"You said you had two drags and had to put it out."

I shrugged. "Same thing. The point is to try things. Anthony said that if you don't try new things, you get nowhere."

"Interesting. I'd never have thought of that myself."

I giggled, then moaned as my head hurt. "We had two bottles of wine."

"Okay, I'm done. And you're really sure you have to go in?"

"Definitely," I said, nodding firmly.

"Fine," Helen relented. "At least you look vaguely human now."

I managed a little smile and left the flat, tossing my hair then regretting it when my head started pounding. An hour later, having gotten on the wrong tube twice, I finally arrived at work.

Max wandered over as soon as I'd sat down, and I looked up at him unenthusiastically.

"I had another thought," he said immediately, forgoing such niceties as *Good morning,* to which I would have replied, *No, it isn't.* It was so typical Max, I found myself thinking. So serious all the time.

"Did you?" I asked, switching on my computer.

"About the research. We need to know the percentage of women with earnings of fifty-thousand-plus pounds a year. Jarvis may already have some figures. But it would also be nice to know the big hitters, too. Women earning over five hundred thousand. It could make some good PR—these are the women that others aspire to be, that kind of thing."

"Absolutely," I said, rummaging in my bag for some more painkillers. "Sounds great."

"You're okay doing that?"

I looked back up at him irritably. "Sure. No problem," I said, tersely. I needed coffee. Lots of it.

"Great. So then I'll leave you to it, then."

Max wandered off and I sighed, dropping my head into my hands. Then I frowned. What was he leaving to me again? Women earning over fifty thousand? What was I meant to be finding out about them?

Slowly, I turned back to my computer.

"Everything all right?" Marcia appeared at her desk, smiling sweetly.

"Fine," I said, not looking up. "Absolutely fine."

"So I hear you had lunch with Anthony."

"Yes," I said, smiling back, "I did."

"Apparently he enjoyed himself."

"He did?" I asked excitedly, then checked myself. "I mean, that's nice."

"Is it?"

Marcia was looking at me curiously, and I blanched slightly. "Is there something the matter?" I demanded.

"No!" Marcia said, shaking her head. "No, nothing at all."

She was scrutinizng my face, and I felt myself tense slightly.

"What?" I asked her. "What is it?"

She opened her eyes innocently. "Nothing. Nothing at all. I mean, if you've got time to have a boozy lunch with Anthony as well as lead a major account then I'm pleased for you. If Project Handbag is in hand, that is."

I nodded. "Yes, I have," I said. "Project Handbag is absolutely in hand."

"Good. Well, that's good then."

Doing my best not to grimace, I picked up my notebook and flicked the pages over to look for the notes from my meeting with Max. Why was everyone so fixated on work all of a sudden? Didn't they know there was more to life? I scanned the notebook as I flicked, then felt myself go slightly white.

Pulp Fiction, I discovered written in sloping handwriting. *All work and no play makes Max a dull boy.*

Underneath, I'd drawn a picture of a handbag.

And that was it.

They were my notes from the meeting.

Okay, so maybe I hadn't been concentrating all that hard.

Frowning, I wandered over to Max's office and tentatively opened the door.

"Yes?" he asked tersely.

I smiled. "Hi, Max. I was just wondering. You know the meeting we had yesterday?"

He nodded. "You've compiled the research?" he asked. "Because we're working against the clock, Jess."

"Right," I said. "Yes. I mean . . . I just wondered . . ."

I bit my lip nervously.

"Wondered what?" Max wasn't smiling. "You're not going to ask me to smile more, are you? Or tell me that work is overrated?"

"No," I said quickly. "I just wanted to let you know everything's in hand."

"Good," he said, turning back to his work. "Glad to hear it."

I walked out again uncertainly. Next to Max's office was Anthony's. I could always ask him, I reasoned. He wasn't grumpy like Max. And it was his company. He'd know what was going on. Tentatively, I approached his office and knocked on the door.

"Come in."

I opened it, and felt better immediately when Anthony grinned at me. I grinned back.

"Jess! Jessica Wild. And how are you today?"

"Fine, I'm fine," I said happily.

"Good, I'm glad. I had Max in here earlier worrying about you."

"Worrying? About me?"

"Oh, nothing serious. He thought you were a bit . . . out of sorts yesterday. Of course, I told him he was imagining things. Told him we'd had a very sober lunch."

"You did?"

"Absolutely." He winked. "For my sake as much as yours. What Max doesn't understand is that it's possible to get pissed on the job and still come back and perform perfectly well. In fact, I negotiated a rather good deal with a printer yesterday afternoon, which just proves my point, and I'm sure your meeting with Max was far less dull than it might otherwise have been."

"Yes, it was," I agreed uncertainly.

"So, what can I do for you?"

"Um, well . . ." I cleared my throat. Maybe now wasn't the best time to ask him what I was meant to be doing on the Jarvis Private Banking account. "Um, well," I said, trying to think of some other reason I'd come to see him. "It's just that . . . you said you were meaning to get up to Islington. So I just wanted to say that if you did want to, anytime, I'd be happy to . . . show you around."

I smiled, nodded purposefully as though my mission had been accomplished, then turned to go.

"How about Saturday?"

I stopped walking, then slowly turned back. "Saturday?"

"I'm at a loose end on Saturday evening."

"You are?" I asked, my voice incredulous. "I mean . . . you are?" I repeated, toning the surprise down a notch or two.

"Are you?"

I gulped. "Um, I believe I am," I said, pretending to mentally check my nonexistent social calendar. I wasn't prepared for this. I didn't know how to react.

"Then it's a date. I'll pick you up at eight PM."

"A date. Right." I cleared my throat.

"Jess?"

I stopped, almost relieved. Of course. It was a joke.

"You'll need to e-mail me your address."

I turned my head, stared at him suspiciously.

"So I can pick you up."

"Pick me up," I said, hardly trusting myself to speak. "Right, then. I'll e-mail it over right away."

"Okay."

I walked out of Anthony's office; as I passed Max's office I saw that the door was open and, without meaning to, I caught his eye.

"Everything okay, Jess?" he asked.

"Okay?" I looked at him blankly. "Absolutely. Things couldn't be better."

Chapter 15

"I CAN'T BELIEVE you actually asked him out! I just can't believe it!"

I looked at Helen worriedly. I couldn't believe it, either. More to the point, I couldn't believe that he'd actually said yes. For the past couple of days I'd been veering between excited incredulity that I was going on a date with Anthony Milton, and utter fear and despair that it was a joke, that it was all going to go horribly wrong, that I'd bamboozled him into it, and that he was already dreading it. Even now, on Saturday evening, with a huge pile of clothes on my bed and my fifteenth change of clothing on, I was still in slight denial. "I didn't mean to. It just . . . came out. Oh God, he's going to think I'm desperate, isn't he?"

"Desperate? No! No way. He's going to think that you're confident, that you know what you want. I just can't believe you, of all people, actually asked him on a date. Ivana's a genius."

"I didn't exactly . . . I mean, it was him who said 'how about Saturday.' I just said I'd show him around Islington sometime."

"That's what I mean. You set up the goal beautifully and still let him score. That takes real talent."

I allowed myself a little smile—lately Helen had taken to watching football on television, owing to a sports quiz show she was thinking of applying for. "So, do I look okay?"

"No. It's the skirt," Helen said, shaking her head. "It isn't tight enough."

"It's absolutely tight enough," I said firmly. "I can barely walk as it is."

"Skirts aren't about being able to walk. They're about what you look like from behind."

"Maybe something longer," I suggested, anxiously turning around to see my rear view. I wasn't entirely comfortable being this much on display.

"No, we need your legs on show."

"My legs? No, no, they're better hidden."

"Rubbish. Come on, Jess. Remember, Jessica Wiiiiild."

She dashed into her bedroom and brought back a twirly red skirt with black buttons. It was short—too short in my opinion—but at least I'd be able to sit down in it. I grabbed it and put it on; then we both looked into the mirror.

"I guess it works," I said dubiously.

"It's great!" Helen agreed. "Who'd have thought?"

Quickly she whipped out some red lipstick and applied it. Then she stepped back.

"Okay, you're done." She looked at me proudly.

"Really?"

"Put on your shoes."

I put on the tall, black, pointed shoes.

"Now turn around."

I duly turned.

"And smile for me."

I grimaced. "I'm not a flipping car model," I complained, but only halfheartedly.

"Smile for me," Helen said sternly, and I obliged. Then she held up a mirror and I gasped. I had smoky eyes and an impressive cleavage and my waist looked tiny. "So what are you going to do on the date?"

I frowned in concentration. "Ask lots of questions and laugh at his jokes."

"And what aren't you going to do?"

"Talk about myself, disagree with him, leave early."

Helen grinned. "My God, I think you're ready," she said, pretending to wipe a tear away from her eye. "I just can't believe my girl has gone and grown up on me."

The buzzer sounded, and we both froze for a second. Then Helen grabbed my coat.

"You'll be fine," she reassured me. "Just smile and be fabulous. And make sure he kisses you good night."

"You think he's going to kiss me?" The thought was exhilarating and terrifying at the same time.

"Well, I bloody well hope he is," Helen said. "I mean, that's kind of the point of a date, isn't it?"

"But I . . . I mean . . . I . . ."

"It'll be fine. It's like riding a bike," Helen said dismissively.

"I never learned to ride a bike," I managed to say, but Helen wasn't listening.

"Just remember, you're gorgeous. You're Jessica Wild."

She did a little impression of Ivana as she said my name, and I forced myself to smile. "Jessica Wild," I said, biting my lip. "I just hope you know what you're doing."

Anthony was leaning against the wall when I got downstairs.

"So, Jessica Wild. Where are you taking me?" He grinned.

"Um, well, Islington," I said. I felt nervous, gawky. All the confidence I'd built up over the years was founded on my belief in myself as an intelligent, serious kind of a person, an independent soul who knew what she wanted out of life. Dressed in a twirly skirt and going on a date, I felt like a fish out of water, like any minute now I was going to be found out and ridiculed.

Anthony didn't look like he was going to laugh at me, though.

His smile was conspiratorial, not sneering, and I felt my shoulders relax a little.

He laughed. "I kind of gathered that," he said, holding out his arm. "Anywhere in particular or are we just going to set up base on a street corner?"

I met his eye and blushed. "Oh, right. Well, there's a bar on Upper Street that's quite good. We could go there? If you want?"

"Quite good?"

My blush deepened. I had no idea what it was like—Helen had given me a list of places to go, most of which I'd never stepped foot in. Never wanted to step foot in, either. "It's meant to be very good," I said. "My flatmate says it is. But we can go somewhere else if you'd prefer . . ."

"No! Let's go and test her review," he said. His arm was still sticking out; I guessed he wanted me to take it, so I did, and a frisson of electricity shot through me. A few seconds later we were walking down the street, me and Anthony Milton, like it was the most normal thing in the world.

"I love your skirt, by the way. Nothing like a flash of red, is there? Reminds me of bullfighting."

"Really? You think it looks okay? I mean, thanks. I mean . . ."

I bit my lip. It was so hard remembering to be the new Jessica Wild, the one who knew how to take a compliment.

"I think it looks divine," Anthony said.

"It's my flatmate's," I said, then kicked myself.

"Then it sounds like we owe your flatmate a debt of gratitude for this date." Anthony winked. "So where's this bar, then? Lead the way."

The debt of gratitude was forgotten as soon as we poked our noses in the bar. It was heaving with people, the music was too loud, and there was nowhere to sit. You couldn't stand still, either, because people kept brushing past you like you were standing in their way, so after being pushed around for twenty minutes we ditched our drinks and left. Helen had suggested a restaurant called Figos that was meant to be super-hip and *the* place to be seen, but we looked in the window and it was really crowded, too, and there was a doorman looking people up and down like a bouncer as they walked in.

"This one of your flatmate's suggestions, too?" Anthony asked, turning away from the window and raising his eyebrows.

I nodded. "She's more . . . well, she's the one who goes out, more," I explained.

"You don't go out so much?" Anthony asked curiously.

"I . . . I don't always have time," I said tentatively. "I mean, I've got a lot on at work and . . ."

"All work and no play makes Jack a dull boy," Anthony said, grinning. "I tell that to Max all the time but he never listens and look what's happened to him. Wouldn't know how to have a good time if you took him to a strip club and shoved a fistful of fifties in his hand!"

I looked at him, slightly shocked. "A . . . a strip club?"

He winked. "An expression, that's all," he said quickly. "I can't abide the places. But you take my point about Max? Obsessed with work. And if you work in a creative industry like we do, you have to live as well as work. You need external stimuli to get inspiration. Need to see people having fun so we know what they're looking for, how to sell to them."

"You mean that going out is like research?" I asked seriously.

He laughed. "Exactly. Research. In fact, perhaps I should expense this evening's entertainment!"

I didn't know if he was serious or not, so I didn't say anything. He, meanwhile, looked around thoughtfully, then nodded to himself. "How about," he said, "we go to a little place around the corner I know? There's no DJ as far as I know, but the food's great and the wine list's as long as your arm."

I nodded with relief, then frowned. "I thought you didn't know Islington?"

"I don't. I mean, not really. But I came here once with a girl . . . a friend." He blanched slightly. "I'm sure the restaurant's up here somewhere."

"You had a girlfriend in Islington?"

Anthony shrugged. "Not a girlfriend. Nothing that serious. And it was a long time ago."

I nodded. Of course he'd had a girlfriend in Islington. He'd probably had a girlfriend in every district in London. Immediately I thought about the girl in the car, the one with the sunglasses, but I forced her from my mind. It wasn't important; Anthony was out with me now.

"So why wasn't it serious?" The words came out before I could stop them.

"Why? God knows. She wasn't my type, I guess."

I nodded again and there was a brief silence. Questions, I thought. Ask more questions.

"So what's your type?"

"My type?" Anthony grinned. "Now, there's a question. You know, I don't think I know. I mean, I'm not sure I'd be able to put it into words. And sometimes people surprise you. I mean, you don't think they're your type and then something happens and you think again."

"You do?"

"Yes, you do." His arm was around my shoulders, and my skin felt hot underneath it. Much as I looked down on women who depended on men for their happiness, I could certainly see the appeal. "Now, I hope you're hungry, because we're here."

He held open a door, and we walked in. It was tiny, just ten or so tables jostling for space as waiters slipped between; there seemed to be more wait staff than diners.

A short little man immediately glided toward us.

"I'm afraid we have no booking," Anthony said, immediately disarming the man with a smile. "But I've been telling Jess here about your wonderful restaurant—I came here a year or so ago—and if you could squeeze us in you really would make our night."

The man smiled, then turned to scan the room. "It won't be easy," he said in an Italian accent. "But I see what we can do, huh?"

"Didn't I tell you? Best restaurant in London," Anthony said loudly, winking at me. Seconds later a table had been brought into the room and space found for it, next to the window.

"Please," the maître d' said, holding out my chair. "Please."

I sat down and remembered Ivana's advice. *Be appreciative. Make him feel like a million dollars.* "That was incredible!" I breathed.

Anthony grinned. "You can get a long way by flattering people," he said, sagely. "Never forget that."

"I won't," I said, allowing myself a slight smile. "I really won't."

The menus were handed to us, and as I tried to make sense of mine, I found my eyes wandering around the restaurant. It was the sort of place where no sooner do you take a sip out of your wineglass than someone is there refilling it for you. Where they call you "sir" and "madam" and tell you what a great choice you've made when you pick a wine from the list just because you like its name.

"So," Anthony said when we'd ordered. "Tell me about Jessica Wild. The real one, not the one who acts like Jessica Rabbit at work, all quiet and demure."

"Jessica Rabbit?" I frowned.

"Frozen in the headlights," he said. "You always look so

earnest, so worried. But now I'm getting to see your other side and I like it."

"My . . . other side?" I asked uncertainly.

"Jessica Rarebit." Anthony grinned. "The Jessica who wins presentations, who drinks whole bottles of wine for lunch, who pretends she isn't a party animal but knows all the most crowded bars in Islington. Tell me about her."

"Oh, well, I mean, I don't know about that . . . ," I said, blushing awkwardly. I had to get off this subject—it was littered with land mines. *Don't talk about yourself. Don't disagree with him.* "I mean, there's really not much to say. But you . . . you must have a lot of stories to tell. About all these girlfriends, for starters."

I looked at him hopefully, and he laughed. "You don't want to know about all my girlfriends."

Not particularly, I thought.

"Yes," I said. "I do."

"Really?" He looked at me incredulously, then shrugged. "Well all right then, I'll tell you," he said eventually, his mouth creasing upward and his eyes twinkling. "But this just reinforces my view of you, Jessica Rarebit. You are unlike any woman I have ever had the pleasure of having dinner with. So, shall I start at the beginning and move forward, or start with the most recent and move backward?"

"Whichever you prefer," I said, smiling brightly with no teeth. "I really don't mind either way."

It took the whole of dinner to get through them. I counted up to forty-two, but I could have missed a couple here or there.

"And you never wanted to stay with any of them?" I asked, genuinely interested now. "Like, not even to see what it was like?"

Anthony shook his head. "I stayed as long as it made sense to. But why settle? Would you settle, Jess?"

"Settle? I . . . oh, no, I mean I . . ." I smiled, feeling myself getting flustered. I'd spent my whole life determined not to settle, convinced I'd never even get married.

He looked at me intently and took my hand. "Would you settle for someone you knew wasn't perfect? Or would you wait for the right person to come along?"

I gulped. "Oh, I think I'd wait," I said, my chest tightening. He was stupidly good looking. Not that I was going to let a beautiful face turn me into jelly. I was far too strong for that sort of thing. I was just going to flirt, like I'd promised I would.

Anthony grinned and let go of my hand. "Exactly. People might look at me and say I'm a philanderer. But I'm not—I'm an incurable romantic, that's all. All I want is the right woman to come along."

"You . . . do?" I asked curiously. "You're not just playing the field?"

The bill arrived and Anthony immediately put a card down, holding up his hand when I attempted to go halves.

"Not at all," he said, looking intently into my eyes. "I want what everyone wants. Someone special to love. Is that naïve, do you think?"

"I don't know. I mean, no, no, it isn't," I said tentatively. Of course it is, I was thinking. Completely naïve. At least I thought it was . . . I kicked myself. Of course it was naïve. I was getting way too carried away. The idea that there was some special love out there just waiting for you was insane. People built their lives around beliefs like that, then wondered why they were disappointed years later.

"Me, too." Anthony smiled. "Although I'm sure some therapist would tell me I'm a hopeless case. Just trying to replace the love of my old mother."

"Your old mother?"

"Dead mother."

My eyes widened. "God, I'm sorry. I didn't know."

Anthony shrugged. "Why should you? It's no big deal. Both my parents died awhile back. To be honest, we weren't that close."

"You weren't?"

Anthony shook his head. "They were ambitious. Thought I should make more of myself."

"More?" I asked incredulously. "But you're a huge success."

"That's very nice of you," Anthony said thoughtfully. "But unfortunately they never saw the rise of Milton Advertising. They . . . they were gone years before."

I nodded slowly. I suddenly felt a kinship with Anthony, felt like maybe at some level I actually understood him. "My parents died, too. At least my mother did. When I was little. I . . . I never knew who my father was."

"Really?" Anthony's eyes crinkled in sympathy. "Poor you. Poor, poor Jess."

I felt a lump in my throat. "Not poor," I said quickly. "I had a grandma who brought me up. It was fine, actually. I'm very lucky."

"How did she die? Your mother, I mean."

"Car crash," I said quietly. "Apparently a lorry plowed into her on the motorway. She didn't stand a chance, Grandma said."

Anthony nodded seriously. "I'm really sorry, Jess. That's awful."

"I guess." I blushed.

"And what about love? Have you found the right person, Jessica Rarebit?"

I shrugged, a little embarrassed all of a sudden. There was way too much attention on me for my liking. I needed to change the subject and quickly. "No, no, I haven't," I said, scanning my brain for new subject matter.

"You mean this boyfriend of yours isn't the one?"

My head jerked up. "Boyfriend?"

Anthony smiled reassuringly. "Max told me. It's okay, I'm not judging. Actually I quite like that you have a boyfriend and you're having dinner with me. I guess it's all part of the Jessica Rarebit mystique."

"Max told you I had a boyfriend?" I started to say indignantly.

"Don't you?"

"No! Why would he say that? Why would he . . ." I trailed off as I suddenly remembered the funeral. The boyfriend I'd invented out of nowhere. What was it with me and imaginary men? "What I mean is," I said hurriedly, "is that I don't have one anymore."

"You don't?"

"No. We split up."

"I'm sorry."

"No need," I said. "Really. It was just . . . you know . . . one of those things."

"So you're young, free, and single?"

I smiled weakly. "Absolutely. Yes, I am."

"Well that's a turn up for the books," Anthony said lightly, a smile playing on his lips. "So, after this, do you want to go home?" He smiled expectantly at me. "Or somewhere else?"

I smiled back nervously. "Um . . . home?" I said, feeling like I was on a game show. *Deal or No Deal. Winner Takes All.*

"Home it is," Anthony said. "What do you say we get a cab? I'm assuming those shoes are horribly uncomfortable because they look fabulous."

"You think? But no, I mean, I can walk," I said, even though the shoes were shooting needles into my toes. "You get a cab, I'll be fine."

Anthony frowned. "Me? Not a chance. We'll get a cab and I'll see you home."

"But it's completely out of your way," I protested halfheartedly. "It'll be really expensive."

"Then it's a good thing I own my own company, isn't it?" Anthony said, his eyes twinkling as he stood up, thanked the maître d' for a glorious meal, then pulled me out of the restaurant and hailed a cab.

"You know, I had fun tonight," he said, leaning back into the leather seat a few seconds later. "I hope you did, too?"

"Definitely." I sneaked a peek over at him; he was looking right at me. God, he was gorgeous. He was making my skin feel all prickly with anticipation. But anticipation of what? Was I actually hoping he was going to kiss me?

"I'm very glad," Anthony said softly.

I sat back, every muscle and ligament on high alert. Of course I was hoping he was going to kiss me, I told myself, doing my best to rationalize the situation. I wanted him to kiss me because that was the plan. That was the point of the date. It was the next step of Project Marriage. And if I was getting a strange ache, an odd feeling of longing deep down at the bottom of my stomach, then it was just that I was in character, that I was taking this project very seriously indeed.

I smiled tentatively; Anthony smiled back, then turned to look out the window, causing my stomach to flip-flop with disappointment. But suddenly I knew what I was going to do. Taking a deep breath, and praying that Ivana knew what she was talking about, I tentatively stretched out a hand and lightly brushed Anthony's. "You know," I whispered, trying not to think too much about what I was doing, "it was really nice to . . . go out with you tonight." My breath still held, I took his hand in mine, and replicated as far as I could the gentle touching that Ivana had demonstrated in Regent's Park. My eyes flickered up anxiously; Anthony's eyes were fixed on my cleavage. Oh my God. It was working.

"The pleasure," he said, his voice low and husky, "was all

mine, Jessica Rarebit." Slowly, his other arm, which had been leaning along the back of the seat, dropped just a bit and touched my shoulder, then wrapped around me and pulled me toward him. Before I knew it, his lips were on mine and his arms were pulling me into him and it was all I could do to remember to breathe in and out.

And then suddenly the car stopped and, to my dismay, he pulled away.

"We're here," he whispered. "Let me come up."

"Up?"

"Up," he confirmed, pulling me toward him again and kissing me. "I don't want to go."

"You . . . you don't?" I raised an eyebrow in surprise.

"No, I don't."

It was a bad idea. I knew it was a bad idea. I wasn't that sort of girl. Not at all. I was going to say no. It was the only sensible response.

Only I wasn't feeling that sensible. I'd never felt less sensible in my life.

"Maybe you could come up for one coffee . . ."

"Coffee. Yes . . ." Anthony grinned and in one seamless movement, he paid the cabbie, got out of the car, and banged it on the side signaling for it to drive away.

We didn't actually have any coffee. To be honest, we didn't go anywhere near the kitchen. We went straight to my bedroom instead. And my clothes didn't stay on very long, either. Nor did Anthony's. It was like I suddenly really was Jessica Wild—by nature as well as name. Anthony Milton was kissing me, and I was kissing him right back, like it was the most normal thing in the world. Being self-sufficient was all very well, but being desired like this was pretty intoxicating actually.

"Wow," Anthony said, an hour or so later, leaning back on his hands and pulling a cigarette out of somewhere. He offered me one, which I declined, then lit his and sighed as he exhaled. "Well, that was something."

"Something?" I bit my lip anxiously. Did he mean *good something* or *bad something*?

"It certainly was. And to think you were going to send me away," Anthony said, shaking his head.

"So you . . . enjoyed it?" I asked tentatively.

Anthony laughed. "You crack me up, Jessica Rarebit," he said. "Of course I enjoyed it. You know, I think you are one of the most unpredictable people I've ever met."

"And that's good?" I wished I didn't feel so insecure all of a sudden. Wished I didn't suddenly feel so vulnerable. I'd never had sex like that in my life. It had been incredible, like in films, like books always made it out to be—passionate and exciting instead of vaguely disappointing. But now all I could hear was Grandma's voice in my head. *No one loves a slut,* she'd say to me whenever I told her about someone at school having a boyfriend, whenever I'd suggested tentatively that I might go out on a date myself. "Look what happened to your mother, if you don't believe me. Left pregnant and alone. No wonder she couldn't cope. She probably drove into that lorry on purpose." I hated it when she said that. Suggesting my mother left me knowingly. But the point stuck. Sluts came to a sticky end.

"Very good." Anthony leaned over me, kissed me, and dug out his cigarettes, lighting another one. I wrinkled my nose, then forced myself not to cough as I snuggled into his chest. There was no need to feel vulnerable, I told myself. Grandma was wrong. Grandma was a bitter old woman who didn't know what she was talking about.

"I had fun tonight," Anthony said softly.

"Me too," I whispered.

Anthony took another drag of his cigarette, then stroked my head; I allowed myself to lean against his shoulder, letting my hand explore his broad chest, his firm stomach. Anthony Milton's firm stomach. If it wasn't actually happening, I'd never have believed it.

"Your bathroom," he said suddenly. "Is it down the corridor?"

I nodded, wishing he didn't have to go, didn't ever have to move. "Just past the kitchen."

He got up and grabbed my dressing gown from off the back of the door. I watched him go, giggling. Anthony Milton. In my dressing gown. Who'd have thought it?

I lay back on the bed, allowing myself to luxuriate slightly. Things could not have gone better. And I couldn't believe that I actually hadn't thought Anthony was that attractive. The man was gorgeous. Gorgeous and charming. Gorgeous, charming, and fun. The opposite of Max. So much nicer. So much better.

A beeping sound disturbed my reverie, and I frowned. It sounded like my mobile phone. Quickly I jumped out of bed and grabbed my purse. But when I checked my phone, there was nothing flashing, no message to read, no voice mail.

Sighing, I got back into bed. And then I heard it again. Beep.

Carefully, I got off the bed, following the sound. It could be the smoke alarm, I thought worriedly. Or some other alarm. I listened again. Beep. It wasn't in my room, I was fairly sure of that. I wrapped a sheet around myself and made my way out into the corridor. Beep. It was coming from the hallway. Slowly, I walked toward it, turning on the light, wrinkling my nose as I tried to work out what it was.

And then I saw what it was. It was Anthony's mobile. On the hall table, where he'd left it an hour or so before. I picked it up and started to mooch back to the bedroom. But then something caught my eye. It was a name, flashing on the small screen. MARCIA.

I frowned. Maybe it was a work emergency. I couldn't think of any other reason Marcia would be texting Anthony in the middle of the night.

Not that I was going to look. It was his phone, after all.

Quickly I went to put the phone back on the table. I would alert Anthony to the beeping when he came out. Who he got messages from was really nothing to do with me. And I certainly wasn't the kind of pathetic person who read her boyfriend's texts.

Not that Anthony was my boyfriend.

Or was he?

The trouble was, either way, I wanted to know. *Had* to know why Marcia had Anthony's mobile number. Why was she contacting him now? I'd never wanted to know something—needed to know something—so much in my whole life.

I shook myself. It was probably a different Marcia, I decided. A cousin, perhaps. An old friend? Feeling a light layer of sweat covering my face, I walked into the kitchen and sat down on one of the kitchen chairs. Marcia. It had to be work Marcia. There weren't that many Marcias in the world.

I heard Anthony clearing his throat loudly in the bathroom, and suddenly, without allowing myself to think about it, I flicked his phone open. Immediately Marcia's message appeared. And I tried not to look, but it was hopeless. I had to. It was impossible not to.

And then, when I'd read it, I almost wished I hadn't.

Hi hon. All going well? Can't wait to hear the gory details xx.

I stared at it for a few seconds. Hon? Anthony was *hon* to her? And *gory details*? Did she mean me?

I felt my heart sink and the next thing I knew, I had dropped the phone for real. Gory details. Of course. This was all some big joke. A joke on me.

"Jess? Is everything okay?"

I looked up to see Anthony looking at me quizzically. I looked down again. Grandma had warned me about men, and she'd been right. I couldn't believe I'd been so stupid.

"Your phone," I said flatly. "It was beeping. I . . ."

"Oh, my phone. Thanks." He leaned down and picked it up. Then he frowned as he read the message. "You . . . you read this?" he asked tentatively.

I nodded. "You should call her," I said, feeling myself tighten, feeling myself close up like a clam. To think I'd thought . . . To think I'd actually believed . . . How stupid. How pathetic. "Only I think you should go first."

"Call her? But it's the middle of the night."

"I'm sure she won't mind."

Anthony went slightly white. "Jess, this isn't what you think."

I pulled my knees up to my chest and wrapped my arms around them. "What do I think, Anthony?"

"I don't know, but I can assure you, there's nothing . . . untoward about this text."

"Untoward?" I rolled my eyes, all my defenses coming slamming down. "I suppose it depends what you mean by *untoward*. To my mind, laughing about someone behind their back is untoward. And I'd like you to leave, please."

"Laugh about someone? About whom?" Anthony looked at me worriedly. "Marcia . . . ," he said, frowning, "she wanted to know the gory details of a client meeting I had today. One of her accounts."

"Sure," I said sarcastically. "I'm sure that's what it was."

"But it was," Anthony said hurriedly. "Jess, honestly, it's nothing to do with you. Marcia didn't even know we were going out tonight."

"She knew about our lunch. And she gave me this little smile on Friday when she told me to have a good weekend."

"A smile?" Anthony shot me a look of mock horror. "Not a smile, surely." He attempted a grin, but I ignored it.

"She knew," I said flatly. "I know she did."

"Fine. So Marcia's nosy. That's all it is. Really."

I shook my head tightly. "Just go," I said. "Please, go."

"Okay. Okay, I will." Shaking his head, Anthony wandered out toward my bedroom; a few minutes later he reappeared wearing his clothes, hastily put on, the buttons all done up incorrectly.

"Well, see you on Monday, then . . . ," he said. "You will be there on Monday?"

I nodded silently.

"Okay, then." Anthony shrugged.

"See you," I managed to say, but he didn't hear. He'd already walked out of the front door, was already on his way down the stairs, no doubt about to call Marcia and tell her they'd been found out. And I didn't care at all. I'd always known this whole marrying-Anthony-Milton thing was a total joke. I hadn't taken it seriously at all. Not one little bit.

Chapter 16

I felt like death the following morning. I wasn't hungover; I was depressed. Humiliated. I'd allowed myself to think that Anthony Milton might actually like me—had slept with him, because I'd believed it—and now I'd discovered that Grandma was right, that I'd been as stupid as all those stupid girls I ridiculed on a regular basis. I was an idiot. And I'd never be able to look Anthony in the eye again. Or Marcia. Or anyone else. Morose, I emerged from my bedroom wearing a T-shirt. I'd picked up my dressing gown, but somehow hadn't been able to put it on.

Despondently, I mooched into the kitchen; to my surprise it was a picture of domesticity, with Helen at the cooker once again, and boxes of cereal laid out prettily on the table with bowls, spoons, and a jug of milk.

"Morning!" she said brightly. "I'm making omelets. Want one?"

I looked at her suspiciously.

"And this is for what, exactly?"

"I reorganized the kitchen last night," Helen said, frowning and turning back to her omelets. "So, how did it go?"

"You reorganized the kitchen? Why?"

Helen sighed. "Because it needed reorganizing. Jeez, it's no big deal, is it?"

"No. I just thought that if you had some spare time you might apply for jobs instead of cleaning." I was taking out my anger on Helen and I knew it, but somehow I couldn't stop myself.

"I would apply for jobs if there were any that I was interested in," Helen said tightly. "Now, do you want breakfast or not?"

"Sure," I said, then sighed. "Look, I'm sorry. I think the kitchen looks great, for what it's worth."

"Well, thank you." Helen brought over the omelet pan and put it on the table, then looked around for a chair. "So come on then, how was the date?"

"It was okay. Do you want some toast?" I stood up and walked over to the bread bin.

"Toast? No. I want to know all about your date."

"My date . . ." I put two slices of bread in the toaster. "My date was. . . ." I felt a lump appear in my throat. "It was . . ."

"It was . . . ?" Helen prompted.

"It wasn't great," I said.

"You didn't get on?" Helen asked worriedly.

"No," I said, shaking my head. "No, we got on really well. At least . . . Look, the truth is that it was all a joke on me. Project Marriage is over, Hel. The whole thing is over."

"Over?" Helen's forehead creased into fine lines. "Okay. You're going to have to talk me through this. From the beginning."

I bit my lip and popped up the toast, then scraped butter on it and returned to my chair. "It started off really well," I said, keeping my voice as matter-of-fact as I could, keeping myself as detached as possible from the story. "I mean, we had drinks, then he took me to this little restaurant . . ."

"Little restaurant? I didn't recommend any little restaurant."

"It was a place Anthony knew. A bit quieter."

"Oh." She sounded put out.

"So, anyway, dinner was good . . ." I swallowed uncomfortably as I remembered the evening, remembered the glow that seemed to surround us all night long, until . . . I grimaced.

"And?" Helen demanded.

"And we shared a cab home and . . ."

"And?" Helen's eyes were boring into mine, and I blushed.

"And he came up," I said quietly.

"He came up?" She sounded amazed.

I nodded as imperceptibly as I could.

"You dirty stop-out!" Helen clapped her hands together in excitement. "And what happened then?"

I felt myself redden. "We . . ." I looked down at my hands, which were clasped together on my lap.

"You didn't!"

I nodded as imperceptibly as I could.

"Oh my God. You did! So how was it? Was the sex not good? I mean, assuming you had . . . or was there a problem there?"

"No, there wasn't a problem," I said defensively. "The sex was fine." I swallowed. "It was really good, actually."

"So what's the problem? What happened?"

"What happened is that . . ." I cleared my throat and told her about Marcia's message.

Helen frowned. "Did you say anything to Anthony?"

"I told him to leave."

"And?"

"And he tried to make out she was texting him about some client meeting. But I knew it was rubbish. So he left. And now it's over. All of it."

Helen digested this information for a few seconds. Then she took a deep breath.

"I think the important thing here is not to panic," she said eventually.

"I'm not panicking. I'm just killing off Jessica Wiiiild. It's easier being the old me."

"Oh, poor Jess."

"Not poor Jess," I said stiffly, remembering Anthony using the same phrase, remembering how it softened my defenses. "I'm not poor. I'm fine. Fine on my own. I don't need Anthony and I don't need Grace's money. My mind's made up."

"You can't give up now," Helen said, shaking her head. "You're just having morning-after anxiety. It's perfectly normal."

"Is a text from Marcia perfectly normal?"

Helen frowned. "Maybe not. But that doesn't mean we give up."

"Yes, it does. He and Marcia obviously thought it would be hysterically funny if we went on a date. They're probably laughing about it now."

Helen shook her head. "You're overreacting." She stood up and picked up the phone.

"You weren't there."

"True, but come on, Jess, the stakes are too high to give up that easily," Helen said, dialing a number. "We just need a bit of help, that's all."

"Not Ivana," I said immediately. "I can't see her today, I just can't."

"Give me a better idea and I'll hang up," Helen said tersely.

"I need more toast," I said, after a pause. "And definitely more coffee."

An hour or so later, Helen and I watched from the window as a bashed-up Mini appeared outside our house and Ivana got out of the passenger's seat. She was wearing a gold lamé dress—the fabric clinging to her ample curves—and her mouth was painted bright red to match her patent-leather stacked heels. Then a lanky man in his thirties got out of the driver's seat and followed her toward our front door. Immediately Helen's mobile rang.

"Hello? Yes, I can see you. I'll press the buzzer."

I looked up, my heart sinking, as Ivana breezed in, followed by her lanky friend. He had a shock of blond hair that hung down over his face and, when you could see them, watery blue eyes. He smiled gauchely; Ivana stared at me, her eyes narrowing.

"You no look good," she said.

"Thanks," I said, rolling my eyes.

"You're welcome. You need more advice. Merrege advice?"

"I need to forget all about marriage," I said, but Helen shushed me.

"Yes, she needs advice," she said quickly. "We need a new strategy."

Ivana nodded and pushed the lanky man forward. "So thees is my friend Sean. He arrange merrege. He know about men. Okay?" Sean smiled bashfully and shoved his hands in his pockets. I nodded again, this time a little uncertainly. Did she mean that Sean arranged marriages for a living, or that he was going to arrange my marriage? And what did he know about men? Just that he was one?

"So, who wants tea?" Helen asked, bustling around and taking jackets from Ivana and Sean. "Or coffee? Orange juice?"

"Bleck coffee," Ivana said.

"Tea, please," Sean replied. "Milk, two sugar. Cheers love."

His accent was a strange mix—one part Eastern European, two parts Manchester. He grinned again and I found myself smiling back; I showed them into the sitting room, where Sean sat down on the sofa, his gangling frame filling the frame, while Ivana remained standing, scrutinizing our bookshelf as though looking for clues.

"So," Ivana said when tea and coffee were duly delivered. "Now, we start."

I looked at her apprehensively.

"We start?"

"Exectly," Ivana confirmed. "You tell me exectly vat happen on your date."

I told her. And then, at her request, I told her about Marcia. I didn't cast her in a very flattering light.

When I'd finished, she whistled, then turned to Sean. "Vat you think?" she asked him.

He frowned. "It's tough," he said.

I sighed. "It's not tough, it's easy," I said. "Anthony must have told Marcia about the date, like it was some joke or something. I've never felt so humiliated in my life."

"Really?" Sean looked at me curiously, then shrugged. "Of course, it's possible that he was telling the truth and she was texting him about a work thing. Or, it could be that Marcia did know about the date and thought it was a bit of a joke but that Anthony didn't. She might just be jealous."

"She might?" I felt a shimmer of hope and tried to ignore it.

"The sex was good?" Sean continued.

I reddened and, despite everyone's eyes boring into me, I couldn't stop a little smile from forcing its way onto my face. "Yes. I mean, I think so."

"And he didn't want to go?"

"No, but . . ." I said defensively. "Look, I saw the text. She called him *hon*."

"Yeah. Yeah, I got that. So look, I think you've just got to play seriously hard to get for a while," he said flatly. "I think things could go one of two ways."

"They could?" Now I was frowning. "How, exactly?"

Sean looked at me strangely as if he thought it was completely obvious. "Well," he said, speaking slowly as though I were a child, "even if this Marcia and him have got something going, he obviously likes you. Yeah?"

"You think he and Marcia have got something going?" I felt myself go white. I hadn't even considered that. Oh God. They probably did. He'd probably slept with everyone in the office. After all, he'd had forty-two girlfriends.

Sean shook his head, his floppy fringe falling from side to side. "Probably not," he said reassuringly. "But either way, you play it right, play it really cool, and he'll forget all about her. You've got to make yourself unattainable so he wants you even more. You get me?"

I frowned. "Not really."

"You've got to rise above it," Sean said, smiling indulgently. "You know, play hardball."

"Hardball?" I asked weakly. I'd never known that love and relationships were so complicated.

Sean nodded.

"But how? What does she do?" Helen interjected.

Sean grinned. "Ah, well, that's easy. You ignore him for a while. Then you flirt with him. Blow hot and cold."

"Ignore him? But I can't. I work with him."

"Even better. Easier to ignore someone when they're right in front of you. Don't mention the date. Go out with someone else. Make him realize that you're not someone to be trifled with."

"Trifled with?" I asked, confused.

"Exactly. Be elusive."

"Except when I'm flirting with him?"

"Exactly." Sean smiled, missing my sarcasm completely.

I looked at him suspiciously. "And how do you know all this? I mean, what is it exactly that you do again?"

"Sean just know," Ivana said quickly. "He in merrege business. But that not how he know. He know because he is men. He know because he know about luff and merrege." She looked at me and at Helen, and then she shrugged. "He know because he is merried to me."

"You?" I exclaimed.

Ivana raised an eyebrow.

"His car, it need service," she said stonily. "It cost eight hundred pounds for new radiator."

I frowned, wondering if this was part of his experience and, if not, what the relevance of this information was.

"You mean, that's his fee?" Helen asked.

Ivana nodded.

"No win, no fee," she said, a smile creeping onto her face again. "No white dress and boom boom with this men, no car service. Okay?"

"Okay," Helen said firmly. "So, Sean, let's run over this just one more time . . ."

Chapter 17

PROJECT: MARRIAGE DAY 16

To do

1. Look fabulous.
2. Be elusive.
3. Put computer cleaning fluid in Marcia's potted plants.

On Monday morning I was at work early. To my immense relief, Marcia wasn't at her desk when I arrived and Anthony didn't appear to be in his office, but every time I heard the door open, I flinched slightly, and every time I heard someone working toward me, I braced myself.

"So, everything going well for the meeting next Monday?" Max asked, appearing at my desk suddenly and making me jump.

"Fine," I said tightly, wondering if he knew anything. "It's all going just brilliantly."

"Good. Because you know this is a really important meeting, don't you? For you as much as the firm. This is really your chance, Jess. So anything you want to run by me, you just let me know."

I sighed. Anthony was right about Max. He was completely obsessed with work. "Sure," I said tersely. "I will."

"Great!" He smiled brightly, and I looked at him suspiciously. Max never smiled. Had Marcia texted him, too? Was I just one big joke to everyone now?

"What?" I demanded. "What's so funny?"

"Nothing!" The smile left Max's face immediately. "I was just smiling. You know how you said I should smile more?"

"No," I said, shaking my head. "I don't remember."

"Oh." Max looked slightly dejected. "Oh, well, I'll just go back to normal then. Are you sure you're okay?"

"Do I look that awful?" I asked, miserably.

"No, not awful. Not at all. Just a bit . . . tired, maybe. Not your usual self."

"Well, maybe I don't want to be my usual self," I said, archly. "Maybe I've had enough of my usual self for a bit."

"Really? Why?" Max looked thoroughly confused. "You have a nice . . . self."

"Yes, well, it's good of you to say that, but you don't have to spend every minute with my 'self,' do you?"

Max thought for a moment. "Now, are we talking about self here as some kind of Durkheimian ego? Or are you talking more about the metaphysical idea of 'self'? Interesting how you've detached the self from you as though they are two component parts. Either you've got a tremendous theory to spring upon the world, or you're verging on the schizophrenic."

"Schizophrenic?" Marcia said suddenly, appearing beside Max. "You know, if you two actually applied yourselves during working hours instead of discussing psychology, you might not have to work late and on weekends. Ever thought of that?"

My eyes narrowed; I stared resolutely at my computer.

Max frowned. "Absolutely, Marcia. And if you didn't spend your days booking facials, you might have a career ahead of you."

Marcia smiled thinly. "Oh, I have a career in front of me, don't you worry about that, Max. So, Jess," she said, turning to me. "How was your date?"

I looked up incredulously. "My date? My date was fine, thank you very much. But then again, I presume you know all about the gory details already?"

She looked at me innocently. "Gory details? So it wasn't good? I happened to speak to Anthony yesterday about a client meeting with RightFoods and he seemed to think your date went really well."

Max's eyes widened. "Anthony?"

"Sure." Marcia smiled. "Didn't you know? Jess and Anthony are dating."

"No, we're not," I said hurriedly. "We had one date. That's it." Then I frowned and turned to Marcia. "You talked to him about . . . RightFoods?"

She nodded and rolled her eyes dramatically. "Nightmare client. Anthony saw them on Friday night and I wanted to know how the meeting went because I've got to call them today."

I bit my lip. "Oh. I see."

"But I couldn't get hold of him because he was out with Jess here," Marcia continued, smiling innocently at Max. I felt my eyes narrowing suspiciously.

"Right, well, interesting as this all is, I'd better be off. Work to do . . ." Max said distractedly.

"Me, too," Marcia said with a shrug. "Far too much work, in my opinion."

"And you're sure you've got Project Handbag under control? You're sure you don't want any help, or feedback?"

"No, Max," I said dismissively. So Anthony had been telling the truth? Marcia had been texting about work all the time? "No, I'm absolutely sure."

"Good. That's good." He turned and walked away. I felt my heart quicken slightly as I turned back to Marcia.

"So, how was it?" she asked.

I wanted to smile, wanted to punch the air, but I managed to rein it in a bit. "Fine."

"Just fine?" she asked. "Oh well. So anyway, I want some coffee. You?"

I stared at her uncertainly. Marcia never made me coffee. She hadn't offered in all the time we worked together. "Coffee? Really?" I heard myself say.

"Yes, you know, hot drink with caffeine in it?" Marcia raised an eyebrow at me, then tossed back her hair. "Look, Jess, I know we haven't always seen eye-to-eye exactly. But I'd like it if we could be . . . you know . . . friends."

"You would?" I stared at her incredulously. "Why?"

Marcia laughed lightly. "Well, first, we work together. Second, it looks like our boss is crazy about you, so it's in my interests that we get on. And third . . ." Her lips pursed. "Third, you're actually okay. You know, once you get to know you."

"Right. I see." Anthony was crazy about me. Had I heard correctly? How did she know? Had he said something? I smiled tentatively. "Well in that case, I guess we can. Be friends, I mean."

"Great. So, coffee?"

"No. No thanks. But thanks, you know, for asking."

"No problem." She stalked off toward the kitchen; moments later, I saw Anthony walking toward me. Immediately I started to type ferociously, my face getting hotter and hotter as he came closer, until he was standing right beside me. Crazy about me. Marcia thought he was crazy about me.

"I . . . um . . . I was wondering if you had a moment," he said quietly. "To talk . . ."

I took a deep breath. "Talk?" I asked, still typing. It was everything I could do not to throw my arms around him and plant my lips on his. Playing it cool was going to be nearly impossible. "Um, okay. But I'm a bit . . . tied up right now. Maybe later?"

"You don't have a moment now?" His voice was soft and serious. I wanted to take his hand, to apologize for throwing him out, to suggest we go right back to my flat now to pick up where we left off . . .

But instead I cleared my throat. "Sorry," I managed to say. "I've just got so much work to do. But maybe this afternoon, if you're free?"

"This afternoon," Anthony said uncertainly. "I guess that would be okay."

"Great. So, I'll see you then?"

I turned back to my computer.

"Any particular time this afternoon?"

"Time?" I was staring at my computer screen as hard as I could, willing myself not to turn around. "Well—"

But before I could finish, the receptionist Gillie rushed over. She was carrying a bouquet of flowers so large they covered her face completely.

"Jess!" she exclaimed. "These arrived. For you. Like a minute ago!"

I stared at her. "Me?"

"Yes! Aren't they amazing! Nicest bouquet I've ever seen. I tell you, you want to hold on to whoever sent you these. Must have cost a packet!"

"Um, thanks, Gillie," I said, taking them from her, my eyes widening as I realized how heavy they were. They were from Anthony. They had to be.

"Shall I get a vase?" Gillie asked, eyeing the card on the side hopefully.

"Oh. Yes please. Thank you." I looked up at Anthony, a big smile on my face, but he looked back at me uncertainly.

Gillie clicked her fingers, and Marie, the other receptionist, arrived with one already full of water.

"We had one already prepared," Gillie explained, grinning as

Marcia returned to see what the fuss was all about. "So come on, open the card. Tell us who they're from."

"The card. Of course." I took it, my hands trembling slightly as I pulled open the small white envelope and took out an equally small card. There was a heart on it.

Slowly, excitedly, I opened it up and read the words inside.

Jess, you're one in a million. Please reconsider my proposal. I'll never let the hedge fund take over my life again—you're the only thing that has ever mattered to me. Sean.

I stared at it uncomprehendingly.

"Sean," Gillie sighed, reading over my shoulder. "He your boyfriend, is he?"

"Um . . ." I reddened, still utterly confused. Sean?

"You've got a boyfriend?" Marcia arrived back, carrying coffee. "I didn't know you had a boyfriend." She looked at me sharply, her eyebrows raised.

"Ex-boyfriend," Marie interjected. "He wants her to reconsider."

"Yeah," Gillie agreed immediately. "Ex-boyfriend. And Jess is the only thing that matters to him. Ahhh. That's nice."

I nodded awkwardly.

"Hedge fund people are loaded, aren't they?" Marie said, with a sigh. "Anthony, you know about stuff like that. Aren't hedge fund people loaded?"

Anthony looked at her strangely. "Yes. Yes, I believe they are."

"A loaded ex who only cares about you," Gillie said dreamily. "I could do with one of those."

"You and me both," Marie agreed.

"Oh, everyone knows hedge fund managers are really boring," Marcia interjected.

"Yes, well," I said, trying to hide my disappointment. Of course they weren't from Anthony. What had I been thinking? "That's all very well, but I think I'd better get back to work. So . . .

thank you. For the vase, I mean. I'll just . . . I'll just put them here, I think." I shifted the vase to the right of my computer screen, blocking my view of Anthony.

"Yeah. Better get back to reception," Gillie said reluctantly, and she and Marie drifted off, turning to look at the flowers every couple of seconds.

"So, this afternoon," Anthony said. "We'll talk then?"

I nodded, then threw him a light smile.

"Great. I'll, um . . . catch you then," he said, and walked back toward his office.

Chapter 18

I followed Sean's advice to the letter and didn't get a chance to talk to Anthony on Monday afternoon after all. Every time I saw him approaching, I found an excuse to leave my desk. Even when I didn't manage to escape, our short conversations were invariably interrupted by my phone ringing and I would shoot him an apologetic look before telling "Sean" that I needed time to think.

"Sean" was variously Helen, Ivana, or Sean—apparently they'd decided not to tell me about the flowers because they wanted me to look genuinely surprised and they weren't convinced by my acting abilities. I wasn't either. Every time I put down the phone from "Sean," I looked around nervously, convinced that everyone knew that there was no ex, that the whole thing was a ridiculous fabrication. But I was wrong. Gillie and Marie kept popping over to look at my flowers and Marcia kept shaking her head as though utterly shocked by their very existence; by the end of the day I almost believed in "Sean" myself.

Tuesday morning saw the Milton Advertising companywide meeting, where everyone gathered in the lobby to hear about highlights (new clients), lowlights (lost clients, failed pitches), and housekeeping issues (the decision to replace the two kettles in the kitchen with a wall-mounted water heater was causing a great deal of consternation and debate). I usually used the opportunity of these meetings to take copious notes and to think of at least one insightful question that I would keep coming really close to asking and then would, eventually, not be able to, because it would mean everyone looking at me, because I'd probably stutter, or because when I said it out loud it probably wouldn't sound that insightful after all. Today, though, I didn't have any questions prepared. Today I was going to be presenting instead, something that would usually have filled me with excitement, with anxiety, with a whole host of emotions. Instead, I felt strangely detached from the whole thing.

Anthony opened the meeting, with his usual pizzazz and enthusiasm, listing clients won, clients lost, upcoming campaigns. Then Max pitched in to discuss the kettle situation, along with the recent change to pension legislation, which inevitably meant that everyone switched off and started checking their phones for messages. And then it was my turn.

Nervously, I stood up. "I guess, really, I just wanted to say that the Jarvis account, Project Handbag, is a really exciting account for Milton Advertising," I said, forcing a big smile onto my face. "And one that I think we can really make our mark with. There's a lot of work to do, but a lot of scope, too. So if anyone has any ideas or suggestions, I'd love to hear them."

I looked around, wondering if anyone was going to ask something; no one did, so I sat down again.

"Great. Thanks, Jess," Anthony said. Our eyes met briefly, and I saw his flicker and forced myself to smile again.

"So, next," Anthony continued, "we've had some great news in the creative department in that we've been nominated for Best Ad Design in the Advertising Today Awards. The ceremony isn't for another six months, but I think this is a tremendous achievement that really demonstrates our commitment to being at the forefront of . . ."

He frowned. "Of . . ."

Anthony was looking at the back of the lobby, where the doors to the street were. "Sorry," he said, a quizzical look on his face. "Can I help you?"

Everyone turned around—four men had just walked in through the doors wearing navy-and-white-striped blazers.

"Does a Jessica Wild work here?" one of them asked.

I gulped.

"Yes, she does," Anthony said. "Do you want to talk to her?"

"Actually, we're here to sing for her."

I reddened and stood up. "I'm . . . I'm Jessica Wild. I'm kind of in a meeting right now, though. Could you possibly come back a bit later?"

The man shook his head. "Would do, but I'm afraid we're booked up all day today."

"Well, look, maybe you could just sing later. Over the phone?" I suggested. Everyone was staring at me, and I could feel myself getting hot. I took a deep breath and managed an unconvincing smile.

"We get paid for personal appearances," the man said, shrugging. "Got to do it properly, otherwise it'll affect our reputation. It won't take long, honest."

"How long?" Anthony asked. People were giggling, and my palms were getting clammy.

"Three minutes, tops."

"Well all right, then. Bit of entertainment for the troops," Anthony said. He was grinning, but I could sense that he wasn't entirely comfortable. That made two of us.

"Right you are. Thanks, mate. Jessica, this comes to you from Sean. Straight from the heart."

The man hummed a note, then they all started to sing.

". . . *Dum dum dum Dum*
My lovely Jess
Dum dum dum Dum
Oh what a mess
You've really got me going with your
To-ing and a fro-ing
Lovely Jess
Dum dum dum Dum
Let me impress
Dum dum dum Dum
Upon you that I love ya
Don't want to live without ya
Lovely Jess
Dum dum dum Dum
I must confess
Dum dum dum Dum
You're all I want in my life
I wish you would be my wife
Lovely Je———ee———ss!"

There was an awkward silence for a moment or two. A couple of the creatives started to clap, then a couple of other people whooped, and before I knew it everyone in the company was cheering them. I even heard someone shout, "Encore." Anthony stared at me uncomprehendingly.

The group's leader grinned. "Sorry, can't do encores," he said, shrugging. "But thanks for listening." Then he did a little bow, and the four of them trooped out of the office, leaving me staring speechlessly after them.

"Well," Anthony said, his eyes flickering over to me and then away again, "that was very . . . entertaining. Does anyone else have any marching bands planning to make an appearance?" His face was smiling, but I could hear the slight irritation in his voice. No one said anything.

"Good," he said. "Then, as I was saying, the Advertising Today Awards are in six months, and we'll be taking a table, so watch this space. Which leaves only the kettle situation in the kitchens to resolve. Now, as Max has just explained, the immersion system we've introduced is recommended under health and safety rules, and really it should make no difference to the quality of tea that can be made . . ." He looked over at the door again. "Yes?" he said, sighing. "Can I help you?"

"Delivery for Jessica Wild." I turned around, along with everyone else, to see a man carrying a vast bouquet of flowers.

"Thank you. Can you just leave them on the reception desk, please?" Anthony said, smiling thinly.

"Needs a signature," the man said.

Quickly I jumped up and squeezed my way to where the man was standing. He had a huge long floppy fringe covering most of his face. A huge long floppy fringe that I thought I'd seen before. I looked more closely. I had seen it before. It was Sean. He'd actually come to deliver the flowers himself.

"So, back to the immersion heaters. I think if we can give them a proper trial—say, a month or so—we'll be in a better position to assess . . ."

"Boyfriend sent you these, did he?" Sean asked, a little grin popping out behind his straggly hair, his voice ringing out loudly into the high ceilings of the lobby.

I nodded, suppressing a giggle. "Ex-boyfriend, actually," I managed to say.

"Ex? Blimey. Not bad for an ex. Trying to get you back, is he?"

Anthony cleared his throat. "Yes, a month will help us assess the pros and cons. I think that wraps things up for today's meeting . . ."

"He is trying," I said, keeping my voice low.

"And you're going to take him back, are you?"

He was throwing his voice on purpose, I realized. Anthony might have closed the meeting, but no one was moving.

"I'm . . . I'm thinking about it," I said self-consciously.

"He's a good-looking chap, your ex," Sean continued, holding out a motorbike shop receipt for me to sign. "If the bloke in the shop was him, that is. Tall bloke. Dark. That the one?"

I nodded, grinning despite myself. "Sounds like him," I said.

"Nice car," Sean said, emitting a low whistle. "What was it—an Aston Martin?"

I giggled. "Could have been," I said seriously. I was beginning to enjoy myself. "That's his favorite."

"Well, enjoy the flowers," Sean said, winking. I nodded and took them from him, turning back into the lobby.

Immediately, as if caught out, everyone started to move back to their desks.

"Your ex-boyfriend drives an Aston Martin?" Marcia asked, sidling up to me. "Thinks he's James Bond, does he?"

I smiled. "I guess. Something like that."

"The thing is," Marcia said, shaking her head, "it's all very well him wanting you back now, but it's too little too late, isn't it?"

She sat down at her desk and I narrowed my eyes at her, uncertainly. "It is?"

"Definitely," she said. "If he wasn't ready to commit before, then I'd ditch him if I were you."

"Only because you want him for yourself," Gillie interjected, arriving next to me carrying a vase. "Here you go. Thought you might need this," she said, grinning.

I took it gratefully. "Thanks, Gillie. You're a star."

"So, going to take him back?" she asked, her eyes lighting up.

"I . . ." I hesitated. Anthony was walking toward me, and I fixed my eyes back on the flowers. "I haven't decided yet," I said, eventually.

"You think he wrote that song himself?" she breathed.

I shrugged. "Maybe. I mean, he's very musical."

"Is he?" Gillie asked dreamily. "Wow. He's good looking, he's musical, he's rich, and he's not afraid of commitment. He must be the most perfect man."

"I doubt it," Marcia said quickly. "Flowers and songs are all very well, but personally I think it's all a bit tacky."

"You wouldn't think it was tacky if he was doing it for you," Gillie said archly. "Go on, Jen, take him back. Or at least invite him here so we can meet him!" Anthony was only a few feet away now, and I realized he could hear us. I looked at her uncertainly. "The thing is," I said seriously, "I'm not sure I can trust him. All this wanting to commit is new. I mean, that's why we split up in the first place—because he couldn't commit."

"But now he's seen the error of his ways," Gillie said excitedly. "He's grown up. And that's so attractive. You know, I've always had a soft spot for married men."

"Gillie!" I said, slightly shocked. "But they're . . . married!"

"Exactly." Gillie sighed. "They're committed. Loyal. Exactly the sort of person you want to have an affair with . . ."

"Gillie, aren't you meant to be on reception?"

She turned around to see Anthony, who was now standing behind her. I quickly turned back to my computer.

"Fine," she said. "But keep me posted," she whispered, winking at me before slinking off.

"Hi, Anthony," Marcia said, batting her eyelids and crossing her arms the way she always did when she wanted to show off her cleavage. I'd started to notice that sort of thing these days. "I'll just leave you two to it, shall I?" She stood up, then smiled at him. "Oh, when you've got a moment I was wondering if you had time to discuss some visuals I'm working on for TheSupermarket dot com."

"Sure," Anthony said easily. "Why don't you go to my office and I'll be there in a moment."

"Great!" Marcia picked up some papers and wandered off.

"So." Anthony turned to me. "Flowers and barbershop quartets, huh?"

I smiled bashfully. "Yeah, sorry about that. I'll have a word with Sean."

"Good," Anthony said. "And . . ."

He trailed off and I looked up at him expectantly. "Yes?"

"Look, we never got to talk. I thought maybe we could have a drink later."

He was looking at me intently; I steeled myself. "Tonight . . . oh, I'm sorry. Tonight's not good for me."

"Tomorrow night, then?"

I hesitated. Blow hot and cold, Sean had said. Well, I'd surpassed myself on the cold. Surely it was time for a bit of warmth? "Maybe Friday?" I said carefully. "I think I'm free then."

"Great," he said, grinning at me suddenly and making me blush with pleasure. "I'll see you then."

Chapter 19

IT'S A VERY STRANGE RULE of nature that the more you push something away, the more it seems attracted to you. The following day I got a single orchid in a vase, and Anthony suggested that we swap drinks for dinner. Thursday afternoon I got twenty cupcakes, which I shared around the office; Anthony walked past my desk fifteen times and sent me no less than twenty-six e-mails, only half of them work-related. I, meanwhile, was finally enjoying this hot-and-cold lark. Every time Anthony started a conversation with me, I smiled flirtatiously, replied to whatever he'd said, then found an excuse to walk off when he was talking. Actually, my excuse was often the same thing, and eventually even Marcia asked me if I had a bladder problem. But it was working—I couldn't quite believe it, but it was. And it wasn't just Anthony who suddenly seemed interested in me—half the men in the office started engaging me in conversation. Guys I'd barely spoken to before suddenly appeared at my desk wanting to know about the Jarvis account, or to ask me if I fancied a drink after work sometime. I was hot property. I was in demand. I was, it seemed, becoming Jessica Wiiiild.

"You ready?" It was 6 PM Friday on the dot; Anthony was standing over me, a hopeful grin playing on his lips.

"Sure." I smiled. "Just give me a moment to finish some stuff off. See you by the door in five minutes?"

Anthony frowned, then shrugged reluctantly. "Five minutes," he said.

Quickly I turned back to my computer and giggled at the Facebook entry Helen had mocked up for me. Wild Child, she'd called me. The only photograph was of a pair of very high heels. Already I'd had fifty friend requests.

I clicked on one of my messages. *Dan Kelly. Hi, Wild Child. Would love to get to know you. Dig the shoes.*

Would love to get to know me. Someone called Dan would love to get to know me. Sure, all he had to go on was a moniker and a picture of some shoes, but that wasn't important. What was important was that I was in demand. I was popular. I was . . .

"Facebook? Are you serious?" I turned around hurriedly to see Max peering over my shoulder. "Tell me this is for research purposes, please."

I reddened. Max and I had often discussed the futility of networking sites like Facebook; we'd rolled our eyes at the time people wasted on them.

"Oh, yes, I mean—" I started, trying to work out a way to justify the screen in front of me.

"Anyone who's got time to waste hanging out with virtual friends frankly doesn't deserve to have a job," Max continued, interrupting me. "And who on earth is Wild Child? I mean, what kind of a stupid name is that? If she was really wild, do you think she'd have time to hang about in front of her computer?" He shook his head, a wry smile on his face. My eyes narrowed.

"Actually, Wild Child is quite popular," I said stiffly. "And you only hate Facebook because you wouldn't have any friends on there if you joined." I knew it was harsh; I knew I was being prickly. But I was sick of Max's constant superiority, his *I'm-the-only-one-who-really-works-around-here* act. He was so serious all the time, so sure that he was right about everything. He was the only one in the office who hadn't been impressed by all my flowers and cupcakes, the only one who interrupted my stories about Sean to ask how I was getting on with Project Handbag. Like there weren't more important things than private bank investment funds for women.

"Ouch," Max said, raising an eyebrow. "Well, maybe you're right. But frankly I think that real friends are worth rather more than Internet ones. Or is reality not something you're interested in these days, Jess?"

His eyes met mine and I felt uncomfortable suddenly. What did he mean? Did he know something? Why did he always have to be so difficult?

"Jess, five minutes has been and gone. Are you coming to dinner or do I have to drag you there?"

Anthony was marching toward me; with relief, I stood up and turned off my computer. "No, you don't have to drag me," I said, shooting a little look at Max. "If there are real drinks and real food on offer, I'm ready to go right now."

"Drinks and dinner," Max said archly. "Sounds very nice." He looked at Anthony. "And is this going to be charged to Chester's account, too, or is this one strictly pleasure?"

Anthony flinched slightly, then rolled his eyes. "Max, haven't you got accounts to scrutinize or something?" he asked, holding out his arm to me in a flourish. "Jess and I are late for a very important engagement."

"Indeed," Max said, walking away. "Indeed."

"Sorry about that," Anthony said as we made our way out of the building. "Max is so anal sometimes. So fixated by the details that he can't see the big picture."

"I know," I said, shaking my head.

"The guy really needs to loosen up," Anthony continued. "I mean, it's as if he doesn't have any life outside the office. He's a mate, but sometimes I just want to shake him and tell him what a loser he's becoming."

"Right," I said firmly. Loser. For spending too much time in the office. Totally different from me, then.

"Like you and me," Anthony said, on a roll now. "We know how to have fun, don't we? We work hard but we play hard, too. We have lives. We have a laugh. But not Max. The guy never goes out. I mean, never!"

I smiled, slightly less certainly now. "Absolutely," I said. "You've got to enjoy yourself, haven't you?"

"Of course you have. Otherwise what's the point? You just become boring. Like Max."

"Right." I nodded, beginning to feel a twinge of guilt at this assassination. "Although he is really good at what he does. And working hard isn't a *bad* thing . . ."

Anthony put his arm around me. "You're very generous, Jess, but come on, let's be honest. You wouldn't want to be stuck in a lift with Max for any length of time, would you?"

A little image flashed into my head of Max and me talking for hours, of me making him laugh—something I'd done only a few times but felt so rewarding because it was so hard—of him letting me lean against him to get some sleep the day after a late night at the office . . . . Then I forced it out. Helen was right—Max was boring and I'd only held a candle for him because I hadn't dared set my sights any higher. Now I could see him for what he really was Now I had Anthony. And now, I was Jessica Wiiild.

"So, champagne?" Anthony asked as he led me into a bar close to the office. I nodded happily, and made my way to a free table.

"Here we are." Anthony reappeared from the bar a few minutes later, brandishing a champagne bottle, a bucket, and two glasses. He opened it and winked as the cork popped, then he poured it into the glasses and handed me one. "To the hedge fund manager's loss and my gain," he said.

I smiled. "Yes. Absolutely," I said, chinking my glass with his.

"So it's completely over? I mean, are we done with the marching bands and flowers, do you think?"

Anthony's voice was light, but underneath his glibness was a serious question.

"Sean, you mean?" I asked. "Well, I can't make any promises, but . . ."

"But you'll tell him where to go if he comes near you again? You'll make it clear that you've got your sights set elsewhere now?"

I looked at Anthony quizzically. I still couldn't quite believe that he was really this interested in me. He had his pick of women. "Well," I said carefully, "I suppose . . ."

"Suppose?" Anthony downed his glass and poured himself another. "What do you mean suppose?"

"I mean . . ." I took a sip of my champagne, trying to remember what Sean had told me to say. "I mean that . . . well, Sean and I were really serious. Until we split up. So I want to be careful before I . . . I guess I want to be sure, that's all."

"Sure about me?"

"And your intentions."

"My intentions." Anthony grinned wickedly. "My intentions, Jessica Wild, are very dishonorable."

I blushed. "That's what I was afraid of," I said, putting my glass down. Dishonorable? Just how dishonorable was he talking here?

"But as for my commitment," Anthony continued, "it is complete."

"Complete?" I arched an eyebrow.

"I'll be devoted," Anthony said, nodding.

"Devoted to me?" I was going off Sean's script now, but I couldn't help wondering why. "When you could have any girl in London?"

"Why would I want to?" Anthony's eyes were glistening mischievously and his hand moved toward my leg.

"But . . ." I stared at him, perplexed, caught between wanting to know why he was interested in me and wanting his hand to keep doing what it was doing. "Why me?"

"Because no one else drives me this wild, Jessica Wild," Anthony said, shifting his chair closer to mine. "Because, unlike Sean, I don't intend to waste my chances."

His voice was soft and low; his mouth moved toward my neck, sending electrical currents down my body. I even seemed to be vibrating.

Then I realized it was my mobile phone in my pocket.

"Excuse me," I said, pulling away briefly and flashing Anthony an apologetic smile.

I had a message from Helen. *RU at drnks now? Sean called to remind you: hot and COLD. Leave early. xx*

I didn't want to leave early. I was enjoying myself.

"Anyway," Anthony continued, resuming his exploration of my neck as I shoved my mobile into my bag, "you fascinate me, Jessica Wild. I feel like I know nothing about you. You're elusive. And I like that."

"You . . . do?" I asked, reminding myself to breathe in and out.

"Of course. Keeps me on my toes."

"Right. On your toes."

"Shall we go back to mine?"

"Yes . . . I mean . . . what? Now?"

Anthony looked up at me, grinning. "I've got food in the fridge. And more champagne. Come home with me."

I cleared my throat. Hot and cold. Maybe I'd just focus on the hot part this evening. Maybe cold could wait until tomorrow. Or the next day. Or . . .

"Anthony?" I looked up and Anthony pulled away.

"Tamara." He smiled easily. "How are you?"

"I'm well. Thank you." Tamara was a tall, elegant blonde who was regarding me rather frostily. She bestowed a large smile on

Anthony, though. "I haven't seen you for ages. Where have you been hiding?"

He grinned back. "Oh, you know. Keeping busy." He grabbed her hand playfully. "This is Jessica. Jessica Wild. And Jess, this is Tamara."

I smiled politely. Based on not very much, I decided I didn't like her; she appeared to have come to the same conclusion about me.

"Delighted," she said, with an expression that suggested she was anything but.

"So how about you, Tam?" Anthony asked, evidently oblivious to our animosity. "What have you been up to?"

Tamara flicked her hair. "The usual," she said. "Going out, staying in, doing a bit of work here and there. Anyway, I'm on my way to Selina's for a party, if you want to come. Everyone's going."

"A party, you say?" Anthony's eyes lit up, and he turned to me. "What do you reckon, Jess?"

"A party!" I said, trying to sound enthusiastic, wishing that Tamara would disappear into a puff of smoke. "That sounds nice. Although, I'm not sure. I mean, I thought maybe I might . . . we might . . ."

Anthony pulled a hangdog expression. "We don't have to stay long. Just a quick meet and greet . . ."

I smiled weakly. "I suppose . . ."

"Great! Tam, why don't you help us finish this champagne?"

"Love to," Tam said, smiling warmly for the first time and sitting down next to Anthony. Anthony shot me a *what-can-you-do?* smile and waved over a waiter to get her a glass.

"You know, Gill, don't stay on my account. If you need to go somewhere." Tamara was smiling thinly at me; I felt myself getting warm.

"Jess. It's Jess," I managed to say. Quickly I touched Anthony's hand the way Ivana had taught me and pressed my arms together. Anthony immediately looked appreciatively at my cleavage.

"She's not going anywhere," he said, squeezing my hand reassuringly.

"You know," Tamara said, leaning in suddenly, "Marc was telling me that you've got some big thing planned. A money-making ruse. Do tell. Sounds very intriguing."

Anthony frowned slightly. "Oh, it's nothing. Just work, you know."

"Really?" Tamara looked disappointed. "He seemed to think you had some hugely cunning plan."

"Well, I'm sorry to disappoint you," Anthony said, winking, "but that's all it is. Just a new deal."

"A new deal?" I asked. Questions. I had to ask questions. "What sort of deal? Are you expanding or something?"

Anthony shrugged and smiled at me. "Oh, something like that. Look, I really shouldn't be discussing it. It's nothing. It's—"

"Work's always boring," Tamara said, faking a yawn. "Like this place. Come on, shall we go?"

"I don't think work is boring," I said pointedly. "I think it's interesting, actually." I looked at Anthony with what I hoped was a supportive expression. But instead of smiling appreciatively, he rolled his eyes.

"It isn't interesting. Not at all. But Tamara's right, this place is. Let's go to the party."

"Now?" I bit my lip. I didn't want to go to a party, particularly if the people there were anything like Tamara. "Why don't we stay a bit longer? We haven't even finished the champagne."

"Oh no!" Tamara said, her eyes widening, then she laughed, drily. "I think if you look at the bottle closely, you'll see that it's sparkling wine, not the real thing. I'm not sure I'm prepared to hang around here any longer for a few sips of this rubbish."

"Too right," Anthony said, standing up. "Let's get out of here. Shall we get a cab to Selina's?"

"Already? I mean, right now?" I asked anxiously. What would Ivana do now? I wondered. Arm-wrestle Anthony to the floor?

"Of course we should get a cab," Tamara said, ignoring me completely and gazing at Anthony. "You know I don't like to walk unless I absolutely have to." She let her eyes rest on me as I stood up, looking me up and down. She didn't look particularly impressed.

And I wasn't particularly impressed when Anthony offered her his arm.

"You know what?" I said, suddenly deciding that now was the time for Cold. Frosty, even. I wasn't even putting on an act this time. "I think I might go. I've . . . I've got a few things I need to do."

"Go?" Anthony looked at me wide-eyed. "Why would you go? We're going to a party. Then we're . . ." He grinned mischievously. "Then we've got plans, haven't we?"

I faltered slightly. Maybe I'd overreacted. Maybe he was just being polite to Tamara.

"Look," I said, pulling him closer. "How about we forget the party and skip straight to our plans," I said in my most seductive voice, giving him a meaningful look.

"You can't miss the party," Tamara said quickly. Evidently she had ears like a bat. "Everyone's going to be there."

I forced a smile. "I'm not sure I know everyone," I said levelly.

"You will if you come to the party," Anthony said, pulling his puppy-dog expression again. "Come on, Jess. It'll be fun."

"Lots of fun," Tamara said in a way that suggested I wouldn't have much fun at all.

"I'm not really in the mood for a party," I heard myself say. I was willing Anthony to tell Tamara we'd give it a miss, desperate for him to leave with me, not her.

"But it won't be any fun without you," Anthony whined. So he was going. With or without me. Of course he was. Had I really thought he might not?

"Tell you what," I said, taking a deep breath. "Why don't I take a rain check. We'll come back to our plans another day. Okay?" Quickly, before I could change my mind, I gave Anthony a little wave and made my way out of the bar.

As I reached the door I heard someone coming up behind me and turned to see Anthony, a quizzical expression on his face. "Jess, what's up?" he asked. "Don't rush off like this. Stay."

I shook my head. "Anthony, I was under the impression that we were having dinner tonight, not going to a party. So now I'm going to go home."

"But we . . . I . . . look, I won't go," he said quickly. "I'll tell Tamara I've . . . well, I'll think of something. If that's what you want. Just say the word and I'll jack."

I looked at him for a moment. "If that were true," I said gently, opening the door in front of me, "you'd already have told her. Bye, Anthony."

I walked down the street as quickly as I could in my high heels. I was almost becoming Jessica Wiiild, I realized.

"Jess?" I looked up, startled, then stopped when I realized who it was: Max. I hadn't registered that I was standing just feet away from the entrance to Milton Advertising.

"Hi, Max. Just leaving work?" I should have been working that evening, I found myself thinking. I still hadn't gotten going on Project Handbag and in the great scheme of things maybe it was more important than Project Marriage. For one thing, Project Handbag had a hope of actually being a success.

Max nodded. "And you? I thought you were out with Anthony." His expression was unreadable.

"I was. I . . ." I shrugged. "Someone called Tamara turned up.

They're going to some party," I said, barely able to hide the irritation in my voice.

"Ah, Tamara," Max said, nodding sagely. "Tall, stupid, and very annoying?"

I grinned. "You know her then."

"Yeah. I can see why you didn't stay. Anthony's choice in friends has always been rather dubious in my opinion."

"You're his friend," I pointed out.

"I suppose," Max conceded. "So where are you off to? Home? Can I walk you to the tube?"

I looked at him uncertainly. Max and I hadn't really talked to each other much lately. Not since I'd started dating Anthony. Not since I'd decided he was work-obsessed and difficult. "Sure," I said. "Thanks."

We started to walk; immediately a silence fell. An awkward silence.

"So how's the account going?" Max said after a few seconds.

"Project Handbag? Oh, great. You know," I said, slightly defensively. The truth was I'd barely looked at it in days; I'd been too busy acting hot and cold and receiving gifts from "Sean."

"Great."

We carried on walking; the tension was becoming uncomfortable. Finally, we got to the tube.

"You . . . coming in?" I asked tentatively.

Max shook his head. "No. I'm going to . . ." He gestured vaguely along the road, and I nodded.

"Okay, well, see you tomorrow, I guess," I said, attempting a smile.

"Yes," Max said. Then he frowned. "Unless . . ."

"Unless?" I looked toward the turnstile, then back at him.

"Unless you . . . you want to go for a drink?" he said suddenly. "If you don't have to get home. I mean, not for long, if you've got other things . . ."

I thought for a moment. "No. I'd like that. I'd like that very much."

"Good!" Max's face lit up. "That's . . . well, good."

"Just one thing," I said, wincing slightly.

"Yes?" Max's face was earnest.

"You mind if we pop back to the office so I can change my shoes? These high heels are killing me."

"Of course," Max looked relieved. "I never understood why women wear those things anyway."

"They make your legs look longer," I said as we turned around.

"But your legs are perfectly long enough." Max caught my eye and blushed. "For walking, I mean," he added immediately. "A perfectly practical length. In my opinion. I mean . . . To be clear, what I was trying to say was that your legs . . ."

"Thanks, Max," I said, smiling to myself as I hobbled along. "I know what you were trying to say. So where shall we go?"

"There's a nice pub around the corner," Max said, shooting me a little smile. "It's nothing fancy but they do a great pint of bitter."

"Bitter?" I raised an eyebrow teasingly. "Don't old fuddy-duddies drink that?"

"Yes, we do." Max grinned. "And what about you? Bitter not good enough for you, is it?"

"A glass of wine will do nicely, thank you." I smiled.

He nodded as we walked. Then, suddenly, he stopped.

"So you're not serious about Anthony?"

I stopped, too. I wasn't prepared for that question. Not from Max.

"Not serious?" I asked. "What do you mean?"

He wasn't looking at me; he was still looking straight ahead.

"I mean, are the two of you serious. In a serious relationship. One that might go somewhere?"

I gulped. Only down the aisle, I was thinking. But that would never happen. Not really.

"I don't think so," I said quietly. "No, I would say that we're not serious."

"Good."

"It is?" I looked at Max tentatively.

"No, not good. Well, sort of good. I mean . . ." Max put his hands through his hair awkwardly. "Good for work relations. You know, no complications. Office politics, that sort of thing."

"Oh, right," I said, a little stab of disappointment hitting my stomach. Disappointment seemed to dog me where Max was concerned: you'd think I'd have learned by now.

"Actually—" Max stopped walking. "Actually, that's not true."

"It isn't?"

"I . . . I had Marcia's style sheet all along," he said.

"Style sheet?" My forehead creased in incomprehension. "Which style sh . . . ?" And then I realized what he meant. What I thought he meant. "You did? I mean, you came . . ."

"To see you, yes."

"Because . . ." I could hardly breathe.

"Because I was hoping that I might pluck up the courage, maybe, to . . . But then I didn't, of course. I bottled it. Like I always do. But sometimes you've got to be brave, don't you think?"

"Yes," I said, my voice hardly audible. "Yes, I think you do."

"So, I'm pleased," he said. "About you and Anthony."

"Yes," I said. Max started walking again and I followed after him, my mind racing. He was pleased. He came to see me. And he was only telling me this now? Why? Why didn't he tell me before. And then I knew why. It was the same reason Anthony was interested in me—because someone else was. Anthony was jealous of Sean; Max was jealous of Anthony. Although jealousy wasn't a bad thing, not always.

Max stopped again. "I just wondered if you . . . if you . . ."

I stopped, too. My eyes met his, and neither of us could look away. His lips were just inches away; if I moved my head just slightly we'd be kissing. It was what I'd hoped for since I met him, what I'd wanted since I'd set eyes on him at my interview to Milton Advertising.

Except it wasn't, I realized suddenly. It wasn't what I wanted, not really. If I kissed Max, if I let him kiss me, everything would change. I'd lose Grace's inheritance. But more importantly, I'd be vulnerable to so much more disappointment. Too vulnerable. And all for a man who was probably only interested in me because someone else was.

Steeling myself, I pulled away. "No," I said, my voice barely audible. "No . . ." And, drawing on every piece of strength in my body and mind, I turned around and ran down the street toward the tube.

Chapter 20

To do
1. Um . . .

The next morning, I was woken up by a loud ringing. Pulling my pillow over my head, I did my best to ignore the sound, which I worked out in my sleepy haze was the doorbell and therefore very unlikely to be anything to do with me. I felt myself drifting back into a delicious sleep. A few moments later, though, I felt the pillow being pulled from my head.

"It's for you," Helen said, her voice strange and brittle.

"For me? What's for me?"

"The door. You've got a visitor."

I stared at her.

"For me?" I asked again stupidly. "Who is it?"

Then I frowned. "It's not Mr. Taylor, is it?" I asked anxiously.

I swung my legs out of bed and lowered my head onto my knees. "Tell him I'm not here," I said pleadingly. "Tell him I'm still out of the country."

"Still out of the country? When did you leave?" Helen asked.

"I told him I was going away a week or two ago," I mumbled. "Please, Hel. Tell him you don't know where I am. I can't face him now. I really can't."

"It isn't Mr. Taylor," Helen said, pulling me out of bed and smoothing down my hair. "But put something on first." She scanned my wardrobe and pulled out some clothes. "Here, put these on."

She handed me a pair of jeans and a pretty cashmere cardigan, and I looked at her cautiously.

"Why?" I demanded.

"Just do it!" Helen said irritably. "Quickly!"

"If it's Ivana with some new activity for me to try, I'm not doing it," I said sulkily. "I'm really not. I need to talk to you about Project Marriage, actually. You see, I've been thinking and I don't think it's going to work. Seriously."

"Fine. Suit yourself. Just go down to the front door."

"You're okay with that?" I asked in amazement. "You don't mind if I abort the whole thing?"

"Not at all," Helen said vaguely. "Whatever you want. Just do me a favor and answer the door."

Curiously, I walked toward the front door and opened it. And just before I did, I got a little jolt in my stomach. Because maybe it was Max. Maybe he wasn't going to take no for an answer and he was going to sweep me off my feet . . .

The hallway was empty. Of course it wasn't Max. Which was good. I mean, it was never going to be him anyway. I didn't know why I'd even thought that.

"There's no one there!" I sighed, turning around to frown at Helen.

"The proper front door. Downstairs," Helen said, urging me toward the staircase.

Tentatively, I made my way downstairs. It *could* be Max. I

mean, it was possible. Slowly, I opened the door. And then my mouth fell open.

"Anthony?"

He smiled awkwardly and presented me with a bouquet of flowers, which I took uncertainly. I could smell wine on his breath. Or maybe it was champagne.

"I know you've had too many of these, but I wasn't sure what else to get."

I looked at him skeptically. "You got these for me?"

"Yes. Yes I did. You see, the thing is—"

He stopped in midsentence, and I looked at him curiously.

"The thing is," he began again, "I got to thinking last night. After you left, I mean."

"You did?"

Anthony smiled uncertainly. "Yes, well. You see, I was at this party, and it was crap, as parties always are, and I got to thinking about my life."

"Your life," I said, squinting against the early-morning sunlight. "Yes, well, it's always good to do that."

"Right. Exactly. And your life, in fact."

I frowned. "My life?"

"You just said no to that party yesterday. You just walked away. I can never do that. If there's a party, I have to go. It's a weakness."

"Maybe you just like parties," I suggested.

"I do!" Anthony's eyes lit up. "But they're never as good as I think they're going to be. That's the point. Things never are. Except you."

"Me?" I looked at him suspiciously.

"Yes. You're better than I thought you were going to be. You see? Better, not worse."

"Right," I said, not knowing whether to be flattered or insulted.

"And then I thought about Sean. You know, missing the boat, full of regrets. And I thought: you know, Anthony? That could be you one day. Running from party to party and missing the boat right in front of you."

I frowned. "You mean a boat party?"

"I mean your boat," Anthony said, his eyes shining.

"I don't have a boat. I'm just ordinary. Look, Anthony, why don't you go home. Why don't you ring up Tamara, or Selina, and talk to them about this?"

"I don't want to talk to them. I want to talk to you."

Anthony was staring at me goofily, swaying from side to side.

"Are you drunk?" I asked.

"A bit. Drunk with love." Anthony grinned.

"You're in love?" I sighed. Of course he was. He was coming to tell me it was over. Good. I wanted it to be over. It would be a relief.

"Yes I am. With you!"

"Good. So, good-bye then . . ." My voice stalled as I realized what he'd said, and I took a step back. "You're what?"

"I'm in love with you. It suddenly became clear."

"In love with me?" I asked incredulously. "But why?"

"Why?" Anthony frowned with confusion.

"Yes," I asked, genuinely baffled. "Why? I'm not a supermodel. I don't like parties. Yesterday we were meant to be having dinner and you went to a party with Tamara instead."

"Exactly!" he said, as though I'd just solved a difficult mathematical equation. "And it was awful. I drank too much, I stayed too long . . . And if I'd stayed with you, I'd be at home now, I wouldn't be hungover, I'd be comfortable."

"You're sure you're not still drunk?" I asked. He wasn't making any sense. He wasn't in love with me. This whole thing was just . . . bizarre.

"Hair of the dog," he said, winking. "Best cure known to man. So anyway, what do you think?"

"Think? About what?" I was beginning to think I needed a drink myself.

"About us? About my proposition."

"What proposition? You haven't proposed anything as far as I can remember."

"Proposition? Oh my God. Has he proposed? Are you two getting married?" I turned, to see Helen rushing toward me, her arms outstretched to give me a hug.

"No," I managed to say before she hurled herself at me. "No, he hasn't. We're not—"

"We could!" Anthony said suddenly, his eyes shining.

"What?" I stared at him in horror.

"Get married," he said, grinning. "Settle down. What a brilliant idea."

"No, it isn't," I said firmly.

"Yes it is!" Helen put her hand over my mouth. "It's a brilliant idea. Wow, how exciting."

"But . . . but . . ." I extricated myself from Helen's grasp. "But . . ."

"But nothing!" Anthony swung around and grabbed me in a bear hug. "Your friend's right. It's a brilliant idea. I'm not going to miss the boat anymore. I'm going to get on the boat."

"*I'm* the boat now?" I asked, reeling slightly.

"We're the boat," Anthony corrected me. "Marriage is the boat. HMS Commitment."

My mouth fell open.

"I . . . I . . ." I looked back at Anthony. "You seriously want to *marry* me?"

"Of course he does!" Helen squealed. "You're going to be Mrs. Milton. Oh, I can't wait to tell Ivana and Sean."

"Sean?" Anthony swung around. "Yes, you tell him. You tell him that she's taken now."

"I'm not taken," I said firmly. "You're not telling anyone anything."

"Yes you are. Anthony just asked you to marry him. I heard him," Helen said immediately. Then she turned to Anthony and stuck out her hand. "I'm Helen, by the way. I'm going to be her bridesmaid, aren't I, Jess?"

I rolled my eyes. "I think there's the small matter of me saying yes."

They both turned to look at me expectantly, hopefully.

I shook my head. "I can't . . ." I started to say, "I can't . . ."

"Can't what?" Helen said impatiently. "You can, Jess. Come on, Deal, for God's sake."

"But . . ." I could feel my heart thudding in my chest. Helen grabbed me and pulled me to one side.

"What's the matter?" she hissed. "You've got everything you want on a plate in front of you. Anthony Milton is proposing. You get him, you get the money, you get the house, you get to fulfill your promise to Grace. Why on earth wouldn't you say yes?"

"Because . . ." I took a deep breath. "Because it's all fake," I said. "I'm not Jessica Wiiild."

"No you're not. Jessica Wiiild is you," Helen whispered, firmly. "Jess, you can't turn this down. Do you really want to walk away from four million pounds?"

"No!" I said defensively. "I just don't want to . . . I don't want to do something I'll regret."

"Regret? Jess, you'd only regret saying no. Marrying Anthony who, incidentally, is utterly gorgeous, is the best thing that would happen to you. And you're going to be a millionaire. What is there to regret?"

I swallowed. Helen was right.

"Nothing, I guess," I admitted.

"Exactly," Helen said, folding her arms. "So?"

I turned back to Anthony. "I can't . . ." I turned back to Helen, who glowered at me. "I can't quite believe it," I continued. And I couldn't. Anthony Milton had just proposed. There was nothing in the project plan to deal with this.

"Believe it," Anthony said, taking my hand. "Jessica Wild, I want you to be my wife."

"Your wife." I said the words, but they still sounded strange in my mouth. Any minute now I expected someone to jump out and shout, *Surprise! It's all a joke!* But no one seemed to be jumping. Not that I could see, anyway. I squinted at Anthony. "You really want me to marry you? Really and truly?"

"Absolutely." Anthony nodded. "It'll be a blast. Everyone'll be gobsmacked. Me, married. Brilliant."

I stared at him for a few seconds, and then I looked past him to the early-morning sky. I couldn't do it. I just couldn't. Could I? Maybe I could. I'd be Mrs. Milton, after all, just like I told Grace. And it would put an end to any dangerous romantic thoughts once and for all. I didn't love Anthony; I didn't have any expectations of him. In many ways it was perfect. If he left me, I wouldn't care. I'd be insulated from disappointment for the rest of my life.

"Okay then," I said, my eyes shining. "What the hell. Let's do it. Let's get married."

Chapter 21

"AND THEN HE ASKED HER to marry him. Just like that!" Helen poured some more champagne into her glass and looked triumphantly at Ivana and Sean, who were stretched out on our sofa. It was Sunday evening and after a weekend spent drinking champagne with Anthony and trying on engagement rings, I was exhausted.

"He ask you merry him?" Ivana looked surprised and I nodded defensively.

"It was all because of you two," Helen said quickly. "You're amazing."

"Yes," Ivana agreed. "Yes, is true."

"And now," Helen said tentatively, "all we need to do is make sure that the wedding happens soon. Like, in twenty-seven days."

"Just under four weeks," I added helpfully, taking another sip of champagne. I found that my comfort with the whole wedding business correlated exactly with the amount of champagne I consumed—if I waited too long before taking a gulp, the doubts and demons all began to surface again.

Ivana raised an eyebrow. "Is not longk," she pointed out.

"Not long at all," I said thoughtfully. "Actually, it's virtually impossible."

"Not impossible," Ivana said firmly. "We find way."

"Tell him you're up the duff," Sean suggested. "Shotgun wedding."

"Shotgun?" Ivana turned to him, her face curious. "We heff shotgun wedding in Russia. But what is point in dead people here? I no understand."

"Not real shotguns," Helen said. "If he thinks she's pregnant, he's more likely to . . . you know, get on with it. The wedding, I mean."

Ivana looked unconvinced. I stood up. "I'm not telling him I'm pregnant," I said firmly. "No way."

"Fine, but do you have any alternatives?" Helen asked.

I shook my head.

"Say you are romantic," Ivana said suddenly. "Say you no want wait."

"A romantic?" I looked at her dubiously. "I don't really see that working, I'm afraid."

Ivana shrugged. "Okay. Maybe you say no boom boom until wedding?"

Sean raised an eyebrow. "*You* could try saying no boom boom period."

"You kip being jealous, you get no boom boom," Ivana said irritably. She turned to Helen. "He know my job. Why now he heff to be jealous?"

Helen smiled sympathetically.

"Fine," Sean said, rolling his eyes. "So, Jess, try asking Anthony. See what he says."

I nodded uncertainly. "Okay. I'll do my best."

"Yes, you will," Ivana agreed. "But if it no work, we need plen." She looked at me seriously, then smiled, gold teeth appearing in her mouth like little stars. "You know, you not doing so bed," she said graciously. "Better than I think you do. So, congratulations, yes?"

She looked around the room, holding up a bottle of champagne and bringing it to her lips.

"Yeah, congratulations," Sean agreed.

"To Jessica Wild," Helen said, grinning. "Or, rather, to Jessica Milton."

On Monday morning, the moment I walked tentatively through the doors Gillie came rushing over (it turned out she could spot an engagement ring at ten paces) and screamed at the top of her voice.

"Sean!" she squealed. "You're marrying Sean! He won you back! Oh my God—was it the barbershop quartet that did it? Or the flowers? Oh, will you look at the size of that diamond. Marie, come over here. Quick!"

Marie duly rushed over and they both sighed reverentially as I held up my left hand for inspection.

"Actually, it's not Sean," I said.

"Not Sean?" Gillie's eyes opened wide. "You dark horse. Who gave it to you then? And do you have any other rich suitors tucked away somewhere to pass to me? I wouldn't mind getting flowers every day, I tell you!"

I swallowed nervously. Ever since Anthony had gone home on Sunday morning (he'd been up for staying all weekend, but I'd made my excuses; as Helen had pointed out, an engagement wasn't a wedding and I still needed some expert tutelage from Ivana and Sean), I'd been half expecting him to call the engagement off, to look at me sheepishly, tell me he was drunk when he proposed, and suggest that maybe we should cool things for a bit. But he'd texted me already today asking how his favorite fiancée was so, assuming the *favorite* bit was a joke and that he didn't have a whole bevy of future wives tucked away somewhere, it appeared that the wedding was very much on.

"Darling, hello!" Anthony swept out of his office and planted a kiss on my lips. "So, what d'you think of the ring?" he asked Gillie, a big smile on his face. "Impressive, huh?"

I watched Gillie's face contort with confusion.

"You? And you?" she asked, looking from me to Anthony and back again.

I nodded, not daring to speak.

"Seriously? You and Anthony?"

I nodded again.

"Getting married?"

"That's right," Anthony said, grinning.

Gillie shook her head in amazement. "But . . ." she said, helplessly. "But I never . . . I mean, you never . . . I never knew!"

"It hasn't been that long," I said tentatively.

"Long enough though," Anthony said, as Gillie looked at my ring again.

I nodded awkwardly. Me. Engaged. It still took a bit of getting used to.

At that moment Marcia arrived through the double doors. Her eyes widened as she took in Anthony's arm, Gillie's rapturous face. Then she saw the ring. A look of uncertainty flicked across her face, but then she smiled, and took my left hand in hers. "You're getting married?"

"We certainly are," Anthony said happily.

"How very romantic. Quite the whirlwind romance."

I looked at her in surprise. "It was quite quick," I agreed.

"And she took some convincing, believe me," Anthony said.

"You knew about this?" Gillie asked Marcia incredulously. "You knew they were an item?"

Marcia smiled smoothly. "Of course I knew. Oh dear. Don't tell me that you were the last to know, Gillie. How awful for you."

"I did know," Gillie said stiffly. "At least, I guessed."

"Really? Only you look like you've been run over by a high-speed lorry," Marcia said. "Anyway, I suppose congratulations are in order. So congratulations."

She smiled again, and I stared at her. I didn't know quite what I'd expected from Marcia, but it certainly wasn't this.

"Yes, congratulations," Gillie said immediately. "This is so exciting. But you need to start planning. Do you want a summer wedding or a winter one? Places book up quickly, you know. Ooh! You should have a wedding like Liz Hurley's. Different locations. Three different dresses. And what about bridesmaids? Got it all sorted, have you? Oh, I love weddings, me. You need any help at all, I'm your woman."

"Great! Thanks, Gillie!" I said, a fixed smile on my face. "But really it's very early. I mean, we haven't really had time to think about any of that stuff yet. Have we, Anthony?"

He smiled indulgently at me. "I suppose we haven't. But that doesn't mean we can't start, does it? You tell me what you'd like, Jess, and let's take it from there, shall we? Summer or winter wedding?"

I felt everyone's eyes on me, and I blushed slightly. Now was my chance. But how could I suggest getting married in under a month? "Well," I said, trying to keep my voice casual and relaxed. "I mean, we could wait and plan something for well into the future, or we could . . . maybe . . . you know, do it quicker?"

"Quicker?" Anthony frowned.

"Sooner, I mean," I said quickly. "You know, just do it."

"Just do it. You mean like Nike?" He was laughing at me, and I found myself blushing.

"I think it's a great idea," Marcia said suddenly. "I mean, overplanned weddings are so boring."

Surprised to have Marcia as my supporter, I smiled and nodded at her. "Exactly. Far better to . . . you know, be impetuous."

"To be impulsive?" Anthony said, his eyes lighting up. "To keep the element of surprise?"

"Exactly," Marcia said triumphantly.

"But what about the planning?" Gillie said uncertainly. "I mean, how quick are we talking here? A few months?"

"Or . . ." I bit my lip hesitantly. "Or a few weeks?"

Anthony thought for a moment, then grinned. "A few weeks. Brilliant. We can book a register office, throw a little dinner afterward—it'll be brilliant."

"A little dinner?" Gillie snorted. "Anthony, you can't get married and just have a little dinner. You have to do it properly. Come on, you're Anthony Milton. People are going to want to see photographs. I bet *Advertising Today* will put you on their front cover again."

"You do?" Anthony looked at her curiously for a moment, then nodded. "You know, I think you're right. Maybe we should think big for this wedding. Get some PR going?"

"PR?" I asked, falteringly. "Really? Won't it be expensive? I mean, a dinner would be fine, really . . ."

"No it wouldn't," Anthony said, firmly. "And don't worry about the money. I'll pay. It'll be an investment. Gillie my dear, you're a genius. But how are we going to organize a huge wedding in a few weeks?"

"A few weeks?" Max emerged from his office and wandered over. "What's happening in a few weeks?"

I felt myself reddening self-consciously. "The wedding," Gillie said, rolling her eyes. "Keep up, Max."

"Wedding?" Max frowned. "Whose wedding?"

Anthony winked at me; my blush deepened. "Just thought of something," he said conspiratorially. "Give me a second."

He disappeared into his office as Gillie shook her head impatiently at Max. "Jess and Anthony's wedding, of course. Do you know nothing, Max?"

Max grinned. "Gillie, one day I really hope to understand your sense of humor. In the meantime I must confess to being completely baffled by it."

"But it's not a joke," Gillie said with a sigh. "Ask her yourself."

"Jess?" Max was staring at me in bewilderment. I swallowed with difficulty.

"We're . . . we're getting married," I said, trying to make it sound less significant. "Anthony asked me on Saturday."

"It's true, Max," Marcia said archly. "Quite the dark horses, aren't they?"

"Look at her ring," Gillie agreed, rushing forward to hold my left hand out. "Nice, don't you think?"

Max looked at the ring, then opened his mouth as if to say something, but nothing came out.

"Surprised us all," Gillie said conspiratorially. "Except me, of course. Nothing surprises me. Nothing at all."

"You're . . . you're getting married? To Anthony? Seriously?" Max looked at me intently. I could feel myself getting hot, feel myself wanting to say, *no, no, not really*, but I steeled myself.

"That's right."

"And you really think this is a good idea?" Max's eyes were boring into me; I could feel his disapproval at the bottom of my stomach.

"Yes, I do," I said defensively. "I think it's a very good idea."

"Right," Max said, nodding, his face suddenly closed, disinterested. "Right. Well. Congratulations. I'm sure you'll be . . . very happy." He turned to walk back to his office, but he was stopped by Anthony, coming out of his office.

"All right, campers. Do we think we can organize a wedding in three weeks?" he said, turning back to me, a big grin playing on his lips.

"Don't be ridiculous," Max said immediately.

"Three weeks?" Gillie asked, her mouth falling open. "Where are you planning to do it? In the local park?"

"Actually I was thinking about the Hilton Park Lane. There's a lovely church around the corner for the ceremony, then we can pack everyone into the Hilton for a huge reception."

"The Hilton?" I looked at him uncertainly. The Hilton Park Lane was one of the largest, most glamorous hotels in London. "Really?"

"Really!" Anthony said happily. "They're a client. I just spoke to the chief exec."

"And they're not booked up?" Gillie demanded.

"Of course they are. They're usually booked up years in advance. But they had a cancellation. Some bride got cold feet, apparently. But her fiancé's loss is our gain!"

"But three weeks? You can't organize a wedding in a month!" Gillie exclaimed. "It's impossible."

"Nothing's impossible," Marcia said, shaking her head. "Is it, Anthony?"

Anthony winked. "Of course it isn't."

Max stared at him. "Anthony, are you insane? Three weeks? You don't think that maybe you might be rushing things slightly? You don't think that marriage is a rather major commitment that should be thought about, planned, prepared for?"

I felt my heart beginning to thud loudly. I was so close, so close to everything working out. So why was I willing Max to persuade Anthony it was a bad idea.

"Strike while the iron's hot, that's what I say," Anthony said quickly, turning away from Max. I caught his eye as he did so, and thought I saw a look of unease, but immediately he grinned, and I realized that it must have been my unease, not his. "Jess, you don't think we're rushing things, do you? You're not scared to rush in where fools fear to tread?"

I shook my head. "Not at all," I said, wishing I felt as sure as I sounded.

"A shotgun wedding," Marcia said. "How romantic."

"Couldn't have put it better myself." Anthony grinned. "So, Jess. You wanted a quick wedding. Three weeks quick enough for you?"

I nodded. "Three weeks sounds great to me," I managed to say.

"Well. Good," Max said tightly. "I'm very glad for you both. And if three weeks is long enough for you to plan a wedding, then I'm sure that three minutes is long enough for you to prepare for our Project Handbag meeting."

I looked at him uncertainly, then looked down at my watch. It was 8:57 AM.

"Oh, right," I said, suddenly remembering that we had a meeting at 9 AM.

"Yes, right," Max said, then turned around and marched back to his office.

Chapter 22

I SAT DOWN at my desk and turned on my computer. Everything was going according to plan. Everything in my life was coming together seamlessly. I was happy. The funny feeling in my stomach was happiness, I was sure of it.

"So, you're ready for the meeting, right?" I looked up to see Max, striding toward me. "Because it's now. Like, right now."

He looked at me expectantly, and I found myself looking away. "Sure," I said lightly. "As far as one can be ready for a meeting."

"What?" Max frowned. "What on earth do you mean? Of course you can be ready for a meeting."

God, he had no sense of humor.

"I mean it's fine," I said. "Just chill out."

"Chill out?" Max's face twisted in distaste. "We have a meeting with Chester Rydall and you're asking me to chill out?"

"Max, for God's sake, Jess has got other more important things to worry about," Marcia said, standing up suddenly. "Jess, ignore him."

Max looked at her for a moment. "I think you'll find she's already mastered that skill," he said levelly, then stalked off toward the meeting room. Sighing, I rolled my eyes at Marcia and followed him.

"Jessica Wild!" Chester, who was standing next to Anthony,

grinned broadly at me as soon as I walked in. "I hear congratulations are in order!" He stood up and enveloped me in a bear hug. "I'm sure the two of you are gonna make a wonderful couple."

I smiled as brightly as I could. "Thanks, Chester. Thanks very much."

"Not at all. And I have to tell you, I'm very excited about this presentation. Folks back at the office are all waiting with bated breath to see what you guys have come up with."

"They are?" I asked happily, shooting a triumphant look at Max. "Well, I'm pleased to hear it."

"Shall we?" Anthony said, winking at me and motioning for everyone to sit down. "So, Jess—the future Mrs. Milton—let's hear all the exciting developments on Project Handbag!"

He grinned at me and I felt myself going slightly pink. "Of course. Thanks, Anthony," I said brightly. "What I wanted to do today was to revisit our thoughts on the campaign and to really establish what it is we want to do."

Chester looked at me quizzically, then laughed. "Oh, it's a joke," he said.

"A joke?" Now I was the one looking confused.

"Yeah. Like you'd bring me here after all this time just to recap. Come on, Jess. I know you like a bit of drama when you're presenting, but give us the meat. The research, the strategies. I'm real excited to hear it all."

I cleared my throat. "The meat. Right."

"Come on, Jess," Anthony said encouragingly. "Tell us all about it."

"Of course!" I said brightly. "Absolutely. Well, we're here to discuss Project Handbag, so let's get right to it. I've got some logos here for people to look at and lots of ideas on the campaign itself . . ."

I managed to pad it out for ten minutes or so, handing around the logos that Max had shown me, flanneling for all I was worth. And actually, I thought it went pretty well. I was Jessica Wiiild, after all. I smiled (no teeth), I flicked my hair, and I managed to sound (in my opinion at least) pretty convincing, even if I had nothing to say, even if I hadn't actually managed to do anything on the account whatsoever.

"So," I said to Chester expectantly, when I'd finished. "Do you have any thoughts?"

Chester rubbed his chin.

"Actually, I do," he said, his brow creasing slightly. "I'm just not sure quite what I've learned today, to be honest."

I nodded. "Learned?" I asked. I was getting a bad feeling in my stomach.

"I guess," Chester said, a slightly pained look on his face, "I was hoping for more . . . detail, today. You know, facts and figures."

"Facts and figures," I said nervously. "Okay. Tell me what you want to know."

"Great." A look of relief filled Chester's face. "Can you tell me, in terms of spend, what's the proportion of print advertising we're planning versus web advertising, and are we expecting direct results from this or just awareness raising?"

I smiled brightly. "Well, that's a good question," I managed to say.

"And what about take-up?" Chester continued. "What actual numbers are we aiming at in months one and two, and what kind of levels of investment? Because that's going to help us crunch the costs of this."

I cleared my throat. "Um, again, a very good question . . ."

"Also, I'd like an update on the celebrity endorsement you mentioned at the pitch meeting. What's the state of that?"

Everyone looked at me and I felt myself getting hot.

"Right, well, yes, that's a good point."

"A point to which you have an answer?" Chester was looking at me curiously.

"Yes, absolutely," I said, swallowing nervously. "Of course I have. Maybe I could e-mail it to you later today?"

"E-mail it?" Chester frowned. "I thought we were holding this meeting so we could discuss these things now."

"Yes, we are. I mean, we were," I found myself saying. "But . . ." I looked around the room. Anthony was looking at me with a slightly fixed smile on his face; Marcia was doodling on her pad. I didn't even dare look at Max. I could feel his irritation from the other side of the table.

Suddenly Max pushed back his chair and I was forced to turn to him. "Chester, you've asked some important questions," he said seriously. "Questions that we have been working through the answers to over the past couple of weeks, although without reaching firm conclusions yet. The truth is that before we present the detail to you, it would be far more worthwhile if you would tell us what it is that Jarvis Private Banking would like to achieve in terms of numbers, and then we can use that to plan the advertising spread. We know, for instance, that you are looking for a growth curve over the first six months as awareness builds—this isn't a cut-price credit card, after all, but a sophisticated financial product that will take time to embed in people's consciousness, but really we need a steer from you on exact numbers."

Chester stared at him for a few seconds. "Right," he said eventually, appearing slightly mollified. "Well, I guess that makes sense. We can crunch some figures and let you have them, if that sounds okay?"

"And then we'll let you have some more detailed information on the logo and its use," Max said quickly.

"Yes. Good. Very good," Chester said.

"And then we can meet again in a couple of weeks?" Max suggested.

Again, Chester nodded. "Well, okay then. Sounds good to me."

Immediately Anthony stood up and ushered him out of the meeting room, followed swiftly by Marcia.

Max and I regarded each other cautiously.

"Well, that was a bit intense," I said, attempting a smile. "Glad you managed to convince him he didn't need the answers to everything right now."

"I didn't convince him of anything. I just managed to stop him from firing us here and now," Max said tightly.

"Firing us? Don't be ridiculous."

"I'm not. The only ridiculous thing today was your presentation. What were you thinking, Jess?"

I reddened. "It wasn't ridiculous. Okay, I hadn't crossed all the *t*'s and dotted all the *i*'s . . ."

"You hadn't done anything," Max said, standing up. "You embarrassed the firm."

"Who embarrassed the firm?" Anthony asked, coming back in. "Max old boy, watch what you say won't you?"

"No, I won't," Max said angrily. "Jess was a disgrace today and she knows it. You know it. And I'm not afraid to say it."

"There are ways and means," Anthony said, his voice low.

"So you think I was a disgrace?" I demanded, staring at Anthony. Bloody Max. Bloody, bloody Max.

"No, of course not," Anthony said immediately, walking over and putting his arm around me. "You were wonderful. Chester's expectations were just—"

"Not met," Max interrupted. "At all."

"Max, have you thought that maybe Jess has had other things on her mind?" I looked up to see Marcia walk back into the room.

She smiled at me supportively. "That she's maybe been a bit pre-occupied, what with Sean, Anthony, the wedding . . ."

"We all have personal lives," Max said coolly.

"Really?" Marcia asked sweetly. "I didn't think it was your bag."

"So is that why your presentation was complete waffle?" Max demanded, ignoring Marcia and turning to me.

"Yes," I said defensively. "I've had a lot on my plate. I guess I just didn't manage to do as much research as I'd hoped, but—"

"As much as you'd hoped? You had nothing," Max said, looking at me in disgust.

"Max, give Jess a break, for God's sake. Marcia's right—it's far too much to expect you to run an account *and* organize a wedding."

"Oh no," I said quickly. "I mean, I can do both. I just—"

"Exactly," Marcia cut in. "It's far too much. Let me help."

"Marvelous," Max said with a sigh. "Why not give the account to Marcia and we can all sleep a bit easier in our beds. I mean, it's only the biggest account we've won in a year."

"Marvelous," Anthony said enthusiastically. "Marcia will take on Project Handbag so Jess can concentrate on organizing cater-ers. Flowers. Whatever else you need at a wedding."

My face fell. "What? No! I mean, there's no need, really . . ."

"Yes, there is a need," Anthony said sternly. "Jess, I don't want you stressed out before our wedding. I want you glowing and blushing. Marcia, you can take over, can't you?"

"Of course I can," Marcia said, a hint of resignation in her voice and a little twinkle in her eye. "More work for me, but hey, I'm sure it'll be worth it."

"But . . . but . . ." I started to say. This wasn't going the way it was meant to. Project Handbag was my account; Marcia would wreck it. I may have been a bit preoccupied for a week or two, but Marcia did nothing *period*. I looked at Max beseechingly—he had to know it was a terrible idea. He hated Marcia. He thought she was a complete waste of space.

But Max didn't look back at me; he just shook his head. "But nothing," he said, standing up and walking out of the room. "Like you said, Jess, you've been busy. Now you're free to focus on what's important. To you, that is."

Chapter 23

OBVIOUSLY I DIDN'T really care about losing Project Handbag. I mean, sure, it was my first account; sure the whole "Project Handbag" thing was my idea; sure it would have been nice to see it through. But in the great scheme of things it really didn't matter; I was going to be Mrs. Milton. I was going to be a happily married millionaire. Or just a millionaire. A happy millionaire who was also married. Either way things were just fine. Really fine.

And anyway, I found myself thinking the next day when Marcia mentioned for the fifth time how pleased she was to help me out with the Project Handbag account, I'd never realized how much organization went into a wedding. There were the invitations, the meal plans, the flowers, the gift list, the dress, the color of the napkins, and that wasn't even the half of it. Determinedly, I flicked through the magazines Gillie had placed on my desk, reading articles like "Countdown to Your Wedding—the 10-Month Plan." Only I had to do it in weeks, not months. I was going to be busy busy busy.

"Look at this . . . flowers for the bride!"

I turned to see Gillie carrying a huge bouquet, which she set down on the middle of my desk. "They're not from Anthony," she said with a glint in her eye. "I checked."

"You checked?"

She blanched slightly. "Just looking out for you, that's all."

Marcia, who seemed determined to become my new best friend, peered over the top of her desk and frowned. "Who are they from, then?" she demanded.

Carefully I opened the card and read it out. *To my darling Jess. A better man has won your heart. I wish you happiness forever. Sean.* I managed to stifle a giggle. "Thanks, Gillie."

Marcia rolled her eyes. "Well, at least he knows the situation. Honestly, Jess, you need to watch him. I think he could turn out to be a stalker."

I nodded sagely. "Yeah, thanks, Marcia, I'll bear that in mind."

"So look, I got you these," Gillie continued breathlessly. From behind her back she pulled out three more wedding magazines, which she spread in front of me. "We've got a lot to think about, you know. Dress, bridesmaids, venue, food, wedding favors . . ."

"Wedding favors?" I asked nervously. "Isn't that what goes on . . . you know . . . on the honeymoon?"

Gillie looked at me for a moment, then burst out laughing. "Oh, you are funny," she said, wiping her eyes. "Wedding favors. Presents for your guests. And you'll need a good photographer, too. Are you going to have an engagement party?"

I looked at her uncertainly. "Um—" I started, but Gillie wasn't listening.

"You have to have an engagement party," she said. "And I think you should make it black-tie . . . I love men in dinner suits, don't you, Marcia?"

Marcia nodded. "Definitely. Engagement parties are de rigueur these days. Aren't they, Anthony?"

I turned around to see Anthony approaching; Gillie pulled herself up quickly. "Hi, Anthony," she said, smiling brightly. "We were just talking about your impending nuptials! So exciting. So much for Jess here to think about. Like, I was wondering if you were going to have an engagement party. A black-tie one?"

"A black-tie engagement party, eh?" Anthony grinned. "Great idea! And I know just the people to organize it. Party Party Party."

"Party Party Party?" I looked at him blankly. Was it a mantra? A philosophy?

"Best event planners in London," Anthony said briskly. "They do all the best weddings. I was on the phone to Fenella, one of their event managers, this morning, and she told me that they said they can take care of the whole lot for us. I mean, if we're going to do it, we might as well do it properly, wouldn't you say?"

"They're going to organize our wedding?" I blanched.

"Oh, fantastic idea," Marcia breathed. "They're the best. Really great. My cousin used them last year."

"Did they?" Anthony's eyes twinkled slightly. "Well, what a great recommendation." He looked at me and smiled. "Apparently they did Elton's wedding, too, although they can't admit it officially. It's perfect—I mean, if we're going to have a big wedding, we need to make sure it's done properly, don't we? So what do you think?"

I cleared my throat. "But I would do things properly," I said uncertainly. Then something occurred to me. "Although maybe it's a good idea to use a third party," I added quickly. "I mean, if they take care of the wedding, that would free me up to concentrate on Project Handbag, wouldn't it?"

Marcia laughed. "God, Jess, you're a scream," she said, rolling her eyes. "Of course you won't have time for Project Handbag. There's still loads to do. You'll have to manage Party Party Party, for starters. I mean, you're still the boss; they're like your team. And there's things like the gift list and your dress."

"Gift list and dress," I said, telling myself for the tenth time that day that my wedding was more important than a silly work project.

"And the flowers," Anthony said immediately. "I think you should do the flowers. Add that personal touch."

"The flowers." I forced another smile.

"Atta girl. Fenella's got your details, so expect a call any minute." Anthony gave me a little punch on the shoulder just as Max wandered over to Marcia's desk; I immediately looked away.

"So, Max," Anthony said. "Coming to our engagement party? I've just signed up Party Party Party to organize it. And the wedding."

"Party Party Party? Sounds expensive," Max said. "Planning to remortgage the company again?"

Marcia looked up sharply; Anthony rolled his eyes. "Maxy, Maxy," he said dismissively. "Don't you worry about the money. Everything's going to be fine."

"I'm sure it is," Max said archly. "But try not to charge the event to the company this time? Tax men don't like it too much, however inconvenient it seems. Now, Marcia, are you free later to talk presentations? Say three PM?"

Marcia nodded vaguely, and Max walked off toward the stairs.

"Don't mind him," Anthony said, rolling his eyes. "He's always been focused on the detail." Winking, he made his way back to his office.

Fenella called twenty minutes later. She had the kind of voice that immediately intimidated me—one of those smart, confident drawls that only very beautiful people with double-barreled surnames seem to have. And while I knew that she was working for me, while she said several times that this was my wedding and that she was just an "enabler," by the end of the phone call I seemed to have promised to abide by her to-do list and assured her that I wouldn't let her down on the planning side. Two seconds after I put the phone down, an e-mail pinged into my inbox:

Jess,

SO great to talk to you just now. I know this is just going to be THE MOST FABULOUS wedding, and I'm really excited to be part of it. My role is to make everything seamless for you and Anthony so anything I can help you with, just let me know. In the meantime, if you could get back to me soonest on the list below that would be just GREAT!

All the best,

Fen

1. Engagement party—what do you think about holding it at Boasters? It's a fresh new private members' club in St. James, very hot, and very free next Saturday (!)—they're holding our reservation. I'm assuming free bar? And I'm assuming e-mailed invitations? It's all a bit last minute, isn't it?!

2. Color scheme. As we discussed, green and red are going to be our critical colors for this wedding. I was thinking of using Pantone numbers 1805 and 3435—can you check you're happy with these? Please check these carefully because once agreed, changes will be incredibly difficult to accommodate. However, I'm sure you're going to love them. I do!

3. Cravats for the groom's party or bow ties? Or shall I run this by Anthony for you?

4. Your dress—can you get me a fabric swatch? Need to make sure it works with the theme. If you want to send me a selection, I'll be happy to give you my feedback.

5. Veil—yes or no? Long or short? Need to know so can replicate on the wedding cake.

6. Rehearsal dinner—would you prefer a dress code of black tie or cocktail dress?

7. Flowers: Anthony said you're doing flowers. Just want to clarify—you're using a florist, right? I'll e-mail over my

recommendations—please ensure you give them the Pantone
numbers and put them in touch with me.

I looked at the list and felt my heart quicken. I had no idea what
my answers were to a single one of her questions. I hadn't covered
any of those things in my project plan.

Immediately I called Helen.

"Do I want cravats or bow ties?" I asked breathlessly.

"What?"

"For the wedding. Fenella needs to know and I have no idea,
Hel. And she wants a fabric swatch of my dress."

"Fenella?"

"My wedding planner."

"You have a wedding planner now?"

"Yes," I said impatiently. "And she's asking me all these questions and I don't know what to say. So you have to help me. Cravats or bow ties and swatches."

"But you haven't chosen your dress yet. We're doing that next
week."

"I know. But she wants everything now. And she's organizing
an engagement party for Saturday night."

"She is?"

"Yes. At Boasters. I don't even know where it is."

"Oh, relax, Jess. I'm sure she'll send you a little map. Anyway,
just remember, in a few weeks you're going to be a millionaire.
You need to get used to people working for you."

"She's given me Pantone numbers."

"Cool! You should get her to decorate Grace's house after the
wedding."

"You think?"

"Sure, put your stamp on it. New sofas, new curtains. Jess, it's
going to be so much fun."

"New sofas . . ." My voice trailed off as an image of me and Anthony moving into Grace's house suddenly filled my head.

"Jess? Are you okay?"

"Sure. Completely okay," I assured her. "I just . . ."

"Just what?"

"You think the marriage is going to work?" I whispered into the receiver. "I mean, I'm actually getting married."

"You've only just realized that?" Helen said, laughing.

"No, but . . ."

"It'll be fine," Helen said reassuringly. "He's gorgeous, you're gorgeous, and it's going to be fabulous."

"You're right," I said, nodding to myself as I forced my eyes to focus back on Fenella's list. Anthony was spending so much money on the wedding—I couldn't possibly let him down. "I'm going to be Mrs. Milton," I said firmly. "And I'm going to be really happy."

"Atta girl," Helen said cheerfully. "Oh, and by the way?"

"What?"

"Cravats. Bow ties are just so last century."

Chapter 24

PROJECT: MARRIAGE DAY 28

To do
1. Go to engagement party.
2. Meet Fenella.
3. Be happy . . .

Boasters wasn't just a "fresh new private members' club." It was the newest, freshest place in London. It was so über-cool that Helen and I couldn't actually find it for half an hour; it was only when Ivana arrived and pointed out the sleek black door with no markings that we realized where it was.

Now, I'll admit that inviting Ivana may not have been one of my proudest moments, but when Fenella rang to apologize that she probably wouldn't be able to meet up with me in person before the party because there was so much to organize but that she was desperately excited and that we'd have coffee "soonest," she asked me to e-mail over my guest list for the party. And even though I figured that everyone from Milton Advertising kind of counted as my guests as well as Anthony's, I just couldn't send over one, single, solitary name (Helen's). She might think I didn't have many friends or something. So I found myself giving her Ivana's, too. And Sean's. Worse than that, I got all intimidated talking to Fenella and found myself making up some utterly crap excuse for my short guest list. I told her that everyone I knew seemed to be out of the country skiing or lapping up some sunshine somewhere, and I was convinced that she knew I was lying, even though she said, "Oh, God, I know exactly what you mean—everyone I know keeps dashing off on holiday, too, and I've only made it to Gstaad twice this year, which is totally unfair, but what are you going to do?"

As we approached the door to the club, Ivana stopped me and narrowed her eyes.

"This your engagement party," she said, grabbing my shoulders. "You no looking like it."

"I'm not?" I asked anxiously

"Your shoulders, they are too far forward," she interrupted me. "They must be back."

I rolled my eyes. "If I don't lean forward slightly, my breasts look like tornadoes," I said, shooting a look at Helen, with whom I'd argued for hours over what I was wearing—she had, eventually, allowed me to wear a demure little black dress but had insisted on squeezing me into a bra that looked like something out of an S&M film.

"Let me see," Ivana demanded, and I duly showed her. "Hmmm. I em liking the bra," she said, scrutinizing me. "The dress not so much. But you . . . No. Is no good."

"No good? Why? Have I got food in my teeth?"

Ivana raised an eyebrow. "No. But you heff look in your eye I recognize. Is fear."

"I'm not afraid," I said defensively. "Just, you know, a bit nervous. I'm meeting all of Anthony's friends. I'm sure he's nervous about meeting . . . well, meeting you."

"Nerrrvous," Ivana said, rolling the *r* for longer than was really necessary in my opinion. "Why nervous? Is yourrrr party. You must think you are sexiest woman in room."

"Right," I said tersely, thinking of all the Tamaras and Selinas who would no doubt be scrutinizing me. "No problem."

Ivana shook her head and looked at Sean, who shrugged for good measure. "This not good," she said dismissively. "Definitely not. So, stand up straight, yes?"

I sighed, then reluctantly drew myself up to my full height. "Okay, can we go in now?"

"Tell me who you are," Ivana said firmly, blocking the entrance.

I looked at her like she was mad. "I'm Jessica Wild," I said as quietly as I could. "And I'm late for my engagement party." I looked at my watch pointedly—I was already twenty minutes later than I'd told Anthony I'd be.

"Jessica who?" Her eyes were flashing dangerously.

"Jessica Wild," I hissed, feeling my cheeks redden. "Look, please, can't we just go in? I'm fine, really I am."

"You are not fine," Ivana said firmly. "You are scared little girl going to own engagement party. Tell me who you are. Tell me you are Jessica Wiiild, crazy sexy woman."

I looked around nervously. There was no one there. Slowly, resignedly, I took a deep breath. "I'm Jessica Wild," I said, looking at Ivana imploringly. "A crazy, sexy woman."

"Now like you are meaning it. Or no go in."

She raised an eyebrow and my shoulders slumped; immediately she stared at them until I'd adjusted my posture. "Fine," I said. Then I tossed back my head. "I'm Jessica Wild," I said, loudly, confidently. "Wild as you like. I'm Jessica Wild, a crazy, sexy woman who's wild, wild, wild. Okay?"

Ivana didn't say anything.

"What?" I demanded. "Not wild enough? Not crazy enough?" I did a little dance, wiggling my hips. "I'm Jessica Wiiild," I yelled.

"Crazy, sexy wild woman of Islington. Lock up your sons, because Jessica Wild is here. Now can we go in?"

"Jessica. Good to see you," a voice said suddenly; I swung around to see Max approaching.

I smiled weakly. "Max. Hi. Um, these are my friends. Helen, Ivana, and . . . Sean."

"And are they wild wild wild, too?" he asked levelly, a little glint in his eye. I blushed furiously. This was all I needed—Max taking the piss.

"That?" I said, attempting a laugh. "Oh that was . . . I mean, I was just . . ."

"She vos doing vocal exercises," Ivana said, turning a huge smile on Max and holding out her hand. "It iys very good to meet you." She batted her eyes, her eyelashes seeming to follow a full three seconds behind her eyelids. Max smiled.

"Ivana," he said, holding out his hand.

"So," Ivana said, her voice deep and low. "Are we going in?"

The glossy black door led to a steep staircase, at the top of which five leggy brunettes were standing, each holding a clipboard with a list of names on it. They looked us up and down dismissively as we made our way up the stairs, then smiled engagingly at us when I gave them my name.

"Congratulations," one of them simpered.

"Have a great night," said another.

I smiled and gulped as they swept back a curtain to let us through; immediately I saw Anthony standing next to Marcia laughing about something. I hesitated for a moment, but then Anthony caught my eye.

"Darling!" He rushed over and kissed me on the cheek. "You're here!"

"Yes. I—"

"You have to come and meet everyone," he said, grabbing me

by the hand and dragging me off. I managed to smile fleetingly back at Helen; moments later I was standing in front of a large group of people, none of whom I'd met before.

"This is Amanda," Anthony said, smiling at a tall girl in a red dress. "And Josh, her boyfriend. This is Saffron, and this is Alexis. And Meg. Charlotte. Clare. Tatiana."

I looked around at the sea of faces and managed a smile.

"And this is my fiancée, Jessica Wild," Anthony concluded. He kissed me on the head. "Back in a tick," he murmured. "Got to go and shake a few hands. Stupidly invited a whole bunch of clients . . ."

He disappeared into the throng and I smiled as brightly as I could at Saffron, Alexis, Tatiana, and the rest of them. "Hi!" I said, feeling more self-conscious than I had on my first day at school. They were all looking at me curiously and I suddenly found myself rather wishing Tamara would turn up. At least I could ask her how the party went.

"So, how do you all know one another?" I said eventually.

"Oh, you know, the party circuit I guess," one of them said.

"The party circuit," I nodded. "Of course . . ."

"And you know him through work, right?" I think it was Tatiana speaking; I nodded and smiled.

"That's right. I'm an account executive at Mil—"

"So are we all going to Henry's after this?" she interrupted, before I'd been able to finish my sentence.

"Henry's?" I asked tentatively.

"He's having a party," she said, frowning curiously as if surprised I didn't know.

"Oh, I see." I looked at her uncertainly.

"Of course we're going," another girl said. It could have been Saffron, but then again, it could have been Meg, Charlotte, or Clare, too. "I mean, we're not staying here all night."

She met my eye and looked slightly sheepish. "We'd love to, of course," she added quickly. "But you know, we can't desert poor Henry."

"Of course not," I said levelly. "You go to his party just as soon as you want."

"So, gorgeous," Anthony said, appearing behind me. "Are you all getting on famously?"

"Absolutely," I said, suddenly feeling guilty for my last comment. Maybe Henry had been planning his party for months, after all.

"I'm so pleased. But I knew you would. My best friends and my best girl!"

I smiled weakly.

"So," Tatiana said, smiling brightly at me. "Tell me the truth, Jess. Are you pregnant? How many months? You can't be more than five months. I mean, you're not showing much at all. Still, I imagine you're already searching for an idyllic country house to live in where your sprogs can run around to their hearts' content. I mean you can't bring up children in London, can you?"

I stared at her in disbelief. "Pregnant? I'm not pregnant."

"And we're not moving to the country. I hate the country, as you know," Anthony said at the same time.

"You're not pregnant?" Tatiana regarded me suspiciously. "But I thought . . . I mean, when Anthony told us . . . It just seemed likely that . . ."

"That I was up the duff?" I asked hotly, turning to Anthony indignantly. "And what do you mean you hate the country?"

He grinned benevolently at me. "Isn't Tats hysterical?" Then he turned to her. " 'Fraid there are no buns in the oven, and we're not moving anywhere. It was just a whirlwind romance."

"*Whirlwind* is certainly one word for it," Tatiana said archly. "I thought you were seeing that other girl anyway. What was her name?"

"No, no one else," Anthony said quickly, putting his arm around me and pulling me away. "Come on, Jess, there's more people for you to meet."

"Do you really hate the country?" I asked tentatively, as he pulled me toward a thin, balding man with very large glasses.

"Absolutely loathe it," he said, grinning. "It's muddy and you can't get anything delivered."

"But if we had a big house," I said, thinking of Grace. "Would you maybe live there then?"

"Not in a million years," Anthony said, winking. "But look, come and meet Ian. Ian, this is Jess. Jess, this is Ian. Old friend from way back when. Works for the *News of the World,* but don't hold it against him. Now, let me get you a drink, Jess. Champagne?"

I nodded, and Anthony disappeared. I looked at Ian hesitantly. He was wearing a suit with wide lapels—he was either very cool and wearing them ironically or very square and unaware that fashion had changed since 1970. I couldn't decide which.

"So, Anthony tells me you've hired the Park Lane Hilton?" he asked. He nodded as he spoke, reminding me of a puppet.

"Um, yes, that's right," I said. "So, you work for the *News of the World.* What sort of stuff do you cover?"

Ian smiled, nodding again. It was almost hypnotic, I thought as I watched him. "Celebs, mainly. You know, pop star caught with her knickers 'round her ankles, that sort of thing."

"Right." I smiled uncertainly. "Well, that must be . . . interesting."

"Not really," Ian said, shrugging. "But it's where the money is, isn't it?"

"Is it?" I asked. I found that I was nodding, too, now. Any minute now we were going to crash into each other.

"Er, yes. That's what I just said," Ian said, looking slightly uncomfortable.

"Of course. Sorry." I looked at him for a few seconds, waiting for him to say something else, but then I realized that he was waiting for me, only I had nothing to say and now it was too late anyway.

"So, *News of the World*," I said weakly.

"Yeah. Well, lovely meeting you. And good luck with every-thing," Ian said, nodding violently as he turned and fled. This, I thought desperately, was why I never went to parties.

Suddenly a drink arrived in my hand. "Darling! Where'd Ian go?"

Anthony put his arm around me and I relaxed into his shoul-der. "Ian? Oh, he . . . he had to go and talk to someone," I said, smiling as brightly as I could.

"How very rude. Now, you've met Fenella, haven't you?"

I shook my head. "Not yet. Is she here?"

"You haven't met Fenella? Oh, you have to. Stay here—I'm going to get her."

"No," I said, slightly too quickly. "I can meet her later. Why don't we talk a bit?"

"Rubbish. You're going to love her," Anthony said, winking. "Wait right here."

Immediately he disappeared into the throng. Five minutes later, when he hadn't returned, I decided to go in search of him. It didn't take me long—he was up at the bar, drinking cham-pagne. "God, I was going to find Fenella for you, wasn't I? I'm so sorry. Got waylaid by . . ." He looked down at his glass sheepishly. "By this. Sorry."

"It's fine," I said quickly. I felt hurt—my cheeks were red and my hair was beginning to frizz at the roots. "I don't need to meet her now anyway. Let's just stay here. I'll grab a stool."

"Perfect." Anthony grinned. "You come and sit next to me. Jes-sica Wild. The future Mrs. Milton. So how are the wedding preparations going, anyway? Do we need to have a stand-up row about the way the napkins are folded?"

I laughed, forgetting my frizz for a moment. "Actually I'm not sure either of us will have a choice. I rather think Fenella's going to be telling me how they're going to be folded."

"Marvelous. That's one argument averted. Using Party Party Party is really an investment in our future, wouldn't you say?"

I nodded. He hadn't realized I was joking. Not that it mattered, I told myself. Seconds later a suited man launched himself on Anthony. "Anthony? Oh, it is you. Wondering where you were hiding. Look, come and meet Gareth, the guy I was telling you about."

Anthony shot me a *what-can-you-do?* look and stood up. "Richard, have you met Jessica? My fiancée?"

The man held out his hand to shake mine. "Great to meet you. Congratulations. Really great stuff." Then he turned back to Anthony. "He's over in the corner. Really wants to meet you."

They wandered off, and I turned back to the bar. Not the worst place to be, I decided. I could do with a drink, after all.

"Jess!"

I looked up reluctantly; it was Marcia. "Great party," she said, smiling. "Are you having a great time?"

"Oh, great," I said, nodding purposefully. "Really great."

"He's a great guy, Anthony. You've done really well for yourself."

I nodded thoughtfully; Marcia frowned. "What's up?" she asked curiously. "You're not having doubts, are you?"

I shook my head. "No. God no. I just . . . His friends. This girl, Tatiana, thought I was pregnant. Thought that was why . . ."

"Tatiana?" Marcia's eyes narrowed. "Don't listen to her. She's just a jealous old shrew."

"You know Tatiana?" I asked curiously.

Marcia blanched slightly. "I've come across her. You know. At parties." Parties, I found myself thinking. Did everyone in the whole world spend their time at parties?

"Jess! There you are!" Helen exclaimed, appearing in front of me suddenly. "We were wondering where you'd gotten to."

Marcia looked her up and down. "Well, I'd better go and mingle," she said, shooting me a little smile. "See you later."

Helen watched her leave then looked at me, one eyebrow raised. "Don't tell me. Marcia?" she asked.

"Marcia," I confirmed, putting my drink down. "She's actually okay when you get to know her. So, having fun?"

Helen shrugged. "I guess. Ivana and Sean are having an argument about something and I've just been propping up the bar really. So who are all these people anyway? Do you work with all of them?"

I turned to stare at the crowd. There were a few faces I vaguely recognized—one or two creatives, a few clients I'd seen in the lobby of Milton Advertising.

"Well, that's Ian," I said eventually, pointing him out.

"The short bald one who looks like a Weeble?" Helen asked, raising an eyebrow.

I giggled. "Okay, well, um . . ." I pointed out a couple of creatives, and Gillie. "And that's Tatiana," I concluded. "She's a friend of Anthony's. She thinks I look five months' pregnant."

"Bitch." Helen frowned in Tatiana's direction, then held up her hand. "There's Max!" she said, waving at him. I looked up and reddened slightly as he caught my eye and walked toward us.

"Jess." He nodded. "And it's Helen, right?"

She nodded and smiled rapturously. He turned back to me. "So, pleased with the party?"

He was smiling, but it wasn't his usual crinkled smile—it was his formal, meeting-with-clients smile.

"Sure," I said. "It's great."

"I'm glad." He looked at Helen, his eyes narrowing. "So, Helen. You're the flatmate, right?"

Helen nodded flirtatiously; immediately Max's eyes started to twinkle. "*Murder, She Wrote,*" he said, grinning. "That was you, right?"

Helen nodded and giggled. "I was watching it purely in the name of research, you understand," she said. "I work in television, you see."

"Television. How interesting. What field?"

I found myself frowning. Television wasn't *that* interesting.

"Well I was a researcher on *Watchdog* for a couple of years, then I worked on this documentary series that told stories about Londoners, then I worked on this diet program."

"And now?"

"Now I'm resting," Helen said, grinning. "You know, waiting for the right job to come along."

"Hence the watching of television during the daytime. Sounds like a very sensible way to spend your time!"

His eyes were still twinkling, I noticed. It was almost as though he were flirting. With Helen. I'd never seen Max flirt before. He'd certainly never flirted with me.

"Max is the deputy managing director of Milton Advertising," I found myself saying. "He set up the firm with Anthony."

"Really?" Helen asked, her mouth opening slightly in a way that I suddenly found very irritating. "Wow, so you're a real entrepreneur, then?"

Max shrugged. "Hardly."

"In Russia, we only call someone entrepreneur if they multimillionaire," Ivana said, suddenly appearing out of nowhere.

"Which confirms my point," Max said immediately. "I'm just a guy who works in advertising, that's all."

"Jess, please stop talking about work," Helen said, rolling her eyes. "Honestly, this is your engagement party, not an office do. Max, tell her to lighten up, will you?"

Max looked slightly perplexed for a moment, then grinned. "You're absolutely right, Helen," he said seriously. "And it's entirely my fault. So why don't you tell us about your ideal job in television?"

Helen opened her mouth to speak, but before she could, a tall, leggy brunette suddenly came rushing up and grabbed her. Her tousled mane trailed down her back and hit me in the face as she passed me.

"Jess?" she asked Helen, batting long false eyelashes caked in mascara. She was wearing a pale pink dress that showed off long tanned limbs, and her long, manicured nails matched her dress perfectly. "Is that you? God, I knew you'd be gorgeous. Everyone is so jealous, and so they should be." She pulled Helen toward her and kissed her on both cheeks. "Fenella. Fen. So pleased to finally meet. Anthony sent me over—so rude of me not to have met you on the door, I know, but you have no idea how many balls I'm juggling here. Now, we must get a date in the diary soonest—so much to go over. I've got some fabulous ideas, some quite off the wall, but now I've seen you I just know you're going to love them . . ."

"Actually," Helen said, managing to extricate herself from Fenella's vise-like grip, "I'm Helen. Jess's friend."

"Helen?" Fenella looked at her uncomprehendingly and flicked her hair, which again landed on my face; I stepped back. "But Anthony pointed at you. He told me to come over—"

"I expect he was pointing at me," I interrupted politely.

Fenella frowned; at least she tried to—her forehead didn't move an inch but her face did take on a slightly vexed look.

"At Jess," Helen said, looking at me pointedly.

"At . . ." The penny seemed to drop and Fenella slowly turned back to me, sweeping her hair as she did so and this time hitting Max. "Jess!" she exclaimed, her voice rising several octaves, a huge smile that didn't quite reach her eyes plastered across her face. "God, how awful. Bad mistake. Well, great to meet you, too." She kissed me, a little too vigorously, on both cheeks and we stared at each other awkwardly for a few seconds. "So, look," she said eventually, "I won't bore you with the same spiel. Just so great to meet you. And same goes. Coffee, soon," she said, seriously. "Lots of things to talk about. Really going to be"— she looked me up and down—"great. Just, you know, fabulous. Oh, you'll be such a . . . blushing bride. You must be the happiest girl in the world right now. And so you should be. Must dash now . . ." She shot one last disappointed look at Helen, then wandered off into the throng, leaving me staring after her silently.

"Who the fuck was that?" Max said immediately.

He looked outraged, and I found myself softening slightly. "That was Fenella. Of Party Party Party."

"That's Fenella? Jesus, you poor thing. You're actually going to have to spend more time with her?"

"She is the best party planner in the whole of London," I said, po-faced.

"So great she doesn't know who her clients are?" Max said wryly.

"Hey, she's got a lot on her mind," I said.

"All that hair, you mean?" Max grinned and I laughed. There was silence for a few minutes; Max and I kept glancing at each other, then looking away again.

"I'm sorry about the meeting," I said eventually.

"Don't mention it. Doesn't matter at all," Max said, shaking his head.

"But it does matter. I let you down. And I'm sorry."

"No, you didn't," Max said immediately. "I totally overreacted. I just . . . I get carried away . . . ." He met my eyes and reddened slightly. "With work," he added. "I get carried away when it comes to work."

"That's a good thing," I said, biting my lip slightly. "Work's important."

"You mean you don't still think that successful people don't work hard?" Max's expression was unreadable. I smiled, then turned when I felt an arm wrapping itself around me. It was Anthony bearing down on me.

"Darling! Remind me never to invite clients to anything again. Except the wedding, of course! So I hear you met Fenella, then?" he enthused.

"Hi!" I put my arm around him, self-consciously. "And yes, I've just met her."

"So you liked her? Isn't she fabulous?"

I smiled weakly. "Fenella? I . . . uh . . . ." I caught Max's eye again and looked away quickly. "Yes! I mean, she seems great. Lovely."

"Not as lovely as you." Anthony winked. "Isn't she lovely, Max? Isn't she just the blushing bride?" He stumbled slightly and I frowned.

"She certainly is," Max said levelly.

"Nearly two weeks away," Anthony continued. "Two weeks!" He held up three fingers to emphasize the point.

"So I understand," Max said.

"And who are you?" Anthony asked, turning to Ivana. "I don't believe we've met, have we?" His voice was slurring slightly; I tried to prize the champagne glass out of his hand, but instead he waved over a waiter to refill it.

Ivana, meanwhile, looked at him and tossed back her hair. "I em Ivana," she said. "Is good to meet you."

"Is very good to meet you, too," he said, grinning flirtatiously. "You're a friend of Jess's?"

Ivana nodded and folded her arms; the action pushed up her cleavage, which Anthony immediately stared at.

"She has a face, you know." My eyes widened as Sean appeared beside Ivana—his eyes were flashing.

"Of course she does," Anthony said, lifting his head quickly. "And who are you, anyway?"

"Doesn't matter," Sean muttered darkly.

Anthony peered at Sean, then turned to me. "He looks rather familiar. Is he a friend of yours?"

I smiled weakly. "Oh, yes, I mean, sort of."

At that moment Gillie appeared next to us. "Jess! Anthony!" she said breathlessly. "You'll never guess who's here. I was talking to this bloke and . . ." Suddenly she stopped talking and her mouth fell open. "Oh, you do know."

"Know what?" Anthony asked. "Who?"

"Sean," Gillie gasped. "That's Sean."

She pointed at Sean; Anthony stared at him. "Sean? You're Sean the hedge fund manager?"

Sean, who had tugged Ivana away, no doubt to argue with her about the attention she was getting, turned around. "Yeah," he said, shrugging. "That's right."

"He was trying to chat me up," Gillie continued. "And when he told me his name, I put two and two together and . . ." She turned to me. "You invited your ex-boyfriend to your engagement party?" she asked incredulously. "I mean, really?"

"You chet her up?" Ivana said, her voice rising. "You jealous of me and you chet up little English girl?"

"No," Sean said irritably as I shrugged awkwardly.

"I did invite him. Sort of. At least—" I began.

"He made her invite him," Helen said quickly. "He's really into her. I guess he just couldn't stay away."

"He couldn't, huh?" Anthony said. "Well, he can piss off now."

Sean's eyes narrowed. "You piss off," he said angrily. "I'm trying to have a conversation here."

"Me? I'm not pissing anywhere," Anthony said, then frowned. "Not pissing off anywhere," he corrected himself.

"Fine. Suit yourself." Sean turned back to Ivana.

"I will," Anthony said. And before I realized what was happening, before I could do anything to intervene, he pulled back his hand and punched Sean in the face. I say *punched;* in reality it was more of a shove. But it certainly made an impact. Sean toppled to the floor, a surprised look on his face.

"That'll teach him," Anthony said, looking very pleased with himself.

"How dare you!" Out of nowhere, Ivana launched herself at Anthony, clocking him on the jaw and kicking him in the knee. Immediately he fell to the floor, too. "How dare you," she said again as she dropped to the floor and continued pummeling him as I looked on in disbelief.

"Ivana! No!" I yelped. "Helen! Help me get her off him."

We leaned down and tried to pull Ivana, but she was having none of it; seconds later, though, she was pinned down on the floor. To my surprise, Max was doing the pinning.

"Right," he said firmly. "I think that some people need to leave. And since this is Anthony and Jess's party, I don't think it should be either of them. Would you agree? Would you?"

Ivana stared at him angrily. "I want to leave anyway," she said, her eyes fiery.

"Me, too," Sean said, pulling himself up. "Crap party anyway."

Max let Ivana go, and she jumped up and dusted herself down, then, throwing Anthony a last look of disgust, grabbed Sean. They made their way out of the club.

"How romantic," Gillie said immediately. "You showed him,

Anthony. But who was the woman? Was that his new girlfriend or something?"

"New girlfriend," I said, looking at Helen, who nodded frantically.

"Yes, that's right," she agreed. "They . . . they started dating a few days ago."

"Well, they deserve each other," Anthony said, pulling himself up and dusting himself down. "Bloody maniac. If I see either of them again, I'll . . . I'll . . ."

"Let her floor you again?" Max said, a little smile playing on his lips.

Anthony glowered at him.

"I need a drink," he said, brushing down his jacket.

"Shall I come with you?" I offered, nervously.

"No," he said flatly. "If it's all the same to you, I'd rather go alone."

A couple of hours later Anthony was nowhere to be seen, my head was hurting from several double vodkas that I'd decided were a necessity to get through the evening, and Helen was slumped on a leather bench. I was sitting at a nearby table with Max. I didn't know if it was the drink or the avoidance of a fight, but all the awkwardness between us seemed to have evaporated and we'd reverted to form, eschewing conversation about normal things and instead talking about work or, more specifically, debating whether Project Handbag should have a celebrity as its figurehead or a leading businesswoman.

"It's for intelligent, together women," Max was saying. "They won't respond to some airhead celebrity. They'll want to see someone together and wealthy whom they can aspire to be like."

"But," I said, wagging my finger at him and realizing I could see two of them, "people aspire to be like celebrities, not businesswomen. Name one famous businesswoman. Go on, name one."

"Anita Roddick," Max said immediately.

I frowned. "Fine, her. But name another one. Someone who's still alive."

"Nicola Horlick."

I took another sip of my drink. "See? You can only come up with two."

"You didn't ask for more. What about Marjorie Scardino?"

"What about her?" I said, shaking my head dismissively. "I mean, look, they're all great. I'd rather be like them than some out-of-work actress any day. But people don't buy magazines because they're on the cover, do they?"

"They do if they're on *BusinessWeek*," Max pointed out.

I rolled my eyes. "People who read *BusinessWeek* probably already have their investments under control," I said, looking at my drink distrustfully. "What's in this thing? I think I might be pissed."

"I think you might be, too," Max agreed, then he smiled bashfully. "You know, I miss this. You and me talking about work."

"You do?"

"Yeah. I like your ideas. I like the way you get so dogmatic when you think you're right."

I laughed awkwardly. "Dogmatic? Isn't that just another word for stubborn?"

Max grinned. "You're convinced you're right. That's a good thing."

"You think?"

"Yes. I mean, take this wedding. Not many people would rush into something like that. But you, you're fearless. You know what you want and you're not afraid to just take it. I'd be far too scared to commit like that."

"You . . . you would?" I asked uncertainly.

"God yes. I mean, marriage is such a huge commitment. When I get married, I want it to be it—you know, lifelong, to have and to hold, all that stuff. I'd have to know that this is the person I want to grow old with, that this is the person I want to wake up next to every morning, who will get my jokes, who will tease me, who I'll never get bored of gazing at. But you . . . you just jump right in. I admire that."

"You do?" I cleared my throat—suddenly I was feeling slightly hot and scratchy. "I mean, marriage isn't always a big deal. Sometimes it's just, you know, like a business deal."

"A business deal?" Max looked at me incredulously. "No it isn't, and you know it isn't. But that's what I admire. You're taking a huge risk and you're not remotely worried about it—which I think is great. Me, I'd be thinking that I'm committing myself to something—to someone—for life, and agonizing over whether I was doing the right thing. For me, for her . . ."

I blanched slightly. "You would? You'd agonize?"

"Yes! But that's just me," Max said quickly. "I don't have your . . . your chutzpah. Your self-belief."

"Right," I said, unconvinced. "Self-belief."

"And anyway, I'm hardly one to talk. I'm thirty-five and single."

Our eyes met, and for the second time neither of us seemed to be able to look away.

"Jess? There you are. I've been looking for you." Max turned his head; mine followed. Anthony was standing a few feet away, his arm extended.

I turned back to Max. "I'd better . . ."

"Yes, you'd better," Max said quietly.

"Right then." I stood up and shot a smile over to Anthony. Then, shaking myself, I walked toward him. Toward Anthony Milton. My future husband. Which I was really happy about. Whatever Max said about marriage and commitment, I was still doing the right thing. In just a few weeks I was going to be Mrs. Milton. Like Fenella said, I was the happiest girl in the world.

Chapter 25

The next morning, I woke up in Anthony's bed with an unsettled feeling in my stomach. It was a huge thing (the bed, I mean, not the feeling)—at least six feet square—and when I stretched out my arms and legs they still didn't even touch him, which seemed kind of apt.

I looked at my watch—9 AM. The engagement party had gone on until about 2 AM—afterward, Anthony had been determined to go to Henry's party (Henry was, apparently, a "brilliant guy" and one that I would love unreservedly on meeting), and I'd gotten a sinking feeling that the whole wedding was all a huge mistake. But then, as he called a cab he'd stumbled and fallen onto the pavement and conceded that perhaps it would be more sensible to go home, so I'd buried my doubts and gone with him.

Tentatively I crept out of bed and out of the bedroom. Anthony's flat was a bit like a magazine spread—all beautifully presented in browns, creams, and a little bit of beige. I tried to imagine myself living here, tried to imagine my things on his shelves. But somehow I couldn't see it. My books, my photographs, my pictures, the pale pink telephone Helen had given me for my last birthday—none of them would work at all. I walked into the open-plan living room/kitchen area. In the "living" space, sumptuous suede sofas surrounded a tasteful cream rug; the kitchen was at the other end, a symphony of stainless steel and glass.

Frowning, I looked around for a kettle and turned it on, then started to rummage in the cupboards for some tea bags. I didn't know where my future husband kept them, I realized. Actually, I didn't know a lot of things about Anthony.

Eventually, I found two cups, tea bags, some toast, and even some jam; putting it all on a tray, I made my way back to the bedroom to wake Anthony up. I wanted to talk to him, have a serious discussion, reassure myself we were doing the right thing.

"Good morning!" I put the tray on the bed and pulled back the curtains to let in some light.

"What the fuck's the time?"

I started slightly; Anthony's voice had become a grunt.

"Um, nine-ish, I think. I've made some tea. And toast."

"Nine AM? What the hell are you doing waking me up at nine AM? Jesus." Anthony grabbed a pillow and shoved it over his head, as he did so, he knocked the tray, spilling tea onto his crisp white duvet cover.

"Shit!" I yelped, trying to salvage it. Anthony rolled over to see what the problem was, forcing the tray onto its side and ensuring that now the toast was also facedown on the duvet cover and the tea was dripping down onto his cream carpet.

"Oh, for fuck's sake. Oh bloody hell," he muttered darkly.

"I'll go and get a towel," I said quickly. "And we can put the duvet cover in the wash . . ."

"It's dry clean only," Anthony said, forcing himself to sit up.

"Right," I said. Anthony's face was dark and angry. I'd never seen it like that. "Look, I'm sorry. I just wanted to . . . I just thought breakfast might be a nice idea."

"It would have been. In a few hours." He lay back against the headboard and sighed.

"I'm sorry," I said tightly. "I won't do it again."

"No," Anthony said, lying back down and this time successfully pulling a pillow over his head. "No, you won't."

"Fine," I said again, this time to myself. "Well, I'll just go then, shall I?" I grabbed my clothes and started to pull them on. My conical breasts looked even more ridiculous at nine in the morning, but I figured in the great scheme of things it didn't really matter.

"Look, you don't have to go." Anthony reemerged from under his pillow.

"Yes, I do," I said, yanking my dress over my head and getting it stuck halfway.

"No, you don't. Don't be angry, I've got a headache, I'm tired. That's all. I'm sorry if I snapped."

He reached out and grabbed my hand, pulling me back onto the bed. "You can't go, anyway," he pointed out. "Not wearing your dress like that. You'll get arrested."

I suppressed a smile. "Actually it's the latest thing, wearing dresses on your head," I deadpanned.

"Interesting. Nice to know you're at the forefront of fashion." Anthony grinned sheepishly.

I smiled back, then bit my lip. "You know," I said tentatively, "marriage is a big step. Are you sure that . . . well, I mean, are you sure you want to? That it's the right thing for us to do?" I knew I was taking a risk, but I couldn't help it.

"The right thing? Of course it is," Anthony said easily. "Look, how about I take you out for breakfast instead?"

I nodded uncertainly. That was it? That was our serious discussion? "Okay. I guess."

"You guess? Doesn't sound like you're that interested. Maybe I'll just go back to sleep," Anthony said, his eyes twinkling.

"No, no, I'm interested," I said, allowing a half smile to creep onto my face. I guessed discussion could, sometimes, be overrated. And didn't they say that actions speak louder than words?

"In breakfast or coming back to bed?" Anthony asked, a little glint in his eye.

"I guess I could be persuaded either way." I smiled.

"Maybe one then the other?"

"Breakfast first?" I suggested innocently.

"Better to work up an appetite for breakfast," Anthony said, pulling me back under the covers. "Don't you think?"

We never made it out for breakfast. Although we did get out of the house in time for a late lunch—a long, boozy affair after which I reeled home, managed to watch *Antiques Roadshow* with Helen, then crashed into bed, exhausted. I couldn't believe how quickly the weekend had gone. Couldn't believe how decadent I'd been—I hadn't done any work, any housework, any anything. And it felt fantastic.

I still felt fantastic the following morning when I arrived at work twenty minutes late.

"Jess!" Anthony grinned at me. "How's my favorite fiancée?"

I grinned back and took a slurp of my coffee. "Oh, you know," I said, nonchalantly. "Not too bad."

"Jess!" Max appeared out of his office. "Listen, do you have a minute? I wanted to have a quick word about the Project Handbag account. Thought you might have some ideas on . . ."

He trailed off as the reception doors flung open and a familiar voice stopped us in our tracks.

"Anthony? Jessica? So sorry I'm late. Do I need to sign in or anything?"

It was Fenella, her glossy brown hair pulled into a neat ponytail, clutching a large file in her hands.

"Late?" I asked uncertainly. "I didn't know you were even coming."

"You didn't know?" She stared at me, then raised an eyebrow at Anthony. "But Anthony and I arranged this at the party. On Saturday night. Anthony, you remember, don't you?"

"We did?" Anthony asked, then nodded, shooting me a look of helplessness. "Of course we did. At the party. Definitely." He pulled a face at me, like a naughty schoolboy. "In which case, let's go to my office, shall we?"

"Well, good," Fenella said suspiciously.

"I'll . . . catch you later, shall I?" Max asked.

"Yes. Probably best," I said vaguely. Fenella was now marching Anthony into his office. By the time I'd followed her in, she was sitting down at his meeting table with an expectant look on her face.

"So," she said immediately. "What was it you wanted to talk about?"

I smiled weakly. "Me? Oh, there's nothing. I mean, you know, whatever *you* want to talk about."

"Oh, but it's not about me," Fenella said seriously. "Whatever you have to say, you must say now—we can't have any surprises later. We've got a tight schedule, so anything that needs to be said must be said now."

Her eyes were boring into mine and I shot a helpless look at Anthony, who shrugged back and looked like he was stifling laughter. "Right," I said, clearing my throat and trying to think of something—anything—to talk about. "Right. Well . . ."

"Yes?" Fenella looked at me expectantly, then got up and walked toward Anthony's desk. "You don't mind if I take a look around, do you?" she asked him, not waiting for an answer. "Helps if I really know the client, you see. I need to get a feel for what you're looking for. Sorry, Jess. You were saying?"

I watched silently as Fenella scanned the desk's surface briefly, her eyes widening slightly at the various piles of paper stacked on top of it. No doubt her desk had no such piles, I found myself thinking. She was probably one of those people who cleared it every night.

"Well," I said tentatively, "well, I mean, there's so much really. You know, all the . . . wedding plans, really . . ."

"House hunting, are we?" Fenella said suddenly, picking up a photograph of a house from Anthony's desk. "Looks lovely. Perfect country retreat." She held up the photograph for us both to look at—it was a honey-colored crumbling house with a bright blue sky behind it.

Anthony got up and quickly moved toward her. "That? Oh, yes. Yes, just something I've been looking at," he said dismissively.

I started. "You are? I mean, we are? I thought you hated the country."

He shrugged and reddened. "And you love it. So I thought, you know, why not have a look."

"Really?" I stared at him incredulously, guiltily. I could hardly tell him we were going to have a mansion of our own in a few weeks. "Let me see!" I held out my hand for Fenella to pass me the photograph; Anthony got there first, though.

"See? No. No, not until I've . . ." he said, taking the photo quickly from Fenella. "It was meant to be a surprise," he added firmly, putting it in his pocket.

"A surprise?" I bit my lip. "That's so sweet. It's . . . really unexpected."

"Anything for you." Anthony shot me a benevolent smile.

"So, anyway," Fenella said, walking back to the table and pick-

ing up her pad. "Wedding plans. You're right, there is a lot to discuss. Shall we start? I've got a list of things to go through that's as
long as my arm, and no doubt you've got one, too. Would you
like to go first?"

"Oh, no, I think you should go first," I insisted. "And I'll fill in
any gaps later. If there are any, that is . . ."

Fenella nodded, seriously. "Good idea. Right, so first, I wanted
to run an idea by you. Lilies. Thousands of lilies everywhere.
What do you think? I mean, the smell alone would be incredible,
don't you think?"

"Lilies," I said vaguely. Anthony was making faces at me and I
was having trouble keeping a straight face. "Right."

"Aren't lilies usually used at funerals?" Anthony asked, po-
faced.

Fenella shook her head. "No. I mean, yes, sometimes. But I
really think that in this day and age one can—"

She was interrupted by the door opening; Marcia's head appeared through it. "Anthony," she said, smiling sweetly. "I need
your help on something. Can you spare a minute?"

"Now?" Anthony looked at her hopefully.

"Yes. I'm sorry," Marcia said. "But it's Project Handbag. I could
really do with your input."

"Right," Anthony said seriously. "Well, okay. If you ladies will
excuse me?"

He smiled at me; I looked at Marcia. "If you want," I said tentatively, "I can help, too. I mean, I'm sure Fenella wouldn't mind
waiting a few minutes . . ."

"Don't be silly!" Marcia exclaimed. "Jess, I wouldn't dream of it."

"No," Anthony agreed. "You stay here with Fenella. I won't be
long."

"Fine," I called after them as they disappeared from his office.
"No problem."

"So, we're agreed on lilies?" Fenella asked, her pen poised over her pad. "Can I tick them off?"

I nodded vaguely. Lilies. Then I frowned. "Um, lilies—they're flowers, aren't they?"

Fenella looked at me uncertainly. "Yes, that's right."

"Right. It's just that I thought I was doing flowers."

"Oh, I see," Fenella said, nodding seriously. "So you wanted to do, like, *all* the flowers? Not just your bouquet?"

I nodded back, just as seriously.

"It's just that flowers are quite, you know, pivotal," she continued.

"No, I know that. But I thought we agreed . . . you know, that I'd do them," I said, tension creeping into my voice. It wasn't like I knew anything about flowers, but suddenly, having control over them felt like the most important thing in the world to me. I'd lost Project Handbag; if I didn't do the flowers, there would be no point to my life. No point to anything.

There was a silence as Fenella looked at her list. "And you definitely want to do all of them? Ceremony, table pieces, bouquets, the lot?"

"The lot," I said, gripping the table with my hand. "Every single one."

Fenella cleared her throat. "Well, fine. But do keep me informed. The more I know, the more I can make sure that things don't slip through the net."

"They won't," I said, crossing my arms defensively. "The flowers are going to be fine. Absolutely fine."

"Great," Fenella said, forcing a smile. "So I can tick off flowers. Next is catering. I've got some menu plans here, and I've highlighted in red the ones that I think would work best. Obviously, it's your choice, but the ones I've chosen will, I think, work best as a whole. And while you're looking at the menus, do you have a sketch of your wedding dress for me?"

"Not yet," I said, scanning the menus. "But I will have. I'm going shopping with my friend Helen today."

"Today?" Fenella said uncertainly. "You don't have one picked out already?"

"No, not yet," I said, my heart sinking as I glanced at Fenella's list and saw that catering was only number two of twenty-five categories. "But so long as we can wrap this meeting up as quickly as possible, I can't see there being a problem."

Fenella nodded dubiously. "Okay," she said. "Now for table dressing . . ."

The Wedding Dress Shop was near Oxford Street and de rigueur for any would-be bride, according to Helen. It promised to have the right dress for every bride in its adverts, and Helen was determined to put it to the test. I was still out of breath from having run up the tube escalator; Fenella had managed to talk about wedding cakes for over forty-five minutes, making me late to meet Helen by the time I finally got out of the meeting.

"And then she took out her list, Hel. It was so long, I thought I was going to die."

"But you didn't," Helen said, opening the doors to the shop. We were met by heavy carpet and walls lined with long white dresses. "And now we're looking at wedding dresses so you're going to have to stop thinking about that Fenella woman."

"I know." I sighed. "But I didn't think I was ever going to get out of that meeting."

"Focus," Helen said sternly as a fierce-looking woman appeared out of nowhere, her eyes fixed on us suspiciously. Her role appeared to be to check fingers for engagement rings, stare down potential interlopers, and ensure that only true brides (with appointments) were allowed to darken their hallowed doors.

"Do you have an appointment?" she asked immediately.

"Yes. Jessica Wild." Helen walked straight past her, seemingly oblivious to the protocol.

The woman's eyes narrowed. "And which one of you is Miss Jessica Wild?"

I smiled awkwardly. "That would be me."

She nodded and let me pass. Immediately, a sweeter-looking woman in her fifties approached me, a big smile on her face.

"Date of wedding?"

I smiled back. "Week after next. April twenty-third."

The woman's eyes opened wide. "The week after next?"

I nodded. "We . . . we're getting married at the Hilton Park Lane," I said nervously. "There was a . . . cancellation."

"A cancellation indeed," the woman tutted. "Well. My name is Vanessa, and I'll be your assistant this morning. It's lovely to meet you. Here at the Wedding Dress Shop, we're all about making dreams come true. So, Jessica, do you have an idea in mind of the sort of dress you're after?"

I looked at her blankly. I wanted a wedding dress. Wasn't that obvious?

"Um, something white I suppose," I said. "Or cream?"

Vanessa looked at me uncertainly. "Full-skirted? Column? Strapless? Lace? Silk?" she prompted.

"Oh, right," I said with relief. "Um, I guess I don't really know, actually."

"Nothing that makes her look like a meringue," Helen said, suddenly appearing at my side.

"A meringue?" Vanessa turned to her with an expressionless face.

"Like the Good Witch from *The Wizard of Oz*," Helen explained.

"The Good Witch," Vanessa said, looking very doubtful. "No. Of course." She looked me up and down. "And you're a size . . . ten? twelve?"

I shrugged. "Somewhere around there," I said. "Depending, you know, on the shape . . ."

She looked at my ample chest. "Yes. Yes, I can see that." Then she moved over to the rails and started to pick up dresses, heaping them over her arm. A few minutes later, almost invisible behind the mountain of dresses she was carrying, she led us into a sumptuous changing room complete with podium. "For the bride," she explained when Helen looked at it curiously.

Deftly, she hung up all the dresses on a rail, then smiled at me. "Try them on, see what you think," she said. "From these we should be able to determine the kind of style that suits you best."

I nodded and stifled a yawn as Vanessa left us.

"Okay, this one first," Helen said, pulling out a huge dress that seemed to have as much fabric as a pair of curtains. I eyed it cautiously.

"Really?"

"Really."

Unconvinced, I got undressed and slipped into it; ten minutes later, Helen had finally secured all the hook-and-eye fastenings and I turned to look at myself in the mirror. Immediately I started to giggle.

"What?" Helen said, crossly. "What's so funny."

"It's ridiculous," I said firmly. "It's too big, too froufrou . . . These sleeves . . ." I waved my arms, demonstrating the impracticality of the huge marshmallows surrounding them. "They'd get in my food. Small birds would fly into them and be unable to escape. They'd nest in there and I wouldn't even notice."

"You're wearing a three-thousand-pound dress, Jess. Try to at least appreciate it a little bit, won't you?"

I felt the blood drain from my face. "Three thousand pounds? Are you serious? You could buy a car for three thousand pounds. It would cover my rent for six months. Three thousand pounds?"

Helen sighed. "That's how much wedding dresses are."

"But I don't have three thousand pounds," I said weakly.

"No, but soon you will." Helen rolled her eyes.

"I'm not spending three thousand pounds on this," I said, pursing my lips slightly. "It's hideous."

"Fine," Helen relented. "Try the next one."

The next one was the sort of thing that Paris Hilton might wear—a tiny column that revealed maximum cleavage and had cutouts to reveal a flat, toned stomach. Only I didn't have a flat, toned stomach; I had *my* stomach and even Helen shook her head as soon as I'd pulled it on.

She pulled out a lacy number, then wrinkled her nose. "This one's only two hundred pounds and you can tell it's cheap," she said dismissively. "The lace feels stiff."

I took it from her. "Two hundred pounds is not cheap and it doesn't feel stiff," I said crossly, even though as soon as it was in my hands I knew she was right. It felt wrong, felt prickly to the touch. I slipped it over my head, and Helen zipped it up.

"It's okay, I suppose," she said, wrinkling her nose. "Shape-wise, I mean. But it's nothing special. I mean, it's just a dress. Not . . . you know . . . *the* dress."

I looked at my reflection. Helen was right. I looked like a bride in a mail-order catalogue.

"Fine, unzip me," I said. "How many more to go?"

Helen counted. "Ten."

She handed me another. And then another, neither of which worked. They either washed me out, made me look fat, or made me look like I was auditioning for a part in a pantomime.

"I'm never going to find anything," I said despondently. "Maybe I'm just not a wedding-dress type of person."

Helen rolled her eyes. "There's no such thing." She handed me another dress, this one made of organza silk that felt soft and but-

tery in my hands. Sighing, I stepped into it. It was strapless, fitted
to the waist, then flowed out in a bias cut.

"Bias cut is never going to work on me," I said dismissively, as
she fastened the buttons. "It'll just emphasize my hips." I stood
back in front of the mirror, not looking up.

"Oh my God." Helen's eyes widened.

"What?" I asked, anxiously. "Is it really that bad?"

"Not bad." Helen shook her head. "Not bad at all."

She turned me around so I was facing the mirror; I looked up
and gasped. It was beautiful. It actually made me look beautiful.
Like a bride. Like a real bride.

The curtain opened and Vanessa peeked in. "Oh. Oh, yes. Oh,
you've found it," she whispered. "Oh, I do love this moment. You
don't choose a wedding dress, you see—it chooses you."

"Oh my God," Helen said again.

I looked back at myself. I did look amazing. Truly amazing.
But somehow, as I stared at my reflection, I felt myself go slightly
white. Then suddenly I felt myself shaking slightly. It started with
my hands. Then my arms were at it, and the rest of my body soon
followed.

"What's wrong?" Vanessa asked in alarm. "What's the matter?"

I felt sick. I felt like I was going to faint. The walls were closing in; everything went dark except the image in front of me—a
bride in a white dress, so full of hope, so full of expectation. So
naïve, so vulnerable.

"Please, take it off," I begged. My hands were pulling at the
bodice; Vanessa rushed to unzip it.

"Are you okay? Can I get you some water?"

I nodded, pulling the dress off with relief. "Water," I whispered. "Water would be good."

Vanessa left and Helen stared at me worriedly. "What's the
matter? You looked amazing."

"I . . . I don't know," I said, my voice small and faltering. I was standing in my underwear and I slowly sank down to the floor, pulling my knees to my chest.

"You don't know?" Helen asked.

"I . . . what if it's a mistake? I mean, what if it doesn't work out?"

"Don't be silly," she said firmly. "You're having wedding jitters. Everyone has them. Just pull yourself together."

"Okay. I will. I . . ." I said, feeling my throat begin to seize up.

"Jess?"

I tried to smile, but instead big fat tears appeared at my eyes and started to roll down my cheeks.

"Jess, what is it?" Helen asked, a look of concern on her face. "What is wrong with you?"

"Nothing. I mean . . . Really, I'm fine," I said, wiping the tears away with the back of my hand. "I mean, people get married all the time, don't they? It's no big deal, right?"

"Not to you, no," she said, frowning. "Come on, Jess. This is a financial transaction. If it works out, that's just a bonus."

I nodded. "A bonus. Right."

"And he's very good looking," Helen pointed out. "And you're having a great time with him, so it all bodes well, doesn't it?"

"I guess," I agreed. "So you don't think marriage is . . . I mean, you don't think it's that important?"

"Of course not," Helen soothed me. "Not to you."

"You keep saying that," I said tightly. "Why isn't it a big deal for me?"

"Because you don't believe in marriage!" Helen said, shaking her head. "I mean, you've always sworn that you'd never allow yourself to lose your independence. You've always said that you have to put yourself first. And that's what you're doing. This isn't a marriage in the normal sense, so you don't have to think about it in the normal way. See?"

"I see," I said tentatively. Helen was right—this wasn't a normal marriage. All that stuff Max had said just wasn't relevant. I didn't believe in real love anyway—I was far too savvy for that nonsense. I didn't need to fall in love and commit to someone through thick and thin, through sickness and health. I didn't need to know that I was loved, completely and utterly. I really didn't.

"So everything's okay?" Helen asked.

I swallowed awkwardly. "Absolutely," I said, trying to convince myself as much as anything.

"And if it doesn't work out, you can always get divorced," Helen pointed out, just as Vanessa walked back in.

"Divorced," I mumbled. "Of course." I was beginning to feel sick again. Divorced. Grandma used to say that *divorce* was another word for *failure*. She used to say it was better not to marry at all.

"Divorce?" Vanessa asked uncertainly. "Who's getting divorced?"

"No one," Helen said quickly.

"Me," I blurted out. "If it doesn't work out. If I have a failed marriage."

"A failed marriage? What way is that to talk?" Vanessa tutted.

"The realistic way," I said flatly.

"You know," she said, eyeing me cautiously, "weddings can be a very stressful time. But you see, it'll all be fine in the end."

I looked at her doubtfully. "I'm not so sure," I said.

"I'm sure it's not as bad as all that," Vanessa said, putting her hand on my shoulder then moving over to the rail to separate the dresses I'd tried. "Everyone has doubts at some point."

"Exactly," Helen said. "You just have to stop thinking about everything so much."

I shook my head. All the vague thoughts and doubts that had been circling in my head suddenly seemed very real. "The truth is that Anthony only proposed because I was following instructions. Because I changed my hair and started wearing high heels. Because of Sean, who we made up."

Vanessa turned and looked at me uncertainly. "Sean?"

"Her ex." Helen shrugged.

"Not my ex. Ivana's husband who pretended to be my ex," I said, folding my arms across my chest.

"Ivana?" Vanessa said weakly. "I see. Well, actually I don't see. But I'm not sure that really matters here. What about your prospective husband. Does he love you?"

I frowned. "I think so," I said uncertainly. "I mean, he's looking at a house in the country, even though he hated it there."

Vanessa nodded. "And you," she asked, "do you love him?"

I shrugged helplessly. "I like him. He's great. I mean, he's charming, we have fun. But is that love? I don't know. I don't think I really know what love is."

"Well, that's okay," Vanessa said soothingly. "Anyway, love is quite overrated when it comes to marriage."

"It is?"

I stared at her in surprise, and she nodded conspiratorially. "Look, you won't read this in magazine articles, but in my opinion, for what it's worth, the truth is that in marriage you should either love someone completely, or not at all. If you love them completely, you'll forgive them anything; if you don't love them at all, you won't expect anything. Not loving someone provides a perfectly sound footing for marriage. Particularly if he loves you. It's better that way."

"Really?" I asked dubiously. "That's not what Max said. He said it was the most important decision I'd ever make."

"Max?"

"A . . . a friend," I said awkwardly, as Helen raised an eyebrow.

"Right. And this friend, he's married, is he?" Vanessa asked.

I shook my head.

"Marriage counselor?"

"No." I shrugged. "No, he knows about as much about marriage as I do."

"Well, then," Vanessa said sternly. "You listen to me. Blissful ignorance or sensible realism, that's your choice. Both work, but for very different reasons. It's the ones who aren't sure that come unstuck. The ones who think they're in love then realize they're not—they can't adjust their expectations, you see."

"Exactly," Helen said, clapping her hands together. "There's nothing to worry about, Jess. Nothing at all."

I bit my lip. "I thought marriage was about being in love, about being best friends, inseparable."

Vanessa laughed. "That's the problem with romantic books and films. They've got people confused," she said matter-of-factly. "Used to be that marriage was about money, land, gene pools, even international diplomacy. People knew where they were then, wouldn't you say? Now they expect thunderbolts—no wonder they're disappointed."

I frowned. "I suppose. So, marrying someone for the wrong reasons . . . it's not necessarily the wrong thing to do?"

"Marrying someone for the right reasons can be just as precarious," Vanessa said.

I nodded thoughtfully.

"So, do you want to try on some more dresses?" she asked kindly.

I looked at her for a moment, then I shook my head. "No, I think I've made my choice."

"The organza?" Helen asked, her eyes lighting up. "Oh, get that one. It's lovely. It's the best of the lot."

"No," I said. "The organza deserves a romantic wedding. I'll take the lace."

"The lace?" Helen's face twisted into a grimace. "Really?"

"Really." I nodded.

"The lace . . . ," Vanessa said, frowning to hide her disappointment as she thumbed the rail. Then she drew out the dress, the dress that said *any old bride,* the dress that scratched my skin slightly. "This one?" she said, brightly.

"That one," I said, nodding firmly, taking it from her to try on one last time. "I think this dress is just the ticket. I think it's going to be perfect."

Chapter 26

PROJECT: MARRIAGE DAY 34

To do
1. Avoid Fenella.
2. Avoid Max.
3. Avoid Mr. Taylor.

I have no idea how people organize weddings without the help of Party Party Party, or while holding down full-time jobs. It was a full-time job just keeping pace with Fenella and her constant demands for information; I barely saw Helen and barely had time to speak to Gillie about the various ideas she had for the big day (doves was her latest one. Lots of white doves. I wasn't convinced; Fenella went into a tiz about the potential for bird droppings and eventually the hotel manager put his foot down and said that no livestock were permitted on the premises). The only way I could keep in touch with everyone was by text message—even Anthony. As for Max, well, I didn't seem to have much time to talk to him at all; it wasn't like I was avoiding him, it was just that I had a lot on. As Vanessa so wisely put it, weddings are very stressful things.

And being busy was good. Getting everything organized felt good and productive, like I was achieving something, like getting married wasn't a big deal at all but just the culmination of a huge long to-do list. I'd gotten used to the sound of Fenella's e-mails pinging into my inbox, demanding answers, confirmations, approvals. And I stopped worrying about the bigger picture because I was too busy thinking about concepts, colors, designs, personalized vows, menu plans, vegetarian options, the first dance . . .

"Have you seen Marcia?"

I looked up distractedly to see Max with a worried expression on his face.

"Marcia? No." I turned back to my computer screen, where an e-mail had recently arrived from Fenella.

"You don't know when she's coming back?"

"I have no idea," I said, barely looking up this time. Fenella wanted to know whether I wanted to arrive at the ceremony in a Jaguar, a Bentley, or a London Taxi painted in white. And whom I would be arriving with. And whether I wanted the driver to wear a cap or not.

"Right," Max said. "I see."

He didn't move. Eventually I forced my eyes away from Fenella's latest list of demands and looked up. "Sorry, Max," I said, with a little sigh. "I wish I knew where she was, but you know Marcia. Is everything okay?"

Max shook his head. "No. I mean, yes, I'm sure it's fine . . ."

"You don't sound very fine," I said, then kicked myself. I'd realized that the less time I spent with Max, the happier I felt about my impending nuptials, and vice versa. Having a conversation with him was really not a good idea. I should have just closed him down, made it clear I wasn't interested in whether or not he was fine.

"Chester's going to be here for a meeting," he said. "In five minutes. Anthony's not here and now I can't find Marcia."

"I'm sure she'll turn up," I said, as another e-mail pinged into my inbox. What color bow ties would we like the ushers to wear, she wanted to know. And had we assigned them each individual jobs or were we happy for her to manage their workload?

Max nodded. Then he looked at me seriously. "For the record," he said, "I think you were right to concentrate on the wedding instead of Project Handbag."

"Yes, me too," I said brightly, then frowned as I scrolled down to the end of Fenella's message. *And the flowers are sorted, I presume. Can you fax me the proposed designs so I can make sure everything coordinates?* Immediately I went white.

"And everything's going okay?"

I looked up in alarm. The flowers. I'd forgotten the bloody flowers. One job. One job that was mine and I forgot all about it. "Okay?" Panic started to rise up within me. "God yes," I managed to say. "More than okay. Everything's just great!"

Max nodded. "Well, I'm pleased to hear it. Weddings are . . . well, they're . . ."

"A big commitment, a huge deal, yes, I know," I said defensively, bringing up Google and typing in *wedding florist London.* "They're also hell to organize, so if you don't mind . . ."

"Of course, sorry. I'd better continue trying to track down your fiancé and Marcia . . ."

"Anthony's at client meetings all morning," I said, hitting on a link to GILES WHEELER, FLORIST TO THE STARS. His client list read like a who's who of the celebrity fraternity. Immediately I started typing him a desperate message. "But as I said, I don't know about Marcia."

"Okay, well, thanks anyway," Max said, then frowned. "Isn't that the lawyer from the funeral?" he asked, looking over at reception. "What on earth is he doing here?"

"Lawyer?" I asked vaguely, hitting SEND.

"Yes, you know, Mr. Taylor, wasn't it?"

My heart stopped immediately and I turned around. Then my eyes widened. Max was right. Mr. Taylor was right there. Talking to Gillie in reception. As quickly as I could, I jumped up and raced toward him.

"Jess?" Max called after me, but I could barely hear him.

"Mr. Taylor," I said, nearly colliding into him in my panic. "What . . . what are you doing here?"

"Ah, Mrs. Milton," he said. "I was hoping to talk to you. You're very difficult to get hold of, you see. I thought perhaps that the mountain should come to Muhammad, so to speak."

"Mountain?" I shook my head desperately. "No, no. I mean, Muhammad will come to you. I will. Just as soon as . . . Just as . . ." I turned my head slightly to see Gillie staring at me curiously. I had to get him out of the building. But more urgently, I had to get him away from Gillie and other prying eyes. "Um, look, why don't you . . . come to the meeting room," I said quickly.

"Lovely," he said cheerfully, picking up a large briefcase that I eyed with alarm. Maybe the meeting room wasn't such a good idea. What if he asked me for identification papers? What if someone came in?

"Jess?" I looked up at Max, who was walking toward me.

"Not right now," I said anxiously. "I'm just . . . I won't be a minute. I'll be in the meeting room."

"But I need the meeting room," Max said, frowning. "Chester's going to be here any minute."

"Ah, Anthony. How nice to see you again," Mr. Taylor said brightly, holding out his hand to Max, who eyed it suspiciously.

"No," he said. "I'm . . ."

"Very busy," I interrupted, tugging Mr. Taylor's arm. This was almost as bad as my dream. If I'd been naked, it would have been. "He's very busy indeed." I looked back at Max uncomfortably. Then I bit my lip. Mr. Taylor thought Max was Anthony, thought we were married. I was so close, I couldn't ruin it all now. "Um, darling, why don't you try Marcia again and see if she's on her way in?"

"Darling?" Max stared at me.

"Not now, sugar," I said, my voice rising several octaves as I felt my hands going clammy. "I'll be with you just as soon as I can."

"He seems rather perturbed," Mr. Taylor said concernedly. "Is he okay?"

"Anthony? Oh, he's fine," I said quickly. "He's just fine and dandy." I pulled him into the meeting room, but as I did so I heard a familiar voice and stopped in my tracks.

"Hey, guys. Great to see you. So, Jessica, how are the preparations going? Anthony tells me you're doing an amazing job."

I turned around abruptly—Chester had just arrived in reception.

"Chester!" Max attempted a broad smile. "Hi!"

My heart sank. "Chester! Great to see you, too."

"Preparations?" Mr. Taylor asked, behind me. "What are you preparing for?"

"A . . . a launch," I said quickly. "A project we're working on." I bit my lip. "Um, look, now isn't really a great time for our meeting. Maybe it would be better if I called you later?"

He shook his head. "Later might be too late, that's the problem."

"It won't be," I assured him. "I'll call you really soon. Very soon indeed."

He looked at me reluctantly as I dragged him back to reception. "You do realize that you're running out of time, Mrs. Milton?" he said, as we passed Chester. "You've got just over two weeks to complete the paperwork. You know that, don't you?"

"Mrs. Milton? Not yet, she isn't," Chester said affably, apparently overhearing what Mr. Taylor had said. "Week or so to go, huh, Jess?"

I smiled weakly. "Oh, something like that," I managed to say.

"Not yet? What does he mean?" Mr. Taylor asked, looking at Chester with confusion.

"He means . . . ," I said, biting my lip and doing my best to walk Mr. Taylor quickly toward the main doors, "that I . . . I haven't changed my name. Yet. But I'm going to."

"You are?"

"Yes," I said.

"I see," Mr. Taylor said thoughtfully.

"So, I'll call you next week?" I said, opening the door for him. "And thanks for coming around. Sorry I couldn't be more . . ."

"Jess!" As the door opened, Anthony swept through, Marcia behind him, both carrying shopping bags. "Hi, gorgeous."

I frowned at him. He'd been shopping? I thought he was at a client meeting. Then I shook myself. Mr. Taylor was this close to finding out the truth and I was worrying about a shopping trip?

I tugged at Mr. Taylor's sleeve and tried to avoid Anthony's eyes but it turned out Anthony wasn't interested in looking at me; instead, he grabbed me and kissed me smack on the lips. Then he looked up and saw Chester. Immediately he let go of me and walked over to clap him on the back. "Chester. Good to see you. How's it going?"

Mr. Taylor's eyes widened as Marcia tottered past him, avoiding my eyes.

"And that is?" he asked, looking utterly baffled.

"Um, that's Anthony's best friend," I said, my mind racing frantically to explain the kiss, the term of endearment. "He . . . he always calls me gorgeous. He's . . . gay," I concluded.

"Gay?" Mr. Taylor asked, his voice suddenly a whisper. "Well, well. Well I never."

"Yes," I said, attempting a smile. "So, there we are. And now you're going to go, and I'm going to see you soon?"

"I do hope so," Mr. Taylor said as I almost pushed him out of the building. "I do hope so very much."

"He thought you were called Jessica Milton," Gillie said a few seconds later, as I passed her reception desk on the way back to my desk. "I tried telling him you were still Jessica Wild for the time being, but he didn't seem to understand."

"No," I said, wiping some drops of sweat from my forehead. "No, he's a bit . . . deaf, I'm afraid. Bit senile, too. Gets confused."

Gillie nodded sagely. "That'll explain it, then."

"Explain what?" I asked tentatively.

"Explain why he looked all funny when I asked him if he was going to the wedding."

"You . . . you asked him that?"

"Shouldn't I have?"

I gulped. "And did you . . . did you tell him when it was?"

Gillie shook her head. "Of course not. I'm not stupid. I figured if he didn't know about it, you didn't want him to know."

"Exactly," I breathed.

"So I pretended I was talking about Liz Hurley's wedding."

"You did?"

She nodded. "He didn't know who she was, either, though." She shrugged. "To be honest, I think he's a few marbles short of a chess set, if you get my drift."

I leaned over the reception desk and kissed her on the cheek. She giggled and pushed me away to answer the phone. "Hello, Milton Advertising? Yes, she is. Just one moment." She raised an eyebrow. "Jess, it's for you. Want to take it here?"

I turned around reluctantly. "For me? Who . . . who is it?"

"A man," she mouthed. "Giles someone."

"Giles? I don't know a Giles. I . . ."

"Says he wants to talk to you," Gillie said, shrugging.

My heart racing, I took the receiver Gillie was holding out to me. No doubt Mr. Taylor had seen through Gillie's tall tales. This was probably him telling me he knew the truth, telling me that Grace's will was null and void and I was going to prison for impersonation.

"Hello?" I asked, hardly daring to speak. "Jessica Wild speaking."

"Jessica Wild. It's Giles Wheeler here. I got your message. I'm so sorry your florist ran out on you. I can't believe a florist would do that. It really doesn't fit with our professional code."

The florist. Of course. The florist who was laboring under the false belief that I had appointed another florist months before, but he'd run off to Bermuda with a former client, leaving me in the lurch. Hey, I'd been desperate. "Your code? Florists have a professional code?"

"Of course we do. Now, I am, naturally, busy on the day of your wedding. I already have two weddings and one party that day. But I can squeeze you in, if we can work quickly. So, are you free to meet later today?"

I thought for a moment. Fenella had sent me an appointment blocking out several hours that afternoon that said, simply: *Pls keep free—I will be with caterers and need to get hold of you.*

"This afternoon's good," I said quickly. "Where are you based?"

"Me? No, I'm coming to you. I want to see where you live, who you are, what you want from your flowers. Okay?"

"Um, okay. I live in Islington."

"Islington," Giles said thoughtfully. "Yes, yes, I think that might work."

"It might?"

"The wedding," he said, ignoring my question. "Is it going to be in Islington, too?"

"No. No, the wedding's going to be at the Park Lane Hilton."

"The Hilton. I see. Urban metropolis meets Islington savoir faire. Yes, yes, I can see this working. I'm loving it, in fact. So, shall we say three PM?"

He sounded so excited, I found myself nodding. "Okay!"

I gave him my address, agreed that there was "lots to think about," then, feeling slightly better about things, turned back to Gillie.

"I have to go home," I said, relief flooding my body at the prospect of getting out of there. "Can you tell Anthony I'm seeing the florist?"

"Sure, no problem." She smiled as I walked back to my computer, deleted Fenella's appointment, and picked up my coat.

Chapter 27

BY THE TIME I got home, my heart was still pounding in my chest and my mind was racing with questions. But, as I kept telling myself, everything was okay. So long as Anthony didn't know about Mr. Taylor, Mr. Taylor didn't know about the wedding, Max didn't know this marriage wasn't entirely the romantic commitment he thought it was, and Fenella didn't know that I had completely forgotten about the flowers until this morning, everything would be okay. Everything would be fine.

So when Giles arrived, looked me up and down, then swept into the sitting room and announced that he'd looked deep into his soul and knew, just knew, that Grecian was the way to go, I found myself agreeing on the spot. In retrospect, I realized that Grecian probably wasn't what Fenella had in mind; in fact I was pretty certain it wouldn't entirely work with her minimalist theme, but I figured it didn't matter in the great scheme of things. He was promising flowers, and that meant I could tick something else off my to-do list.

"By Grecian, do you mean togas?" I asked curiously, handing Giles a cup of tea. He'd been in the flat only a few minutes, but he was already spreading out photographs on the sitting room floor. He was tiny—about five feet tall—skinny, and wearing a pin-striped suit with a bright pink shirt and cowboy boots, which, I realized, meant that without them he was probably only four foot ten.

He rolled his eyes. "Darling, this is not the 'eighties. I mean vine leaves. I mean decadence. I mean maximalism. Grapes. Wine. Huge overflowing table displays and restrained walls. I want twigs, tall twigs, like trees, around the reception hall, with little fairy lights that come on as the sun goes down. Like an enchanted forest. Magical. Like *A Midsummer Night's Dream.*"

My eyes lit up. "I love that play. And I love the idea of an enchanted forest. You know?" An image floated into my head of me as the Fairy Queen, all ethereal and dream-like. I felt Giles's eyes on me and reddened slightly. "But it's not exactly . . . Grecian, is it?" I asked.

He looked at me reproachfully. "You have to think outside the box," he said, shaking his head. "We're talking classical. Magical. Aphrodite. Titania. They are one and the same."

"Which would make me Bottom?" I giggled. "Or would that be my future husband?"

Giles raised his eyebrows, and then his face turned serious again. "There is a lot to do," he said soberly. "But before we get started, I have to know. Why was it that you turned to me to do your flowers? When you were so dreadfully let down? It helps me, you see, to understand what it is you're looking for. Did you choose me because of my attention to detail, because of my vision? Was it my creativity, my flair? And who recommended me to you? Was it Antonia Harrison? Or Isabella Marchant?"

I smiled weakly, not sure I could admit that I'd found him through Google, not now that he was going to build me my own enchanted forest, a dream-like stage for an unreal wedding. "So many different people," I said, eventually. "Every time I mentioned flowers to anyone, your name came up."

"Yes," Giles said, nodding, his eyes shining gratefully. "Yes, that happens. It's a responsibility, you know. I make people's dreams come true, and it's not an easy job description. But I always succeed. So, let's get going, shall we?"

"Absolutely," I agreed. "Let's sort out those Grecian classical mythological Shakespearean wedding flowers."

Giles looked at me suspiciously for a second, then shrugged. "So," he said. "Talk to me about colors. Tell me the colors that you love, that you want to surround yourself with."

I thought for a moment. *Orange*, I wanted to say. Orange is my favorite color—it's bright and warm and friendly without being overpowering or bossy or placid or weak. But instead I pulled out the Pantone numbers Fenella had sent me. I owed her that at least.

"We were thinking red and green," I said unenthusiastically. "We've got these Pantone numbers."

"Pantone numbers?" Giles looked at me strangely. "You know flowers don't really conform to Pantone numbers?"

I blushed. "I know . . . I just . . ."

"You're in advertising, right?" Giles grinned.

I nodded.

"So that's all I need to know," he said, taking the Pantones. "I'll do my best to match them. And I'll send you drawings in the post. Now, talk to me about the ceremony and reception. I need dimensions of the rooms, I need photographs, I need numbers of guests. And then I need to see your dress. And shoes. I need to measure your arms. I need to know what lipstick you're going to wear. I'm going to turn you into a princess, Jessica Wild."

"So I can live happily ever after, The End?" I asked, forcing a grin and doing my best to ignore the lump that had appeared in my throat.

"So you can live happily ever after, The Beginning," he said, shaking his head. "Weddings are not the end, they are the start."

"The start," I said quietly. "Of course it is. Let me . . . go and get my dress."

I ran to my bedroom and pulled the white lace dress out of my wardrobe. Giles frowned when I held it up for him.

"This? This is your dress?" He was looking at it the same way I had when I first saw it. He had a shrug of an expression on his face.

"Yes," I said, slightly defensively. "I mean, it's okay, isn't it?"

"Of course! I love it!" Giles said immediately. "It's just not what I was . . . expecting. It's lovely, though. Really . . . lovely."

He took it from me and hung it from the picture rail on the sitting room wall. As I looked at it, I remembered the lace that itched slightly, and conjured the image of myself in the mirror when I'd tried it on, looking like any other bride, looking anonymous.

"I mean, there were nicer dresses," I said, trying hard to explain. "But this one, you know, was nice, and . . ."

"And I'm sure it's beautiful on," Giles said, smiling just a little bit too brightly. "Really beautiful. Anyway, it's your wedding, right? And that's one day of your life you should have everything just the way you want it."

"And you think I can look like a fairy princess in this dress?"

"Exactly like one," Giles said firmly.

He measured my arms, then analyzed the contents of my makeup bag. I gave him a file Fenella had given me, labeled PARK LANE HILTON DETAILS, which held not just measurements and photos but also the names of everyone who worked there, their policy on music and dancing, and menus from each of their restaurants. Then we spent an hour or so looking through photographs of flowers and twigs—me saying yes, no, or maybe to each one—and for the first time in a long time I realized I was enjoying myself. I got interested in the different types of fairy lights;

I listened seriously as Giles explained the different types of twigs and their connotations. And by the time he was packing up his things, I really didn't want him to go.

"I'm so pleased you found me," he said, clutching me in his arms as I said a reluctant good-bye. "I have a wonderful feeling about this wedding. It's going to be magical. Pure fantasy."

"Fantasy," I said, allowing myself a little smile. "You know, I think you might be right."

Chapter 28

To do

1. Do whatever Fenella tells me to do.

The next week or two went by in a blur and before I knew it, there were just two days until the wedding and Giles was at my flat to deliver a rehearsal bouquet. It was huge—long-stemmed white roses, lots of leaves and twigs, a couple of deep red roses that smelled divine, and a whole load of other flowers I didn't know the names of but would never admit as much to Giles.

"It's . . . beautiful," I breathed. "So perfect."

Giles smiled. "It is rather good, if I say so myself," he said, excitedly. "Now, remember, carry the flowers to your left as you walk up the aisle."

"Okay," I said seriously. "Flowers to the left."

Giles frowned. "You're looking thin," he said. "Have you lost weight? You're not on one of those ridiculous pre-wedding diets, are you?"

"Diet? No, no of course not," I said quickly. "It's just, you know, stress. Wedding stress."

Giles nodded. "Gotcha," he said. "Well, probably not a bad thing. You can always pile the weight back on during your honeymoon. Eat, shag, sleep, shag, eat, that's all honeymoons are for, isn't it?" He winked, and I nodded as enthusiastically as I could. He was right—the honeymoon would be great. Sure, Anthony and I had been busy lately; sure, we never seemed to have time for much of a conversation, but that was normal. Organizing a wedding in weeks was stressful, and Anthony had his hands full at work. It didn't mean anything.

"So where are you going?" he asked.

"Where are we going?" I looked at him blankly.

"On your honeymoon."

"Oh, right." I leaned back against the wall, trying to remember what Fenella had written in the e-mail titled HONEYMOON. "Um, France. The south of France."

"Nice," Giles said approvingly. "Nothing like jet lag to spoil a good holiday. Keep it simple, then you only have to enjoy each other."

"Yes, that's right." I smiled brightly. "You know, I really can't wait. It's going to be just . . . wonderful."

"You all right?" Giles looked at me in concern. "You look a bit white."

"Me?" I shook my head. "No, I'm fine. Completely fine." I forced a big smile to emphasize just how fine I was, just how relaxed and not at all exhausted I was.

"Helloooo." I heard the key in the door; moments later Helen appeared. She sighed heavily and sat down on the sofa, then frowned at Giles. "And who's this?"

"This is Giles," I said. "You know, the guy who's doing flowers for the wedding. Giles, this is Helen, my flatmate."

"No, I didn't know," Helen said pointedly. "I guess you forgot to tell me."

I blanched slightly. "Really?"

"You've been busy." Helen shrugged. "It's no biggie."

"Well, it's good to meet you." Giles jumped up immediately and formally took Helen's hand.

"Yeah, likewise," Helen said, pulling herself up again. "So, anyone want a drink? Cup of tea? Gin and tonic?"

Giles arched an eyebrow. "Gin and tonic. Ooh, yes, I think so. Thank you."

She got us all a drink, then turned to Giles. "So come on then, talk me through the floral displays," she said. I thought I could sense a bit of tension in her voice, but shrugged it off. If anyone was tense, it was me, not Helen.

Giles's eyes lit up and he started to talk Helen through the bouquets, the table arrangements, the enchanted forest.

"There are going to be little fairy lights in the twigs," I found myself saying. "They're going to come on when the sun sets."

"Nice," Helen said appreciatively. "That'll be really nice."

"It'll be more than nice," Giles said immediately, then he grinned. "Well, you'll see for yourself, won't you? Day after tomorrow."

Helen sniffed. "Yeah, actually Jess, I was going to talk to you about that. I've got this interview, you see. So I might be late."

"To the wedding?" I felt the blood drain from my face. "But it's on a Saturday."

Helen blanched slightly. "Yeah, I know, but it's this job . . . I . . . Look, you're the one who keeps telling me I should focus on my career. And I'll do my best. I just can't, you know, guarantee I'll be there at the beginning."

"Right." I nodded. "Right, no problem. I mean, it's a job interview. That's important."

"Yes it is," Helen said.

I bit my lip. "So you're sure you can't get out of it? The interview, I mean?"

Helen shook her head. "It's a really good job. And you always say that work's really important," she said.

Giles frowned. "But . . ." He looked at me curiously. "Isn't Helen your bridesmaid?"

Helen shook her head. "No. I mean . . . well, no, I'm not."

"But Jess"—Giles's voice was an octave higher than usual as he flicked through his book—"this isn't right. You said you wanted a bouquet for . . . for . . ." His eye scanned the page in front of him. "Yes. Here. It says Helen."

"It does?" Helen stared at me. "I was under the impression that you didn't want me as a bridesmaid," she said defensively. "I mean, I dropped enough hints and you never said anything . . ."

I met her eyes awkwardly. "I hadn't . . . I mean . . ."

"Look, it's no problem," Helen said quickly. "I mean it's no big deal. And I do have this interview anyway, so . . ."

"You have to come. Hel, I can't do it if you're not there." My voice caught slightly.

"Of course you can," Helen said matter-of-factly. "So, who's going to be your bridesmaid? Just out of interest?"

"I'm not having one," I said tightly.

"Not having one?" Giles's eyes widened. "But why? We have flowers for a bridesmaid. It creates a symmetry. Without one, the design—it's not going to work. It will be lopsided!"

"No bridesmaid," I continued, biting my lip and looking at Helen tentatively. "I was going to ask you to . . . to . . ." I took a deep breath. "To give me away."

"You want me to give you away?" Helen's eyes opened in surprise.

I shrugged awkwardly.

"Seriously?" Helen was staring at me now. "You seriously want me to give you away?"

I nodded. "But it's fine, if you can't," I said quickly. "I mean, if you're busy . . ."

"I thought you didn't care," Helen gasped. "I thought you had Fenella now and you didn't need me around anymore."

I stared at her incredulously. "Fenella?"

Helen reddened slightly. "She's all you talk about. Fenella this, Fenella that . . . I mean, you don't need two bossy boots in your life, do you?"

I giggled. "You're the only bossy boots I want," I said, taking her hand. "Honestly, Hel, you have to be there."

"Well, then, looks like I will," Helen said, biting her lip. Then she punched me lightly on the arm. "I can't believe it. Why didn't you ask me before?"

"I should have," I agreed. "I just kept forgetting, I've had so much on my mind . . ."

"I could have gone to a frigging job interview, you realize?"

"I know. I'm sorry," I sniffed. "You know this is all down to you. All of it."

"No it isn't. It's down to you, Jess. You pulled this all together."

"So you still need the bouquet?" Giles asked uncertainly.

"Definitely. A big one," Helen said, her eyes shining. "The best you've got. I mean, you know, after Jess's . . ."

Giles nodded and waved his hand to his eyes. "Well, girls, this is all getting a bit emotional for me. So much as I'd love to stay, I've got work to do," he said, rolling his eyes indulgently. "Jess, I'll be at the hotel on Saturday morning at six to get the flowers set up; after that I'll do the reception flowers. It starts at eleven AM, right?"

I nodded.

"So that's the day after tomorrow, right?" Helen said suddenly. Giles and I both nodded.

"Right," Helen said sagely. "It's just that, as far as I know, you haven't had a hen night. Have you?"

I squirmed slightly. "Hen night? Uh, no. And I don't want one, thanks very much."

"But you have to have a hen night," Helen said immediately. "In two days' time you're going to be married. You're going to be moving out."

"I am?" My heart quickened. "I mean, yes, I am." I didn't know why the fact hit me like a bolt out of the blue; Anthony and I had already had the conversation. I'd be moving in with him after the wedding. Fenella had even offered to have his place redecorated. But it had all felt a bit surreal, like I was talking about someone else—about Mrs. Milton, not Jessica Wild.

"So this is our last night in the flat as . . . flatmates," Helen continued, her voice cracking slightly.

"Um, yes. I guess it is." My throat was constricting again.

"So then we need to have a party. Giles, can you be a girl for the night?"

Giles looked at her uncertainly then shrugged, grinning. "Sure. Who am I kidding. I *am* a big girl. I'm a florist, for God's sake."

"Jess? Any objections? Not that I'll accept any, but do your best anyway."

I looked at her for a few seconds, then grinned. "Fine. But I can't get too drunk," I said sternly. "And no strippers."

"No strippers," Helen said, seriously, then winked at Giles. "Giles," she said, smiling sweetly. "I think we're going to need more gin."

We didn't have strippers. We did have Ivana, though. And Sean. And lots more gin, Kylie Minogue, and dancing. Lots of dancing. At one point I was dancing in my wedding dress. Actually, I fell asleep in my wedding dress with Ivana next to me. We woke up at the same time, our eyes opening to find themselves gazing into each other's, just an inch or two apart. Immediately we both pulled away and stared at each other warily; a second later we realized what had woken us up as the intercom buzzed again. Sleepily, I ran toward it and picked it up.

"Hello?"

"Jess, it's me," a familiar voice said curtly. "In the car. Ready?"

I looked down at my watch in alarm. It was already the middle of the afternoon.

"Fenella! Hi! Um, give me a minute, okay?"

"A minute? Jess, we don't have a minute. There are things to do, checklists to check . . ."

"Just wait there." I put the intercom down and turned around. A sleepy-looking Helen was mooching toward me. "Who was that?" she asked, yawning.

"Fenella. It's the rehearsal today. I'm meant to be ready."

Helen looked me up and down. "You're wearing your wedding dress," she pointed out. "I don't think you're meant to wear that to the rehearsal."

I looked at her levelly, then pulled a face. "Yeah, thanks for pointing that out. And help me get out of it."

Twenty minutes later, dress back in its bag, smelling, admittedly, slightly of gin, my clothes packed, me washed, and Ivana safely in the kitchen, I hugged Helen good-bye.

"You're sure you can't make the rehearsal?" I asked imploringly. Helen had managed to shift her job interview forward a day; she shook her head.

"I'm sorry," she said sadly. "But I'll be there first thing tomorrow. And you'll be fine. Honestly you will."

I nodded. "Thanks, Hel. For . . . for everything," I said.

"Oh, don't be silly. You don't need to thank me for anything."

"You can still come and live with us, you know. When we're married." My voice caught slightly, and Helen's eyes widened.

"I keep forgetting you're not going to be living here anymore," she whispered, then bit her lip. "You're going to be married. You're going to be Mrs. Milton."

We reluctantly disentangled ourselves and I made my way downstairs where Fenella was standing, her mobile phone clamped to her face. She looked up at me irritably, then forced a smile.

"Okay, time to go. Otherwise we'll be late!" she said, her voice slightly shrill.

"Sorry. Just . . . you know, last-minute stuff," I mumbled apologetically, putting my bag in the boot and jumping into the passenger's seat.

"Jess!" I turned around to see Helen running toward me, her face white, her expression anxious. "Mr. Taylor's on the phone," she said, her voice barely audible. "He says it's urgent."

I gulped. "Mr. Taylor?"

She nodded.

"Tell him I'm out," I whispered. "Tell him I'm going away for the weekend."

"I did," Helen said, her eyes wide. "But he just said it was really important that he got to talk to you today. He said I had to track you down. He mentioned the W-word."

"W?" I asked, confused.

"Wedding!" Helen mouthed. I felt my heart beginning to pound in my chest, and I moved out of Fenella's earshot. He knew. He knew everything.

"You have to do something," I whispered desperately. "You have to keep him away. He could ruin everything."

Helen nodded seriously. "Leave it with me," she said. "I'll . . . I'll tell him the wedding's in Manchester. That should keep him busy."

"Manchester," I said, grabbing her to give her one last hug. "Or, you know, Scotland. Scotland's even farther away . . ."

Helen nodded. "Scotland it is," she said forcefully. "Absolutely. You leave it to me. No problem at all."

Chapter 29

The reception room was a hive of activity and looked utterly beautiful—table upon table covered in crisp white linen, with gold and red upholstered chairs surrounding them.

"Right, I need to find Anthony," Fenella said as soon as we arrived. "There are some problems with some invoices I need to clear up."

"Sure," I said vaguely, as she marched off, her mobile phone pressed to her ear. I was standing still at the doorway, taking in the vision before me. My wedding. My wedding to Anthony Milton. Tomorrow. I felt slightly faint.

"Jess! Hi!" I looked up to see Marcia walking toward me, a large pair of sunglasses positioned on the top of her head, a huge grin plastered across her face. "How exciting—bet you thought this day would never come."

"Absolutely," I said, hoping against hope that Mr. Taylor was on his way to Scotland at that very moment.

"So, last day of being single," she said, winking.

"I guess," I managed to say. Everywhere I looked, people were carrying things, rearranging things, discussing tomorrow's events in low, urgent voices. All for me. All for my wedding. Jessica Wild, the girl who always insisted she'd never get married, and look at me.

"And then I guess everything will be different," Marcia continued. "I mean, you'll be a Mrs., won't you? You'll be Mrs. Milton . . ." She trailed off, then smiled again. "Just like I'm sure you've always wanted to be," she finished.

"Right," I said, looking at her slightly strangely.

"You're not getting wedding jitters, are you?" Marcia said, laughing slightly. "Not going to do a runner are we?" Her eyes were glinting slightly.

"Of course not," I said too quickly, shaking my head. "Why would I?"

"Good." Her eyes rested on me for a few seconds. "Well, see you later."

I nodded. Wedding jitters. Maybe that's what my churning stomach was all about. It would calm down, I was sure of it. I was just worried about losing my independence. It was perfectly normal.

"Jessica!" I looked up sharply to see Max at my side. "So, coming to the church?"

"Church?"

"For the rehearsal," Max said, looking at me curiously. "You okay, Jess?"

I nodded. My legs were feeling slightly weak. "Me? Fine.

Really fine. So, yes. Church. Let's . . . Only I should probably wait for Fenella."

"Fenella?" Max raised an eyebrow. "The girl with the hair?"

I giggled, immediately feeling better. "She's actually very nice when you get to know her. At least she's okay. I mean, she means well . . ."

"She means well? Are you sure about that?"

"Fine, I'll come," I said, grinning. "I'm sure she'll find me if she needs me."

"I'm sure she will," Max said, holding out his arm. The church was just around the corner from the hotel.

"So, excited?" Max asked as we walked.

"Terrified," I said before I could stop myself.

He laughed. "Can't be that bad," he said.

"No, no of course not." I bit my lip. "I meant that I'm terrified in a good way. You know, like any bride."

"Jess, it's okay to be nervous, you know," Max said gently. "Marriage is a big deal."

"I know," I said, wishing it wasn't. "So how come you . . . I mean, did you never think about getting married yourself?"

Max shook his head. "No. Not for me."

I remembered saying that myself. Before . . . well, just before. "You mean you don't ever want to . . . ?"

"Never say never," he said, winking. "I just . . . well, it would have to be the right person, wouldn't it? I mean, you can't rush into these things."

He met my eye and blanched slightly. "I didn't mean you're rushing into things," he said quickly. "I know that you and Anthony are doing the right thing."

"You do?" I asked, uncertainly.

"Yes. I think you're going to make a great team."

"Really?"

Max nodded and pulled my arm around his more tightly; it felt nice. Felt reassuring. I hadn't felt reassured like this in a long time. With Anthony I felt excited sometimes, felt like Jessica Wiiild, but I didn't feel . . . comfortable, necessarily. Didn't really feel like I could relax. "You'll have fun together," Max continued. "And support each other. Be there for each other. You know, all the things married people do that single people like me pretend don't matter. Even though they do. Very much."

"Right." I nodded, aware that my chest was constricting slightly. We *would* have fun, I told myself. We *would* support each other. Wouldn't we?

"Jess? Are you okay? Jess?" Max was looking at me, concern splashed all over his face, and I realized I was holding his arm in a vise-like grip.

I let go immediately. "Yes. Yes, I'm fine," I said quickly. "Although . . ."

"Although?"

"Although not all marriages are the same, are they?"

"No, I suppose they're not," Max said.

"Right. So there's no right or wrong way."

"Of course not. So long as you love each other, you can make it up as you go along."

"Love. Right." My heart was clattering in my chest and I took a deep breath.

"Jess?" Max stopped walking. "Jess, what's up? What's going on?"

He was looking at me intently, and I felt myself weaken. "What I mean is," I said, looking down at the ground, "that some marriages are based on . . . other things. You know." Like money, I was thinking. Like lies. I thought of Grace. Like not letting someone important down.

"I suppose," Max said. He sounded confused.

"Right," I said, trying to convince myself as much as anyone. "And ends justify the means, don't they? You know, generally."

"I guess so." Max frowned.

I nodded. "Yes. You see, sometimes you do things that may not seem entirely like the right thing, but they are because if you don't do them then you'll be doing the wrong thing. Right?"

I looked up at him hopefully; his face crumpled slightly. "I'm not entirely sure I'm following you. Can you be more specific?"

"I mean that right and wrong, well, they can be interlinked, can't they?" I gulped slightly. "And sometimes what seems to be the right thing is actually the wrong thing and what might feel wrong is actually right . . ."

"It is?" Max looked perplexed. "Jess, are you having doubts?"

I shook my head. "No, of course not. I mean . . ."

"You mean?" Max was looking at me intently.

"I mean, no . . ." I started to nod. "Well, maybe . . ."

"Jess? Oh, thank God, there you are. Look, the rehearsal is about to start and I've lost Anthony."

It was Fenella—at the sound of her voice I went bright red.

"Fenella! Hi!" My voice was slightly too high to sound natural.

"I was chasing him for some payments—apparently the hotel's invoices haven't been paid—and he said he was going to call his bank and now he's disappeared," Fenella said agitatedly. "Do you know where he is?"

I shook my head. "No. No, I haven't seen him. Not since we got here."

"Wonderful." Fenella sighed. "A rehearsal with no groom."

She peered at Max. "You. Who are you?"

"This is Max," I said, forcing a bright smile onto my face. "You met him at the engagement party, remember?"

"Max." Fenella looked at her list. "The best man?"

"I like to think so," Max joked, but Fenella didn't even attempt a smile.

"Well, Max, could you go and see if you can find Anthony? Perhaps you'll have more luck than I did."

"I could . . . ," Max said tentatively, his eyes still on me. "But . . ."

"But?" Fenella sighed.

His eyes were boring into mine. "You were saying?"

"I was saying I'm fine," I assured him, suddenly feeling foolish for wanting to get his approval, for having such a moment of weakness. I was having far too many of them. And always around Max. "You go and get Anthony. Thanks, Max."

"Well, if you're sure," he said.

"Quite sure." I nodded.

"God, it's like herding cats," Fenella sighed as Max disappeared back toward the hotel. I felt his absence as if a comforting blanket had been whipped off me. "Now come with me and meet the vicar. He's . . . not what I expected, but I'm afraid he'll have to do."

She led me into the church. "So, here we are," she said. "Have a wander around to familiarize yourself with the layout. Aisle is here, obviously, altar over there. There's a room at the back for Anthony and the best man tomorrow morning. You'll come through these doors and when you do, the organ will start to play."

I followed her as she took me on a brisk tour, doing my best to keep up, doing my best to take in what she was saying. Then, eventually, she steered me toward a small, squat man with a big bushy beard, pale blue jeans, and a dog collar. He didn't look much like a vicar, I found myself thinking as he held out his hand.

"Vicar, this is Jess. Jess, this is the vicar."

"Jess. Great to meet you."

"Hi!" I said uncertainly. "You're the vicar?"

"Call me Roger." The man grinned. "I prefer to keep things informal if that's okay?"

"Sure." I noticed Fenella's expression—it appeared that *infor-*

mal was not at all okay as far as she was concerned. "I mean, great!"

"Of course, he'll be in his robes, tomorrow," Fenella said, smiling tightly. "Won't you, Roger?"

Roger winked. "Oh, I'll see what I can do," he said jovially. "Who knows, I might even mention the Bible in my sermon. What do you reckon?"

Fenella raised an eyebrow at him, then turned to the doors—which were opening to reveal Max, rather breathless.

"I . . . I can't find him anywhere," he said. "Anthony, I mean."

"What do you mean, you can't find him?" Fenella said irritably. "Are you quite certain?"

Max nodded. "He's not in the bar, or the reception, and he's not in his room, either."

Fenella took out her mobile and dialed a number. "Anthony? Fenella. We're waiting for you in the church. Please call me the second you get this message."

Then she turned to me and stared at me accusingly. "Do you know where he is?" she asked. "Do you?"

I shook my head. "He was at the bar a few minutes ago. Marcia saw him."

"And where's Marcia?" Fenella asked, looking at me accusingly, as though I'd hidden them both on purpose.

"I don't know," I said redundantly.

"Of course you don't." Fenella sighed. "Well, it looks like I'm going to have to go back to the hotel to look for him myself."

"Good luck," Max said levelly. "Because I can promise you I had a good look."

"Everywhere?" Fenella looked unconvinced.

"Everywhere." He nodded firmly.

"Okay, well, guys, we may have to think of a Plan B, because we're going to have to clear the church for the evening service soon," Roger said, clapping his hands together.

"Plan B?" Fenella looked at him in alarm. "There is no Plan B. We need to have the rehearsal. We have to wait for Anthony."

Roger's brow wrinkled. "Thing is," he said apologetically, "evensong doesn't really wait, if you know what I mean."

"But we have to rehearse," Fenella said, the stress evident in her voice. "We have to have a run-through."

Roger shrugged hopelessly.

"Fine," Fenella said, crossing her arms. "Max, you'll have to stand in for now. I'll wait outside and usher Anthony in if I see him."

"Max? Stand in for Anthony?" I gulped.

"Only for the rehearsal," Fenella said irritably. "It's no big deal. Come on, people."

Max looked at her uncertainly. "Really?"

"Makes sense to me," Roger said. He winked at Max. "Of course, it is the best man's job to stand in for the groom if he goes missing, you know."

Max caught my eye and I blushed. He shook his head, then shrugged. "Well, okay, then. If I have to. So, what, I just go . . ."

"To the altar," Roger said. "And Jessica, you go to the door. That's right. Okay, so cue the music . . ." He started to whistle a badly out of tune "Here Comes the Bride" as everyone else took their places.

"You want me to . . ." I looked at him uncertainly.

"To walk down the aisle, that's right," Roger said encouragingly.

"Down the aisle." I nodded and walked toward the door. I wished Helen were here now for me to cling to. Wished the altar weren't quite so far away. Taking a deep breath, I started to walk, focusing on putting one foot in front of the other, slowly, unsteadily. Max was facing the front of the chapel; from the back, he could have been Anthony. Tomorrow it would be Anthony, I thought to myself, and felt my hands go clammy.

And then he turned around, and our eyes met, and he grinned reassuringly at me, and suddenly it didn't seem quite so scary anymore. So I carried on walking, and soon I was standing next to him and Roger was saying, "Dearly beloved, we are gathered here today," and I found myself thinking that this wasn't going to be so hard after all.

"So," Roger said, "you have to repeat the vows after me. We won't go through them all now, but let's just try the first one to make sure I don't go too fast, okay?"

I nodded.

"Right. So, I, Jessica . . ."

"I, Jessica . . . ," I repeated.

"Take thee Ant—" Roger frowned. "Well, since he's not here, we'll skip over that line. So, to have and to hold . . ."

"To have and to hold . . ."

"To love and cherish . . ."

I could feel Max's eyes on me, and my cheeks started to burn up. I couldn't say these words tomorrow. Not to Anthony. Could I?

"To love and cherish . . ."

"In sickness and in health . . ."

"In sickness and in health . . ."

I looked up briefly, and then looked away, but my eyes were drawn back to Max's almost immediately. He was hot, too, I noticed.

"And so on and so forth."

"And so on and—" I stopped myself from repeating what he'd said word for word just in time.

"Okay," Roger said, his eyes twinkling. "So then Anthony will say his stuff, and then, if I'm feeling generous, I'll tell him he can kiss the bride."

I imagined kissing Max and my flush deepened. Max's did, too. I wondered if he was thinking the same thing, then shook myself. Of course he wasn't. He was probably just embarrassed. Probably wondering what was wrong with me. I was, too; my hands were hot and clammy and my face felt like a furnace. Max, meanwhile, was pulling at his collar.

"And then," Roger continued, "you'll go and sit over there and sign the marriage certificates while I give the congregation a scare with my sermon." He laughed, then, seeing that no one else was joining in the joke, he shrugged. "Okay, then. After that, we'll finish the service, you will walk back down the aisle a married couple and, hopefully, the booze will start to flow. Sound good?"

I managed to nod.

"Great, so if you and Max can make your way back down the aisle?"

Max looked at me uncertainly and held out his arm; I took it, equally uncertain. Just touching the sleeve of his jacket was shooting little electrical currents all around my body; as I hooked my arm around his, I felt his muscles tighten. We walked silently down the aisle until we reached the bottom where we stood, waiting, although I wasn't sure what for. All I knew was that I didn't want to let go.

"Great! Okay, well, I think we're done," Roger said. "If you're happy with that?"

"Yes. Yes, of course," I heard myself say.

"That was great!" Fenella said, walking toward us. "Okay, so now you need to go back to the hotel to get changed for the dinner. It's in the conference suite—starts in forty-five minutes. Okay?"

We both nodded, silently, and carried on walking, down the aisle, out of the church, around the corner. It was only as we were approaching the hotel that I realized I was still holding Max's arm.

"Well, that went okay," Max said, as we walked through the main doors. "I'm sure tomorrow will go perfectly."

I nodded. And tears started to prick in my eyes and I didn't know why so I wiped them away irritably.

"If you want it to," he said tentatively.

"If I want it to?" I repeated.

"If it's really what you want to do."

"Is it what you want me to do?"

"Me?" He stopped, and I suddenly realized what I'd said.

"You? No," I said quickly. "No, I didn't mean . . ."

"What did you mean, Jess?" Max was staring at me, and as he did his eyes seemed to go darker, more intense, and I could feel the heat of his body, even though he was several inches away from me, and suddenly I didn't want to be Jessica Milton, I wanted to be Jessica Wild, here, with Max. And I don't know if I moved closer to him or if he moved closer to me, but suddenly we were touching, from our legs to our shoulders, and before I could even think a coherent thought his lips were on mine and my arms were around his neck and it felt so incredibly right. And suddenly I knew. Knew without any doubt that I didn't want to marry Anthony. And that it had nothing to do with hating marriage, nothing to do with my desire for independence. It was because I was in love with Max. I was in love, just like my mother had been before she had me, just like all those silly girls my grandma used to roll her eyes at, like *I* used to roll my eyes at.

"I can't do this." Max pulled away and I felt my heart thud with despair. And then I pulled myself together. Of course he couldn't. Nor could I.

"No, of course not," I said immediately, my voice slightly shrill. "No, I can't do this either. I don't even know what happened then . . ."

"You don't?" Max's expression was unreadable.

"No," I said quickly. "No, it must be wedding jitters. I'm sorry. I really should go . . ."

As I spoke, I heard a familiar voice from across the lobby. "Jess? Maxy," Anthony called. "There you are. Sorry I missed the rehearsal—I was on the phone. Work got in the way, I'm afraid. So, drink? What do you say? I think I need a stiff one, myself."

"Anthony," I said, turning guiltily. "Hi!"

"I looked everywhere for you," Max said. He was trying to smile but it didn't reach his eyes. "We had to do the rehearsal without you."

"Well, so long as you don't do the same with the wedding I think I'll survive." Anthony grinned.

"Marcia said there was a problem with payment," Max continued. His voice was expressionless, like nothing had happened, like we hadn't been clinging to each other just seconds before. I was suddenly aware of a big, empty feeling in my stomach, but did my best to ignore it. It was just weakness on my part. I'd get over it.

Anthony smiled easily. "Max, it's kind of you to worry, but believe me it's all under control. So, drink?"

I looked at Max.

He looked at me.

We both looked at Anthony.

"Actually, no," Max said. "No, I think I need to do some work on my best man's speech if that's okay. You . . . you have a drink together. If that's what you . . ." His eyes flickered over to mine; I looked away.

"Yes! Absolutely. You work on your speech," I managed to say. "We'll see you later?"

"Of course," Max said, looking down at the ground as he spun around and marched off toward the lifts.

"Come on, Jess," Anthony said affably. "Looks like it's just the two of us."

"Yes," I said, looking up at him. "I guess it is."

Chapter 30

Helen arrived the following morning with Sean and Ivana in tow to find me still in bed. It was, I realized, the last time I would wake up alone, the last time I would have my own bed—even if it was a hotel one—and I wanted to make the most of it. Plus I had a bit of a headache—one drink had turned into quite a few the night before; somehow it seemed the right thing to do, and Anthony certainly thought it was a good idea. He kept saying how tomorrow was a big day, how any problems would disappear, and even though I wasn't sure entirely what he was talking about, I found myself nodding vigorously and telling myself he was absolutely right.

Ivana inspected the room, nodding curtly as she noted the smart plasma television screen, the writing paper, the large shower, the huge bed I hadn't been able to pull myself out of.

"Is nice room," she said. "Good bed. But is now time you get ready." She sat down on the bed and lit a cigarette. Immediately I got up and opened a window.

"So how did the rehearsal go?" Helen asked.

"Oh, you know, fine really," I said, attempting a smile.

"You no seem like excited bride," Ivana said, her voice deadpan. "No big smile and screaming."

I shrugged. "I'm screaming on the inside."

Ivana raised an eyebrow and picked up the remote control, flicking on the television as she and Sean took over the double bed, leaning back against the headboard and stretching out their legs. "Ah!" she shouted. "Ah! Is perfect film. Is wedding film. We watch."

I looked at the screen to see Hugh Grant and Andie MacDowell in a restaurant talking about the number of lovers they'd had.

"Maybe *Runaway Bride's* on the other channel," I heard myself say, a little smile playing on my lips.

Helen looked at me uncertainly. "You're not . . . having second thoughts, are you, Jess?"

Ivana turned up the volume.

"Because . . ." Helen came over to me and took my hand. "Look, I want you to know, Jess, if you are, then that's fine. I've been thinking . . . you know . . . I mean, marriage is a big deal. I know I said it isn't, but it is. And I'd hate to think I pushed you into anything you don't . . . you know . . . want to do . . ."

"You haven't," I said quickly. "This is my mess, not yours. You haven't pushed me into anything. You've just helped me, that's all. And I am grateful, you know. I do appreciate it."

"Really?"

"Really." I nodded. "Come on—this time tomorrow I'm going to be a millionaire!" I forced a smile, tried to make myself feel happy and excited.

"Oh, thank God." She smiled in relief. "So listen, how would you feel about being on TV?"

"TV?" I looked at her uncertainly.

"My interview yesterday," she said, grinning. "This producer asked me for an idea for a television show and I was thinking about you and the wedding, and I just, you know, came out with it. And they loved it!"

"Came out with what?" I demanded.

"How to turn your life around in fifty days."

"What?"

Helen sighed. "Like you did," she said patiently. "You see, I was in this job interview and I was having one of those out-of-body experiences where I realized that I didn't really want to work on a program about fishing and that I was missing your rehearsal."

"Right," I said doubtfully.

"I mean, I was thinking about how amazing the whole Project Marriage thing had been—you know, making all your dreams come true."

"My dreams," I said, thinking of Max, then kicking myself. "And?"

"And I thought, you know what? Anything's possible," Helen continued. "Don't you see?"

"Anything?" I sighed inwardly. "I'm not sure about that."

"Yes it is! Jess, we completely turned your life around, didn't we?"

I nodded. "You're right. We did. So you got the job?"

"No, I didn't," Helen said excitedly. "But after the interview I went for a coffee and ended up at the same table as a producer. And I told him about my crap interview and about you, and about my idea for a series based on people changing their lives completely. And he loved it! Commissioned it right there and then! And the best thing is, you can be our first show, so it's virtually already in the bag. I mean, ideally we'd have filmed the wedding, but there just wasn't time to get a crew down here."

"You were going to get a crew down here?"

"Well, not without asking, obviously," Helen said, rolling her eyes. "But it was all down to you. So you have to be in the show. Don't you?"

"Can I think about it?" I asked tentatively. "Maybe after the wedding?"

Helen shrugged. "Sure. I mean, you know, whenever works for you . . ."

I smiled weakly. "Okay, time to get dressed."

"This dress?" Ivana had moved off the bed and was now looking at my wedding dress, which was hanging on the back of the door, rubbing the fabric between her fingers. "Is no good dress. Febric is itchy."

I took a deep breath. "Well, it's my dress. It's the one I chose."

Ivana shrugged. "Funny choice, to me."

"Yes, well, I didn't ask you," I said.

"End there is no ashtray in room," Ivana continued, apparently not noticing the stress in my voice. "Where am I putting cigarette out?"

Helen looked at me warily. "Tell you what," she said, walking over to Ivana. "Why don't the two of you go downstairs to the café? You can smoke there; I'll stay here with Jess and help her get ready."

"Downstairs?" Ivana asked dubiously.

"That's right," Helen said, helping Sean off the bed. "We'll see you in the church, okay?"

Ivana opened her mouth to speak, then shrugged. "We put coffee on your room teb. Maybe even full breakfast."

As Helen closed the door, she turned back to me with raised eyebrows. "She means well," she said tentatively. "They both do."

"I know," I said quietly. "But thanks for getting rid of them."

"No problem. So look, let me do your makeup before you put the dress on, okay?"

I nodded silently, my eyes drifting over to the plasma screen showing *Four Weddings and a Funeral* as Helen smeared creams over my face. When she was finished, I picked up my wedding dress. It took awhile to fasten, but eventually it was on and I turned to look at myself in the mirror. I was a bride. I was a bride wearing a dress that didn't do much for me, that was uncomfortable against my skin, that even a Soho prostitute turned her nose up at. But to me it felt right. The wrong dress for the wrong wedding to the wrong man.

"I got you this." Helen handed me a garter belt. "It's blue. And if you give it back, it's borrowed. Plus it's new. So that's covered three out of four."

I gave her a hug and put the garter on, pulling my dress right up in the process.

"Your knickers," Helen said.

"My knickers?"

"They're the old thing, right? I mean, they're not new, are they?"

I reddened slightly. I'd bought some new silky lingerie weeks before from a shop that Fenella had recommended (actually, she'd insisted I go there—at one point I thought she was going to march me in there herself). But somehow I hadn't been able to put it on this morning. My old graying cotton panties seemed somehow more appropriate.

"No one's going to see my knickers," I said.

"No one?" Helen raised her eyebrow.

I shrugged and opened my eyes wide because I could feel the prick of a tear and didn't want to encourage it.

"Jess, are you okay?" Helen put her hands on my shoulders—her expression was anxious. "Are you sure you want to do this?"

I nodded. "Of course I do."

"Really?"

"Really," I nodded. "I'm just . . . emotional, that's all."

"Good. Just checking." She held out her arm, and I hooked mine over it. "So, ready to go?"

I looked back at the television, briefly, to watch Hugh Grant getting punched by his bride in front of a whole congregation of his family and friends.

"Ready," I whispered.

Slowly, silently, we left the room, walked down the stairs, out through the hotel lobby, then around the corner to the church. It was a warm day, but I was shivering.

"To the future Mrs. Milton," Helen said, giving me a wink. And as she spoke, the doors to the church opened, the organ started to play, and suddenly we were walking through the doors, down the aisle.

"Perfect timing!" I turned to see Fenella right next to me. "Okay, I'm going to the hotel to get everything ready. Good luck!"

She dashed off; I looked ahead, uncertainly, and saw Anthony, who was standing in front of the altar. He turned around and winked at me. Next to him was Max; our eyes met briefly and my stomach flip-flopped, then he looked away. As we approached the altar I could see on one side Ivana and Sean, who both offered me a thumbs-up, and on the other side, Marcia and Gillie.

Giving me a little squeeze, Helen prized my arm out of hers and went to sit down. Roger, who, as promised, was wearing the full regalia of gowns, gave me a beaming smile, and the organ changed its pace and suddenly everyone was standing up and singing a hymn.

And then the singing stopped. "Dearly beloved," I heard Roger say. "Or rather, ladies and gentlemen. Good morning. And what a morning it is. A morning for celebration. A morning for being thankful for God's bounty—for love, for devotion, for friendship, for support—for all the things in fact that make up a good marriage. Because, as we all know, marriage isn't something to approach lightly, not something to jump into out of boredom or because it seems like a good idea. Marriage is a lifelong commitment in the eyes of God. It requires faith, trust, love, commitment, honesty, and hard work. It means enjoying the good times together but also working through the difficult ones, supporting each other. The phrase we all know is *in sickness and in health*— but it's more than that. It's in poverty, in uncertainty, in dark times when the only light at the end of the tunnel is the belief that it's there. That's real love. And that's what we're here to celebrate today. The wedding of Jessica Wild and Anthony Milton."

He smiled at me and I tried to smile back, but I felt like the world was closing in on me.

"And so," Roger continued, apparently oblivious to my glassy eyes and greenish skin, "without further ado, let's get this show on the road, shall we? Although, first of all, and please excuse the official language, but I am required to ask anyone present who knows a reason why these persons may not lawfully marry, to declare it now."

I turned around, involuntarily, just in case someone had something to say. But they didn't. Quickly I faced front again.

Roger smiled at me. "Anthony and Jessica, the vows you are about to take are to be made in the name of God, who is judge of all and who knows all the secrets of our hearts: therefore if either of you knows a reason why you may not lawfully marry, you must declare it now."

I gulped, and Anthony winked at me.

"Great!" Roger said. "Well, it's always a relief when we get that bit over with, isn't it?" There was a murmur of laughter from the congregation. "And now for the important bit. Anthony, will you take Jessica to be your wife? Will you love her, comfort her, honor and protect her, and, forsaking all others, be faithful to her as long as you both shall live?"

"I will," Anthony said seriously. "Definitely."

There was another little murmur of laughter. Then Roger turned to me. "Jessica, will you take Anthony to be your husband? Will you love him, comfort him, honor and protect him, and, forsaking all others, be faithful to him as long as you both shall live?"

He smiled at me encouragingly. I forced myself to smile back. "I . . . I . . ." I could hear voices in my head—Grace, telling me about the importance of real love, Helen yelling *Deal or No Deal,* Ivana shouting *Jessica Wiiiiild.*

"Stage fright," Roger said, beaming at the congregation. "Happens all the time." He looked back at me and smiled again. "As long as you both shall live?" he prompted.

"I . . ." I took a deep breath. I had to do this. For Grace. I owed her. I forced myself to think about how she'd placed her trust in me, forced myself to picture the house I was going to inherit, the house I had to protect, the house that . . . Suddenly I frowned. The house. I'd seen it somewhere else. I racked my brain but drew a blank.

"Jess?" Anthony asked. "Are you okay?"

I nodded and swallowed awkwardly. "I . . . ," I said, then stopped. I knew where I'd seen it. On Anthony's desk. The photograph. The house he'd been looking at, the photograph Fenella picked up. It was Grace's house. I was sure of it.

I looked at him uncertainly.

"The picture on your desk," I whispered, my voice slightly strangled. "It was Grace's house."

Roger cleared his throat. "As long as you . . . ," he started to say again, but I waved him aside.

"The house," I demanded. "Tell me about the house."

Anthony frowned. "Grace's house? I don't know what you're talking about," he whispered, smiling strangely at me. "I don't even know who Grace is. Jess, we're getting married, darling. Can't this wait?"

I thought for a moment. He was probably right. I was imagining things. There were lots of houses like that in the country. I was just looking for an excuse to stall. "Sure," I said. "Sure, it can wait."

"Atta girl." Anthony winked. "Sorry, Vic," he said, turning to the congregation to give them a wry smile. "Just a little disagreement over the flowers. All sorted now."

There was a low level of laughter and Roger turned to me again.

"Okay, then," he said, grinning broadly. "Jessica, will you take Anthony to be your husband? Will you love him, comfort him, honor and protect him, and, forsaking all others, be faithful to him as long as you both shall live?"

I looked up at him, then at Anthony.

"I . . . ," I started; then my eyes caught Max's. He was staring at me intently, and I felt brittle suddenly, like I might crack down the middle. I didn't love Anthony. And suddenly I knew that this wasn't what Grace would have wanted—she wanted me to fall in love and be happy, not to marry someone just to inherit her estate. And it wasn't what I wanted, either. Not at all. I didn't care if it made me a ridiculous romantic; I didn't care if Grandma would roll her eyes and say, *I knew it, I knew you'd cave eventually.* I was in love with Max, and even if he wasn't in love with me, I couldn't marry Anthony, not for all the money in the world.

I looked back at Anthony. Then I took a deep breath. "No deal."

"No deal?" Roger was looking at me uncertainly now. "What do you mean?"

"I mean no deal," I heard myself say. "I mean I'm not doing this. I'm not getting married."

Chapter 31

THE GREAT THING about films is that something dramatic can happen—let's say, Hugh Grant gets punched at the altar—and then the scene cuts and the next thing you know, he's back in the safety of someone's house being comforted by his friends. In real life the dramatic event happens and moments later you're still standing there as people stare at you, incredulously. At least Anthony and Roger were staring at me, and I kind of assumed everyone else was, too. I felt myself getting hot and my cheap wedding dress felt like it was made out of thistles.

"You can't?" Roger asked eventually, and I nodded. Now that I'd actually said it, I felt strangely detached, like this was all happening to someone else.

"Of course she can," Anthony said, the irritation evident in his voice.

"No, I can't," I said firmly.

"Then perhaps you'd better come around the back," Roger said. "I think we need to talk, don't you?"

Gratefully, I nodded; Roger turned to the congregation. "Slight hitch," he said, grinning warmly. "Just need to clarify one or two things, then we'll be right back with you."

Silently, I followed him. I felt like I was wading through marshmallow as I walked; it seemed to take forever. Anthony walked ahead of me, quickly, his shoulders tense; behind him was Max.

"Right," Roger said, opening the door to the crypt and waiting for us to follow him in. "Why exactly can't you do this?"

There was a chair near the wall and I headed for it, then sat down. "Because I'm not in love with Anthony," I said quietly. "And he's not in love with me. He's in love with Jessica Wiiild."

Anthony stared at me. "But *you're* Jessica Wild," he said uncertainly.

"No, I'm Jess," I said, suddenly feeling very calm. "The girl you fell in love with was fabricated. She doesn't exist. Sean, her ex-boyfriend, doesn't exist. Just me. Just Jess."

Anthony's face crumpled in confusion, and he put his hand through his hair. "Okay," he said, taking a deep breath. "Look, Jess, I don't know what's going on. Maybe you need to see a shrink. Maybe you've got multiple personalities or something. But let's just get the wedding over and done with, shall we? Then we'll deal with your . . . issues. Okay?"

I shook my head; Anthony sighed with exasperation. "For fuck's sake," he said, irritably. "Jess, stop being so bloody immature."

"I'm not being immature."

"Okay," Roger said, attempting a smile. "Come on, guys. Let's see if we can't work out what this is all about."

"Or we can just get on with the bloody wedding," Anthony said irritably. "There are people waiting out there."

"Let them wait," Max said. "Look, if Jess is having doubts, why not postpone? There's no need to rush into anything."

I shot him a look of gratitude, but he didn't reciprocate; our eyes met fleetingly, then he looked away again.

"Yes, there is," Anthony said firmly. "And Jess isn't having doubts."

"Not doubts, no," I agreed, feeling lighter suddenly, as though I'd finally taken a huge rucksack off my back. "It's more than doubts. I know I don't want to marry you. And you don't want to marry me. Not really."

"Yes, I do." Anthony looked at me in annoyance, then forced a smile onto his face. "Jess, darling, come on. Don't make a scene, okay? Let's just do this."

"No. I don't love you, Anthony." It felt good, finally telling the truth, like a weight had been lifted from my shoulders.

"Right," Roger said, looking slightly taken aback.

"Fine. You're right. You don't love me and I don't love you. But who cares? Love's got nothing to do with it," Anthony said, his eyes narrowing slightly. "It doesn't matter. We can still get married."

My mouth opened in surprise. He didn't love me? Then I kicked myself—that really wasn't important right now. "That's what I thought, Anthony. But it does matter," I said quietly. "It matters a lot. It . . ." I looked over at Max again, but suddenly the sound of clacking heels made him turn his head away from me; seconds later, Helen and Ivana emerged from behind a pillar, Sean in tow. With them was Marcia.

Helen immediately rushed to my side and grabbed my hand. "Are you okay?" she whispered; I nodded in reply and squeezed her hand back.

"Vat is going on?" Ivana demanded. "We are here to see mer-rege. Why you no say *I do*?" She was looking at me accusingly, and Anthony nodded.

"My question exactly," he said sharply. "Why, Jess?"

"I've just explained why not." I stood up as I spoke; my legs were feeling wobbly underneath me and I steeled myself. "Anthony, listen to me. I'm not the person you think I am. And marriage isn't something that should be rushed into . . ."

"You didn't mind rushing before," he said, his eyes flashing with anger. "In fact, if I remember rightly, it was you who wanted us to get married so quickly. What's changed?"

"I've changed." I reached out to take Anthony's arm tentatively. "Anthony, I'm doing you a favor, honestly. Marriage should be based on love. And we're not in love. We're really not."

"Love?" Anthony rolled his eyes and pulled away from me. "Oh, don't be so naïve. Marriage isn't about love. It's about convenience and boredom, about money, property, family alliances . . ."

"Maybe for some, not for me," I said, then stopped. "Property?" I stared at Anthony as something popped into my head. Then I shook myself. No, I was imagining it.

"Yes, property." He was staring at me with a look of malevolence in his eye, a look I hadn't seen before.

"The picture," I said, a feeling of unease sweeping through me. "The picture of the house on your desk. It *was* Grace's house, wasn't it. You had a picture of Grace's house on your desk."

"No I didn't," Anthony said, looking away as though I were a tiresome child. "You're talking rubbish."

"You did. It was her house," I insisted. "Why wouldn't you let me look at it?"

"I don't know what you're talking about. It wasn't anyone's house. It was just a house I was looking at buying, and I didn't want you to see it because it was a surprise." Anthony sighed. "Jesus, Jess, what is with you? You're embarrassing everyone."

"No, she isn't embarrassing anyone," Max said, his voice serious. "Anthony, what's going on? What's this about a house?"

Anthony folded his arms tightly. "I have no idea," he said tensely. "No idea at all." His eyes rested on me for a few seconds—suddenly their blueness didn't look so attractive anymore. They were cold, hard eyes. And as I looked into them, I realized something. Something that made my heart sink down into my stomach.

"You knew," I gasped. "You knew about the will. That's why you asked me to marry you."

"Will?" Anthony feigned ignorance, but his eyes flickered slightly. "What will?"

"He didn't know about any will," Marcia said suddenly, then reddened. "I mean *doesn't,*" she corrected herself quickly. "Doesn't know."

I stared at her, my eyes narrowing. "What's any of this to do with you anyway?"

"Me? Nothing. I just happen to know that Anthony doesn't know anything about any will," Marcia said, pouting guiltily.

Suddenly I found my eyes drawn to the top of her head. "Your sunglasses," I said, frowning. "I've seen them before."

"Sunglasses? Jess, are you okay? I think you're going mad." Marcia tossed her hair, but I could sense her unease.

Finally the image I'd been scanning my memory for popped into my head and my mouth fell open. "You were wearing them in the car. In Anthony's car. The night he drove past me. You were in the car."

Marcia blanched. "I don't know what you mean."

"You were in the car," I said agitatedly. "It was you. You and Anthony . . ."

I stared at her in disbelief, but she didn't say anything.

I turned back to Anthony, utterly confused. "But how did you know? How could you know that . . ."

"That what?" Max asked, but I ignored him. My brain was working overtime.

"Marcia!" I swung around accusingly. "You spoke to Mr. Taylor."

"I did?" Marcia rolled her eyes. "I speak to a lot of people, Jess. I can't remember all of them."

"You spoke to him and you told Anthony." I was on a roll now. "You must have."

"So Anthony did know?" Helen's eyes widened incredulously. "This was all a setup to get the money?"

"What money?" Max said, his face now a picture of confusion. "What's everyone talking about?"

"Grace." My voice was barely audible as I took in the reality of the situation. "Grace left me her house. Her money. And Anthony knew. He was only marrying me because . . ."

Anthony regarded me stonily. "Because you'd be rich? Well of course. Why else would I be marrying you?"

"You bastard!" Helen stared at him incredulously. "You manipulative bastard."

Max moved toward me. "Anthony, I can't believe you," he said, icily. "All this time you've been using Jess. I take it this is your big moneymaking plan?"

"Oh, grow up, Max," Anthony said angrily. "At least I showed her a good time. Shagged her. She had the time of her life."

"You . . . you . . . you *are* a bastard," Max said, stepping forward, his eyes blazing with anger.

"I just can't believe this," Helen said, her eyes wide with indignation. "So the two of you cooked up this little scheme together?"

"What, like your little scheme, you mean?" Anthony asked, a cruel little smile on his lips. "Project Marriage, wasn't it?"

I felt the blood drain from my face.

"Project Marriage? What was Project Marriage?" Max asked, but everyone ignored him.

"It was on your computer," Marcia said, folding her arms and shooting me a triumphant look. "You didn't hide it very well."

I gulped. My life was over. I'd never been so humiliated. "I thought you . . . I thought . . . ," I said, trailing off, unable to complete the sentence.

"Thought he was madly in love with you?" Marcia laughed. "Oh, Jess, get a grip, will you? Why on earth would someone like Anthony fall madly in love with you? I mean, really."

"You cow!" Helen said, outraged. "You total cow! Why shouldn't Anthony have fallen in love with Jess?"

"Because he's already in love with me," Marcia said. "Please keep up."

"In love with you?" Anthony shook his head dismissively and turned to me. "I'm shagging her, that's all. Come on, Jess, be reasonable."

"Shagging me?" Now it was Marcia's turn to look at him in disbelief. "I set you up to inherit all that money and you say you're just shagging me? You bastard! Helen and Max are right. You are a total bastard."

"Let's forget about who's shagging whom, shall we?" Anthony said, looking at me intently. "The fact of the matter is that you still need to marry me to get the money. Whatever has or hasn't happened is water under the bridge now. Just say *I do* and we can discuss the division of assets later, okay?"

"Division of assets?" I couldn't believe what I was hearing.

"Well I'm hardly going to let you have the lot, am I?" Anthony smiled thinly. "Now for the last time, let's go back to the altar and hear you say *I do*. Two words, Jess. Just two words. You can do it."

I took a deep breath and turned to Anthony. "Never," I said, not a tremor in my voice. "Not in a million years."

"Yes," Marcia said, with passion. "Not in a million years."

"Yes you will," Anthony said, ignoring her, his voice tense. "You don't have a choice. We both have a lot to lose here, Jess. And neither of us will win if you walk away. Think about that. Think very hard."

"I am thinking very hard," I said, flatly.

"Then do the sensible thing."

"Oh, but I am doing the sensible thing. I'm walking away. You know, Anthony, I used to think that love and romance were a waste of time, an admission of weakness. But they're not. Faking love is what's weak. Marrying for the wrong reasons is weak."

"So's leading people on," Marcia offered.

"No," Anthony sneered. "Letting people down is weak. Marcia, just butt out, will you? And Jess, you're pathetic."

"She isn't pathetic," Helen said hotly. "She just doesn't love you. And after what I've heard, I'm bloody relieved. I'm pleased she isn't marrying you."

"No, you are not," Ivana said, rolling her eyes. "No merrege, no money, remember."

"Okay, I've had enough of this. Would someone please explain what's going on?" Max said suddenly. "I thought Anthony was marrying Jess for her money. Why does she need to get married?"

"I don't," I said, blanching. "At least . . . I don't want to. Not anymore . . ."

"Not anymore?" Max's eyes were staring into mine and I looked back at him uncomfortably.

"I . . ." I bit my lip.

"Grace, Jess's little old lady friend, thought Jess was married to Anthony," Marcia said. "So she left her money to Mrs. Milton. Jess had to marry Anthony to get her hands on the money." She shot me a little smile, which I ignored.

Max's eyes widened. "But why would she think Jess was married to Anthony?"

I went red.

"Because she told Grace she was married to him, that's why," Marcia said with a sigh, as though it were common knowledge. "Keep up, Max."

"But . . . but . . . that's ridiculous," Max said incredulously. "You didn't, did you Jess?" He was looking at me imploringly and I wished with all my heart that I hadn't, wished I could come up with a reason, an explanation that didn't make me appear a total loser. But I couldn't.

"Yes, I did," I said, biting my lip. "But only because Grace wanted me to be happy. Because her idea of happiness was . . . was . . ."

I trailed off, unable to finish the sentence. Marcia was right. I was a total loser.

"Okay, so you were left the money as Mrs. Milton, and so you . . ." His forehead creased in concentration. "And so you decided to marry him for real?" he said, eventually, his eyes wide. "Oh my God." Suddenly, Max recoiled from me. Then he looked from me to Anthony and back to me again, shaking his head in disbelief. "All that bollocks last night about doing the wrong thing to do the right thing . . . I thought you were talking about something important. But you were talking about this. About marrying someone for money."

"Don't be so bloody moral, Max," Anthony said, rolling his eyes. "Money's a perfectly good reason to get married, isn't it, Jess?" He looked at me meaningfully. "Four million pounds, isn't it? That's a lot to walk away from."

"Yes," Ivana said loudly. "Four million pounds is very good reason to get married. Say yes and then we cen all heff drink."

I shook my head.

"Um, sorry, guys," Roger said tentatively. "But I'm not sure I'm really following this."

I looked at him for a moment, then sighed. "I was left some money in a will," I said quietly. "Only, Grace—she was the one who left me the money—she thought I was married to Anthony. So she left the inheritance to Jessica Milton. Mrs. Jessica Milton."

Roger rubbed his forehead. "I'm still not sure I entirely understand," he said nervously. "Who's Grace?"

"Grace is my friend," I whispered. "Was my friend. She died."

"Your friend?" Anthony looked at me contemptuously. "Grace," he said, carefully, "was my mother. If anyone should have her house, it's me, not Jess."

There was a shocked silence. "She was your . . . your mother?" I asked, my voice faltering. "But how? I mean . . . what . . . I mean . . . You don't have a mother. She died. You said she died . . ."

"She did," he said, his lips thin. "To me, anyway. Cut me off without a penny, just because I hocked a few paintings for some cash. Didn't even know she'd died until I read about her funeral. Then when you said you were going to a funeral, I thought that was rather interesting. And when Marcia spoke to your friend . . ."

"Mr. Taylor?" I asked breathlessly.

"Mr. Taylor," Anthony said, nodding, "she told me about their interesting conversation and we decided that we'd help you along a bit."

"Help me?" I said, shaking my head.

"Exactly," Anthony said firmly, grabbing my arm tightly and making me flinch. "Look, this is a win–win situation. And I need that money. If I don't get my hands on it pretty quickly, there are going to be creditors banging at the door. It's mine. I'm owed it. Come on, Jess, do the right thing here. Do it."

"I . . . I can't," I said, shaking my head. "I can't marry you, not now. But I'll pay you back for the wedding. I'll take out a loan . . ."

"A loan?" Anthony snorted. "Jess, it's not just the wedding I owe money for. I'm in debt up to my eyeballs."

"The firm," Max said levelly. "It's in debt, too?"

Anthony sighed. "I thought it would be okay. I thought when my mother died . . . I thought she'd leave it all to me." He turned to me and grabbed me. "You have to marry me," he said bitterly, his hands tightening around my shoulders. "You have to. You owe me."

"All right, easy does it. It doesn't look like she wants to say *I do,* does it?" Sean said suddenly, stepping forward and trying to separate us. "Just give it up, yeah? Leave her alone."

Anthony's eyes widened and he let me go, turning his attention to Sean instead. "Bloody hell, it's you, isn't it?" he said angrily. "You're her ex-boyfriend." He turned back to me. "You invited Sean? You invited him to our wedding?"

I looked at him incredulously. "Yes, and *that's* the problem here. If it weren't for Sean, everything would be just fine, wouldn't it, Anthony?"

"Still," Anthony said, narrowing his eyes at my sarcasm. "No reason why I should put up with his presence." He squared up to him. "Get out," he said menacingly. "Just get out, before I make you."

Sean raised an eyebrow. "What, you going to hit me again?"

Anthony nodded. "Yes. Maybe I am. Maybe I'll just . . ." He pulled back his fist. But before he could do anything with it, Ivana launched herself at him, pushing him to the ground and pummeling him.

"No one punch my husband," she said angrily as her nails headed for Anthony's face. "No one."

"Your . . . husband? But he's Jess's ex . . . ," Anthony managed to say before she landed on top of him.

"No," I pleaded as Roger and Max did their best to separate them. "No, he's not. He's . . . he only pretended to be my ex. He isn't really . . ."

"Another lie," Max said bitterly as he managed to prize Anthony out of Ivana's clutches. "Any more you'd like to confess to while we're at it? Is your name really Jessica Wild, or is that a lie, too?"

"No. I mean yes. I mean . . . ," I said desperately. But before I could work out how to explain, the sound of more footsteps echoing toward us halted me in my tracks. When I looked up to see who it was, I felt my head roll back on my neck.

"I'm very sorry to interrupt," a worried-looking Mr. Taylor said, rushing toward us. "I meant to come here earlier. Ended up in Scotland, I'm afraid. But I wonder if I might delay proceedings a little. I'm afraid that I need to talk to Miss Jessica Wild as a matter of some urgency."

Roger the vicar stared at him, then at Max, then at me.

"Another matter? Or is this about Grace, too?"

"About Grace?" Mr. Taylor said curiously. "Well yes, I suppose it is."

"I suppose you want to stop Jess from marrying this young man, too?" Roger asked weakly.

Mr. Taylor frowned. "This man?" he asked, looking at Anthony in surprise. "But this man is gay. No, I want to stop her from marrying that man," he said, pointing at Max. "Anthony Milton."

"I'm Anthony Milton," Anthony said angrily. "And I'm not gay."

"You're not?" Mr. Taylor raised his eyebrows. "Are you sure?" He peered at Anthony. "You know," he continued, "perhaps I can see the resemblance, after all. It's been such a long time."

Anthony pulled back his fist; quickly, Max restrained him.

"Sorry to interrupt," Roger asked, "but do I take it that this marriage is off? Because if it is, perhaps I should let the congregation know."

I nodded. "Yes. Yes, it is," I said.

"Wait a sec," Helen said, coming forward and grabbing my hand. "Jess, do what you have to do. But you do know that if you don't marry him, you'll lose everything. I mean, if you marry him, at least you'll get fifty percent. That's something, isn't it?"

"No," I said, shaking slightly. "If I don't marry him, I'll lose the money and the house. I know that. But if I do marry Anthony I'll lose a lot more." I looked at Max; for a second, he stared at me intently. Then he looked away.

"I've had enough of this, I'm afraid," he said tightly. "I think it's time I left."

"No! Don't! Max, let me explain," I called after him. "Max, I only did it to protect Grace's house. I thought . . . I thought . . ."

But my words were lost; Max didn't turn around. He kept on walking, right out of the church.

I could feel tears pricking at my eyes, and I wiped them away distractedly. It was over, I realized. It was all over. Then I looked at Mr. Taylor and cleared my throat. "Mr. Taylor, I'm afraid I can't accept Grace's inheritance after all. She left her money and house to someone she thought she could trust to look after it, and I've proved that I'm not that person." I felt a lump in my throat develop. "So I'm afraid I won't be able to complete the paperwork after all. You see, I'm not Mrs. Milton. I never was. Never will be, either. I let Grace down. And I'm really sorry."

Mr. Taylor shook his head and tutted to himself. "Oh dear," he said. "Oh dear me, I knew this was a mistake. I knew . . ."

"Of course you knew," I said in a strangled voice. "You suspected from the start, didn't you? God, I've been such an idiot. I've been such a complete prize idiot . . ." I let my head fall into my hands. "This is all my fault," I said, big fat tears beginning to roll down my face. "It's all my stupid fault. And I'm so sorry. I'm so very sorry."

"Actually," Mr. Taylor said, his voice tentative, "actually, I don't think it is your fault, Ms. Wild. I told Grace it was a bad idea, but she wouldn't listen. She did like her little schemes, you see. She did so like to interfere . . ."

Chapter 32

IT TOOK A FEW SECONDS to register what Mr. Taylor had said. Then, slowly, I lifted my head and wiped my eyes with the back of my hand.

"Grace?" I asked. "What do you mean?"

"I mean," Mr. Taylor said anxiously, "I had a feeling this would not end well. I did try to warn Lady Hampton, but she wouldn't listen."

"Warn her about what?" Helen asked, frowning. "What wouldn't she listen to?"

"Reason," Mr. Taylor said, looking around vaguely.

"Would you like to sit down?" I asked, standing up and offering him my chair.

He nodded gratefully. "Thank you. I . . . if you don't mind. Yes, yes, I think sitting down would be a good idea. I think . . ."

He lowered himself into the chair, his head shaking from side to side. Then he leaned forward and looked at me, his face crumpled and serious. "When she first heard you talking about Anthony Milton, she couldn't help herself," he said. "She hadn't heard from him in years, and suddenly she could find out all about him."

I stared at him uncertainly. "You mean he really is her son? Was, I mean?"

Mr. Taylor nodded sadly.

"So what you're saying is that . . . that our friendship, everything was just . . . just a ruse so she could hear about Anthony?" I was frowning in disbelief.

"No, no." Mr. Taylor shook his head. "At least it might have been at first, but not for long. She liked you. Loved you, of that I have no doubt. But at first, she was also very curious. And then, she started getting ideas. Plans. Plans that I'm afraid you allowed yourself to walk into, my dear."

"Plans?" I asked, confused. "I don't understand."

"Nor do I," Anthony said irritably. "What the hell are you talking about?"

Mr. Taylor raised an eyebrow. "Yes," he said, looking Anthony up and down. "I can see what Grace meant about you." He turned back to me. "She thought that if you and Anthony were to get together, you'd be a restraining influence on him. She became quite obsessed with the idea."

"Me and Anthony?"

Mr. Taylor nodded again as I digested the news.

"So when she thought we'd gotten married?" I asked tentatively.

Mr Taylor smiled. "I'm afraid she knew you weren't married," he said wistfully. "The Anthony you described was just too different from the Anthony she knew. She asked me to . . . to check up on the situation. And I did."

I gulped. "And you discovered . . ."

"That you weren't married? Yes, I'm afraid I did. But Grace didn't seem to mind. She saw it as a grand romantic challenge. One in which she might play Cupid."

"So she knew?" My voice was barely audible. "She knew it was all lies?"

"Dreams, she preferred to call them," Mr. Taylor said gently. "Dreams that she hoped might come true with a little . . . encouragement. It was her dream, too, you see. That you and her son . . . that the two of you might be happy together."

"You mean she left the money and house to Jess to get me to marry her?" Anthony said, shaking his head incredulously, a grin appearing on his face. "She wanted me to have it all along?"

"No. She was clear that she wanted Ms. Wild to have the money," Mr. Taylor said, shooting a reproachful look at Anthony. "But she assumed that Ms. Wild was in love with you. She wanted you both to be happy. And she hoped that under Ms. Wild's influence you . . . you might reform your ways."

"Really? Because that's not the way I see it. Or how a court will see it," Anthony said dismissively. "The money's been left to Mrs. Milton. So whoever I marry will get the money, right? I'm going to challenge the will and I'm going to win."

"You can have the money," I said, my shoulders hanging heavily. "I don't want it. I don't deserve it."

"Oh but you do. Mrs. Hampton wanted you to have it," Mr. Taylor said gently.

"But . . . but I'm not Jessica Milton." I faltered. "And I'm not in love with her son."

"No, you're not," Mr. Taylor agreed. "Which is why there is a clause in the will stating that if Jessica Milton is, in actual fact, still Jessica Wild, then the moneys and property should pass to her anyway."

"But that's outrageous! That's vindictive." Anthony said angrily, turning on Mr. Taylor. "You blame me for trying to get what was mine early? I knew she'd stitch me up. Total cow."

Mr. Taylor regarded him coolly. "There's also a trust of two million pounds to go to her son, so long as he doesn't contest the will," he said quietly.

"Two million pounds?" Anthony's face changed suddenly, his blue eyes regaining their twinkle, all signs of anger evaporating.

"Two million pounds."

"Well, why on earth didn't you tell me before?" Anthony smiled. "We could have avoided all of this, couldn't we?"

"Yes, we could," Mr. Taylor said patiently, "but that's not what Grace wanted. She rather hoped that you'd marry Ms. Wild here. She wanted you to find out about the two million afterward."

"Right. I see." Anthony nodded seriously. "Well, that's . . . that's very interesting. So when do I get the money? Do I need to sign something?"

Mr. Taylor reached into his pocket and brought out a check. "You need to sign these forms," he said, handing a piece of paper to Anthony. He grabbed it greedily and handed it back. Mr. Taylor folded it, put it in his pocket, then handed Anthony a check.

Anthony took the check immediately; I was still staring at Mr. Taylor in disbelief. "But why didn't you tell me? You said she hadn't left any money to her family. You said . . ."

"I told you what Grace asked me to tell you," Mr. Taylor said apologetically. "I advised her against it. I pleaded with her, but she was convinced the plan was worthwhile. Either you would find love, she said, or you would find something else just as important."

"She said that?"

Mr. Taylor nodded. "And did you?" he asked tentatively. "Did you find something else just as important?"

I bit my lip. "I don't know. I don't know if I did."

"Yes you did," Helen said suddenly. "You didn't marry him, did you? You found out that you weren't a total cynic after all. That you do believe in marriage. You know, for the right reasons and everything . . ."

"I . . . I guess," I said uncertainly. "I'm still not sure I deserve the money."

"I don't think you deserved what my client put you through,"

Mr. Taylor said firmly. "The inheritance, well, I think she knew what she was doing."

"Well, fun as this has been, I'm afraid that I really do have to leave," Anthony said suddenly. "I've got two million pounds to spend and a honeymoon to take. Marcia, fancy a trip to the south of France?"

Marcia shot him a look of disgust. "You expect me to go away with you now?"

"It's all paid for. And I didn't mean what I said earlier. I was just playing around. I adore you. You know that, right?" He held out his hand, his eyes twinkling flirtatiously; Marcia stared at it for a few seconds, then tossed her hair back.

"Fine," she said, taking his hand. "But I want separate bedrooms. Separate beds, at any rate . . ."

"Whatever you want," Anthony agreed. "Jess, see you back at the office?"

Marcia grinned. "Yes, do you mind taking back Project Handbag for me? I promised Chester I'd have some mock-ups with him next week and I really don't think I'm going to have the time."

I stared at her in disbelief. "You think I'm still working for you?" I asked Anthony. "You think I want anything to do with Milton Advertising?"

"Frankly I don't really care." Anthony shrugged. "I'm not sure I want much to do with it myself now I'm rich. Max won't mind. Give him my best, won't you?"

"But the paperwork," Mr. Taylor said falteringly. "You will sign the rest of the paperwork?"

"Sure." Anthony waved as they left. "Send it to me in France."

Roger scratched his head. "Well, I suppose I'd better go and tell everyone," he said nervously, walking out toward the main church. "Wish me luck."

"Yes," Mr. Taylor said distractedly. "I'd better go, too. Get Mr.

Milton to sign . . . I'll . . . I'll be in touch, Ms. Wild. I'll be in touch very soon."

"Thanks," I said vaguely. "Thanks very much."

He walked out of the church; Helen immediately put her arms around me.

"You did it, Jess," she said, grinning. "You did it!"

I shook my head. "Hardly."

"You did it! And you should be a bit more cheerful." She frowned. "You've got the money and the house and you didn't even have to marry Anthony."

"I suppose," I agreed despondently.

"So let's go and celebrate!"

Helen's eyes were shining, and I shot her a halfhearted smile. "You go," I said. "I'll see you later. Okay?"

"Really? Why?" Helen said uncertainly. "Are you all right, Jess?"

"Fine," I assured her. "I just need some time alone."

"Alone," Helen said looking like I was mad, then she shrugged. "Well, okay, if that's what you want. I think I'll go and tell Fenella what happened." A wicked glint appeared in her eye. She tugged at Ivana's arm. "I think you guys better come with me—I might need some help when she finds out the wedding's off."

Ivana nodded. "I can restrain if required," she said, her voice low. Then she turned to me. "So, you heff the money? Without merrege?"

I nodded. "Looks that way."

"Clever," she said, a look of something approaching respect crossing her face. "Money with no boom boom. I like idea of this."

"Money *with* boom boom's even better, though," Sean said, winking. "If it's the right boom boom."

Ivana shrugged. "Maybe." Then she grabbed Sean and kissed him. "For you, I would have boom boom and no money," she said. "But only you."

"Thanks," I said, as they turned to leave. "Thanks for everything . . ."

"No problem." Sean grinned. "It's been . . . unreal."

I followed them out of the church, but instead of walking back to the hotel, I hung around outside. There was a small patch of grass to the right of the door, and I made my way toward it. Then, taking a deep breath, I took out my cream clutch bag that Helen had given me as a last-minute present that morning, dug out my mobile phone, and dialed a number.

"Hello?"

"It's me, Jess," I said.

"Jess."

"Yes." I took a deep breath. "Just . . . look, I want to say something to you, and I want you to listen, okay?"

"You're giving me orders?"

I cleared my throat. "Look, I've behaved terribly, unforgivably. So badly, I expect you really dislike me right now. But I have to say something to you so, yes, I'm giving you orders, if you don't mind."

"Yes, you have behaved terribly. And I do mind. I mind a great deal. But I will listen. Go ahead."

I took another deep breath. My palms were sweating so much, I was worried I was going to drop the phone.

"Thank you," I said uncertainly, "okay, here's the thing. I . . ." I hesitated, then closed my eyes. I couldn't believe I was really going to do this. But then again, I had nothing else to lose. "I like you, Max. I like you very much. Always have. Since I met you. And I know that romance and love are unreal and dangerous and that you get your heart broken. I mean me. I'll be the one to get my . . . Oh, it doesn't matter. What matters is . . . Well, I just wanted to say it. Because I used to think it was strong to not. Say it, I mean, or even feel it. But now, now I think that maybe it's stronger to do the opposite. To take a risk. Even though things might go wrong. Like now. I mean, they could go awfully."

"Awfully? You mean like the wedding? Or nonwedding, I suppose I should say."

I gulped. "That would, I suppose, count as awful, yes," I said.

"You told Grace you were married to Anthony."

Max's voice was level, unreadable. "It was stupid," I agreed. "But I never thought . . . I mean, I didn't know she'd leave me her estate. I just wanted her to be happy, that's all . . ."

"Yeah, that's not what I'm concerned about."

"It's not?" I asked worriedly. "Well, I'm sorry about everything else, too . . ."

"Hmmm. You see, I just have one question."

"You do?" I asked.

"You were really going to marry Anthony? I mean, you were actually planning to go through with it?" he asked, his voice soft now. I was pressing the phone to my ear as tightly as I could.

I shook my head. "No. I mean, yes, but : . . I thought I had to. For Grace. And then I thought he really wanted to . . ."

"But you couldn't actually go through with it?"

"No. No, I couldn't. I thought I didn't believe in marriage, but I do. When it's real. When it means something."

"I see," Max said.

"And it was all a setup." I sighed. "Grace had it all planned . . ."

"I know."

"You do?" I frowned. "How?"

"I was listening to you, in the church."

"You were there?"

"I still am." I felt someone next to me; slowly, tentatively, I turned around to see Max looking at me. "It was two setups, actually, if you think about it," he said, one eyebrow raised. "First Grace, then Anthony. They both set you up."

I nodded dismally. "Two setups." I felt my face getting hot, my hands getting clammy; I dropped my phone.

"You know, to fall for something like that once, well, that's almost understandable. But twice?"

He was so close I could almost feel him breathing. But did he hate me? Did I think I was an idiot? I had no idea.

"So, the question?" I asked, my voice catching as I spoke. "You said you had a question."

"Ah, the question," Max nodded. "Yes, I do have a question."

"Which is?"

He pulled back slightly. "Why Anthony? Why did you tell Grace you were in love with Anthony?"

I swallowed with difficulty. "Because it wasn't true," I said. "Because it made the whole story ridiculous in my mind. It made the whole story easier to tell because it was so obviously fiction."

"So you weren't in love with him? Even a little bit?"

"Not even a little bit," I said, my voice catching slightly.

"I see," Max said thoughtfully. "Even when you thought he was in love with you?"

"No," I said firmly. "I knew he was never in love with me. I thought he was in love with Jessica Wiiild, who had shiny hair and high-heeled shoes and who had an ex-boyfriend called Sean. God, I can't believe I was so gullible."

"I don't think you were gullible. He might have fallen in love with you."

"No, not with me," I said, shaking my head awkwardly. "I'm not his type. And he's not mine."

"And I am?"

"No," I said, then bit my lip. "I don't have a type. I just like you."

"I'm not made up."

I met Max's eyes; I felt like a furnace. "No, you're not."

"And you really like me?"

I nodded. "But it's okay if you don't . . . I mean, last night you said you couldn't . . . Which is fine . . ."

"Last night you didn't let me finish my sentence. You were too busy telling me that you couldn't, either, that you were getting married the next day."

"I . . . I didn't?" I asked, catching my breath.

"No, you didn't," Max said. "I was going to say I couldn't believe you were marrying that idiot," he said. "I was going to say I couldn't bear to watch you walk down that aisle tomorrow."

"You were?" My eyes opened wide. "Really?"

Max put his arms around me. "Really."

"So you actually like me?"

Max nodded. "You did a good impression of being in love with Anthony, though," he said archly.

"I told you, that was just . . . you know, a project," I said, embarrassed.

"Not the project. Before that. I thought you were in love with Anthony when you first joined."

"You did?" I asked incredulously.

He shrugged. "Everyone did. You walked into a glass door after your interview."

"The wall . . ." I gasped. "That was you, not Anthony."

"Me!"

"You grinned at me."

"I did?"

I nodded sheepishly.

"Like this?" He grinned at me, his eyes twinkling, his arms pulling me closer.

"Just like that." I felt short of breath suddenly, like the world was going into slow motion.

"So let me get this straight. You like me, you're single, and you're rich?"

My own mouth started to inch upward. "Sounds about right."

Max nodded thoughtfully. "Well, in that case, perhaps you might agree to have dinner with me? Your treat?"

"Dinner?"

"You might want to get changed first, of course. But yes, dinner. If you're free?"

My eyes lit up. Actually, my whole body lit up. "I . . . I may have to check my calendar," I said carefully.

"I already have," Max said, his voice suddenly husky. "There was something about a wedding in your diary, but I figured it wasn't important, right?"

His arms were wrapping around me and I nodded, my eyes shining.

"The wedding?" I managed to say, as his lips moved toward mine. "Absolutely not. You see, Max, there are more important things than getting married. As I've been trying to tell you, in the great scheme of things, getting married really isn't that important at all."

GEMMA TOWNLEY is the author of *When in Rome . . .* , *Little White Lies, Learning Curves,* and *The Hopeless Romantic's Handbook.* She lives in London with her husband, Mark, and son, Atticus.

ABOUT THE TYPE

ITC Berkeley Oldstyle, designed in 1983 by Tony Stan, is a variation of the University of California Old Style, which was created by Frederick Goudy. While capturing the feel and traits of its predecessor, ITC Berkeley Old Style shows influences from Kennerly, Goudy Old Style, Deepdene, and Booklet Oldstyle, all of which were also designed by Goudy. It is characterized by its calligraphic weight stress, and its x-height, now described as classic, is smaller than most other ITC designs of the day. The generous ascenders and descenders provide variations in text color, easy legibility, and an overall inviting appearance.